Chase Wilde
Comes Home

He took her mouth in a deep kiss, sliding his tongue along hers, tasting her on his lips and tongue and needing her to feel all that she made him feel.

Her hands came up to cup his face, and she whispered his name like a prayer as their bodies moved together, their lips touched, and their hearts beat as one.

That connection they shared cocooned them. It lived and breathed around them. It was up to them to keep it alive just like this, both of them open and honest and giving everything to each other.

He pressed his forehead to hers, stared into her eyes, and saw everything in his heart reflected back to him. Love. So overwhelming and impossible and wonderful and frightening and perfect.

Her eyes went bright, and he knew she saw it and felt it, too.

Also by Jennifer Ryan

Chase Wilde Comes Home

A Wyoming Wilde Novel

JENNIFER RYAN

AVONBOOKS

An Imprint of HarperCollinsPublishers

First Avon Books mass market printing: March 2022

Print Edition ISBN: 978-0-06-311140-0
Digital Edition ISBN: 978-0-06-309460-4

Cover design by Nadine Badalaty
Cover photograph © Rob Lang
Cover images © iStock/Getty Images; © Shutterstock

FIRST EDITION

Printed in Lithuania

22 23 24 25 26 SB 10 9 8 7 6 5 4 3 2 1

For all the readers, bloggers, reviewers.
None of this would be possible without you.
Thank you for your time and support.
I appreciate it so much.

Author's Note

Dear readers,

I often tackle tough topics in my books. I want readers who have faced these challenges, are in the midst of dealing with them, or know someone who is going through it, or has been through it, to know that you are not alone.

While Chase and Shelby's story was difficult to write, I knew it had a happy ending. But to get there, Chase had to take control of his addiction and learn to manage his PTSD. Shelby had to face her biological father, her mother's rapist, and come to terms with her past and how it shaped her.

If you, or someone you know, needs help, you deserve it, you are worth it. Please contact . . .

Substance Abuse and Mental Health Service
Administration - National Helpline
www.samhsa.gov
1-800-662-HELP (4357)

National Sexual Assault Hotline
1-800-656-4673

You can have and deserve your own happy ending.

XO
Jennifer

Chase Wilde Comes Home

Chapter One

Chase sat on the edge of the twin bed in his rehab room and stared blankly out the window, wondering what the hell came next. He had no home. He didn't have a dime to his name after sixty days of rehab and the extra week he tacked on after . . . the unimaginable happened.

Choked up, thoughts of Juliana filled his every thought.

Her dropping to the floor.

Him giving her CPR.

Something overtaking him until he collapsed beside her.

When he woke up in the hospital, the cops told him she'd OD'd on fentanyl-laced heroin. He'd done the same when the drugs from her skin absorbed into his as he gave her mouth-to-mouth. She'd been dosed intentionally, him by accident. Fentanyl was fifty to one hundred times more potent than morphine. She died. He lived.

He'd cheated death. Again.

His brothers, Hunt and Max, showed up unannounced and unwelcome at the hospital last week. They eagerly pointed a finger and accused him of wasting two months and all his money on rehab if he was just going to use the second he got out. Even after being told the OD was an accident, Hunt and Max still left angry and skeptical.

They didn't see how determined he was to get back to his little girl.

They didn't care.

Sometimes it felt like no one cared about him anymore.

He should be grateful his brothers bothered to check on him at all. It didn't go well. They'd come because their mother would have wanted it. But she was also the reason they wanted nothing to do with him. So they did their duty to appease their conscience for Mom's sake, then delivered Chase once he was released from the hospital back to rehab for another week to get his head straight with little faith he'd changed or gotten his act together. They left, basically washing their hands of him yet again.

All Chase wanted to do was see his little girl, and that meant facing her mom, Shelby, and convincing her he'd changed his ways and wanted to put Eliza first.

He prayed he could make Shelby believe him.

He pulled out his phone and scrolled through pics of Eliza. Shelby had sent him a new one every day since Eliza was born. One look at her sweet, smiling face and all the tension went out of his chest.

It wasn't just the photos Shelby sent that made his day. Shelby had even hooked up a private webcam in Eliza's nursery. He could log in with his password anytime and see his little girl in her room. Some days, the pictures and seeing the livestream had been all that kept him sane while he was serving overseas. He'd spent every night in rehab watching his baby sleep.

It went a long way to stitching up his bleeding heart.

Shelby never called to talk to him about anything except Eliza. But since he got out of rehab and ended up right back in, she'd left him several messages he hadn't listened to because if her reaction to him OD'ing again matched his brothers' responses, he was in deep shit.

He didn't want to hear her tell him not to come back this time.

"Mr. Wilde," a nurse called from the door. "I see you're all packed up and ready to go."

He wished he knew exactly where he was going.

"There's someone in the lobby to see you."

Definitely wasn't his brothers. His dad wanted nothing to do with him either.

It had to be his buddy Drake. Chase wondered if Adria, Drake's girlfriend and Juliana's sister, was holding it together after losing her twin.

Maybe she came, too. He wanted to talk to her and tell her how sorry he was for not being able to save Juliana. He'd tried but failed miserably.

"I'm headed out now," he told the nurse.

"Good luck. And remember, take it one day at a time." She smiled and left.

He rubbed his hand over his aching chest, swallowed down the guilt, stuffed his feet in his boots, laced them, stood, grabbed his duffel bag, and headed out the door. He'd already had his last session with his psychiatrist and picked up his meds at the pharmacy. All he had left to do was figure out where he was going and how he would get there.

Back to Wyoming to see his kid first, then . . . he didn't know.

He walked down the hall, out the door, and into the lobby, expecting to see Drake, but he stopped in his tracks and stared at the woman who stood staring right back at him.

Her gaze swept over him from his head to his boots and back up, leaving a warm caress all over him. "Chase."

His name on her lips would always be the sweetest sound. "Shelby."

Just looking at her made him ache. He wanted to be what she wanted. But hell if he knew what that was, because they were still practically strangers.

Strangers who had seen each other naked and left not one centimeter of skin untouched.

He didn't know Shelby before the night they got stupid drunk and had a one-night stand. He didn't take the time to get to know her afterward either because he'd only been home on leave for ten days, and spent most of that in a bar, regretting spending those few days in his hometown where his family didn't want him. He met her his last night home. She made those ten miserable days worth it.

She didn't know what that night meant to him.

How he relived it over and over in his mind and that sometimes it was the only thing that kept him sane.

She didn't know how much he appreciated her letting him into her life through Eliza. How that webcam and the pictures she sent while he was overseas, and now, meant everything to him.

When he returned the last time, wounded in body and mind, she'd let him visit Eliza. They'd played in the backyard or at the park in town. But then she started shutting the door in his face when he showed up stoned out of his mind. He'd made an ass out of himself too many times to count, and Hunt showed up in his patrol car and dragged Chase back to the apartment that was dinky in size but felt like a huge empty black hole.

She'd known which days to send him on his way and which days, wasted and desperate, he needed Eliza or he wasn't going to make it through the night.

Her actions spoke volumes.

She got him.

She never raged at him even when he'd given her good reason.

She never judged him.

In her quiet way, she showed him patience and understanding and compassion without pity.

She kept Eliza safe and made her happy and loved her when Chase wasn't there and couldn't do those things for her, too.

No, he didn't know Shelby well, but God, he loved her.

Still, he couldn't believe his eyes. "What are you doing here?" He glanced around the empty room. "Where's Eliza?"

"Back home with the sitter. I took the bus up last night, stayed in a motel, and came here to drive home with you."

That blew him back a step. "Why?"

She tilted her head, her soft green eyes filled with sympathy. "Because after all you've been through, I thought you might like the company."

He loved the company. But she didn't know that.

A month into counseling, he realized that somewhere between their one-night stand, them having a baby together, her holding down the fort and parenting duties the whole time he was overseas serving his country—and even when he came back—he'd fallen in love with her.

"You came all the way to Montana to drive home with me?" He really couldn't believe it.

The last thing she'd said to him still rang in his head. *Get help, or you will never see Eliza again.*

He couldn't wait to see Eliza.

She needed him. She wanted him. She was the only person in his life who loved him. Because she didn't know who her father really was deep down inside, or what he'd done, she accepted him as-is.

He had a chance to be the man she needed, because at two, she didn't know that there were bad things in the world, and he was one of them.

He wished he could undo the past and make everything right.

All he could do now was accept that all the bad shit in his past happened because he'd done the best he could each and every time he'd been faced with impossible decisions.

He hated that when it all got to be too much, he'd hidden in a prescription drug haze meant to kill the pain, but it just made things worse.

And nearly cost him everything.

It was never about some high. He needed an escape from his thoughts, to turn off his brain, so he didn't have to remember or feel or do something he couldn't take back and end it all.

Eliza needed him to *be* better. So he was going to *do* better.

He'd learned his lesson.

He wouldn't make the same mistake again.

Shelby gave him a shy smile. "I have a surprise for you."

He didn't think she came all this way and smiled like that because she had a restraining order tucked in her purse to keep him the hell away from her and Eliza, so he ended up completely lost. "I'm definitely surprised to see you."

A pretty blush flushed her cheeks. "*I'm* not the surprise."

"Yeah. You are."

She surprised the hell out of him all the time.

The night they met in the bar, she'd sat next to him and somehow ended up turning his whole world upside down in the best way.

It didn't feel that way at first, but now . . . with her standing here picking his ass up from rehab . . . he wanted to hug her for being so thoughtful and kind after all he'd done—and hadn't done for her. But he refrained because he was lucky she wasn't handing him that restraining order.

She took a tentative step closer. "It's better than me. You'll see."

He took her in with one sweeping gaze and remembered every curve and line of her body even though it was hidden beneath an oversized black hoodie and leggings. And beneath all that beat her beautiful heart. "There's nothing better than you."

She sucked in a surprised gasp.

He held her gaze, letting her see how much he meant that.

"Um, ready?"

"I'd follow you anywhere," he admitted, because he

wanted things between them to change. As co-parents, they were okay, mostly because she took the lead while he'd been gone and messed up. He wanted to show her she could count on him. He wasn't the same guy leaving rehab as the guy she'd slammed the door on when he wasn't fit to see his baby girl.

She gave him a look that clearly said she didn't believe him, then headed for the door, her long, dark ponytail bouncing. "Come on. I promised Eliza she'd get to see you today."

Shelby led the way out of the building and across the parking lot to his truck. He pulled the key fob out of his jeans pocket and unlocked the doors. He held the passenger door open for her and waited for her to climb in and stow her backpack between her feet on the floorboard, then closed the door. It only took a minute to round the truck, open the door, toss his duffel bag behind the seat, and climb behind the wheel. He started the truck, put it in Drive, then stared at the gas gauge and swore under his breath.

"We'll need to stop for gas." He prayed his credit card didn't get declined, because he only had about forty bucks in his wallet, and that would not get them home.

"We can grab some snacks for the trip. I'm starving. I wasn't sure what time you planned to leave this morning, so I skipped breakfast and got a taxi over to the rehab center to be sure I didn't miss you. Because you haven't answered my calls," she pointedly added.

He slammed the truck back into Park without ever backing out of the parking space and looked at her. "I'm sorry. I . . ."

"Had a lot on your mind. Other stuff to deal with. You needed some time and space. I get it."

"There's no excuse for my bad behavior. You called. I should have answered. It won't happen again. Ever."

She eyed him. "Things happen, Chase. Things that are out of our control. I won't hold you to that promise, just like I won't hold it against you that you didn't return my calls. I was worried about you after what happened. I'm sure your brothers weren't very supportive or kind when they came to see you."

This time, Chase put the truck in Reverse and got them going on their way. "You could say that."

"I'm sorry. I know what it's like not to have family you can count on." Shelby lost her mom when she was a baby, and her grandparents had passed a few years ago, if he remembered right. He didn't know anything about her dad. "It's a long drive back. I didn't want you to do it alone. It's a lot of miles. A lot of time to think. I thought you could use a distraction." She did get it.

"I appreciate that." But he wondered. "Are you here to also make sure I don't stray, and I get to where I'm supposed to be?"

She turned her gaze to him. "Chase, you can go and do whatever you want. I'm not the boss of you. I have no say in your life. But for Eliza's sake, I hope you want to go back to Willow Fork to see her. At least for a little while."

"I want to be there for the both of you." He hoped she believed that.

He pulled into the gas station with a minimart, cut the engine, and sighed. "What do you want to eat?"

She picked up her backpack, opened the door, and then glanced back at him. "I've got this." She hopped out and stuffed her credit card into the pump before he made it around the truck.

"Hey. You didn't have to do that."

"I know." She pulled the nozzle off the holder and held it out to him. "What do you want from inside?"

"I can—" He cut off his next words at her glare. "Something with caffeine."

The smile he loved so much was back. "Okay. Salty or sweet snacks?"

He shrugged. "Both." He really didn't care. He just wanted to spend the next few hours with her by his side, soaking up her sweet smile and how she looked at him and at the same time tried to make it seem like she wasn't staring at him.

She spun around and headed inside the minimart.

He placed the nozzle into his tank and stared across the truck bed at her zipping back to the cooler to grab a couple sodas. She disappeared down the aisles, her head barely visible as she shopped. She stood in line at the checkout. The guy behind her kept checking out her ass. He couldn't blame the guy. She had a great ass. But he wanted to kick the guy's teeth in for looking at her the way he loved to check her out.

He knew exactly what she looked like naked. How she tasted and smelled and felt against his skin.

His flesh remembered that one night they shared all too well, and the memory had him hard behind his fly. "This is going to be a long ride home."

Home. For him that wasn't a place anymore. It was with Eliza and her mama.

For now, that would have to be enough, until he figured out what came next. If all he had was them, he was a lucky man.

Not that he and Shelby were anything to each other

right now except Eliza's parents. He hoped to change that. Soon.

His throbbing dick agreed.

It had been a damn long time since he'd had his hands on Shelby, or any woman for that matter.

She walked out of the store, a bag in hand and a grin for him, but the smile slipped when she met him next to the truck.

"What's wrong?" He didn't get the concern in her eyes.

"Did you sleep at all last night? Or this past week?"

He made a vow to himself when he went into rehab to never lie to her again. "Not really. Maybe two or three hours a night."

She held out her hand. "I'll drive. You can take a nap."

He wanted to say he was fine, but his anxiety about leaving rehab and not knowing exactly what came next combined with being nervous about her being here sapped his energy.

She tipped her head back and stared up at him. "I just want you to be able to kick back and relax and not worry about anything for a while. That's all, Chase."

The way she said his name always did something to him.

He dropped his keys into her hand, brushing his fingers over her wrist as he did so. "I don't know what I did to deserve this."

"It's not a punishment."

He quickly shook his head. "I mean having you show up here to get me and being so damn nice about it after what I put you and Eliza through."

"We're fine, Chase."

Yeah. Fine without him. He was the outsider.

Shelby took care of Eliza on her own. He sent her child support while he served, and visited when he was stateside and had time off from base, a few days here, a week there over the past two years. Then he got out of the military, and everything in his life went to shit.

Actually, it happened years before he'd met Shelby and just got worse. Not because of her. She and Eliza were the only bright spot in his dark world.

After his mom's death, his father banished him from their ranch. His mom asked Chase to promise to make his dad see reason and let Chase rebuild and repair the failing business. She wanted all of them to always have a home at Split Tree Ranch.

Their family tree had definitely split, leaving his branch broken on the ground while his father and brothers stood against him and kicked him off the ranch and out of their lives.

But he'd kept his promise to his mom and left them all with a business plan and the money to carry it out. The only way to get his hands on a chunk of money without putting them further in debt had been to join the army and take the big bonus they offered him at enlistment. He needed to escape their hatred and anger and find a place to go and a purpose. He got both, and a new kind of family with his brothers-in-arms. Knowing he wasn't welcome at home but he was needed in the service, he reenlisted after his first term ended and sent the bonus he got for that to the ranch, too.

At the time, he thought his service and helping his family were his penance.

They turned out to be his undoing.

He'd served, and served well, but the battles left him

scarred, battered, mentally unstable, and ultimately addicted to the very painkillers they gave him for the wounds that healed on his body but not in his mind. That kind of pain never ceased.

"Chase. You okay?"

He shook himself out of his thoughts. "I'm getting there."

She'd put away the nozzle and took the receipt from the pump. "Then let's head out."

He hated that she'd paid for the gas and snacks, but it was her silent way of telling him she knew he was broke. How did she know? Because he was behind on paying his child support.

The guilt piled up quick in his world.

Shelby told him before he left for rehab that he didn't need to pay her until he was back on his feet.

Shelby had the biggest heart of anyone he knew.

He didn't deserve her. That didn't stop him from wanting her.

They climbed into the truck. Shelby had to move the seat way up to touch the pedals.

It made him smile. "You sure you want to drive this thing? It's a lot bigger than your SUV."

She looked like a dwarf behind the steering wheel. "I've got it. No problem."

Nothing ever seemed to faze her.

He pushed his seat back as far as it would go to accommodate his long legs and ease the ever-present ache in his back. He settled in the seat and left her to it. They didn't talk as she negotiated the streets in town and hit the highway.

Without the distraction of driving, he found himself fidgeting, folding his arms over his chest, then dropping them again, his mind spinning out with thoughts about the war, Juliana, Shelby, what the hell he was going to do, and where he was going to live.

"Chase."

He glanced over at her profile. "Yeah?"

She met his gaze. "Relax. Everything will work out."

He still couldn't believe she was here with him. He had so many things he wanted to say. He went with what needed to be said. "I'm sorry."

"For what? You don't owe me an apology."

"Yeah, I do. I lost it when I came home. I wasn't there for you and Eliza. In fact, I made things worse."

"You were in pain. You were hurting inside and out. I'm so glad you got the help you needed. But I'll ask again. Are you okay?"

"No. Not really."

Juliana's haunting face filled his mind. Watching her die . . . She wasn't the first person he'd seen die right before his eyes. But seeing a young woman, so bright and fresh with so much life left to live, drop dead right in front of him broke the last shred of whatever he'd been hanging by these last many months.

"Do you want to talk about what happened last week? Why you didn't come home as expected?"

He owed her an explanation. "I'm sorry about sending you a bunch of texts about OD'ing, instead of calling. I know that had to have been a shock after I'd just gotten out of rehab the day before."

"You said it wasn't your fault. Someone dosed your friend. And you got dosed when you gave her CPR."

He scraped his hand along his scruffy jaw and dropped it back to his lap.

"My buddy Drake, we served together in the military, he's the one who got me into the rehab center. His girlfriend Adria's sister, Juliana, went there, too. We met a couple times in group. She was cool. She got out before I did. Anyway, she was working at her sister's store. Adria let me stay in the apartment upstairs so I could get my head together before I drove home. There was a commotion in the shop. I went in to see if I could help, because Juliana sounded really pissed. Turns out another guy who worked there wanted to party and get Juliana loosened up because she wasn't into him. He shoved a bunch of heroin under her nose, not knowing the heroin was laced with fentanyl. The drug suppressed her breathing, and Juliana's heart stopped. I gave her CPR and got dosed, too, without knowing it. In fact, I thought I had some kind of panic attack or something, and she died because I blacked out."

Shelby reached over and touched his forearm. "Oh, Chase, it wasn't your fault."

"The cops told me they saw the whole thing go down on the surveillance video." He glanced out the side window. "Adria rushed in just as I hit the floor. Juliana was already gone. Adria gave me two doses of naloxone."

Her hand contracted on his arm. "She saved your life."

"Yes. The cop said she didn't even try to give Juliana a dose. She knew Juliana was gone." He put his elbow on the window frame and planted his head in his hand. "If I'd gotten there a little sooner . . . Maybe if I'd been able to continue CPR . . ."

"Don't do that to yourself. Don't put those thoughts in your head. You did everything you could to save her and nearly died trying."

That's what his psychiatrist told him. It was not his fault. That didn't stop the pain and guilt.

What happened with Juliana left him reeling. He knew the only way to get through it was to feel it, no matter how bad it hurt.

Having Shelby here, telling her what happened, it helped.

"It's a tragedy she died the way she did when she'd worked so hard to get clean." Shelby looked at him. "Is that why you went back to rehab, because you OD'd and feared you'd relapse?"

"No. I swear to you, I will not use again." He held her gaze for a moment so she could see he meant those words with everything in him. "Her death messed with my head. I thought I had a handle on everything when I walked out last time, and then . . ."

"You lost her." The way she said it made it sound different than him failing to save her life.

He shifted toward her. "Shelby, there was nothing going on between me and Juliana. I barely knew her really. I just couldn't deal with another loss. The grief and guilt were too much. And Hunt and Max showed up at the hospital accusing me of blowing it again, but I didn't. I'm committed to staying clean. But I needed to sort out the overwhelming grief I felt about Juliana and all the others I lost overseas, and that meant going back to the counselors who knew me."

"I can't imagine all you've been through. I know the past sixty days away from Eliza have been a challenge for you."

He missed his little girl. He wanted to move on with his life. But his past kept dragging him under. "More than you know." Sitting next to Shelby and not having the kind of relationship he wanted with her sucked big time.

"But you survived."

That's what I do.

Though sometimes he'd wished he hadn't.

But that was behind him—he hoped—even if the nightmares were still fresh in his mind.

"You could have died," she whispered, tearing at his heart.

"I know exactly what I want for my future and what I have to lose if I let my demons loose." Shelby. His daughter. And the life he wanted with both of them. "I will prove to you that you can trust me. I want us to be a family."

She didn't even look at him when he dropped that truth bomb between them. "Why don't you try to get some sleep? You look exhausted."

He was, though talking to Shelby about Juliana actually made him feel a little better. He shouldn't have waited so long to tell her his reasons for the extra week at rehab and that it had nothing to do with him using again.

He closed his eyes, thinking about what came next. He and Shelby would finally have some time together to figure out how to be partners in raising Eliza. He'd jump through any hoop she put in place. He'd do whatever it took. He'd show her he wasn't a deadbeat dad. He cared. More than she knew. Because even if she didn't know it, she'd saved him.

It didn't take long for him to drift off. Shelby had a way of making everything seem okay, and her presence always settled him, though it also amped up the desperate need he had for her.

The peace only lasted so long, because sleep opened the door to the many nightmares stored up in his mind.

Something strong gripped his arm and shook him. "Chase! Wake up!"

Chase's eyes shot open, and he sat bolt upright with the echo of the *rat-a-tat-tat* of automatic gunfire and the blast of explosions going off in his head. Not real. Just a series of horrific memories now. He pressed the heels of his hands into his eye sockets, and the gruesome scenes turned into a new fresh hell as the ghostly image of a beautiful blonde stared at him with dead eyes and blue lips.

Juliana.

He dropped his hands, opened his eyes, sucked in a ragged breath, and stared at the unfamiliar house in front of him.

"Are you okay?"

He hated that Shelby kept asking him that, but he guessed he hadn't slept peacefully. He never did. Not for long.

The concerned look on her face confirmed it.

"I'm fine."

Worry turned to doubt in her beautiful eyes.

"Where are we?"

"This used to be the Hudson place. Now it's the Wilde place."

He stared at the white house with the covered porch, black-trimmed windows, and dark green front door, not understanding at all. "What?"

"This is your new place. Welcome home." She gave him a brilliant smile that made him want to soak up all the good and wonderful things she was, but two trucks pulled in behind them and set his teeth to grinding.

His father and both brothers climbed out of the trucks.

"Fuck me." Chase climbed out of the truck ready to battle his family again, but they didn't come after him. Instead of chewing him out, his dad went off on Shelby.

Chapter Two

SHELBY CLIMBED down from the truck and faced off with three very pissed-off Wilde men. She should have realized when she spotted them in the driveway at Split Tree Ranch down the road that they'd come and start trouble. She knew why they were here, even if Chase was completely clueless.

All she wanted to do was surprise Chase and make him happy. He deserved it after everything he'd been through. But no. His family had to come and ruin her surprise.

She knew exactly what this was about. Still didn't make it any easier.

No one believed Chase, the handsome high school football star, prom king, valedictorian, and college grad with a bright and successful future, who could get any woman he wanted, had slept with *her*.

Chase's father, Wayne Wilde, took the lead and didn't mince words. He never did. "You're not going to get away with this, girl."

Chase stopped right beside her, gaze bouncing from his father to her.

"I did get away with it." She'd pulled it off days ago right under his nose.

She'd been working on it ever since she overheard someone talking in the diner where she and Eliza had Pancake Tuesday. Nobody ever really paid her any attention in this town, so she tended to hear a lot of things people said, not realizing she was right there.

They thought her quiet. Shy. Odd.

Someone to whisper about behind her back.

Stained by her mother and father's past.

She was all those things.

But for one glorious night, she'd been Chase's.

And now she was Eliza's mom. And Eliza thought she was awesome. And that felt really good.

Because growing up, she'd always felt like something was wrong with her. Her grandparents reluctantly raised her, providing for her needs but never loving her. They tolerated her. She'd been the unexpected burden they didn't ask for and didn't want. Not after all they'd been through with her mother.

Her birth had not been a happy day. No one celebrated. In fact, no one, including her mother, wanted her to exist at all.

She was the living reminder of a man's brutality and a woman's ruin.

The scandal had rocked the town.

People don't forget things like that when there's a sordid tale that goes with it.

Her grandmother told her that Shelby's father broke her mother, and that's why she committed suicide. But Shelby knew another truth. Her mother went crazy staring at Shelby, the living proof of what happened to her, and couldn't take it anymore.

Even her own grandparents could barely stand the sight of her.

She reminded them of the daughter they lost and the man who took her from them.

It was a sad tale.

It was a sad life.

One Eliza would never have to endure, because Shelby showered her with love and attention and tried to make each day a happy one.

Even if that meant slamming the door in Eliza's father's face once in a while.

And Shelby refused to apologize for who she was when she'd done nothing wrong. So she looked Mr. Wilde in the eye and said, "You're just mad I beat you to it."

Mr. Wilde stared daggers at her. "There's no way you could pull this off on your own."

"That's what you think, because you don't know me at all."

None of them did.

Not Max, who side-eyed her in town every time they crossed paths. Not Hunt, who refused to help her with the man who kept harassing her, despite the fact he was a cop.

And Mr. Wilde, who'd tossed his son out on his ass for doing what his mother asked of him, for daring to set the ranch on a better course, and for leaving despite not being wanted, he didn't know her either.

"What the hell is going on?" Chase asked, his gaze ping-ponging back and forth between her and his family.

Damn but they were all the most gorgeous men she'd ever seen. All tall, dark, and handsome. Mr. Wilde's hair had gone gray at the temples. They all had his striking blue eyes, though Chase's were more denim blue than ice blue. Each one of them was lean and toned. Again,

Chase stood out because of his bulk. The military had honed those muscles well.

But looks could be deceiving.

Each one of them wore a scowl to match their bad tempers.

Mr. Wilde bullied to get what he wanted.

Hunt had the authority and bearing of his position as a cop.

Max was mild-mannered, until you pissed him off. Then, watch out. She'd seen him practically take a guy's head off in the high school parking lot years ago when a girl tried to push the guy away and he got handsy instead, pinning her against his car. Max and the girl started dating the following week. Of course the hero got the beautiful girl.

Max probably didn't even remember Shelby from high school. He'd been way out of her league and in the stratosphere of social circles. She bet she could count the people who remembered her on one hand unless they were reminded of the sordid tale about her parents that never seemed to fade from anyone's mind for long.

And Chase. He really was the wild card in the family. Smart. Thoughtful. Practical. Tough. A little dangerous when angry. But she bet he had the biggest heart of them all.

She'd seen it when he was with Eliza.

She'd heard it when he talked to Eliza.

She knew it because of the way he opened up to his little girl.

Mr. Wilde glared at her. "She's going to screw you over just like she screwed us."

Shelby smiled at Mr. Wilde. "You got exactly what you deserved."

Chase looked at her. "What is he talking about?"

She held Mr. Wilde's menacing gaze. "I made them pay for what they did to you." She met Chase's inquisitive and astonished eyes.

"What did you do?"

"She stole the Hudson property right out from under us."

Chase eyed the house. "You bought this place."

Mr. Wilde pointed his finger at her. "And you probably used Chase's money to do it."

She grinned. "Which is why the property is in *his* name."

All the Wilde men gasped in shock.

Chase found his voice first. "Shelby, why would you do that? The money I sent you is for Eliza."

She rolled her eyes. "I keep telling you, you send me too much. What are you sending me, like half your paycheck?"

His face said he sent her more than half.

"Seriously, Chase, I appreciate that you want to take care of Eliza . . ."

"And you," he interjected.

"I didn't ask you to do that."

His gaze softened. "You didn't ask for anything. But I'm her dad, and taking care of her is my job."

"And now you're here to do it. Because the money you sent was way too much, I saved it. When I found out about the property and how your dad planned to sneak in and buy it cheap before the county put it up on the auction block, I beat him to it." She looked past Chase to Mr. Wilde. "I got it for a steal. The house had just been renovated before the guy who owned it lost his job. He and his wife inherited the house, but lost it when they couldn't pay the taxes. So I bought the house and land for twenty-six thousand dollars and some change. It is worth way more than the money your family took from you to save the ranch." She met Chase's gaze again. "You can take a loan out against the property and start your own ranch. Or sell it to your dad and make him pay what it's worth. Do whatever you want to do, because you aren't broke anymore, Chase. And you have a place that is yours, and no one can take it away from you."

Chase closed the distance between them.

She didn't know what to do and stepped back a few steps, but he quickly caught her in a hug, buried his face in her neck, and whispered, "Thank you."

She didn't know what to do with her hands, but they somehow ended up on the outside of his shoulders. She patted him awkwardly, but when he hugged her tighter, she wrapped her arms around him and hugged him close.

Her whole body went molten hot in his embrace. She remembered every tiny detail of their night together. She didn't care what anyone said about being drunk and forgetting things. Her mind had imprinted that night on her brain and heart.

He released her, only to take her face in both his big hands. "You amaze me."

"They shouldn't have turned their backs on you. You didn't do anything wrong."

"He took his mother away from us." Mr. Wilde's eyes held a world of hurt behind all the anger.

Chase released her and turned to his dad. "She didn't want to suffer anymore, and you wouldn't let her go. You held on so tight. I get why. You loved her. But all it did was force her to do something drastic to stop the pain."

Mr. Wilde's face flushed red with anger and some-thing more. His breathing became erratic.

Chase didn't dismiss it so easily. "Get back in the truck and go home, old man, before you have a heart attack."

"Another one, you mean." Max didn't look at all sorry for spilling the beans on that.

Shelby heard about the heart attack two weeks af-ter Chase had gone to rehab. Of course, none of them told Chase. She'd kept it to herself, knowing Mr. Wilde had recovered well enough to go home with medication, and Chase needed to focus on his own health and well-being.

Chase looked at both his brothers, pain and anger in his eyes. "I guess I didn't need to know about that."

They all looked defiant, making Chase shake his head. "Just go. Apparently I own this place, and I don't want you here."

Mr. Wilde spoke directly to Chase for the first time in probably the last seven years. "We aren't leaving until she finally tells you the truth."

Chase looked at her, then met his father's gaze with rage in his eyes. "She always tells me the truth."

Shelby fell back a step at the absolute vehemence in his voice.

Hunt took a step toward her and planted his hands on his hips. "Do the DNA test. Give him legal partial custody *if* he's the father."

Shelby held Chase's stunned gaze. He had no idea this wasn't the first time Hunt asked for a paternity test.

Chase took two long strides toward Hunt, his hands fisted.

Shelby couldn't let Chase fight her battles and rushed

to him just as he was about to throw a punch. She ducked between Chase and Hunt and pushed with her feet, her chest to Chase's, and held him back the best she could.

The second her cheek pressed to his neck, he went still.

"Stop," she pleaded. "He wants you to go after him so he'll have another excuse to lock you up and force you to do what he wants."

Chase's hands went to her arms. He rather gently set her aside, then took a step closer to Hunt and got in his face. "This is bullshit, Hunt, and you know it."

Mr. Wilde hooked his hand on Chase's shoulder and made him turn toward him. "Can't you see she played you? You're just a payday for her."

"You're the one who got paid, old man. I seem to remember leaving here empty-handed while your account was flush. You have a roof over your head and all that land because of the promise I made to *Mom*. The ranch is thriving because of the plans *I* put together for it."

"I did the work," he shot back.

"Really? You? Or Max leading the crew and Hunt taking up the slack?"

She couldn't believe he'd give his brothers credit. Judging by their faces, they couldn't believe it either.

"The ranch was built on my blood." Chase all of a sudden tore his T-shirt off over his head. "I've got the scars to prove it."

While they got a look at Chase's front, Shelby gasped at the sight of his back. Two large round scars, one high on his left shoulder, the other an inch in from his right side on his lower back. She'd seen the one on his forearm, where he had a small scar on the front and a big one on the back where the bullet went through. There was another long line that stretched from his back and wound around his side just under his ribs. She wondered how far around his front it went.

Hunt and Max stood staring, transfixed.

Mr. Wilde put a hand to his mouth. "I didn't want this for you."

"You threw me out. I had nowhere to go. The ranch needed an influx of cash, and a loan would only sink us faster. So I did what had to be done. Just like always. You got to keep your ranch, but you should know what it took to keep it. Four bullet wounds. A piece of shrapnel the size of a Frisbee in my side. A collapsed lung on two occasions. Eight total broken bones. And a lifetime of nightmares. I went to hell and back. I fought to come home to *my* little girl, and all you want to do is call the woman who saved me a liar. Are you fucking kidding me?" Chase rubbed his hands, T-shirt and all, over his face. "I am so fucking tired of this bullshit." Chase turned and looked at her with such sorrow and remorse, but he spoke to his family. "She gave me the greatest gift, and then she kept on giving. She had the nurse video call me during the birth. I got to see my little girl come into this world while I was halfway around the globe, surrounded by death. She set up a webcam in the nursery so I could log in anytime I wanted to see Eliza. I spent so much time just watching my little girl sleep. And every time I did, everything else faded away."

"That doesn't make it true. And how dare she give that baby your mother's name." Mr. Wilde's angry words sent one of the tears swimming in Chase's eyes down his cheek.

His family couldn't see it. Only she could see his pain.

Chase dragged his T-shirt back on over his head, at the same time wiping away those tears and his pain, so that when he faced them, all they got was his anger. "She did that for me because she knew how much I love Mom. How much I miss her. Because the night we were together, all I talked about was Mom, because *she* was willing to listen."

Chase turned to Hunt. "But you weren't willing to listen to Shelby. She asked you for months to get in touch with me to tell me about the baby. But did you? No. She had to steal your phone to get my number. How could you?"

"I'll apologize for all of it as soon you get a DNA test to prove that baby is yours."

"No." Chase shook his head. "All you guys do is push family away. You started with Mom, then me, and now you won't even accept Eliza. She's mine. I don't need a fucking test to tell me that when I know it all the way to my soul. So fuck all of you." He turned to her, took her hand, and pulled her toward the house.

Shelby tried to keep up with Chase's long strides, but finally ended up pulling her hand free so she didn't stumble. "Slow down. They're not chasing us."

They'd actually gotten into the two trucks and left.

"I cannot believe you." The words didn't sound like an accusation, but she took it that way.

"What did I do?"

"Saved my life. Again."

She didn't know what to say to that.

Chase stopped in the middle of the path up to the front door, turned, and moved in close. He smelled like the sun and wind and him. An intoxicating mix that made her want to snuggle up to him.

"Shelby."

It took her a second to meet his gaze. "Yeah?"

"I don't deserve you."

She clasped her hands in front of her so she didn't reach out and touch him. He wasn't hers to touch. But she did know one thing. "You're a good man, Chase."

"No, I'm not. But I'm trying to be for you and Eliza." With that, he turned back and headed for the house again, leaving her wondering exactly what he meant by that.

She scolded herself for sprouting dreams about a one-night stand turning into a life with an outcast Wilde that would never be reality.

Chapter Three

CHASE STOOD on the porch of his new house and felt the weight of his family driving back to Split Tree Ranch, a place he'd never be welcome again, crushing down on him. The pain in his chest left by his family's abandonment ached anew.

But he had a chance to start fresh and build a new life, thanks to Shelby.

Wholly aware of the woman beside him, he tried to ignore the echo of having her pressed up against his body.

Shelby pulled her phone out of her purse. "I need to call the sitter and let her know I'm going to be late." She tapped the screen and put the phone to her ear. "Hi, Abby, I'm so sorry. I'm going to be about half an hour late picking up Eliza. If you need me to call Tom to pick her up now, I will."

A shot of jealousy washed through Chase.

Who the hell is Tom?

"Okay, great. Tell her I'll be there as soon as I can, and I have a big surprise for her." Shelby smiled. "Yes. Her daddy." Shelby glanced at him. "You can come see her, right? I promised her."

"I'm all yours." He meant it. Though he didn't think

shy, sweet Shelby believed him. Why would she? His family acted like they hated her. They didn't even know her. Hell, he was still trying to get to know her. All he really had was the limited video chats with her from overseas, when they mostly talked about Eliza.

Seeing her as a mom to his little girl endeared her to him in a deep and meaningful way, but he knew there was so much more to her.

All those days away, he'd clung to that feeling of connection and understanding she'd left him with after their night together.

And then he came home and found he still wanted her just as bad as the morning they'd said goodbye. He hadn't seen her in person as often as he wished he could between deployments over the last nearly two and a half years. When he came home for good nine months ago, he'd never had a chance with her when she saw the way he was struggling and relying on the pain meds the doctors gave him after his surgeries to get him through one hour after the next, each and every day, even after his body healed.

He'd given her no choice but to keep him at arm's length, even though he caught the longing looks and hope in her eyes when he was relatively sober. They had a handful of good times they shared where he felt the friendship and bond between them strengthen. But then he'd ruin it by not showing up for days at a time, forgetting they were supposed to meet up at the park or he was supposed to watch Eliza. He'd wallow in the pain and his misery in his dark apartment, chasing oblivion. The pain he saw in her eyes when she'd laid down the law and ordered him to go to rehab or lose his daughter still tore him to pieces. It had felt like he'd let her down by not returning from the military and really being able to show her that he'd come back for her.

"We'll be there soon." She looked up at him. "Ready to go inside?"

He blurted out the question repeating in his head. "Who the hell is Tom?"

"My next-door neighbor." She said it matter-of-factly, telling him nothing of consequence. At least to him.

He left it alone for now, hoping she'd say *my boyfriend* if that's what he was. "I'm sorry about my family. They had no right to ask you for a DNA test."

Why the hell did Hunt have to butt into everything Chase did these days? Why did his father go after Shelby and make it infinitely harder on Chase to earn back her trust? And how dare they treat Shelby like a liar and a thief.

Anger roiled in his gut, and all he wanted to do was thump Hunt's head off a wall.

She stared out at the land beyond the side porch. "It doesn't matter." He hated the resignation in her voice.

"It matters to me. That's not the first time it's come up, is it?"

Shelby sighed. "Hunt stopped by the hospital the day after I gave birth. I thought you sent him to check on me." The last she whispered, her words filled with hurt and disappointment.

Chase hung his head. "You thought *I* wanted the DNA test?"

"No."

Relief rushed through him.

"Hunt made it very clear why he was there and how

he wanted to protect you. I'm not surprised he hasn't dropped it. For all their anger toward you, Chase, they still care about you."

Chase thought about all the times in the months leading up to him going to rehab that Hunt would show up at the bar or Shelby's house and drag his ass back to his lonely apartment instead of dumping him in a cell. He'd threatened it enough, but never did it.

Then he OD'd trying to save Juliana and woke up to Hunt and Max at his hospital bedside. Yes, they'd been pissed before they knew the OD was an accident, but they showed up.

He had to make amends to Shelby, but he also hoped to make amends with his brothers and father one day.

"I meant what I said. I don't need the DNA test, because I know she's mine."

"Hunt's a cop. He wants proof." Shelby shrugged it off, but it bothered her. She didn't deserve nor had she ever done anything to warrant being called a liar.

"You should have told me he asked for it. I would have told him to go fuck himself." He loved the little smirk that earned him. "You can count on me, Shelby. I will always have your back."

She folded her arms under her breasts, pulling the oversized sweatshirt tight and making him wonder why she always hid her curves. "You had enough going on in your life. I knew how hard things were for you over there, and you wanted to be with Eliza, and you missed your mom, and your family sucked. I didn't want to add anything onto your already overburdened shoulders."

"How do you know things were hard for me?" His heart jackhammered in his chest. There were things in his past he didn't want anyone to know. Things he'd seen. Things he'd done. Mistakes. Miscalculations. His anxiety-fueled mind conjured a million scenarios.

She held his gaze. "Because I heard you talking to Eliza over the webcam."

He shifted from one foot to the other, uncomfortable knowing she'd heard him pouring out his thoughts to his little girl when he'd catch her awake in her crib waiting for her mom to come in and get her in the morning or after a nap.

He'd been honest. But he'd held back on the darkest stuff, even if he had said things to Eliza he hadn't shared with anyone else.

The compassion in Shelby's eyes touched him. "I felt bad for listening and intruding on your time with her, but you had to know I could hear you."

"I guess I just didn't really think about it. She was there, my captive audience, and I could whisper all the things cluttering my mind. I wanted her to hear my voice and know that I was there, even if I couldn't be right there in the room with her."

"You tell really great stories. I love how you changed the dangerous things that were happening to you into other things, like you being swarmed by trolls shooting bees at you."

"I got stung a couple of times."

"Five times," she corrected him.

"Four," he reminded her.

"Five if you count the one that grazed your thigh." She gave him a pointed look. "Stingers are still stingers even if they only cut and not impale."

"Okay. So, seven by your way of counting."

Her head whipped back, her eyes wide with shock. "Jeez, Chase."

"I'm a little worse for wear, that's for sure." Epic understatement.

"How are you now?" The softly spoken question held an inquisitive tone and not a trace of accusation that maybe he hadn't changed at all.

"I don't know." And that was the absolute truth.

He'd been good coming out of rehab. Hopeful. Excited, even, to start a new chapter of his life with Eliza. And Shelby, if she'd have him.

Then everything went to shit when Juliana died, and he'd ended up in the hospital with one more senseless death haunting him.

He needed to find his way back to hopeful.

He turned and took in the house she bought him. "I haven't had a real home in seven years."

She put her hand on his arm. "Eliza will always be your home. You need her as much as she needs you. I saw that when you came home all those months ago. Despite the time you needed to heal and you not being in the right frame of mind to be present for her, I could still see how much you wanted to be her dad. I never had one, but I want it for her. You hated your apartment. I think you felt trapped there in that tiny box, surrounded by things that weren't yours. You talked about getting a place just like this, a place you could put down roots and call your own, and know no one could kick you out. So when I heard about this house and property, I knew it was just what you wanted and needed. This is yours, Chase. Settle in. Make it yours. Make good memories here with Eliza."

It touched him deeply that she'd known how much he needed this. He'd been adrift for too long. "It's mine because you were looking out for me. You had my back."

He missed that after leaving the army. He needed it. And Shelby had given it to him.

"I will always have your back, Chase. You're Eliza's dad. We are bound together by blood through her. You are not alone. And the next time you feel that way and you're nose-diving toward the bottom again, you let me know, and I will be there to hold out my hand and pull you back up."

Because you want me?

He didn't ask. But he hoped so.

"Eliza needs you, Chase."

Do you need me, the way I desperately need you?

He knew he could count on her. He wanted her to know she could count on him. "What do you need, Shelby?"

She stared at the house she practically stole for him. "I have Eliza. She's all I need."

He saw in her eyes what he'd felt for a long time. She didn't have anyone else.

He'd felt exactly the same way, except now she'd made it clear he had her. At least as far as him being important because of their connection to Eliza. But he wanted Shelby to want to keep him close for much more personal and intimate reasons.

He wished she knew she had him, too. So he tried to remind her of that, took a chance, and brought up something they'd never talked about. "You and me, we were good together that night." Good didn't begin to cover what they shared. Great. Amazing. Special. His mind couldn't come up with a word that defined that night in her arms.

If he hadn't been watching her so closely, he wouldn't have seen the ever-so-slight nod. But she contradicted her agreement. "I'm not the person you end up with, Chase." The defeatist tone surprised him.

"Why not?" He really wanted to know. Because of his past? Because he'd screwed up and dove headfirst into a prescription drug bottle and never wanted to come out? Until he did. Because of her.

"Because you're Chase Wilde."

That didn't explain anything.

"You could have any woman you want."

He wanted her.

"You don't end up with the girl who was ruined before she was ever born. Your father knows that. Your brothers, too." She moved past him and went to the front door, putting her back to him and shutting down the conversation.

Ruined? What the hell does she mean?

He turned to her as she pulled a set of keys from her purse. He stopped dead in his tracks and stared down at the mat she stood on in front of the door that read, "Welcome Home," with "Wilde" underneath the greeting.

"A housewarming gift. To remind you this is yours. This is home now."

How the hell did she keep surprising him like this?

Choked up, he mumbled, "Thank you."

She unlocked the door, then handed him the keys. "You first. It's your place."

Chase opened the door, pushed it wide, and held his hand out for her to go in first. Manners, yes, but also because he wanted to see *her* in *his* place.

And even though they stepped into an empty wide-open combination family room, dining room, and kitchen area, all he wanted to look at was her.

She'd changed over the last nearly three years he'd

known her. Of course after their night together, he'd obsessed over every little detail of their time together. He spent seven months kicking his ass for not getting her number and wishing he was stateside so he could talk her back into his bed. Then she called him out of the blue and dropped the bomb. He was going to be a father. By the time he wrapped his head around that, they'd shared several phone calls leading up to the birth, talking mostly about the pregnancy, how the baby was doing, and what Shelby needed to do to prepare to bring Eliza home alone. He'd felt a million miles away and mostly useless because he was overseas and could only support Shelby by sending a check and sympathizing with her sore back and swollen feet. Their calls were often too short for them to really get to know each other, but he loved all the little tidbits he pulled out of her. And he shared things with her about his family, his work, some of the cool things he'd seen and done being stationed overseas without boring her with details about drills or scaring her with recounts of his missions. But she always seemed to know how lonely he was away from home, and it drew him to her even more.

Several women hit on him in the bar the night they met. None of those other women captured his attention the way Shelby did, though at first he didn't think she noticed him at all. Something about the way she didn't seem to belong there hooked him. He'd bet she'd never been in the place. But he liked the way her plump ass filled the stool beside his and how her brown wavy hair spilled over her shoulders and hid her face and that she sat there quietly drinking some fruity cocktail. Three different ones, if he remembered right, while he knocked back one whiskey shot after another, trying to drink away the memory of how he got a bullet through the shoulder, one sliced across his thigh, and how he couldn't call himself stupid enough for coming home on leave where no one wanted him.

He was on the last night of his stay before he had to fly back to base and report in. And he hadn't wanted to spend it alone. But a night with a girl who didn't so much as even try to engage him in conversation and who tried really hard not to be noticed . . . Well, she seemed like the perfect match to his need to shut off everything and just be quiet—and naked—with someone.

Shelby stared at him, her eyes filled with concern. "Chase? Are you okay?"

"Do you remember that night?" He needed to know if it meant as much to her as it did to him.

She held his gaze, her cheeks tinted pink, then turned for the kitchen. "You'll need to buy a washer and dryer for the mudroom off the back."

"So we're not ever going to talk about it?"

Still she didn't look at him. "Do you want to see this place or not?"

"The way you're avoiding talking about it makes me think you've got something to say." He hoped it was something good. He hoped it was, *Let's do it again.*

She opened the fridge door. "I put some essentials in here for you. Eggs, milk, butter, frozen pancakes and waffles, a few frozen pizzas, and TV dinner things I thought you might like." She slammed the door. "You should replace the fridge, too, by the way." Her cheeks were an even brighter shade of pink that made him think she was imagining that night. "I put some canned goods up in the cupboard," she said to her toes, then started walking toward the hallway. "It's three bedrooms, two baths. The main bedroom is pretty big."

He followed her down to it, stopped just inside the room, and stared at the king-size bed backed by the most amazing wood design going up the wall.

"Do you like it?" The shyness was back.

He didn't know what to say about the stunning display.

"I saw something like it on one of those home improvement shows. I'm not that great with tools, but Tom showed me how to use the chop saw. It was actually kind of fun. My grandpa had a huge pile of lumber in the shed behind the house and I thought . . . Well . . . Do you like it?" The nervous words tumbled out her mouth, and all he could do was stare at her in wonder.

"I think you're amazing."

Her blush turned even the soft shell of her ears pink.

Trying to alleviate some of her nerves, he focused on the wood. "Did you stain it all yourself, too?"

"Sanded, stained the boards in three different tones to give it this pretty pattern of lights and darks, laid it all out the way I thought it looked best, then nailed it up. The mattress store was having a big sale, so I got you a bed." Her cheeks blazed red. "I mean, you need to sleep somewhere."

"In my house is a good place." Her bed would be infinitely better. It had been a damn long time since he'd slept with anyone. He barely slept at all most nights. And since he found out she was pregnant with his child, he'd attempted to go out and find some comfort, but always ended up going home alone, because no one compared to her. No one could come close to what they shared that night.

He wondered if Shelby had any idea about the kinds of feelings he had for her.

"Shelby, honey, you didn't have to do all this for me."

Her eyes went wide at the endearment before her gaze dropped to his chest. "I did what needed to be done. You need a home. You need a bed. The rest you can do on your own. But I wanted you to have something to come home to, because the last time . . ." She choked up, turned her back on him, and pretended to straighten the hunter-green comforter she'd bought for his bed to go with the white sheets.

"The last time I fucked everything up," he readily admitted. "Including being Eliza's dad and showing you that you can trust me."

Finally Shelby met his gaze head-on. "Don't disappoint me this time, Chase." There was so much hope in those words.

"I wish I could make you that promise. I'm sure to disappoint you in some way. But you can be sure, I won't ever use again." The OD last week proved how lucky he was to still be alive and how even one slipup could take everything, even his life, from him.

"I'm sorry about the woman you tried to save who died. I can't imagine . . ." She turned away again, and he barely heard her say, "We almost lost you."

That was the second time she'd said it, making him believe she really did care about him as more than just Eliza's dad.

He closed the distance between them and set his hands on her shoulders. "I've got a lot of making up to do. I have a lot to prove. I'm not saying I'm a hundred percent. I know I'm not. After Juliana's death . . ." He still couldn't believe she was gone. He didn't know how to process it, and every time he thought about her and what happened, the depression he'd fought so hard to claw his way out of threatened to take him under again. "I don't know if I will ever be who I used to be, but I'm working on being the guy you and Eliza need."

"Chase, let's face it. All I know about that guy is that he was charming and sad and a little lost but had a world of possibilities waiting for him. What I liked most about him, *you*, is your strength and determination to do what needs to be done to get to where you want to be. It took a lot of guts and hard work to get through rehab. I know you put in the work. I heard something different and optimistic in your voice when you called to talk to Eliza."

He turned her to face him. "She's two, Shelby. Our conversations are *me* talking to *you*."

Her eyes went wide with surprise and something else he glimpsed. Then she hid her emotions away before he could really say it was interest.

"You barely give me a chance to have a real conversation with you. You always put Eliza on, which I appreciate, but I needed you to hear that I was working on my shit and I was getting better, so you wouldn't stop me from seeing my little girl."

When he arrived home for good, he and Shelby decided they didn't need to go to court for any sort of legal visitation. Shelby said he could see Eliza anytime he wanted. Since he hadn't been working, just recovering from his wounds, he stuck to seeing her every weekend and two nights during the week so he didn't mess up her schedule. But then he started losing track of time, showed up on the wrong night, or didn't show up at all for days on end. He'd even been stoned enough to show up late at night, pounding on her door, demanding to see Eliza well after her bedtime. He'd made a fool of himself making passes at Shelby that were sloppy and stupid. She hadn't taken him seriously.

Drunk and stoned, he was an asshole.

Her eyes pleaded with him to understand. "I hated telling you that you couldn't see her, but you left me no choice."

"I know. You had to protect her. And I hate that you had to keep her safe by keeping me away." He ran his hand over the back of his tense neck. "I'm so damn glad she's too young to know what happened, how far I fell down the rabbit hole, but I promise you, it won't happen again."

"I hope you keep that promise. For your sake, Chase. I don't want to see you self-destruct again. I didn't know how to help you. I didn't think you'd even want my help." She'd been a quiet, steady presence he could count on.

"You did exactly what I needed you to do and made it clear that if I wanted to hold on to the one thing that actually mattered in my life, I'd have to fight for it."

"And you did."

"Yeah. And just when I thought I could come home and we could"—*be together*, he wanted to say but didn't because they weren't there yet, so he went with—"find a way to be a family, everything got messed up. I wasn't using again," he swore. "I didn't OD because I took something." He needed her to believe him. Unlike his brothers.

She put her hand on his arm, trying to reassure him. "I believe you. You tried to save her, Chase. You did the right thing." Her gaze fell away. "And I'm so glad you survived."

He'd come damn close to losing his life. Again.

He thought that was over now that he wasn't in a war zone, but he'd come damn close while he was using the months he'd been home recovering from his latest set of wounds and adjusting to a new life outside of the military. Then he'd very nearly died trying to save Juliana.

That was one too many close calls.

He came back here because this was where Shelby and Eliza were, but he didn't feel the kind of peace he needed because he'd still felt adrift while trying to find his place in their lives and his own.

This time, he planned to do better.

And thanks to Shelby's help, getting him this home and welcoming him back without any hostility or anger for what he'd done in the past, he hoped they could start again and build something together.

He just wished he knew if she wanted to do that with him.

He knew he meant something to her. She'd gone above and beyond getting him this place and revenge on his family. He found that exceedingly hot. No woman he'd ever been with had done something so badass and important to him.

"We better get going. Eliza is waiting for us."

He stopped her before she exited the room. "Shelby."

She turned to face him.

"Thank you."

She gave him one of those shy smiles he loved. "You're welcome."

They stared at each other for a moment, something poignant passing between them.

She turned away first, but not before her gaze landed on the bed behind him, then darted away.

He grinned for the first time in a long time, and a

spark of hope lit in his chest. Then he followed her back down the hall toward the family room and kitchen.

She stopped outside one of the two bedroom doors they'd passed on the way to the master bedroom. "I think you should make this Eliza's room. It has really great light and a fantastic view of the trees out the window."

Stunned, he stared at the empty room and mentally decorated it with a toddler bed, a soft rug for her to play on, and something fun on the walls to make the place seem cheerful. "You'll really let her stay here with me sometimes?"

"Yes. Eventually. But that's a long talk we'll have soon about shared custody and taking care of her. After what happened, and the fact you're still working on setting up a new life for yourself, I hope you understand it's going to be a slow process."

Yeah, he didn't really know how to take care of Eliza on his own. But he'd learn. And the best way to do that was to spend time with Eliza—and her pretty mom.

Chapter Four

SHELBY AND Chase pulled up in front of the babysitter's house. He drove, giving her time to think about everything that happened between them.

He looked a hell of a lot better than his first day home after being discharged from the army, when she thought he'd be hopeful about starting a new life and being a dad to Eliza. But he'd still been healing from his wounds, in pain physically and emotionally, after being shot and probably losing more friends, though he never went into any depth about his experiences overseas. Eliza was the only thing that really made him smile and leave his apartment to do things other than wallowing on the couch, drinking and taking far more than the prescribed amount of pain meds.

At first, he always seemed happy to see Eliza. But the more time that passed, the worse he got.

He made Shelby the bad guy, because she wouldn't allow him to see his daughter, and she didn't want that to happen again.

He swore this time would be different. He'd even said he wanted them to be a family. While that made her heart beat faster and her wish for things that seemed impossible, she understood that Chase wanted them to raise Eliza together. She connected them.

He'd used Eliza as a lifeline when he was using, desperate to see her, so he had something good in his life when he was destroying it at the same time.

Eliza couldn't be the glue that held Chase together. He needed to find that within himself and build a new life, one that gave him a sense of accomplishment and satisfaction.

That's why she'd gotten him the house and property. He needed a solid starting point. What he did with it was on him. Success or failure was up to him.

She loved that she'd been able to shock him with her surprise. She'd never done anything so daring. But when she heard about the property and knew that she had a rare favor she could call in at the courthouse, she didn't hesitate to snap up the land.

She wanted Chase to have a safe and nice place to live so that Eliza could have longer visits with him. A drab apartment or motel room wasn't going to cut it. And after he'd served his country, had spent all his money on rehab to be better for himself and Eliza, and had given his bonuses to his family to save their ranch, he deserved something good to happen to him.

She couldn't believe he'd brought up that night. Her cheeks heated just thinking about it.

Why now? They'd never spoken about it.

She understood it had been a onetime thing. She didn't expect Chase to want her just because they had a child. But it seemed like that night meant something to him. Though maybe she was reading too much into it. Growing up in a home with two people who obviously loved each other, but were cold to her, she'd internalized how much she wasn't wanted. She was a burden to her grandparents. An obligation.

She didn't want to be that to Chase.

The tie that bound them together was the only thing they needed to focus on. Eliza. Shelby appreciated so much that Chase stepped up immediately and took responsibility for Eliza. And even though he'd been serving overseas, he took every opportunity to call, video chat, and engage with Eliza over the webcam.

Shelby thought it sweet and probably cathartic for him to talk to someone who hadn't learned to talk back. He'd taken the time and made a point to let Eliza hear him and feel his presence during those calls. He may not have been with her, but he'd found a way to connect with her.

Now, every time she heard his voice, she yelled, "Daddy." *Dada* had been her first word.

And they talked, too. Shelby always gave him an update when he managed to link in during the morning or evening. She let him know about Eliza's checkups and the new things she was doing. When Eliza started babbling, crawling, and toddling, Shelby made sure he got to see it.

She remembered so many calls where she'd see Chase's haggard and weary face and how he'd smile the second he saw Eliza, even if she was asleep.

She hated that his family thought she lied about Eliza's paternity. She wondered if Chase questioned it as well, but simply didn't care, because he needed Eliza to be his so he had something good in his life.

She wondered how much of their night together he actually remembered. They were up practically the whole night. He had to be as sober as her by the early morning light when they'd run out of condoms, rolled the dice, and said thank you and goodbye with their bodies. There'd been no thought to consequences because they were so caught up in each other before she silently slipped out of bed, dressed, and left without a word exchanged between them.

She'd left a piece of herself with him.

She'd taken a piece of him with her.

But did he believe that?

She slipped out of the car and met Chase on the sidewalk.

"What is it?" He looked concerned, reading the raw emotions swelling inside her. "Did you change your mind about me seeing her?"

"No. Of course not."

"Then what?" He gave her a second. "Just say it, Shelby, because I can't take this tension right now."

She couldn't meet his eyes and stared at the concrete. She wanted him to believe her, but would understand if he didn't. "Do you want the DNA test?"

His black work boots came into view, his shoes nearly touching hers he was so close now. "Shelby, you've seen me naked and done untold wonders to my body. Surely you can look at me."

That made her head pop up. She stared at him, wide-eyed and dumbstruck. Then he smiled, and she got it. He was trying to remind her they'd been intimate, and she needed to relax. Still, memories of that night, what they'd done together and to each other, made her head tilt down again as embarrassment heated her whole face.

He caught her chin with the tip of one big, rough finger and tipped her head back up. "I will always tell you the truth. After all we've shared and the fact that we have a kid together, don't ever think you can't look me in the eye and say whatever the hell is on your mind and I won't listen." He took her hand and walked with her toward the door. "And no. I don't need a test to tell me she's mine." He knocked on the door. "I could never forget that night. How you sat quietly next to me, ordered three different drinks, like you hadn't ever had one before and couldn't decide what you liked."

"I'd never had a drink before, so I tried a few." She'd been celebrating. Alone. And he'd been the gift she never expected but dared to make hers—at least for one night.

He chuckled and shook his head. "I wondered about that, but then it just made you seem more interesting. And bold, to mix so many different kinds of alcohol, and maybe a bit reckless. After your third drink, you finally spoke to me."

"You were so quiet. And sad. It didn't fit your outgoing, take-on-the-world reputation."

"Well, the fourth drink you ordered loosened your tongue even more, and after we talked for a while, you said it would be a good idea if we left together. After that, I was shocked to be the first."

She liked and appreciated Chase even more for not teasing her or questioning why she'd waited so long to be with someone. It was her choice, and she'd picked him. Still, she blushed from her toes all the way up to the top of her head.

Her embarrassment didn't deter him from going on. "Given that, I don't imagine you got a taste of something good and rushed out for more after you'd waited that long to try it. You're still blushing just as much around me as you did then, and all we did was bring up that night."

"Nothing could compare to that," she said under her breath, remembering the many ways and times they did it that night. The last time, after they'd gone through the three condoms he had on him, they came together and didn't just have sex. It was a slow, mesmerizing connection that branded his imprint on her body, heart, and soul. She'd never forget it.

And Eliza was the proof that it wasn't just a fantasy, but it really happened.

This time Chase cupped her face and made her look at him. "Christ, Shelby. You can't say something like that and not expect me to not only remember but want to show you how good it can be all over again."

The door opened, and Abby stood there staring at Chase. "What are you doing again?"

"Nothing," Shelby blurted, stepping out of Chase's warm hands, and catching Eliza under the arms as the toddler launched herself into Shelby's chest. She stood with her little girl in her arms and hugged her close.

"Is this him?" Abby asked, still staring at Chase. She couldn't take her eyes off him.

No woman, young or old, could ignore Chase's gorgeous face and tall, strong body.

"Chase Wilde, Abby Clarke."

"Daddy!" Eliza held her arms out to him.

He plucked her from Shelby's arms, breathed her in, closed his eyes, and sighed. "Hey, baby girl. Did you have a good day?"

"You 'ate."

"I'm sorry, I'm *late*. Mama and I got held up talking to your uncles and granddad."

Abby raised one eyebrow. "Everything okay?"

"Fine." Shelby wanted to forget the whole thing happened.

"Good. You've got enough on your plate right now."

Shelby touched her hand to Abby's arm and gave her a pointed look to stop her from saying anything more.

Chase eyed her. "What else is going on?"

"Nothing," she said too quickly to make it believable. "We need to get this little one home for dinner."

Abby seemed a little confused. "So you're going home? Together?"

"Chase is moving into *his* new place tonight."

"I still can't believe you got that one over on them." Abby beamed, then turned to Chase. "Do you love it?"

"I'm completely blown away. As always, Shelby surprises me in the best ways."

Abby gave her a knowing smirk. "If only she'd stop holding herself back from everyone."

Shelby side-eyed Abby. "I'm . . ."

"A loner," Abby filled in the blank Shelby left. It was hard for Shelby to describe how difficult it was for her to connect with others, because she always feared the same cold rejection she got from her grandparents. "Closed off."

Shelby scoffed, but knew it was true.

Abby gave her a soft smile. "And amazing to those very few of us you let in."

That made Shelby blush again.

Chase stared at her for a long moment. "I'm damn happy to be one of those lucky few. But why are you so . . . guarded?"

Because being rejected sucked, but being rejected by you after all we shared would hurt more than all the hurts I've suffered growing up.

"Fly, Daddy."

Saved by the toddler!

Chase shifted Eliza in his arms so she lay across both of his, then walked down the path, flying her up and down in the air, leaving Shelby alone with Abby for a moment.

"Seriously, Shelby, he's . . . oh my God gorgeous. And look at him with her."

Chase tossed Eliza in the air and caught her to his chest.

Eliza laughed and tapped her hands on his shoulders. "Again."

Shelby's heart melted, and another part of her went hot and needy.

Chase did as Eliza ordered and tossed her in the air again.

Shelby held her breath, even though she knew Chase would never let her fall. Still . . . "Chase. Your back. Are you sure you're okay to do that?" The last thing she wanted was for him to get hurt, start taking meds, and not be able to stop himself again.

Chase held Eliza close. "I'm fine."

She believed in second chances and that Chase knew best when it came to his physical limitation due to his past injuries. She nodded at him, then turned to Abby. "Everything okay today? Did you go to the park?"

"Same as yesterday." Abby held her gaze, worry in hers.

Relief, sharp and heady, went through her. Thirty-seven days ago, everything in her life changed. Again. But not in a good way. In a way that had her looking over her shoulder and worried about her little girl. "Okay. Let me know if anything changes."

"What's going on?" Chase looked from her to Abby.

"Nothing," she said, only making his eyes narrow more with not just curiosity, but frustration now. "Would you mind strapping her in her car seat?" They'd stopped by her place a few blocks away and grabbed the extra safety seat on the way to pick up Eliza.

Chase eyed her for another moment, then carried Eliza to his truck.

"You should tell him what's going on."

The last thing she wanted to do was talk about her parents with him. She didn't want him to look at her differently, the way others did when they realized she was *that girl*. "He's got enough to deal with right now. And like you said, nothing has changed."

"Creepy is still creepy. You don't know if this situation is going to escalate or not."

"If you're nervous about taking the kids to the park, keep them here and play in the backyard."

"They love the park. Though it's not easy to keep three toddlers corralled. Adding in keeping track of someone else makes it harder."

"I know. I'm sorry. But Hunt has so far been no help."

"He's a police officer. If he won't help, go over his head." Abby pushed because she cared. And because she was responsible for Eliza and didn't want to get blamed if something happened on her watch.

"Hunt has a point," she reluctantly admitted. "He can't do something about someone who hasn't actually done anything." Still, showing up, watching them, it creeped her out.

Abby pressed her lips into a flat line. "I don't like it."

"You and me both."

Chase stood on the sidewalk staring back at her, Eliza already strapped in her seat.

"Thank you for watching her today. See you in the morning."

"I hope you have a really good night." Abby winked, then closed the door on a giggle.

The butterflies were back in her belly as she approached the big man leaning against the side of the truck.

"Everything okay?"

"Yep."

Chase folded his arms over his broad chest. "Why are you lying to me?"

"I'm not," she shot back. "Everything is fine." She hated lying, but seriously, Chase had enough going on, and this was her problem. "Let's celebrate your home-coming with Eliza."

Chase gave her a sad grin. "You're always looking out for me, helping me be a part of Eliza's life. You pushed me into rehab." He held up a hand to stop her from defending her actions and ultimatum that if he didn't get help, he couldn't see his daughter. "Believe me, I know I needed the shove. What I'm trying to say is that if you need my help, I'm here for you no matter what else is going on in my life. Helping you might actually help me feel like I'm not useless and you're not carrying ninety percent of the load all the time with Eliza."

She sighed, unable to stop her heart from softening toward him even more. "I don't feel that way. I love being a mom. It's not a burden."

"I see that. But doing it mostly on your own has got to be hard."

She couldn't deny it. Occasionally she really needed a break and some time to herself. And she loved seeing Chase with Eliza.

"I'm here to stay, Shelby. I want to share the load. I

want more time with her. And what I'd really like is for us to spend time together as a family."

Right. They were Eliza's parents. Nothing more. And she'd like Eliza to see them together, able to be the family she deserved even if they weren't a couple. "Then let's get our girl home and have dinner together."

Eliza needed her dad. And Chase needed his little girl. She hoped this time he'd conquered his demons and stepped up, because she hated denying him access to Eliza. She hated the disappointed look on her daughter's face when she asked for her daddy and he wasn't around.

She grew up without her parents. Thank God. They were terrifying in different ways, in horrible ways. She was better off without them. But that didn't stop her little girl heart from wishing and hoping she'd had loving parents just like the other kids.

Chase looked wiped out from the long day, but his eyes brightened with joy at the invitation. "I'm really looking forward to having dinner with you."

He didn't mean with her, she reminded herself. He meant with them, her and Eliza.

"You look like you could use a home-cooked meal."

"Definitely. And being with you and Eliza is a hell of a lot better than being alone, even in my new place."

Exactly. He needed her to be a friend and to spend time with his daughter.

"Once you're really moved in and settled, it will feel like home." She glanced up and down the street, looking for a familiar car and breathing easier when she didn't see it.

"Are you going to tell me what's got you unnerved? Or is it me and you just don't want to say so?"

"What? No. It's not you." Well, him being so close did make her wholly aware of him and the strange way he always made her feel. But he didn't make her uncomfortable in a bad way, just . . . so *aware* of him. Like she could feel him next to her. But she couldn't say that without sounding like a crazy person and tried to come up with a reasonable explanation. "I guess I'm just unsettled. I thought Hunt dropped the paternity test thing right after Eliza was born." She really needed to stop lying to him. He didn't deserve that, and it made her feel terrible.

Chase's shoulders sagged. "I'm really sorry about that."

Great, now she'd made him apologize to her. "It's not your fault."

"Yeah. It is. I don't know why they're pursuing this DNA thing."

"They're standing up for you." She wondered what that felt like.

"I don't need their protection."

"I would never lie to you about Eliza," she assured him, because she felt guilty for holding back the real reason she was on edge. Yes, being around him brought back all kinds of memories and made her long for things that would never be more than yearnings. Chase gave her the best night of her life but never promised more. He was home to start over, and she would give him the time and space to do that because he'd been through enough. And now he got to decide what he wanted for his future.

She wouldn't put her wants and desires on him to try to build the family she'd never had but wanted for her little girl. His family had forced Chase to make desperate attempts to save the ranch and his family relationships. And because of his efforts, he'd nearly lost his life—several times.

He deserved to be happy. And that meant letting him find that happiness on his terms.

Right now, he needed the attachment to her and Eliza to ground him. But once he found his footing, once he had his balance back, he still had a world of possibilities in front of him. And she couldn't stand in his way or force or expect him to choose her just because they shared a child.

She liked her life. She was fine with it being just her and Eliza. She didn't need anyone to make her feel fulfilled.

But sometimes, she did get lonely.

Chapter Five

KYLE WALKED into his family home in Willow Fork, excited to share his news with his parents. They didn't want to be here. They'd moved down south after he was arrested and incarcerated. They couldn't stand the gossip and hateful looks people gave them. They wanted to live where no one knew what he'd done. But he'd forced them to come back with him.

They'd told him a dozen times to stay away from Shelby and Eliza, that he didn't have a right to see his own child and grandchild because of what he'd done.

They didn't understand.

After all the years he missed with them, sitting in a locked cell, he needed to see them.

Maybe if his parents had shared news about them while he was away, the need wouldn't be so great to learn everything he could about them.

He went up the stairs to their room, opened the door, and stared at the two people who were never on his side or let him do what he wanted. "I saw Eliza today with Shelby. They're both so beautiful. Shelby looks so much like her mom, my Rebecca."

"Leave them alone," his mother warned. "If Shelby sees you, she'll call the police again."

"That's why I parked on another street and watched from behind a tree. I'm not stupid."

"You'll be caught, just like the last time." His father sounded so sure, and it grated.

"She didn't see me. Neither did that guy she's with."

"He's ex-military. He will fight to keep you away from *his* family." His father looked all too happy about that.

"They're *my* family."

Shelby and Chase looked like they were getting really close. You could tell by the way they stood near each other and kind of leaned toward each other. They had a lot to say to each other. He wished he knew how Chase managed to get her to forgive him for screwing things up.

Kyle had done some digging and discovered Chase was back home from rehab.

Shelby didn't look the least bit concerned or upset with him about it.

If he read his daughter right, it was easy to see how she felt when she looked at Chase when he wasn't looking at her. She had real feelings for him.

That could be a problem if Chase got in Kyle's way.

"Shelby will come around. I know she will. I'm her dad. She just needs a little more time."

"Stay away from her," his mom ordered again. "She won't forgive you."

"She will! You don't know anything. We can be happy together!" He slammed the door on them and walked away, knowing he was right.

Shelby had a good heart. She'd see how much he loved her mother, Rebecca, how much he loved her and Eliza, and she'd want them to be a family.

Chapter Six

CHASE PARKED the truck in front of his new house, the headlights spotlighting the front door, emphasizing the loneliness of the place. Out in the middle of nowhere, everything quiet beneath the sparkling night sky, no other lights for miles, and an empty house with no one waiting for him.

But he finally had a place to call home again.

A fresh start, just like he'd wanted coming out of rehab.

He still hadn't fully processed how Shelby had done this for him, but he owed her big time for finding him a place to live.

Not some barracks or container housing unit in another country. Not some cheap motel room. Not a dingy apartment where you could hear your neighbors' TV and shouting and smell their cooking.

This was a place you settled down in and made a life.

He understood that was her message to him.

And she was right. He needed to get his shit together.

But it was damn hard to forget what happened last week and really believe that Juliana was gone.

He needed to call his buddy Drake and tell him how

sorry he was for the loss. Adria, Juliana's twin sister, must be devastated.

He needed to thank her for saving his life.

It seemed the women who came into his life took better care of him than his family.

Shelby and Eliza were the best distraction. He'd loved having dinner with them tonight. A simple meal together at the table eased him in a way he hadn't expected. He'd felt connected to Shelby in a way he'd never felt before. And watching her with Eliza the last two years, knowing she was the mother of *his* child, set off a protective instinct inside him.

Hunt overstepped asking for the DNA test and court-ordered visitation for Chase. Where the hell did he get off interfering in Chase's relationship and straining an already tenuous agreement he had with Shelby?

Because Chase knew she was watching him. Any wrong move, any sign that he was slipping back into old habits, and she'd cut him off from Eliza again.

He blamed himself for keeping Eliza, not necessarily a secret, but to himself, and not sharing her with his family. Not that he had a relationship with them anymore, but a child was something he should have told them about and at least sent pictures of her to them so they couldn't deny her.

Finding out about Eliza floored him. But it didn't necessarily surprise him.

He'd been the one to pull Shelby back into his arms right before dawn broke the night sky and brought on the day he had to return to the military life he hadn't exactly wanted but embraced. But he found himself hesitant to leave the woman who surprised him with her shyness at the bar, then her easy way of following his lead in bed and giving herself over to the experience, wanting to please him but also discovering she could feel just as good as she made him feel.

And so he said his reluctant goodbye to her without any barriers between them, both of them holding the other close, taking their time to memorize every detail of each other's body until the magic that happened between them overtook them and they were both lying in each other's arms in wonder. He saw it in her eyes. He felt it in his heart. And though he never intended to get her pregnant, nine months later that magic came into the world, not crying, but quiet and watchful like her mama, taking everything in with her beautiful gray-blue eyes that over those early months turned greenish-blue, a mix of her mama's greenish-gold and his blue eyes.

The generous heart Shelby showed him the night they were together continued to shine on him from the day his girl came into this world to today. Shelby made him a part of their lives. And even though he'd let his past, the nightmares he carried, and the pain from his injuries overtake his life and drown him in addiction, she still welcomed him back with an open heart.

He didn't deserve her. But he was going to work damn hard to be worthy of everything she showered on him while still maintaining the strange cordial we're-not-exactly-friends-but-have-seen-each-other-naked thing they had going.

Of course, she didn't look like she used to look. The pregnancy had changed her body and her mindset. She told him over the very healthy dinner of grilled chicken, steamed broccoli, and garlic mashed potatoes that she'd exchanged her bad habits for good ones for Eliza's sake. She wanted to deliver a healthy baby and be a good example for their daughter. It showed in her leaner body and soft curves.

She even seemed happier.

Being a mom looked good on her.

But there was something about her that nagged at him. He felt like he was missing a few key pieces that would tell him why she seemed on edge. Why she held back. Because it didn't seem to be him and his presence in her life. Something else made her . . . he didn't know what it was, but it was something.

She and Abby, the babysitter, were talking about something without actually spelling out what.

And Shelby just seemed . . . jumpy.

He'd figure it out. She'd learn to trust him again. He'd earn her trust.

Starting with getting this place in order. He wanted Shelby and Eliza to feel comfortable here. He wanted Shelby to feel like she could leave Eliza with him and not worry.

Until now, he'd been the fun dad, the one who showed up for a few hours and played and spoiled, then left again.

He'd never had Eliza overnight or all to himself for even a few days. He wanted to be that kind of dad, the one who was there and knew his kid inside and out. But Shelby saw how he was spiraling, and she'd rightfully put her foot down and said she wouldn't endanger Eliza just so he could prove he wasn't up to taking care of her.

It hurt to believe that then and think about it now.

Chase couldn't sit in his truck all night. He got out and walked the path to the porch steps, his gut tight and dread sinking in. He hadn't been good alone in a long time. He didn't expect tonight to be any different.

He unlocked the door with the keys Shelby gave him. He'd left the spare set with her and told her she could come by anytime she wanted.

For him, the place felt just as much hers as his because she'd gotten it for him and made sure he felt welcome.

Plus, he hoped they grew closer together as parents and friends and something more. Right now, he felt her still holding back, using her shyness and his past to keep a wall up between them.

He just wanted someone, her, to see that he'd changed, that he was trying to be better and move on with his life.

But that would take more than a day out of rehab and an OD he never saw coming to prove to everyone.

He walked in the door and stared at the place like he was seeing it for the first time. He needed furniture, a TV, lamps, and something to break up the white, sterile walls. He loved the caramel-colored hardwood floors. He'd get a soft carpet for the living room so Eliza could play and roll around on the floor without hurting herself. He'd set up a corner in the room for her toys and maybe a small table with a chair where she could color or whatever, like Shelby had in her house.

That sparked several more ideas.

He'd loved being in Shelby's place. It felt bright and cheerful and inviting.

She had one big wall in the living room painted a soft sky blue with a gorgeous seascape painting. He could do something similar here. Maybe in a pale green with a picture. Something with trees.

He loved the black touches she had in each room in

her house. The door pulls and handles in the kitchen, along with the sink fixtures, the lamps and chandeliers.

He looked from the living room, through the dining room, to the kitchen. All the fixtures were a mismatch even though the last owners had updated the house. He could fix that.

He pulled out his phone, found his memo app, and started making a list of what he wanted to buy and what he needed to fix in the house. Tomorrow, he'd walk the property, check out the garage and barn, and see what else he needed to do around the place once he had the money.

It hit him the second he finished the list and stared at the house again, imagining what it could be.

Shelby didn't just get him a place to live. She gave him a place to start building a new life.

He tapped the icon on his phone and punched in the password so he could check on his little girl. The camera covered a good portion of Eliza's room. She wasn't in her crib. Instead, Shelby sat in the chair next to it with Eliza in her arms. She must have woken for some reason. Shelby gently rubbed Eliza's back and brushed her cheek against Eliza's soft hair.

The red light on the camera would alert Shelby that he was watching and listening. She never seemed to care. After all, she'd set up the camera for him.

"Dada come back," Eliza whispered.

Shelby kept rubbing her back. "He'll be back to see you real soon."

Chase tapped the microphone and whispered to his little girl. "I'm here, sweetheart."

Eliza raised her head, looked at the camera, and smiled. "Dada."

"Shh, baby," he said. "Go to sleep for your mom. I'll see you tomorrow."

"Now."

"Tomorrow. Promise. 'Night baby." He logged out and left Shelby to settle Eliza back into bed, wishing he was there with both of them. Wishing for more than maybe he deserved.

He'd drop by the bank and see about getting an equity line of credit on the house to get him started on his new life. Then he'd run his errands, pick Eliza up from daycare, and spend some time with her again. He'd start looking for a job, too.

In rehab, they told him to establish a new routine. He'd make Eliza and Shelby his priority.

He walked down the hall to his room and tossed his duffel bag on the floor at the foot of the bed. He stared at the amazing wood wall, still surprised by Shelby's skill and that she'd go out of her way to do something like that for him. Although this room still needed a rug, some bedside tables, and something on the walls to finish it off, she'd made it feel warm and welcoming. Plus, he didn't have to sleep in a lumpy motel bed where who knew how many people had slept and fucked their way through a night in a place that always felt temporary.

This place was his. That bed was his.

And although he'd be sleeping in it alone, he'd still be dreaming of the night he spent with Shelby, wondering if they could ever have that again.

CHASE WOKE UP the way he usually did, in a cold sweat, nightmare images overlapping in his mind, the sound of gunfire and bombs and the screams of those he couldn't save.

The silence of those he couldn't reach in time.

Shaken and fatigued from yet another restless night, he untangled himself from the sweaty bedsheets, sat on the edge of the bed, and gave himself a minute to orient himself and focus on reality. Then he stood naked, stretched his aching back muscles, and rummaged through his duffel until he found a pair of sweats.

He walked down the hall, stopped at the thermostat to turn on the heat because the house felt like an icebox, then went into the kitchen and realized not only didn't he have any coffee, but he also didn't own a coffeepot at the moment. He'd left his phone on the bed but mentally added both those things to his purchase list.

He opened the fridge and found the staples Shelby promised along with a six-pack of cola. Needing the caffeine, he grabbed a can and headed for the front door to investigate the strange creaking sound.

He walked out onto the porch and found his dad's truck parked next to his in the driveway and his old man sitting in one of two rocking chairs that hadn't adorned his porch last night.

"I heard you talking and thrashing in your sleep all the way out here."

Chase finally recognized the rocking chairs as two of the many his mom had on the front porch and back patio area at Split Tree Ranch. "I don't really sleep." He relived hell.

His old man probably thought he deserved his nightmares for helping his mom end her life the way she wanted to end it.

His dad turned his gaze from the cold misty morning to Chase standing next to him. His eyes fell on each of the round scars marring his torso and arm and the many other lines of scars he'd accumulated in war. "I had no idea what you'd been through over there."

"You wanted me to pay for what I did. I hope you feel like you got it, because I'm done paying." He took a sip of the sugary soda even though it didn't wash away the bitterness inside him.

His dad stared back out to the grass and trees. "I didn't want anything bad to happen to you, son. I wanted you to understand what you took from me."

"The cancer took her."

"She had more time."

"She was done!" He wished his father could understand how it felt to be in that kind of pain and how desperate it felt to make it stop. Chase understood it all too well. "You and Hunt and Max weren't ready to let her go, but she was done fighting a losing battle. You guys wanted her to stick it out to the bitter end. She wanted to say goodbye and end things on her terms with all of us beside her."

"I didn't want her to give up."

"What was the use of fighting when the end result wasn't going to change? Why are we more humane to our pets and livestock than we are to the ones closest to us?"

"It's not the same. I loved her. I wanted more time."

"She felt the same way about you. About us. But it was never going to be enough. She didn't want to be bedridden and lost in a drug-induced haze without the ability to think clearly and say goodbye with a clear and open heart. She held on as long as she could. She tried to say goodbye to you, but you wouldn't let her. You, Hunt, Max, and me could have had that moment with her, but you guys just kept begging her to hold on a little longer. That was for you, not her. So when she asked me to take her away, that she wanted to see the ocean before she died, and listen to the waves crashing on the beach as she took her last breath, I did it. Not because I wanted to, but because it was her life, her decision, and I couldn't watch her suffer anymore."

Silence stretched as the mist hung in the air, clouding everything beyond the edges of the house his father had wanted but Shelby stole right out from under him.

Chase took the chair next to his father's, letting the cold seep into his bones and the silence that had lived between them for so long expand.

And then his father said the unexpected. "I should have listened to her. I should have given her what she wanted. What she desperately needed. I see that now. But it's too late to go back and fix it. And it makes me angry." Maybe the heart attack had actually mellowed his father. Or caused brain damage. Either way, Chase had never heard his dad talk like this.

Chase took that in, absorbed the surprise of his father's words, and how heartfelt they sounded. Maybe the near-death experience gave his dad some much needed insight and perspective on his life. That it was precious. And short. And you never knew what was going to happen.

"She knew the kind of man you are. You hold on to what you love. She wasn't angry at you about that. She understood why you wanted her to fight to stay with you."

"Everything always had to be my way." His father shook his head. "She must have said something like that to me nearly every day we were married." His dad gripped the chair arms in both hands. "She was right. I let my stubbornness drive her away. I think of all the times she asked for something she wanted and I denied her it. Another child," he confessed. "She wanted to try one more time for a little girl. I told her we had three strong boys to help run the ranch. We didn't need a girl."

Chase's heart ached, and he thought of something whimsical, but that felt all too real. "She sent that little girl to me."

His dad unlatched his hands from the rocking chair and used one to rub at the back of his neck.

Chase recognized the gesture as one he did himself all the time.

"It would be just like her to do something amazing like that. She loved you boys more than anything." His dad glanced over. "How did you and Shelby even end up together? She's nothing like anyone you've ever dated."

He didn't want to get into the details with his dad. Yes, Shelby wasn't like anyone else he'd ever dated. She wasn't the type to jump into a stranger's bed. She wasn't the type to party and see where things led. She'd never been with anyone.

But that night he'd gotten lucky, and for whatever reason, she'd chosen him.

He thought Shelby would be a distraction and a final goodbye from this place. Instead, she'd anchored him here again.

"Shelby and I . . ." He tried to come up with something benign to tell his dad, then went with the truth. "The best night I ever spent with a woman, I shared with her. No, she's not like anyone else. She's special. She's the mother of my little girl. And if you and Hunt and Max don't leave her the hell alone, you'll answer to me."

His dad looked him in the eye. "You really believe that girl is yours."

"I *know* she's mine. Shelby's never lied to me. She has no reason to. And if you're still thinking she wanted money from me, then why the hell did she spend almost everything I gave her to buy this place out from under you?"

His dad's mouth drew into a tight line. "She outmaneuvered me." Judging by the look, his old man didn't like it one bit and really couldn't believe she got one over on him.

Chase tried to hide the smile and his pride in Shelby. "Yeah, and that pisses you off, so you think you can treat her like shit. Never again. I'm back. And I'm trying to make amends to her for losing my shit and not being there for Eliza."

"About making amends . . ."

Chase barely refrained from crushing the half-full can in his hand. "I'm done with you. I've given all I've got to make you understand that what I did for Mom, I did for her. Not against you."

His dad's hand settled on Chase's arm, over the bullet scar. "I understand that now. I'm sure you, of all people, understand that when you face death, things have a way of becoming clear in your life. You want to be a good father. I want the same thing. I don't want to fight with you anymore. I want what I've always wanted, us working together on the ranch."

Chase tried to interrupt, but his dad squeezed his arm.

"I know we can't go on the way we have in the past. I need to be different. And I'm trying. That's why I came here this morning, to deliver your housewarming gift, something that your mom picked out for our place and brings a little of her here to yours."

Chase sighed, fighting back a wave of emotion, letting that sink in, and releasing some of the anger he harbored for his dad.

As peace offerings went, the porch chairs were a pretty damn good one.

"I also want you to know that I found out you and Max have been corresponding back and forth all these years, working together for the benefit of the ranch. You left us with a good plan."

"That you didn't fully implement."

"And I should have," his dad admitted. "Max fought for me to do what you laid out."

Chase rolled his eyes. "Of course, you didn't listen to him either."

His dad sighed. "Change isn't easy for me," he snapped. "But I'm trying. Maybe you could give me a break."

"You never gave me one." Chase couldn't ignore the way his dad slumped back in his chair, still keeping his hand on Chase's arm. The man was trying to connect with him. And Chase was acting like a bratty teenager, instead of the man he wanted to be. "If you're trying, then I'll try, too." He owed it to his mother, who'd hoped that after her death, they'd all find a way to come back together and be a family.

His dad leaned close. "Does that mean you'll come back to work at the ranch?"

"What?" Chase didn't have a plan for work as of yet. Now that he owned this property, he could start his own ranch, or find work in town. He had a college degree and a lot of skills after working in the military, including some tech and security expertise. He'd even thought about opening a branch of the security business Drake started in Montana here and being his partner.

"Hear me out, son. I'm getting older. My health, well,

it's okay, could be better, but I can't do all the work that needs to be done. Your plan, it showed a vision for the ranch, one that could take us into the future for generations." His dad glanced around the yard again. "If we expanded onto your land here, we'd have the extra water source we need to increase the herds."

Disappointment crushed what little hope he had that his dad came because he truly cared. "So that's what this is about. You need this land and the water on it."

"No. Well, yes, we need the extra water, but I really want you back at the ranch." It sounded sincere.

"Why? Max can handle things just fine if you give him a chance to step up and truly manage the place."

"He's doing well, but he still relies on you and your know-how. And I want you there. That place is as much yours as it is ours. To prove it . . ." His dad pulled out an envelope from his back pocket and handed it over.

Chase took it and stared at his dad. "What is this?"

"Your cut of the ranch profits from the time you left to today, minus the money we put back into the business per your instructions for the expansion."

They'd never spoken about the money. Chase never expected to get anything back. Why now? "Are you trying to buy me off?"

"No." His dad's frustration rang through loud and clear. "I'm trying to tell you, you were right. Okay?"

His dad had changed a lot if he was admitting that out loud.

"After Elizabeth got sick, everything around me seemed to fall apart. I didn't pay enough attention to the ranch, the bills piled up, that early freeze took part of the herd, and I didn't care about any of it. I just wanted your mom to live. That's all that mattered until I realized we were about to lose the ranch, too. I didn't want her to worry about anything, so I made some rash decisions that only made things worse. Without the money you put into the ranch and the plan you had to dig us out of the mess I'd made . . . You earned that money, son. You saved us."

Chase sank back in the chair, his chest tight with a swirl of emotion, and stared up at the ceiling. "Well, damn, hell just froze over."

His dad crossed his arms. "It *is* cold out here. Don't you have a sweatshirt or something?" Coming from his dad, that was the equivalent of *I love you*.

"I wasn't expecting a porch visit this early in the morning." Or for his dad to practically apologize and bare his soul all at once. "Do you want to come inside?"

His dad leaned forward, ready to get up. "I gotta get to work. You coming?"

Chase leaned his forearms on his knees and stared at the wood decking that needed to be sanded and restained. "I appreciate the offer, the welcome back, and the money."

"I was going to wait on giving it to you after . . ."

After he'd had to go to rehab.

"But I thought you needed it now, seeing as how you did the right thing and put what you had into getting better. You are better, right?"

"I'm still working on it," he admitted.

"Yeah, well, that thing with that girl up in Montana . . . that was bad luck what happened to her. You did what you could . . . I'm real sorry it didn't work out for her and her family, but I'm proud of you for stepping in to help."

Obviously Hunt left his hospital room thinking Chase

had screwed up and OD'd all on his own. But being a police officer, he'd probably contacted the local cops up there to verify Chase's story and to see if Chase faced any charges in Juliana's death and got the whole story that way.

Of course, Hunt hadn't said anything to him about being sorry for accusing him of using right out of rehab, but whatever.

Chase swallowed back the wave of regret and the lump in his throat over Juliana's death. Adria and Drake had to be hurting right now.

"You've got a lot on your shoulders, Chase. Don't carry that one, too. You did everything you could to save her. That's all anyone can ask. I'm just glad . . . Well, I'm glad it wasn't you."

Another dad *I love you* Chase never expected.

He tried to reassure his dad. "Like I said, I'm working on being better and rebuilding my life."

"This place is a good start. Coming back to work will give you a purpose. You didn't have that when you came back the last time. I should have seen that you needed it."

"I do. But I need a few days, maybe a week to get this place fixed up the way I want so that Eliza can be here with me when it's my turn to have her."

"You really should have a legal agreement in place to make sure you get to see her."

"Don't start. Shelby's never denied me access to Eliza unless I didn't deserve it."

His dad's nod made it clear he understood that Shelby had reason in the past to keep him away from his daughter.

"You'll do better this time," his dad encouraged him.

"That's my plan, because Eliza is the most important thing in my life. I won't lose her again." Two months in rehab away from her had felt like forever, even longer than the time he'd been away in the army.

"Then you'll start next week." His dad nodded like it was all decided.

Chase guessed it was because he needed a job. Maybe going back to the ranch would mend fences with Max, who'd kept their calls and correspondence to ranch business and not much else. While Hunt made it plain how he felt about Chase and how he'd helped their mother, Max's feelings were harder to read.

Chase didn't want to be at odds with either of his brothers.

All he wanted to do was put his life back together. He just wished it wasn't so damn hard.

He glanced at his dad watching him and answered the question he hadn't asked. "I'll start next week."

His dad placed his hands over Chase's ears, leaned down, and kissed him on top of the head. He hadn't done that since Chase was a very small boy. "Good to have you home, son." His dad walked down the porch steps, climbed into his truck, and left.

Chase stared out at the misty morning, wondering if he was still dreaming, because nothing that happened this morning seemed real.

Except for the envelope in his hand. He tore it open, pulled out the check, and stared at the figure. The check was for his share of the profits the family had earned, plus the exact amount of money Chase had put into the ranch when he joined the army.

His dad paid him back every cent and then some.

His chest went tight. He didn't know if he should be

happy or sad or even angry it took his dad this long to finally do what was right and acknowledge that without Chase's help, he'd have lost everything.

But Chase remembered what he'd said: that after his mom got sick, nothing else mattered to him, except her getting well. And when she didn't, and things turned bleak . . .

It wasn't that his father didn't care. Didn't love. He did. He just had a hard time showing it.

He'd done a lot better today with Chase, and he couldn't deny that it made a huge difference and changed things between them.

Still, if his dad didn't accept Eliza and Shelby as part of the family, then Chase didn't want back in.

Chapter Seven

SHELBY LOVED her job most days. Helping people made her feel good. As a physical therapist, she helped people regain mobility after an injury or surgery. In the beginning, she'd had to work hard to overcome her shyness and aversion to being really close to people.

Most days now, it didn't bother her. But sometimes with a male client, she got nervous and tried to stay ultra-focused on the task and not them, and sometimes that made her seem unfriendly, but all she was trying to do was be professional.

Not a bitch, like some clients thought.

Including the guy she was working with now. "You could smile or something, so it doesn't seem like you want this to be over."

She eased his leg out of the stretch she held him in due to a hamstring injury. "What? No. That's not it. I was just concentrating." She gave him a weak smile, but didn't meet his intense gaze.

"That's a little better."

She gently held his leg and pushed it back into the stretch.

"You never wear your hair down."

With him on his back on the mat, her practically between his legs, and her holding one of his legs aloft, she felt far too up close and personal in his space to be talking about her smile and hair during a session.

"Um. It gets in the way when it's down."

"I bet it's really pretty down."

She felt her whole face flush at the inappropriate compliment. "Thank you," she mumbled. She was so not good at talking to people sometimes.

And for the life of her, she didn't know why they were having this conversation in the first place.

She eased his leg back down to the mat, thankful time was up. "That's all for today. Be sure to make your next appointment at the desk. Practice the stretches. Alternate ice and heat if you're sore later."

He rolled up to a sitting position next to her and draped his arms over his upright knees. "Are you off now? Maybe we could get a smoothie next door."

"Um . . ." She never dated clients. She never dated anyone, because no one ever really asked her out. Partly because she never gave them a chance. "I . . . Thank you, but I have to pick up my daughter at the sitter."

He stood and shifted his weight to ease the pain he was still experiencing. "Well, I did get you to smile at me. Maybe next time you'll take me up on the offer." He walked toward the front desk, not giving her a chance to respond in any way.

Not that she could form words right now.

She didn't know what to make of him asking her out. She played out the scenario like she always did when someone wanted to get to know her better. They'd go out, chat about work, life, and eventually they'd ask about her family, where she came from, and that meant saying something about being raised by her grandparents. Then they'd question why, and that led to questions about her parents. If the person had been in town long enough to know the infamous story, they put the pieces together and looked at her most often with pity and sadness, and she didn't like it. Not one bit.

They wanted to hear all the sordid details. Then she didn't know if they were interested in being her friend or just getting the scoop.

That's part of why her grandparents had kept her close to home, never allowing her to just be a kid without what happened hanging over her head. She'd known from a very young age that something about her made people whisper and look at her funny. She'd spent most of her young life believing people simply didn't like her.

Of course, having a mother with severe PTSD and mental health issues also explained a lot about why people looked at her strangely. And after her mom committed suicide, people said things like, "Maybe it was for the best," to her grandparents. They nodded like that made perfect sense and that her mother dying so young was a good thing. It just reinforced everyone's belief that in order to erase the past, you needed to get rid of all the evidence it ever happened.

But Shelby was still here.

She often thought of leaving this small town, where everyone knew her business. But would it really be any different for her anywhere else? People would ask about her, her life, where she came from. She didn't want to lie. She didn't want to hide parts of herself just to feel like she wasn't damaged by her past and how she was raised. People could see it in her.

Besides, she'd never been anywhere but here, and leaving everything she'd ever known—even if it wasn't always healthy—scared her. She'd hesitated again and again.

And then she met Chase in the bar and had that amazing night with him, and Eliza came along, and she'd stayed right here—waiting like a lovesick fool for him to return, despite knowing he'd never pick her.

Once Chase was well again and had his head on straight, he'd find someone who matched him in every way.

Not every ugly duckling gets to grow up to be a swan.

Sometimes, you're just an ugly duck.

Chase would see that now that he was back, clean, and thinking with a clear head again.

He didn't seem to know about her past, but that wouldn't last long. His father, or any number of people in town, would remind him of the story that never died in this town because it was just good gossip, filled with intrigue, the downfall of a beautiful young woman, and the evil that took over a favored son, who had everything and destroyed it all.

Laura sidled up to her. "Please tell me you're kicking yourself for not accepting that invitation and you're just working up the courage to go over there and say yes."

"Um. No." She let out a nervous laugh.

"Why the hell not? He's cute. He's got a job." Laura eyed him. "He's got a great ass."

Shelby laughed again. "He's a client."

"He won't always be one. You should let him know you're interested."

"I'm not." He was really good-looking and seemed nice, but . . .

Laura side-eyed her. "Chase is back, isn't he?"

"Yes. But that doesn't have anything to do with me not accepting a date from a client."

"Uh-huh. Right." The knowing grin on Laura's face made Shelby blush.

"Chase and I had dinner together last night." The giddiness inside her came out with that blurted admission.

"So you two are finally dating." Laura married her high school sweetheart ten years ago and lived a happy life with her adoring husband and their two boys. Everyone loved her because of her bright, cheerful personality. It didn't hurt that her mom and dad ran the diner and everyone adored them, too.

Shelby was the opposite of Laura. Quiet. Guarded. And truthfully, sometimes too lost in her grandparents' notion that she was something to be hidden and ignored.

"Chase is not and never will be mine."

Laura arched a brow. "Are you worried about him using again?"

"No. Yes. I don't know. He's dealing with a lot right now. The last thing he needs is me pushing my feelings on him."

"Maybe he'd be happy to know you have feelings for him," Laura suggested, like that could be a real thing. "Shelby, as your friend, I'm going to say something I feel you should know."

"Okay." Maybe she didn't want to hear this.

Laura put her hand on Shelby's arm. "Anyone you want to be with would be lucky to have you."

Oh, that made Shelby's chest tight and her heart soar.

"You're sweet and kind," Laura said, "and I would kill for your body, because let me tell you, two babies make everything drop, and that last ten pounds just never goes away."

Shelby grinned. "I don't see your husband complaining, or you when you come in here smiling all the time."

"My man likes to wake me up and send me on my way a happy girl. Still, we're talking about you, and how you don't put yourself out there. You've told me a few things about how growing up with your grandparents left you feeling like you didn't matter. But you deserve every happiness, even if they made you feel like you don't because of what happened to your mom. And really, that makes no sense. What happened to her was tragic, but that doesn't have anything to do with you."

"I know that. Now. But growing up, it felt like somehow it was my fault. And I try to make myself believe that my grandparents' feelings toward me were their grief and anger over what happened, but still, when you're treated like that for so long, it just somehow becomes who you are."

"Then shift your focus. That guy, and probably Chase for that matter, didn't look at you that way. He didn't treat you that way. He thought you were attractive and nice and worth asking out on a date."

"I guess so."

"And Chase, you never talk about your night with him, but it had to be something, because I know you want more with him. You told me you asked him to be with you that night."

It had been the boldest thing she'd ever done.

Laura leaned in and held her gaze. "He wouldn't have said yes if he didn't want to be with you, too."

They were both drunk. But Chase had made that night so special. He didn't just take what he wanted and leave. He stayed for more. Lots more.

"Chase and I . . . we're complicated."

"Maybe. But how much of that is because you keep him at arm's length the way you do other people? Hell, it took months before you felt comfortable talking about more than work and the weather with me." Laura was teasing, but she was right.

With everyone Shelby came into contact with, she kept the interactions to everyday pleasantries. Working with Laura allowed her time to get over her insecurities and see that Laura really liked her and wouldn't see her past as some stain on her. When it came to talking about their kids, they connected so easily. Laura had been a huge help when it came to raising Eliza and figuring out what to do for her when Shelby got overwhelmed and felt inadequate. Laura assured her every parent felt that way and always offered up suggestions for whatever dilemma Shelby faced.

"It's easier talking to you than Chase. I don't want to screw that up because we have a kid to raise together."

"All I'm saying, Shelby, is that being a mom is great, but you deserve more. I know you're lonely. How can you not be when you give so much to your daughter, your clients, those few of us you call friends? You deserve someone in your life who takes care of you."

Shelby had a hard time even imagining it.

"I know you have feelings for Chase, and that's complicated because of his situation. You're worried about him relapsing, and you should be. It's a valid concern. But don't use it as an excuse not to be honest with yourself and him about what you want and need out of the relationship. Because whether you realize it or not, you are in one with him. You just have to decide and allow yourself to be as close as you want to be with him."

"You make it sound so easy."

"I know it's not. But it's also not as hard as you think."

Shelby couldn't help but think about it. "Thank you for the advice and insight. I'll keep it in mind." She checked the time. "I have to pick up Eliza. See you tomorrow."

It only took Shelby a few minutes to wrap up her paperwork, grab her stuff, and walk out of the clinic into the bright late afternoon. Temporarily blinded by the sunlight, she gave her eyes a second to adjust before she headed across the parking lot. The second she could see clearly, she hoped she was hallucinating the tall man standing by her car.

But no. He didn't disappear. He simply shifted his weight, folded his arms across his chest, and waited for her to come to him.

She mustered her courage for the upcoming confrontation, walked across the lot, stood right in front of Mr. Wilde, and matched his stance with her arms crossed. "Let me save you your breath. You want me to stay away from Chase. You want me to admit I lied about him being Eliza's father. You want me to disappear from the face of the earth and never go near your family ever again." She shook her head. "No. To all of it. Now I've got to pick up my daughter from the babysitter. Excuse me."

He repeated what she'd said. "No. To all of it. I didn't come here to issue warnings or demand anything."

She sighed, because whatever he wanted couldn't be good. "Then we have nothing to say to each other. You've made it plain how you feel about me and what you think of me. I don't need to hear it again."

"But you deserve to hear this." He waited for her to meet his gaze. "I'm sorry."

She actually dropped her arms and took a step back, shocked *he* of all people would apologize to *her*.

"I spoke to Chase early this morning. We talked about the past, my wife, and *you*." Mr. Wilde rubbed his hand over the back of his neck in a familiar gesture she'd seen Chase do countless times. "I really couldn't believe you outmaneuvered me on that deal and bought the house and property for Chase. I thought you wanted it for yourself and used his money to take it."

"Chase is a generous man, but he gives away everything he has because he feels like he doesn't deserve it. I want him to support his daughter, but I don't expect him to pay more than his fair share, and he sent far more than that. I know he feels like he lost everything important to him, and no matter how hard he tries or how much he wants it, he can't get it back. He returned after he got out of the army, but he didn't have a home or his family. Eliza helped to anchor him, but he knows she belongs with me, so he felt like she wasn't really his family either. And then I took her away from him."

"He wasn't in a good place and couldn't take care of her. You did the right thing."

She appreciated that he agreed with her on that point. "Still, it broke something inside him. I never wanted to, then or now, hurt him."

Sorrow filled Mr. Wilde's eyes. "He's been hurt enough."

"And now, just when he's finished rehab and was ready to come home and start over—again—he lost someone he knew. Again."

"What happened to that girl was tragic. Chase did what he could to save her."

"For Chase, that's not enough. She's gone. He blames himself." She glanced at the ground, then at Mr. Wilde again. "How was he this morning?"

Mr. Wilde didn't hide his concern. "Exhausted. I arrived before he woke up. Sounded like he got a night full of nightmares instead of sleep."

She nodded, wishing she could help Chase, but knowing nothing she said or did would take away his pain. "I bought that property for him so he'd have a home to come back to, a place that was his, that no one could take from him, or make him leave. I wanted him to have a place where he could make memories with Eliza. A place close to you and his brothers, because even though you kicked him out, you all love him and want him back."

Mr. Wilde nodded. "Believe it or not, that's exactly why I wanted that place."

"Not for the land and water on it?" She raised a skeptical brow.

"Smart girl. But it really was for him." Mr. Wilde rubbed at his neck again. "Everything you said is true. I want him back at Split Tree Ranch and in my life." He held her gaze. "I want to get to know my granddaughter."

"But let me guess. First you want a DNA test to prove it." It stung that he, Hunt, and Max believed her a liar.

He shook his head. "Whether or not she's Chase's doesn't seem to matter to him. He believes she's his, and he loves her. He says she's his, so that makes her family."

She wanted to believe him, but the bad blood between them couldn't be erased so easily. "But will you treat her like she's a Wilde, or like she's the unwanted stepchild of a woman you find lacking?"

Mr. Wilde pressed his lips tight. "It's come to my attention that sometimes I judge people too harshly and push them away because I believe I'm right, even when I'm not."

She couldn't believe he'd made the admission. "You either get to be right or keep your friends and family."

"So I've learned. And I'm trying to wise up. I already lost my wife. I can't fathom the number of times I nearly lost my son."

"Those scars on him really hit home." Even now, just thinking about them, her gut went tight, and her heart ached for Chase.

Mr. Wilde rubbed at his neck again. "You hear something happened to him, but it just doesn't compute. He downplayed everything, and I never thought it was that bad." He got lost in thoughts and probably regrets. "I have a chance to make things right with him. I started this morning, but I know it's going to take some time before he believes I'm sorry and I want things between us to be better."

"I'm sure he'll be open to that because it's what he wants, too. He needs his family."

"Like everything else in Chase's life, he's been stingy with the details about your relationship."

"Chase and I are Eliza's parents. There's nothing beyond that." She thought it would make him happy to hear that she and Chase weren't together.

Instead, Mr. Wilde narrowed his gaze. "Well, it's interesting that you think that, because I know my son, and there's a hell of a lot more between you than you think."

Her heart raced with . . . hope. But she squashed it, because wishing for impossible things never worked out. "What does that mean?"

"He told me the best night he ever spent with a woman was with you. You know what I did when that happened to me?"

She stared in shock at him, completely confused by his words.

"I married her. So I guess I'll be seeing you again soon." Mr. Wilde left her dumbfounded, standing in the parking lot as he drove away, a knowing grin on his face.

He couldn't be right. Chase didn't feel anything for her except maybe friendship because they shared Eliza.

Right?

Her heart felt like it might beat out of her chest. She took a breath and got in her car, but she didn't start it. She held the steering wheel and tried to ignore the feelings of hope that sprang up in her mind.

Mr. Wilde didn't know what he was talking about. He didn't know she and Chase only had a one-night stand. They hadn't touched each other since. There'd been no hint Chase wanted a repeat of that night. As far as she knew, he only spent time with her because of Eliza.

Right?

Right. She wouldn't let her imagination, or her emotions, run wild.

Someone knocked on the driver's side window. She jolted out of her never-going-to-happen thoughts only to be confronted by the very man who made those dreams unrealistic and impossible.

"Shelby. Are you okay?"

She didn't acknowledge him. She turned the key in the ignition, threw the car into Reverse and got lucky there were no cars behind her, blindly pulled out of the parking spot, and hauled ass out of there.

Maybe you can't run from your past, but you can drive away from it.

Chapter Eight

KYLE WATCHED Shelby tear out of the parking lot, frustrated but convinced she just needed more time. He needed to be patient. He'd waited twenty-eight years for this. He could give her a little more time. Shelby would come around and give him a chance. She'd been told the worst about him, that's all. Her grandparents, the press, everyone had poisoned her against him. But they didn't know him. They didn't know what really happened between him and Rebecca. Her parents, the police, everyone wanted a villain, and they turned him into one.

They called him a monster.

He wasn't. He loved his little girl.

She reminded him so much of his beloved Rebecca.

And he was a grandfather now.

That meant everything to him.

He had a chance to be a part of Eliza's life and watch her grow up. He'd missed so much with Shelby. This was his chance to make things right and show Shelby that he could be a good father and grandpa.

They needed time to get to know each other.

The only way to do that was to spend time together. So far, she'd refused. He'd let her.

But soon, he'd get what he wanted.

He always got what he wanted.

We're family.

And family should be together.

Chapter Nine

CHASE CLOSED the last open window in the house and turned back to the living room to survey his work. The paint smell still lingered, but the pale green wall turned out great. He loved the color. It went well with the brown leather sofa and love seat he bought and hauled home in the back of his truck today. He still needed to put together the wood entertainment wall unit, unbox his new TV, and call the satellite company to get him hooked up. The dining room table, rugs, and bedroom furniture for his room and Eliza's was due to be delivered tomorrow afternoon.

In addition to his furniture shopping spree, he'd hit the big box store an hour away and picked up a bunch of household essentials. He'd put the new outdoor grill he ordered to good use once it arrived.

He appreciated Shelby buying him some basic groceries, but he needed to make a run to the store, too. Maybe he'd do that after he stopped by her place to check on Eliza and make plans with Shelby. They needed to come up with a schedule for him to see Eliza that worked with her already established routine. He didn't want to disrupt either of their lives, but he wanted his time and for

Eliza to know she could count on him to be there on a regular basis.

He didn't want to give Shelby a reason to slam the door in his face ever again.

He wanted to be invited in and welcomed like he was a real part of the family. Even though they weren't together, like he hoped they could be soon, Shelby and Eliza were his family.

Chase checked to be sure he'd cleaned up everything, then grabbed his keys off the counter. He'd spent too much time alone in the quiet today. His anxiety and negative thoughts were starting to push their way in. He needed a distraction and to talk to someone. And the only person he felt comfortable with these days was Shelby.

She listened without judging him. She offered advice but didn't chide him if he didn't take it. Mostly he did, because she was usually right.

He just liked being with her.

When he'd been away, just the idea of her, back home, eased him. Her constant presence in his life made him feel like he knew her. Now he wanted to really get to know her—and his daughter—by being *in* their lives.

Chase walked out the front door, locked up, then headed down the porch steps to his truck just as Hunt pulled in and rolled down his window.

"We need to talk."

Chase unlocked his truck door, but didn't climb in. "After the way you treated Shelby, I have nothing to say to you."

"I'm trying to protect you. There are things about her that you don't know."

That's exactly why he was trying to spend more time with her, so he could learn everything about her.

"I don't need to be protected from her. Drop this, or the next time I see you, I'll drop you." Chase turned his back on his cussing brother.

He didn't want to hear Hunt's suspicions. He didn't believe them anyway.

All he wanted to do was put the past behind him and live his life with his beautiful daughter. And her mother, if she'd have him.

Right now, she didn't have a reason to even think his head and heart had gone in that direction. He needed to fix that and do something to show Shelby that she mattered to him.

He caught glimpses of interest from her, but she hid her feelings well. Sometimes he caught himself before he outright demanded that she simply tell him what she was thinking. Because he really wanted to know. She held everything personal back from him. She didn't share anything that wasn't about Eliza.

He wondered if that's why she didn't date. Other men found her standoffish when she was really just shy. They didn't see what he saw in her, a woman who wanted to connect with others but found it hard to put herself out there.

At least, that's how she seemed to him.

He had an in with her because of Eliza, but he wanted her to see him as more than just Eliza's dad.

It would take time. She probably wondered if he'd hold his shit together this time.

He'd have to prove himself.

Hunt caught up to him before he climbed into his truck, grabbed his shoulder, and spun him around.

"If you won't watch your six, then I'll have to do it for you."

"Shelby is not pulling one over on me. She isn't lying about Eliza. She didn't even keep all the money I sent her. She used it to buy me this place. So tell me, Hunt, what are you trying to do other than drive a wedge between me and Shelby?"

"Like before, I'm trying to protect you from yourself. You need time to focus on your recovery. Starting a relationship now . . . it's not a good idea."

"I know what I want for my future, and it's Shelby and Eliza. I want us to be a real family. I've made a lot of mistakes. I've been away far too long. My mental health, recovery, and me are better off with them in my life. And I've waited a damn long time to be with them and nearly didn't survive to make it happen. I've lost enough time with them. I'm not waiting until someone else thinks it's a good idea. I have my meds and my appointments with my psychiatrist. I'm doing everything I need to do to be healthy for myself and them. So thanks for the fucking concern, but what I could really use is your support."

"Then do this the right way. Get the DNA test, a legal custody and child support agreement, and for God's sake stay clean."

"Why the fuck do you care what I do? I thought you washed your hands of me long ago. But you keep showing up, pushing."

"Because it's what Mom would have wanted me to do." A world of pain and loss filled those angry words.

Chase shook his head. "I'm going to tell you the same thing I told Dad. I did not kill her. The cancer did. Yes, when she was ready to end her life, I took her away, so she could do that on her terms." And it hurt Chase just as much as it hurt the rest of them. "She died the way she wanted to die. You and Max and Dad . . . You wouldn't let her go."

"We wanted her to fight."

Chase sighed. "That is so easy to say and so difficult to do sometimes. You have no idea how hard it is to keep fighting against something that wins every damn time." Chase held back the nightmares filling his mind with thoughts of Eliza. But it didn't always work. Eventually, the nightmares always won and eviscerated everything good in his mind, heart, and life. They left him with guilt and shame and anger and terror. Then the grief set in and swallowed him whole.

Hunt's lips went flat. "She could have come to me and told me she was done."

"She told all of us she was done. You, Dad, and Max just didn't want to hear it. You didn't want it to be real. Neither did I. Could she have lasted longer? Sure. But what kind of end would that have been for her, enduring all that pain just so we had a few more days or weeks, while she was miserable? She wanted one last adventure, to see something she'd never seen in person, so I gave that to her because it was what *she* wanted."

Hunt glared. "Yeah, and you got to be with her when she died and none of us did."

Chase had never spoken to any of them about what happened with their mom. Not in any detail. They only ever wanted to rage at him for taking her away. They never wanted to know what really happened. But Chase confessed, "I wasn't there either."

Mom left this world without them by her side but always in her heart.

That's the only thing that gave him comfort, and something Hunt would never understand.

Hunt swore. "You're an even bigger asshole than I thought."

His mother's death was the one thing that didn't haunt him. He didn't care what Hunt thought about it. He'd done the right thing. He'd done what she'd wanted. And when she called him that last hour and told him how proud she was of him for doing the hard thing, he'd stayed on the line with her until she breathed her last breath and he'd given her the only words she'd wanted to hear from him, *I love you*, because that's all that mattered.

She wouldn't be proud of what he'd done to himself these last many months, but she'd understand his pain and how he'd fought to get through it but finally gave up the fight to find some peace. Though in his case, that precious oblivion he sought never lasted long and came with a ton of consequences.

"I found her a hospice with a beach view. She sat on the terrace, listening to the ocean, and called each of us. First you, then Max, then Dad. She didn't want us to watch her die. She wanted us to remember how she lived and loved us. You got the goodbye. You had a chance to tell her you loved her. And while I was the only one on the phone with her as she passed, in her heart, we were all with her, Hunt. I get that you're angry, but it's not really at me. You want her back just as much as I do, and she's not coming back, and that hurts like hell."

There were too many people in his life he'd lost.

"I'm sorry, Hunt. I really am. Now I have someplace I need to be." He had someone who wanted his time and attention.

Chase climbed into his truck and left Hunt in his driveway. The drive gave him too much time to think about Hunt, their mom, his chat with his dad, and what came next. It amped up his anxiety.

Shelby wasn't expecting him per se, though he hoped they could do the dinner and bedtime thing again tonight.

He parked in front of her place in town. The cottage-style two-bedroom, two-bath house sat on a half-acre lot. It had belonged to Shelby's grandparents before they passed. Shelby had been raised by them after her mom died. All other questions about her family went unanswered. She had a way of changing the subject every time he brought up her past.

She knew practically everything about his.

He wanted to know everything about hers.

He understood how losing your family would make you afraid of losing even more people in your life.

He thought of the night he met Shelby. She'd seemed lonely then. Not as much now because she had Eliza. But still, he sometimes caught glimpses of it in her eyes.

Chase got out of the truck and headed for the path up to the house, but stopped when he spotted her neighbor taking out the trash. Chase smiled, remembering how he'd felt a spurt of jealousy when Shelby talked about her neighbor helping her out. He didn't think he needed to worry about the seventysomething guy next door, and that was a relief.

He knocked on the door.

Shelby opened it and gave him a warm smile that turned to a concerned frown. "Did you sleep at all last night?"

"Some." He vowed not to lie to her. Ever. It was the only way he knew how to make her trust him again. "Rough nights are normal for me now."

She stepped back. "Come in. You're just in time for dinner. Eliza is in her high chair."

Chase walked in the door to the welcoming scent of spaghetti sauce and garlic bread. "Are you sure?"

"I made plenty. Eliza has asked, 'Where Dada,' several times since we got home."

"You should have let me know. I'd have come over sooner."

"You're here now." She waved her hand for him to go ahead of her.

In the small house, it only took a few long strides to enter the tiny kitchen and spot his girl.

"Dada!" She held her spaghetti-sauce-covered hands out to him.

He dodged her hands, leaned down, and kissed her on the head. "Hey, sweet baby. Did you get some of that food in your mouth?"

She picked up a handful of sauce-drenched noodles and stuffed them in her mouth, smiling as a long noodle stuck to her chin.

"Good job, baby."

Shelby came to the table with a loaded plate for him. "Sit. Eat."

He took the seat across from her and next to Eliza. "Thanks for inviting me in."

Shelby held his gaze. "You're always welcome, Chase." Shyness overtook her, and she busied herself with breaking up a piece of garlic bread for Eliza, who stuffed two small pieces in her mouth.

"One at a time," he and Shelby said in unison.

Shelby smiled. He laughed, enjoying that they were in sync on something.

"Eat," she coaxed him. "You need to take better care of yourself."

This is where he'd hoped to steer the conversation so they could talk about their future. "I'm working on it. I had an omelet for breakfast and a big sandwich and an apple for lunch, thanks to you stocking the fridge. I'm going to hit the grocery store tonight on the way home and fill the cupboards. Um, if you could make me a list of things Eliza likes, I'll keep them stocked at my place for when she visits me."

Shelby finished chewing, making him wait with his breath held for an answer. He hoped she didn't refuse to let Eliza come to his place.

"Sure. She's a little picky at this age, so having what she likes will make things easier on you. Less tantrums," she added.

"Really?"

She raised a brow. "You'll need to feed her, right?"

"Yeah. It's just . . . I wasn't sure you'd let me take her."

Shelby's head tilted. "We need to talk about how this is going to work. She's only spent the one night I came to get you away from me. Are you prepared for her to sleep over?"

"Not yet. I bought furniture for her room. It will be delivered tomorrow. I got her a twin bed. I think I'll put it up against the wall. I bought a bed rail to put on it so she doesn't roll out the open side."

Shelby twirled her fork in the pasta. "It's about time I got her a big girl bed here, too."

He let out a sigh of relief. "I thought maybe you'd say it was too soon for a twin bed."

Shelby shook her head. "Even if I thought that and you got the bed, we could simply put the mattress on the floor or something for safety, but I think the bed rail will work just fine."

Another wave of relief hit him, and he sank back into the chair. "Okay. Good."

Shelby's gaze softened. "Chase, relax. You don't have to be perfect at this. I'm not."

"From my perspective, it looks like you are."

"That's only because I've had the last two years to learn how to be Eliza's mom. You've been gone more than you've been here." She held up her hand to stop him from defending himself. "You were working, and then you needed help to put your life back on track. I understand. You weren't expecting her. I didn't expect you to change your life for us. I only wanted you to be a part of her life in whatever way you can."

"I want to be a real and present part of her life, not just a weekend dad. I want you to know you can count on me to be there for her when you need me."

Shelby leaned forward. "I appreciate that. I'm so used to doing everything on my own, I just do whatever needs to be done. I realized when you went to rehab that maybe I'd been part of the problem. You were trying to reintegrate yourself here at home and spend time with her. We didn't set up a specific custody schedule. I didn't include you in decisions I made for her. I didn't even ask you to go to her pediatric checkup with me. I treated you like a guest instead of her father."

He appreciated that she understood where he was coming from and that he had in fact felt like an outsider. But he'd contributed to that and forced Shelby's hand. "I wasn't in a good place. You had every right to exclude me from those things and limit my time with her. But I want things to be different this time."

She stared across at him. "Okay. Let's start with your plan."

"I'm going to let you lead with her. She has a routine, I get that, but I want to be included in it."

Shelby shook her head, making his stomach drop. "No. What is *your* plan to stay clean and get better?"

He sat back. "Oh. You think I'm going to relapse." It stung that she didn't have faith in him.

"I never said that. You're still recovering, Chase. Rehab didn't solve all your problems or eliminate what made you start abusing your meds in the first place. So what is your plan to work on the things that led you to need an escape?"

He appreciated her patience and understanding. "I have a video conference with the psychiatrist Drake recommended twice a week. The shrink at the rehab helped, but I know I need someone to continue the work I started at the center. Dr. Porter is ex-military and works with vets with PTSD. He helped Drake. I'm hoping he can help me."

"That's great. I really hope he can assist you in reconciling what you've been through. Trauma doesn't just go away. It fades into the background. But I'm sure you know anything can trigger it when you least expect it, and it feels all too real and present again. You don't just deal with it once and it's gone."

This time he tilted his head and studied her. "What kind of trauma have you suffered?" It sounded like she not only got it, but had been through it.

"We're not talking about me." She stuffed a huge bite of garlic bread in her mouth to end that line of conversation.

He dropped it. For now. Because he needed her to know that he was stable enough to be a good father to Eliza, who was using her spaghetti to finger paint swirls on her high chair table.

"Okay, we'll stick with me. For now. Counseling twice a week. I'm taking my anxiety and depression meds. They help a lot, but we're still dialing that in to find the right combination so I feel like myself and not . . . off." He didn't know how else to describe it. He didn't want the side effects to be worse than the cure, but he needed the meds to keep his head on straight. "I learned some meditation techniques at rehab that helped me sleep, but the last couple days, I haven't done them. I know sleep is important to my overall health and mental state, so I'll get back to that. If it doesn't work, over-the-counter sleep aids can do the trick, too. I just don't want to rely on a drug to get me to sleep."

"Try some chamomile tea. Limit screen time at night. Exercise helps."

"I'll get plenty of that when I start work at the ranch next week."

Her head whipped back. "What? Really? Your dad didn't mention that when he ambushed me today."

"What the . . ." Chase fell back in his chair and rubbed his hand over the back of his tense neck. "Tell me what happened."

"It's not what you think. I mean, I still can't believe he went from wanting DNA proof Eliza is yours to asking to get to know his granddaughter in a day, but . . ." She shrugged.

"Wow." Chase had no idea his dad was this serious about them fixing their broken relationship. So much so that he reached out to Shelby. "I had some doubts after we spoke, but him going to you, asking to be a part of Eliza's life, I guess he really does want to make things right."

"It seems that way." She brushed a stray strand of hair behind her ear. "At least as far as you and Eliza are concerned."

"What does that mean?"

"It's obvious your father and brothers don't think very much of me."

"They don't know you the way I do."

"Oh, I think in some ways they know more than you."

That got his attention. "What do you mean?" He felt like he was missing something that everyone else knew.

Shelby took a sip of water. "Sorry. I didn't offer you a drink. Do you want water? A soda? Iced tea?" She always avoided talking about herself.

He just wanted to get to know her. "I want an answer to my question. It feels like you're purposely not telling me something I should know."

"Your whole family thinks I tricked you, or lied to you, or whatever, about Eliza. Hunt went out of his way to keep me from getting in touch with you."

"I know. I'm sorry about that. I should have given you my number that morning before you left."

"Why? That's not how one-night stands work. When it's over, it's over. No promises or expectations."

"Except it wasn't over," he pointed out.

"We didn't know that. You were going back to base. I went back to my life, such as it was."

"What does that mean?"

"Nothing." She rolled her eyes. "I'm just saying that it's nice your dad wants to make amends with you somehow and that he's dropped this whole Eliza-isn't-yours thing."

"He said he's sorry in more ways than one." Chase pulled the check out of his back pocket and slid it across the table to her.

She leaned back and stared at him. "What is that?"

"The money you paid for the house and land you bought me."

"Did you take out a loan? You shouldn't have done that. That was your money I spent." She pushed the check back to him.

He shoved it back in front of her. "No loan. My dad paid me back what I put into the ranch, plus my share of the profits over the last seven years I was gone. He admitted that without the money I put into the ranch and the plan I left him and Max with, they'd have lost everything."

Her whole expression softened. "I guess seeing your battle scars really got through to him."

"And he hasn't seen the rest of them."

Her eyes went wide. "There are more?"

"Want to see them?" he teased, even if he hoped she'd say yes.

"Oh, Chase." Her eyes glassed over.

He reached across the table and put his hand over hers. "Hey, I'm okay. Really, the other scars aren't that bad. I'm mostly healed up."

"Mostly?"

He gave her the truth again. "My head's a little out of sorts. My back is still killing me most of the time. And when it's cold, my bum hip and knee ache like a son of a—" He cut the last word off for Eliza's sake. "It's hell getting old."

Her lips pressed into a tight line. "Your age has nothing to do with what the war did to you."

He sighed. "It's hard to accept that I left the war but it hasn't left me."

Opening up like this didn't come easy, but she made him feel like he could say anything to her.

They let the moment stretch, both of them looking at the other. He didn't know if she realized she'd linked her fingers with his, but it felt so good to be connected to her again, even in this small way. Her hand fit his to perfection. Her skin was soft, and the warmth in her spread up his arm and washed over the rest of him. He could sit here all night holding her hand.

He flinched when a blob of spaghetti smacked him in the chest.

Eliza giggled beside them.

Shelby gasped, covered her mouth with her free hand, and hid a laugh that filled her eyes.

He glanced down at his black T-shirt, then pretend-glared at Eliza. "Not cool, baby." He grabbed his napkin and wiped the mess from his shirt, then made a silly face at Eliza, who laughed again. Shelby joined in.

And for the first time in a long time, his heart felt light.

It tripped when Shelby squeezed his hand and her gaze met his again. "You look good laughing. That might be the first real smile I've seen on your face."

"That's because it was dark in our room that night."

She tried to slip her hand free as that same shyness that drew him to her came back, but he tightened his hold to stop her.

"Every time I think about you or see you, I smile. Maybe not always on the outside, but definitely on the inside. When I was overseas and things were going downhill fast, I'd think about you, what we shared, how great I felt that night, and everything didn't seem so bad. I'd think about coming home, hopefully getting a chance to see you again, and I'd have something amazing to look forward to. Then you called and told me about Eliza, and I knew that no matter what happened over there, I had to get back here. To you."

Her fingertips brushed back and forth against his skin. "Chase. I don't know what to say to that. We never spoke about . . . us."

"You made it clear you wanted to keep the focus on Eliza. I wasn't here, so I understood that you were trying to make sure the limited time I had for a call or video chat, I spent it with Eliza. When we talked, it was about her, but I also wanted to hear about you."

"Why?"

He chuckled under his breath. "You're the mother of my child. You're the woman I spent an amazing night with and left even though I really wanted to stay."

Astonishment lit her eyes. "You did?"

He wanted her in his arms right now. "Why does that surprise you so much? We were great together. I wanted to see what more we could have, but I couldn't ask that of you when I was walking out the door and would be gone for God knows how long."

"But you're . . . you. And I'm . . . not the person you'd pick."

He didn't like that she felt that way. "I picked you that night," he reminded her, trying to figure out why she didn't think he'd want her beyond a one-night stand. Granted, sometimes people didn't make it past that, but they didn't have to be those people.

"That was just sex." She sounded like she was trying to convince him and herself of that.

"Was it?" Maybe he'd read things all wrong. Maybe he was feeling things she wasn't. "I'm interested in you, Shelby. If you don't feel the same way, I'll let it go." He rubbed his thumb over the back of her hand, which she still kept in his. "But if you want to take a chance on a slightly broken and definitely battered guy who really loves his little girl, then let's work on getting to know each other better."

That same wonder he'd seen a moment ago filled her eyes. "You're serious."

He leaned forward. "Put me out of my misery. I don't think I can take the rejection right now."

She laughed. "Have you ever actually been rejected?"

"Yes. Of course." Hadn't everybody? With women, it didn't happen to him often. He'd usually been the one to walk away. But his whole damn family sent him packing, and that really stung. "I plan to do a hell of a lot better with you."

"I can't imagine any woman saying no to that face. And the rest of you," she added, her expression serious and thoughtful.

"My mother used to say she had a hard time saying no to me, too. I'm irresistible. So please stop resisting and say you'll date me."

Her eyes went wide. "Seriously?"

"Yes," he said, exasperated, but with a smile. "What did you think I was asking?"

She shrugged that shoulder again, and a smirk tried to tilt her lips, but she fought it.

She had him thinking about their night together, but he wanted a hell of a lot more this time.

"It might not be the usual dating thing since we'll

have a chaperone." He cocked his head toward Eliza, who watched them while gnawing on a piece of bread.

Shelby laughed under her breath. "I . . . I really didn't expect this." She thought he wanted another night, or just some superficial no-strings-attached sex.

Why?

Why didn't she expect more from him?

Did she think him shallow?

Did she think he didn't deserve her?

Maybe he didn't, but he'd show her that he'd be good to her. For her. They could be good for each other.

"I'm going to figure out the *why not* about you not expecting me to be interested in you one of these days, but right now I just want you to say something to the effect of, 'Yes, Chase, I'd love to date you.'"

"What if it doesn't work out?"

"I want to build a solid friendship with you no matter what. If we do this and it doesn't work out for whatever reason, let's promise to always be friends."

She shifted her hand in his so they were shaking hands. "Deal. Yes, Chase, I'd love to date you."

He let out a huge exhale. "Thank God. I didn't want my little girl to watch her dad crash and burn."

Shelby laughed again. "We wouldn't want to disappoint her."

"I'm the one who'd be disappointed. She'd be embarrassed her dad couldn't get a date."

Shelby's smile dimmed to a soft frown. "If you're doing this thinking having her parents together is just for her, then—"

"Stop. That's not what this is. At all. I don't know how to make it plainer than to say I'm more attracted to you now than the day we met. I'm interested in you and who you are, other than Eliza's mom. This is personal. This is what *I* want. *You're* who I want."

Shelby stared at their joined hands. "You do realize I have no idea how to do this . . . that I've never done this."

He'd been surprised to be her first lover. He was even more shocked to discover she'd never dated anyone. "Wasn't there ever some boy or guy?"

"Sure. Kinda. It's just . . . I have a hard time believing guys are interested in me."

"Really? No kidding," he teased, then turned serious again, so she'd know he really wanted to be with her. "But seriously, that makes no sense. You're beautiful and kind and shy, yes, but not rude or dismissive in any way."

Her cheeks pinked. "Well, thanks. It's just . . . the way I was raised . . . my past. People remember the story and want me to spill all the salacious details. Instead of wanting to know me, they want to know about that, and . . ." She didn't go on even though she'd basically told him nothing.

"What story?"

Shelby looked at Eliza. "A long one, better left to tell another time. She needs a bath and story time before bed." Shelby slipped her hand free of his, stood, and took his empty plate and hers to the sink.

"I want to hear that story. I feel like it will answer a lot of questions and tell me a lot about you."

"Then we'll see if whatever it is you think about me appeals to you still holds."

He purposely let his gaze drop and roam over the curves she tried to hide beneath her oversized work polo that did nothing to display her perfect figure. The boxy black scrub pants were a bit too long and didn't show the curve of her hips, her heart-shaped ass, or her toned legs, but he remembered mapping those curves and her legs with his hands and tongue. Her hair was pulled up into some kind of knot at the back of her head. He remembered how silky soft it felt running through his fingers. Her skin felt like a rose petal and smelled fresh and clean with the barest hint of citrus. Her eyes held an honesty and warmth that always pulled him in. And when she touched him, it was like she needed the contact and connection that buzzed between them.

She couldn't deny it, just like he couldn't keep ignoring it.

She offered him her support and understanding, and there was something so easy about her that made him relax and just be himself around her.

"There's nothing you can tell me that would change the way I feel about you. You'd still be beautiful." He didn't just mean her looks. He meant her spirit and heart.

Her eyes locked on him. "No one would call me beautiful, Chase, especially if I'm standing next to you. You're gorgeous. You're the one every woman stares at and wants and dreams about."

It had been a while since he felt like that was true. "You're the only woman I dream about. Night after night after night. You probably think I spend so much time watching the monitor because of Eliza. I do, but it's also so I can look at you. I'm fairly certain I've memorized every curve of your face, the slope of your neck, the way your hair falls on your shoulders and brushes the tops of your breasts. I know the way you breathe, how you sigh with contentment when Eliza falls asleep in your arms, and how every time you lay her in her bed, and right before you turn to leave her room, you look at me with the barest hint of a smile. I've lived on that few seconds every night when your attention turns from her and you acknowledge that I'm there and it makes you happy in some way. I hope it's because you remember that night we spent together and that I did one thing right and made you want more of me."

He'd laid it all on the line. He'd bared his soul to her. If she didn't believe him now, that he truly wanted a chance to see if they could turn something that was amazing into something that was forever, then he didn't know what else to say or do.

Except maybe show her how good they were together again. If she'd let him.

Shelby stood in the kitchen still as could be and stared at him, her eyes misty again.

The last thing he wanted to do was make her cry, though he had no idea what he'd said to bring on the tears.

Finally she moved, and he breathed in, hoping she'd say something to let him know how she felt.

She came up beside him. So close, but still too far away. "I've only ever had that night with you. And if there's a chance that I could have that again . . ."

He wrapped his arms around her waist and drew her close, her hips to his chest. With her standing and him in his seat, he stared up at her and gave her another bold truth. "You can have it every night if you want it."

She cupped his face, her soft hands rubbing against the stubble he hadn't shaved this morning. "I want you." She whispered it like a secret.

He heard it like a wish come true.

He stood, keeping her close, and gave her a second to change her mind or back out before he kissed her. She met him halfway, going up on tiptoe to wrap her arms around his neck and draw him to her. He went anxiously and settled his lips over hers. And just like that, passion flared as it did the first time he kissed her. This time, he didn't want to stop. He didn't want it to end.

But Eliza had other plans. "Dada. Dada. Hug 'Liza. Me, too," Eliza squealed from her high chair behind him.

Shelby broke the kiss and stared at him wide-eyed and a little dazed. "She wants you."

"She's not the only one." He wanted Shelby to know he felt how much she wanted him, too. "But I guess her mom has to wait, and so do I."

"I think this time, we should slow down and get to know each other better."

"I'm hoping we can do both."

"Dada! Dada, up. Up." Eliza held her hands out to him.

He reluctantly released Shelby, took the table off the high chair, unbuckled his girl, and picked her up. She wrapped her little arms around his neck and pressed her sticky face into his cheek. "I think we both need a bath now." His shirt needed to go into the laundry. The front had been smeared with sauce, and now she had her sauce-covered hands on his back.

Shelby smiled at them. "She looks so much like you."

"I see you when I look at her."

Eliza gave him a wet openmouthed kiss on the cheek. "Dada."

Shelby grinned. "She's happy you're here."

"And you?"

"And me," she assured him. "Do you have time to stay and do her bath and books?"

"Absolutely. I want to spend as much time as I can with both of you."

Concern filled her eyes again. "You also need to get some sleep."

"I will. I feel better that you and I are on the same page now."

"I'm still trying to wrap my mind around . . . this."

"Us," he clarified. "I know you're worried about me. I am, too. My head . . . it's mostly a mess again because of . . . what happened." He didn't want to talk about all the details. He didn't want to think about how he'd failed Juliana, or how Adria must blame him for not getting to her fast enough or being there to stop that asshole from drugging her sister in the first place. Everyone told him he did what he could, he'd tried, but it felt like one more failure. One more life gone he wished he'd saved.

"You need to talk about it."

He shook his head. "Right now, I need you and Eliza. You're my priority. You're my future."

"Chase, you can't ignore everything that's happened to you."

"I'm not. I've got my call with my shrink tomorrow." Not that he really wanted to talk about any of it anymore. But he'd learned in rehab that holding it all in made things worse.

He just wanted everything in his life to go back to normal, although realistically he didn't know what that looked like anymore.

He'd only been home a couple days, he reminded himself. Still, he knew he was off, and Shelby was seeing that in him.

"Come on, baby. It's nearly your bedtime." Chase took Eliza to her room, feeling Shelby's gaze on him as he left. He didn't like worrying her. But he loved that she cared about him. And wanted him. And that was a good place to start.

Chapter Ten

SEVERAL DAYS later, Shelby answered the knock on the door, excited Chase had changed his mind about coming over tonight. They'd had dinner together three times already, but he'd said he had a lot to do, including putting together Eliza's bed and decorating her room. She offered to help, but he said he wanted to do it on his own and surprise them. She loved that he was taking such an interest and initiative, but as each day passed, her worry about him grew. He didn't look like he was getting enough sleep. She caught him lost in thought more often than not. But what disturbed her most was the look of sadness and desolation she sometimes saw in his eyes.

He tried to hide it. He brushed it aside with assurances that he was okay.

When she asked how his session went with his psychiatrist, he clammed up. She wasn't even sure he kept the appointments, or how the sessions went if he did.

She opened the door with a smile, hoping to get Chase to return it and see that she was happy to see him.

But the person standing on the other side of the door only got a fierce glare from her instead. "What are you doing here?"

Hunt stood with his thumbs hooked in his jeans front pockets. "If you actually care about my brother, you'll help me out. Please."

Well, she didn't expect that.

"I got a call from the bartender at Cooper's. I asked him to keep an eye out for Chase. It appears my brother is out looking for a good time." Did Hunt want her to believe not only was Chase out drinking, but looking for a woman, too?

"Go down there and take him home," she demanded, knowing Chase at a bar didn't add up to anything good when he was struggling emotionally, even if he didn't want to admit it.

She wanted to believe he hadn't thrown away his sobriety and went out drinking, but doubts creeped in and cracked her heart.

Hunt pressed his lips tight and sucked in a breath to stave off his obvious frustration that he'd had to come to her. "I would, but that would only end badly. He's not talking to me and even threatened a beatdown the next time he saw me."

She didn't want Hunt to have any reason to arrest Chase. "I'll call him and see what's going on."

Hunt took a step closer. "You need to go down there and get him out of that place and home before he fucks everything up again."

She didn't want to believe Chase had started drinking again so quickly after coming back from rehab. He seemed so hopeful about the two of them building a relationship, even if they were taking things slow this time.

Nearly nonexistent really. Her fault entirely for the platonic dinners, where she kept him at arm's length because . . . She didn't really have a good excuse, except that she kept waiting for him to change his mind or meet someone better than her.

She worried about him finding out about her past and him looking at her differently.

But maybe she should just tell him and let the chips fall where they may before things got even more complicated and she started believing in things that weren't ever going to be real.

"Please, Shelby. Go get him. Make him see that the bottom of a bottle, whether it's a whiskey or pill bottle, won't solve anything." The *please* made her believe that Hunt really cared.

"I'll have to wake Eliza and—"

"Don't. I'll stay. She'll probably just sleep and never know you're gone." Hunt sounded sincere, and if he wanted her to go help Chase, then the least he could do was watch Eliza while she did it. Still, she didn't quite believe his motives and wondered if he was up to something.

"I'll just sit and watch TV until you return. Seriously, the longer we wait, the deeper Chase gets into trouble. I'd hate to see him have to spend another two months in rehab."

If that's what it took to get Chase better, then that's what needed to happen.

But she really didn't want to believe Chase would throw it all away again when he'd been so earnest and determined to get it right this time.

"Fine." She grabbed her purse off the table beside the door and stepped back so Hunt could come inside. She eyed him. "If this is a trick of some kind . . ."

Hunt gave her a half frown and glared at her. "I'm only here about my brother. That's all."

She huffed out a breath. "Sit. Watch TV. Don't touch anything."

Hunt held his hands up in surrender.

"If Eliza happens to wake up . . ." It dawned on her that she was leaving a man Eliza didn't know, granted a cop and her uncle, to watch her child. "She's not going to know who you are. She'll probably be scared. Call me. I can talk to her over the phone and assure her you're not a bad guy."

Hunt gave her a sincere look. "I'm not, you know. I'm just trying to protect my brother."

"In your mind, it comes from a good place, but your methods and accusations are not appreciated. I'm not the bad guy either."

He raised a brow.

She huffed out a breath to ease her frustration. "If Eliza wakes, call me." She turned to the door. "You have my number, right?"

"I know everything about you," he assured her, but that didn't ease her mind.

Right now, she had bigger problems to deal with. She got in her car and drove to the bar, hoping she wasn't too late to save Chase from himself.

She wondered if getting involved with Chase in a relationship meant a lifetime of watching him struggle to contain his addiction.

Is that the kind of life she wanted?

She hoped it wouldn't be like that, because she really liked Chase. She tried not to think about how deep her feelings ran for him, because she didn't want to feel the disappointment if things didn't work out. She remembered how the days and weeks after their night together felt. Lonelier than she'd ever been in her life, and she had spent most of her life feeling alone. But missing him . . . it ached in a way she couldn't explain after only having shared one night with the man and barely knowing him.

Still, she couldn't help but dream of a life together with their little girl and how wonderful it could be if he was happy and healthy and actually loved her.

That dream died the second she walked into Cooper's bar where they met, and she spotted him in a back booth with the waitress leaning into him, whispering something very close to his ear.

Chase spotted her standing in the middle of the walkway between the bar and tables, and his eyes went wide a second before he smiled. Whatever the waitress said must have sounded good to him.

She spun on her heel and walked toward the exit, not wanting to get involved after all in Chase's night out.

Truthfully, she thought Hunt sent her on this mission for some nefarious reason. Apparently his hint that Chase was out looking for a woman didn't only ring true. It looked that way, and sliced at her heart.

She didn't make it to the door fast enough.

Chase took her arm and tugged her to a stop. "Shelby, wait. Where are you going? What are you doing here?"

"I'm going home. Apparently Hunt has thought up new ways to humiliate me." It hurt to see Chase with another woman.

Chase's eyes narrowed. "What are you talking about?"

"Nothing. Enjoy your night." She turned to go, but he took her hand.

"Stop. What's wrong?"

She kept her back to him and stared at the door, hoping he didn't see the hurt she couldn't hide. "Nothing. I don't want to spoil your fun."

He rubbed his thumb back and forth across the back of her hand. "You'll spoil what looked like was finally going to be a great night if you leave."

"I'm sure your friend will make it up to you, and you don't need me—"

He cut her off with a kiss that nearly buckled her knees, but Chase held her up with one arm banded around her waist, the other hand softly pressed to the side of her face. He ended the sweet kiss with a brush of his nose against hers. "My need for *you* is overwhelming."

She stared up at him, completely confused. "I don't understand. You were flirting with that waitress."

"Um, no. Not even close. I'm not interested in her, or anyone else but you." He traced his fingers down the side of her face and held her gaze, his earnest and honest. "Full disclosure, I do know her, but we've never . . . you know. She welcomed me home, but I'm pretty sure she wanted to thank me for my service without using words." He eyed her, making sure she got his meaning.

She rolled her eyes and tried to pull away.

He held her close. "I was about to tell her thanks but no thanks, when I spotted you and my whole day got a hell of a lot better, until you turned to leave."

The smile had been for her.

"Seriously, Shelby, nothing is going on here. I came in to get dinner. I've been welcomed back and thanked for my service by half a dozen people here, including Deb, the waitress."

"I thought you had stuff to do tonight."

"I do. But the walls started closing in on me, it was too quiet, and I just needed a change of scenery. I thought it was too late to drop by your place because Eliza is probably already in bed and I didn't want to wake her.

This place makes the best steak sandwich in the state, so I came to get some food and be surrounded by noise that wasn't all in my head."

She put her hand on his chest and sighed. "I'm sorry you're having a hard time."

He put his hand over hers and squeezed. "I was until you walked in the door." He hooked his arm around her shoulders and walked with her back toward his table. "Sit with me while I eat and tell me how you even knew I was here."

She slid into the booth, and Chase took his seat across from her. She stared at the platter overflowing with French fries and a thick sandwich filled with thinly sliced medium-rare steak that looked delicious.

"Want one?" Chase asked.

"I already ate."

"Not what I asked." He grinned at her.

She stared at the soda in front of him and wanted to kick her own ass for thinking the worst of him when he'd done nothing wrong. "I'm sorry, Chase. I came here thinking you'd gone off the deep end."

He frowned and glanced around the place. "Maybe a bar isn't the best place for me right now, but I have to learn to live my life the right way. I get that I haven't given you a reason to believe I've changed."

She reached out and put her hand over his. "You also haven't given me a reason to think you're looking for an escape either. You said you wanted to start dating, but the second I see a woman flirting with you, I think the worst."

"I don't mind a little jealousy when it comes to you, honey."

"And you do that, and I feel even worse."

"Do what?"

"Call me something sweet. Even if it doesn't mean anything and you'd rather be with someone who suits you better—"

"Better than what? You?" He shook his head. "Why can't you allow yourself to see and believe that I want you?"

She stole a fry and put it in her mouth, needing a distraction and a moment to think. And find some courage. "My whole life, no one really wanted me. Not my mother. Not my grandparents. They took care of me out of obligation, and every day I knew that, even if they tried to hide it."

"Why would you believe that?" Chase had been loved by his family his whole life even if they had gone through some hard times. Of course he didn't get it.

"It's true." It was the truth she lived with every day. Chase needed to know because eventually he'd find out, and she'd rather he heard her truth than town gossip. "Do you know who I really am?"

"Shelby Payne. Mother of our daughter." He leaned in. "The woman who seduced me in a shy, quiet way that left me changed and wanting more than I deserve."

Those words sank into her heart, deep, and rooted there, making her want to believe they'd sprout into something she never thought she'd have. Love.

"You're the woman I want to kiss and make smile and thank for saving my ass too many times to count and in ways I can't name. That's you, Shelby. Whatever else you want to tell me about yourself won't change any of that or the other things I think about you. Like how pretty you are when you're trying not to let me see how much you want me. Or how you shine when you're playing with Eliza. How you care so deeply for her and me. You find the strength to be bold and stand up for us even when you can't seem to do that for yourself and accept that I want you even though you seem to feel like you don't deserve to find happiness. You think I deserve it despite what I've done. You think I'm good enough for you, but you aren't good enough for me. And I just don't get it, because you're the best person I know."

But he really didn't know her. "My biological father is Kyle Hodges," she blurted out.

Chase tilted his head. "Okay." He shrugged like it meant nothing to him.

She pressed her lips tight. "Do you know who that is?"

"The name sounds familiar. I seem to remember the Hodges family was well-known in these parts because of their . . . lumber business, I think."

"Yes. Lots of money. A big operation. Lots of people who relied on them for jobs." Some of those folks still looked sideways at her because they hadn't recovered after the loss of the industry in town.

"Didn't they move the lumber operation further south?"

"Yes. After the scandal. As far as I know, they're still living down there and running the business."

Chase eyed her, his gaze turning thoughtful. "The son got into some trouble."

That mild statement didn't cover even one percent of the trouble and pain Kyle Hodges caused. "He went to jail for raping a girl he'd been obsessed with for months. He stalked her, kidnapped her, and held her for three days in a remote cabin where no one could hear her screams for help. He thought she'd think it was romantic. He thought he could force her to love him. In the end, he drove her mad, and she killed herself while trying to also drown the little girl who reminded her every day of what happened to her."

Chase stared at her for a long moment, sorrow and understanding in his eyes. "Rebecca Payne." He remembered her mother's name and sighed out his sadness. "She was found with her wrists slit in the bathtub holding . . . you . . . under the water."

"My grandfather found us. He gave me CPR and I survived, though I'm not sure he thought me living was better than if he'd let me go and that would have been some kind of mercy for me and my grandparents. What happened to my mother . . . she thought what that man did to her left a stain on her she couldn't erase or escape.

"I think my grandparents felt the same way. And I believe it did leave a mark because I always felt it when they looked at me or I looked at them. It was just always there. They couldn't escape the sadness everyone held for them. The town couldn't forget what happened. They couldn't escape the living reminder under their roof. I didn't know how to be anything but the reminder of what happened and what it cost them."

She sighed and continued. "Kyle paid for his crimes, but he didn't pay for the torment he caused her, or them. He sat in a cell, and they buried her. He lived. She died. And I existed and tortured them with the memories of how I came to be the ghost of her and the evil of him."

"Shelby." Just her name and the way he said it with such sorrow touched her.

"My grandparents are gone now. I've never met Kyle's parents. My grandparents never spoke about them. I've tried to move on from the pain my presence caused them. I've forgiven my mother for not wanting me and trying to kill what drove her mad day in and day out. I remind myself that just because my grandparents made me feel unwanted and unloved doesn't mean that I am."

"That is not true at all, Shelby." His earnest words touched her deeply.

"It took a long time for me to believe that, though some days those old feelings seem all too real. But Eliza reminds me every day that I'm enough. It's just hard sometimes because every time I think people have forgotten, it comes up again. I can't escape it. I can't escape him."

"None of what happened was your fault. Not your mother's inability to see you for who you are and not how you came to her. Not for your grandparents' grief and anger and tolerance of you instead of accepting you. *Who* you come from doesn't make you who you are. You are not your parents' violent tendencies, mistakes, and mental issues. You aren't what they were. You're you, and that's damn good, honey. If others don't see you as someone who is kind and amazing, that's their loss."

"You don't know what it's like to have people look at you your whole life and only see how you came to be."

"There is nothing wrong with you. Except maybe that you're always trying to hide. You shouldn't."

"Hide?" She didn't think she was doing anything of the sort. She lived her life. She stayed in her lane and tried to keep out of everyone else's way.

That's what she'd done with her grandparents. She spent a lot of time in her room, studying or reading, trying not to put that sadness in their eyes every time they looked at her.

"Yes. You hide. You keep your head down, so you

can hide in all that gorgeous hair. You don't wear anything that would attract attention. You don't engage with anyone unless you have to, and even then you hold back. You don't believe anyone could be interested in you. Me included." Chase squeezed her hand. "*You* are worth knowing, honey. And I'm happy that I'm one of the lucky few you let in, even if it is only a little bit so far. You keep trying to push me out, but I won't let you. And now that you know that, we can finally move forward." Chase picked up his sandwich and took a huge bite, chewing and watching her with a cocky grin on his too handsome face.

He was right. She had held back really letting herself believe they could be more to each other because she'd been waiting for him to look at her and see what her grandparents saw, but that was their problem not Chase's. Which meant all she had to do was take a chance with a man she really wanted to be with and put her heart on the line, knowing Chase wasn't out to hurt her.

She'd been alone and lonely for so long, she didn't know what it would be like to have someone in her life who really wanted her.

"It sucks what happened to you. I hate that your grandparents used their heartbreak and grief and anger to make you feel like something was wrong with you. It made them unable to love you the way they should have and you deserved. But that wasn't because of you. It was because of them and their inability to separate what your father did, what your mother suffered, from you, an innocent caught up in it all. As for you and me, sweetheart, let's just do us and ignore what everyone else thinks. Fuck them. I only care about what you think."

"Are you sure? Because Hunt is the one who sent me

down here. The bartender called him and said you were here. Hunt made it sound like you were sinking fast and I needed to rescue you."

Chase chewed another bite of his sandwich and looked thoughtful. "Hundred bucks says Hunt hasn't given up on the DNA test thing and he's getting a sample from Eliza right now."

She tried to scoot out of the booth to drive home and give Hunt a piece of her mind, but Chase tugged on her hand.

"I'll deal with Hunt. I know you're pissed and hurt by what he's doing. I am, too. But at this point, let him run his fucking test. You and I both know what it will say. Tonight, we have a babysitter for Eliza. You and I can sit here and enjoy our food, I'll get you a drink, and we'll spend some time together and let Hunt stew about what's going on while we have fun."

She slid back in her seat and faced him with a smile. "Is it diabolical of me to hope that Eliza wakes up and gives him a really hard time about going back to sleep?"

Chase picked up his phone. "I could log in to the webcam and wake her up."

She gave that a thought for a second, letting her wicked smile show, then shook her head. "Then I'd have to deal with a cranky toddler tomorrow."

Chase waved Deb the waitress back over. Then he asked Shelby, "What do you want? A peach vodka cocktail thing? I think that's the one you liked best the last time we were here."

She couldn't believe he remembered. "That one was my favorite that night, but I'm driving."

"One drink. You'll be fine. Especially if you keep eating all my fries."

She popped the one in her hand in her mouth.

He leaned in. "You don't have to skip the drink for my sake."

She didn't want to make him uncomfortable, but she would whether she ordered a drink or didn't, so she went with something simple. "I'd love an iced tea, no lemon."

"Sure thing," Deb said.

Chase frowned, so she assured him, "It's really what I want. I'm not that big of a drinker, despite the display you saw the last time I was here with you."

Chase settled back and relaxed.

The waitress hovered. "Can I get you something to eat, too?" The bar had a decent small menu.

Chase made another suggestion. "How about a slice of cheesecake with strawberries? We'll share it." The same dessert they shared that night.

She nodded, and the waitress went to fill the order. She stared across at Chase. "Trying to re-create the night we hung out at the bar."

"Reminding you that everything good we had that night you can have again."

"Obviously we both agree that night was . . ."

"Amazing," he supplied.

"Yes," she agreed.

"I know I'm not the safest bet because of what I put you through the last nine months, but I swear to you I've changed. And I'll prove it to you. I just want to do that while we're seeing each other because life is short and I screwed up the last nine months instead of showing you how much I wanted us to be together." Chase polished off the rest of his dinner while she watched him, taking her time to really look at him.

She believed he really meant to make a go of them, stay clean, and rebuild his life.

The waitress dropped off her iced tea and the cheesecake. She took a sip, then blurted out, "I've missed you."

Chase went still, his gaze locked with hers. "I missed you, too." He sighed. "I'm really tired of missing you."

She gave him a shy smile, then tucked her hair back again because she'd automatically let it fall forward to cover her face. She held his gaze and took a chance. "We should spend more time together."

He smiled and chuckled under his breath. "That's a great idea." He'd been asking her for that since he came home, but she'd been holding him off, protecting her heart.

It couldn't get broken if she didn't put herself out there.

She also couldn't have what he was offering if she didn't.

She pushed her drink across the table, slid out of the booth, and sank into the seat next to Chase, who scooted over just enough to give her room to sit.

Their thighs touched. He draped his arm around the back of her, leaned in, and kissed her on the side of the head. "I like you close."

She took a sip of her iced tea and admitted, "You make me a little nervous."

He hugged her to his side. "You'll get used to me, because we're going to spend a lot of time together from now on."

She turned her head and looked at him, his face inches from hers. "You make me want . . . a lot of things."

"Name it and it's yours."

Forever came to mind, but she went with the most demanding urge inside her. "Kiss me."

The arm banded around her back tightened. His other hand cupped her face. He slowly leaned in, watching her as he drew closer until his lips touched hers in a soft caress that made her sigh and lean into him.

"You taste like heaven." And with those whispered words against her lips, he took the kiss deeper, his tongue sliding along hers.

She went willingly into the fire, knowing most of the people in the bar were probably watching them. She didn't care. Chase showed her with one kiss what he'd been saying to her for days. He wanted her and he didn't care who knew it.

Chase broke the kiss before their clothes caught fire. "Damn. I may have to thank Hunt for being an asshole."

Which reminded her that she'd left her toddler at home with a stranger. "I need to get back to Eliza."

Chase didn't release her. She didn't really want to leave him.

"Hunt is acting like an ass, yes, one hundred percent, but he'll be putty in Eliza's hands. He loves kids. Always has. So stay a few more minutes. We'll share dessert and pretend we don't want to go next door and get our same motel room again for the night."

She leaned her forehead to his. "You are more tempting than dessert."

"I'm sweet and naughty in a whole other way."

She couldn't help the giggle or admitting, "Yes, you are." She touched her fingertips to his lips. "I love it when you smile."

"You're the only thing lately that makes me want to smile." He handed her a fork, took the other one, and dug into the decadent treat. "Eat, honey. Hunt can handle Eliza if she wakes up."

"Can he handle her pissed off mom when I get home and go after him for making me worry that something happened to you?"

Chase placed his big hand on her thigh. "Like I said, you made my night. I'm good."

"If you're really not . . ."

"I'm working on it," he assured her. "And now that I have your full attention and participation in us being together, things are looking up."

They finished the creamy cheesecake, and she immensely enjoyed being close to him again.

Reluctantly, she slid out of the booth and grabbed her purse off the bench on the other side. "I better get home."

He tossed some bills on the table and stood beside her. "I'll follow you home and deal with Hunt. He's my problem. Not yours."

"You don't have to do that. You should go home and get some sleep."

"I want to take care of this for you, instead of you having to do everything and deal with the problems on your own all the time." He put his hand to her back and ushered her to the door.

They stepped out into the cool night breeze. She wrapped her arms around her waist to ward off the cold. Chase drew her close, his hand at her waist, as he walked her toward her car in the parking lot. She burrowed into his side and soaked up his warmth. He kissed the side of her head. It felt so normal and right and easy to be with him.

A sense of well-being and happiness came over her. This is how things could be between them now. It would only get better the closer they became.

"Shelby." That voice sent a chill down her spine and flipped on all her defenses.

Everything inside her ran cold.

She spun out of Chase's embrace and faced the man who couldn't take a hint and leave her the hell alone. "I have nothing to say to you."

"Hear me out," he pleaded, reaching out his hand to touch her.

She backed up into Chase. "No." She rushed to her car, fumbled with the guts of her purse, and found her keys. She unlocked the door with a shaking hand.

Chase was right there next to her, standing close, protecting her with his big body from the man she usually dismissed without a word. "Honey, who is that?"

"Kyle Hodges." She spat out his name to Chase. "A fucking monster."

The monster's eyes went wide, then narrowed. "I'm not. I'm your dad, and I just want to talk to you."

She ignored him and focused on Chase, who stood between her and the man she both loathed and feared. "Follow me home or don't, but I'm leaving." She slipped into the car, slammed the door, barely managed to get the key in the ignition her hands shook so badly, and started the engine.

Chase stared at her through the window, concern in his eyes. He faced off with Kyle. "You heard her. She has nothing to say to you. Stay the hell away from her, or you'll deal with me."

She appreciated so much that Chase stood up for her and put himself between her and someone who didn't deserve a second of her time, yet took up far too much of it.

Kyle stared at her for a long moment, holding her captive in his penetrating gaze, turned, and finally walked away.

Chase climbed into his truck the second she pulled out of the lot. His headlights came up behind her car as she turned onto the main road and headed home, her heart still pounding, adrenaline still rushing through her system, making her anxious and antsy. He followed her the whole way, and it eased the fear turning her insides sour.

They pulled up in front of her house. She parked in the driveway.

Chase parked on the street, but he made it to her car door the second she opened it. "Want to fill me in on what just happened? Because it feels like that's not the first time he's approached you."

"They set that monster free six weeks ago." She pushed past a stunned Chase and headed for her door like the hounds of hell were after her.

Chase came up behind her. "Is he harassing you?"

"He tries. I keep dodging him. Like tonight."

Chase put his hand over hers on the doorknob. "He's stalking you?"

The door opened and Hunt filled the entry. "Are you drunk, stoned, what?"

"Fuck you," Chase snarled at Hunt, then focused on her again. "I want an answer."

"He shows up places and attempts to talk to me, but I keep shutting him down." She glared at Hunt. "But no one will stop him."

Hunt hooked his thumbs in his jeans pockets. "Kyle Hodges served his time, was released, and since then hasn't broken any laws. He hasn't even threatened you."

"His existence is a threat to me. He sits in his car and

watches Eliza when her babysitter takes her to the park. He sits outside my home. Watching. Waiting. He follows me during the day and shows up whenever the hell he wants. He knew I was at Cooper's tonight with Chase and waited for me to come out."

Hunt eyed her. "Did he threaten you? Did he put his hands on you? Did he do anything besides say a few words to you?" When she didn't answer, he added, "I can't do anything unless he does something illegal."

"Right. That's exactly what the cops said to my grandparents when he was stalking my mother. And when he finally did do something, what good were the cops to her when he held her hostage for three days, torturing and raping her, and they assured my grandparents they were doing everything they could to find her? Too little, too late."

Hunt's gaze softened. "I'm sorry, but I have to follow the law. So far, he hasn't met the threshold for a stalking charge to stick. You can certainly ask for a restraining order, but that means you've got to document everything so you can show the record to a judge."

She fumed. "Do you really think someone like him is going to let a piece of paper stand in his way?"

"No. But it gives me a reason to arrest him."

Frustrated beyond reason, she snapped, "Get out of my house."

Hunt turned to Chase. "Do you need a lift home?"

"I'm stone cold sober, asshole. Did you get what you came for?"

Hunt tilted his head. "I don't know what you mean."

"Yeah, you do. Do you want a sample from me, or will you just test Eliza's DNA against your own to see if there's a familial match?"

Hunt narrowed his gaze. "Why do you have to make this so hard? Don't you want to be sure?"

"I already am. But go ahead. Run the test. But be honest, Hunt. You're not trying to protect me. You want that test to say she's not mine because you know how much I love her and you want to take her away from me the way you think I took Mom from you. You just want to get back at me. So go ahead and try, but you won't get your revenge through my daughter."

Hunt actually looked hurt and offended. "That is not what this is about."

"Keep telling yourself that while you try to break up a family. I'm the only dad Eliza knows. I'm the only dad she's got. And while I'm working on being the best one I can be to her, you're hell-bent on putting a wedge between me and Shelby. I get it. You don't want me to be happy."

"Not true," Hunt shot back.

"You think I don't deserve anything good in my life. I probably don't after the shit I've done, but I'm trying to survive for that little girl. And her mom. So get the fuck out of her house. Go run your test. And stay the hell away from us."

Hunt walked past her and down the steps, shaking his head at Chase as he passed him. "You've got this all wrong."

"I think it makes you uncomfortable and sorry that I have it so right." Chase took her hand and walked into the house, pulling her in after him. Then he closed the door with purpose, but didn't slam it because Eliza was sleeping. "I'm sorry," he said to her, raking his fingers through his hair.

She put her hand on his chest. "It's okay."

He covered her hand with his. "No, it's not. None of this is. Hunt. Your father."

"That monster is not my father," she spat out. "I don't have a father. Or a mother, thanks to him." She sucked in a breath and tried to calm down. "Sorry." She didn't want to take out her anger and frustration on Chase.

He put his hand to her face. "You're right. I spoke without thinking."

She leaned in to his touch. "It's just . . . a lot. Your brother. Him. Us."

"Us?"

She met his gaze and reassured him, "I'm excited about us. I just need time to settle in, for it to feel normal. And real."

He leaned down and kissed her softly. "Real enough for you?"

The kiss made her a bit light-headed and left her wanting more. "Yeah. And our first date was mostly lovely."

"That wasn't a date."

"You bought me a drink and food, showed me to the door, and kissed me good-night. That's a date. And including our dinners the past few days, it's as close to one as I've ever had aside from awkward get-togethers as a teen that ended in disaster and a coffee here or there with someone who seemed nice and interested but turned out not to be right for me at all. Or I ruined it by being too . . . guarded."

"Then lucky me, I get to be the one to show you what a real relationship is all about. Not that I've been that successful at it, but you and me . . . I feel very good about us."

"I feel the same way. And it's nice to see you hopeful."

"You and Eliza are the best things in my life." Truth. The sincerity in his voice and words made her throat tight and her eyes glass over.

"Let's check on her."

Chase followed her across the living room to Eliza's door. They peeked in and found their girl sound asleep, knees tucked up under her, butt in the air.

"I wonder how Hunt got the sample without waking her."

She didn't know either. "I'm just glad she's still asleep. It's not easy to get her down after she wakes up in the night."

Chase took her hand and tugged her to follow him back into the living room, where he wrapped her in his arms and kissed her again. "I should go." It sounded more like a question.

She wanted him to stay, but things seemed to be moving fast, and they hadn't really taken the time to settle into this new relationship. "What's your day like tomorrow?"

"I have an appointment with my shrink, and I need to finish putting the furniture together and decorating Eliza's room."

"I can't wait to see it."

"Come over to my place tomorrow night for dinner. I'll cook. You can see what I've done with the house." He leaned in close. "We can spend more time together." He smiled down at her. "Plus, I'd like Eliza to start getting used to being there."

"That's a great idea. We'll see you tomorrow night."

"I'd like to be seeing all of *you* tonight." His lips were warm and soft and oh so tempting as he kissed her again and again. She got lost in the taste of him and found herself wrapping her arms around his neck and holding him close. His big hands swept up her back and down her sides, his thumbs brushing the outside of her breasts. "You make it really hard to say goodbye."

She felt exactly how hard she'd made him against her belly. It thrilled her to know he reacted to her so quickly and desperately and that she wasn't the only one feeling this way. "I know it's hard, but we should call it a night." She tried to hide the smile those double entendre words evoked, but failed.

Chase chuckled. "I'll survive, because I know it won't be long before you and I are sharing a bed again."

She traced her finger along his sternum, up and down, staring at its path. "You understand that it's not that I don't want to . . ."

Chase cupped her face and made her look up at him. "I know. And you deserve a little romance. Dinners out. Flowers. Sweet words that aren't me just talking you into bed."

"I'd love all that, but really I just want us to spend some time together and give ourselves a chance to let this build into something that will last."

"That's all I want too." He planted a sweet kiss on her lips that held a lot of promise, then released her with a reluctant sigh, and left the house. She stood in her living room, feeling how empty it seemed without him there.

She got that same feeling every time he left.

So why the hell was she waiting to move things forward when that's what she really wanted to do? Because going to bed alone sucked when she knew what going to bed with him would bring her. Sheer and utter happiness.

But would it last outside the bedroom?

That's what she really wanted. A real relationship that turned into a lifetime of memories of them together as a family.

They'd get there.

She just hoped his demons, his family, and her past didn't get in the way.

Chapter Eleven

K<small>YLE</small> <small>RETURNED</small> home to his parents and stared at them, hoping this time they'd see things his way, that they'd be happy for him. He hoped they'd encourage him, instead of always telling him how he'd failed and that he was no good.

"I saw her again tonight. She looked happy. She and the guy she's seeing, Eliza's dad . . . they looked like they were getting closer."

Kyle felt uneasy about the guy, but he wanted Shelby to find someone who made her smile the way she did tonight when she was with him.

His parents remained silent, seemingly uninterested, and it pissed him off.

"She wouldn't talk to me tonight. In fact, she called me a monster." He fisted his hands at his sides and tried to breathe through the rage brewing inside him. "The guy—Chase—he stepped in between us. He got in my way. I won't let that happen again. Yes, I want Shelby to have the happiness she deserves, but why does he get to come back into her life like nothing's happened? Why does he get to be a dad and I don't?"

His parents stared at him, silent and disapproving.

"I get it. Chase just wanted to show Shelby how much

he cares about her. He protected her tonight because Shelby thinks I'm some sort of threat. She doesn't know yet that I love her. That's why I took Rebecca away with me, so I could show her how much I cared, that I'd protect her and love her always. But then that hunter and the police interfered."

His parents still refused to talk to him.

"I don't need your silent judgment." He slammed the door on them.

No one was going to get in his way this time.

If Chase did again, well, then he'd just have to remove Chase from his path.

Chapter Twelve

I'M GLAD things with Shelby and your daughter are going well." Dr. Porter's face stared at Chase from the laptop screen. "You seem excited to spend more time with Eliza and work on building a stronger, more intimate relationship with Shelby."

He definitely wanted things to get a hell of a lot more intimate. He loved spending time with her. He appreciated that she trusted him with her story about her parents. It couldn't be easy to grow up knowing your very existence reminded everyone close to you about a tragic event and the cost and consequences that followed even though you didn't have anything to do with it.

Most of all, he enjoyed spending time with her and Eliza. He felt like he was really becoming a part of their lives.

"Things are good." Understatement, but he didn't want to get his hopes up too high because he had a lot of work to do to get to where he wanted to be personally and in his relationship with Shelby and Eliza.

"Those things are good. Shelby's made it easy on you because she wants what you want. But you need to talk about what's not working right now, because for all your enthusiasm about them, I can see you're not sleeping.

Since things with you and Shelby are new, and you've said you're taking things slow, that tells me she's not keeping you up at night and something else is. Things from your past. That's what we need to focus on."

"Focusing on the good things in my life is keeping me from drowning in my past and losing myself in depression over the people I couldn't save."

"Couldn't save, or tried your best to save but circumstances made it impossible to do so?"

"Using circumstance as an excuse doesn't change the fact they're gone. I see it in my mind and all I can think about is, what if I'd been faster, shot better, gotten there sooner, seen what was coming?"

"You can't predict all of that in the seconds you have to react in war. Like the time your Humvee hit an IED, or a sniper picked off three members of your unit during a raid, or when your team got hit by an RPG."

That rocket-propelled grenade came out of nowhere. "I should have been watching the rooftops and windows."

"The enemy uses the element of surprise to catch you off guard, just like you try to do to them. Shit happens."

Chase sighed, reluctantly agreeing. "Logically, I know all that, but reconciling it with someone getting hurt or killed and I'm still standing . . . I can't seem to get past that." He thought he'd made progress on that in rehab, but then Juliana died, and he was left standing yet again.

Why him?

Why did he get to live and others died?

Dr. Porter spread his hands over the thick file in front of him. "I read the notes from your therapist at rehab. He spoke to you about survivor's guilt."

"Again, I know logic has nothing to do with my feelings. I can tell myself I did the best I could, made the decisions I made because I thought they'd work out, but when they didn't . . . That's on me." It felt like his fault. It felt like he'd cheated death because other people had died instead of him.

"When your feelings seem too big to handle, that's when you need to use that logic to remind yourself of the truth. You didn't do anything wrong. You did everything you could in the moment to save yourself and others. And you need to remind yourself, you were worth saving. You deserve to live. You didn't take someone's place when they lost their lives. You are simply living *your* life. And it is the only one you get, so make it count. Live it for those you've lost. Show them their sacrifice mattered to you. Don't wallow in what-ifs and I should have done x, y, z. You can't change the past."

He knew that all too well. "I'm trying to leave the past behind, but the images won't stop repeating in my head. I lived it once. I don't want to keep seeing it over and over and over again until all I see is blood and death."

"I know you want a cure-all that will wipe it away. You tried that with drugs. It didn't work. Nothing really will."

Chase appreciated the truth, even if it sucked to hear it.

"Time is the only thing that will fade the memories. Most of all, living in the present, staying focused on your goals and what you want for your future, and doing the work we are doing here. Talking about what happened, how it is affecting you, that will help."

He didn't need to be talked into therapy. It helped, so he was willing to do it, even if some sessions were easier than others. Opening up, recounting the things he'd seen and done, it wasn't easy. But it did eventually help.

"Let's talk about recent events. It can't have been easy to go through rehab, really put in the time and effort to get through it and come out the other side clean and ready for a fresh start—"

"Only to end up dosed and OD'ing," he interrupted, frustrated and angry about what happened to Juliana and him. If not for that selfish, destructive asshole, Juliana would be alive, and he'd be in a better headspace than he was now.

"Juliana lost her life. You suffered a setback in your recovery."

"I'm not using again. I know I can't. That OD really scared me, just like the near miss I had before Hunt arrested me and I went into rehab. But doing drugs, self-medicating and self-destructing, it's not the same as what happened to Juliana. That guy went after her. He practically shoved the drugs up her nose. He wanted to get her high and loose so he could take advantage of her. He didn't know the drugs were laced with fentanyl. Doesn't excuse what he did to her. When she dropped to the ground, I tried to save her, gave her CPR, and the fentanyl got on my skin. I was done for, if not for Adria saving my life. I wasn't the target, just collateral damage."

"Is that how you see it?"

"How else am I supposed to look at it? I tried to save her, but in doing so, I got drugged."

"Exactly. For all your efforts to do the right thing, unforeseen circumstances made it impossible for you to save her. That's not your fault."

"It feels like it is. If I'd taken the time to assess the situation ... ."

"She'd still be dead. Nothing you could have done would have saved her."

Adria used the naloxone to save *him*. What if she'd given it to Juliana instead? It might have made a difference.

"I see you playing the what-if game in your head. Let me repeat: nothing you could have done would have saved her."

"Why do I get to live and she didn't?" He couldn't stop asking himself that question. "What have I done to get to live my life and she lost hers?" He could ask the same question about the men and women who died fighting with him overseas.

"Maybe it is as simple as you having another chance to live your life and possibly helping or saving someone else along the way."

He didn't want to hold another person's life in his hands. The responsibility was too great to bear, because if he lost someone else, he didn't know if he could take it.

"You have a chance to be happy and make others happy."

He thought he could be happy with Shelby. He wanted to make her happy. She deserved it. She didn't deserve to be judged by her father's cruelty or mother's downfall.

He'd be the one person in her life who always saw her.

"You get the chance to achieve your dreams and help others realize theirs."

He wanted to watch Eliza grow into the beautiful, smart, strong woman she was meant to become because she'd have her mom and him to guide her. He wanted to see his little girl happy and healthy and thriving and becoming whatever her heart desired.

Dr. Porter replied as if he'd read Chase's mind. "Make your life about that instead of what you can't change for the ones you've lost."

"I'm working on it."

"I think this is a good place to stop. Our time is nearly up. Is there anything else you want to discuss before we end the call?"

Something else was on his mind. "My dad made this big gesture and really opened up to me about my mom and wanting to fix things between us. I think we made up, but I'm not sure how to move forward with him." He didn't want to go back to the way things used to be. It felt like they'd both changed and were different now.

"Just like everything else, Chase. One day at a time. Ask for what you need. Set boundaries when you need to. Be open to possibilities and new things. You never know what could happen. You might actually find your relationship grows stronger because you've been able to reconcile the past and forgive each other."

"For all our strife, we love each other. We always had each other's backs. I know they're still trying to do that for me even if I have made it hard on them these last many months. I didn't expect my dad to come to me the way he did, but I'm so glad we were finally able to talk openly and honestly with each other. I found out he had a heart attack while I was in rehab. I think about what it would have done to me if I'd lost him and we had still been at odds."

"That didn't happen. You have a chance to be a family again. That's a regret you don't have to carry with you."

"No. But I'm still at odds with my brothers."

"Now that you're home and have a clear head, you can work on those relationships, too."

"I will." He'd keep trying to break through Hunt's resentments and anger. He'd poke at Max until he opened up about how he really felt, because Max liked to keep things to himself, but Chase needed to know where he stood with Max.

"Thanks for the talk, Doc." Chase felt nothing had changed or been accomplished on the call, but he knew from experience that this would slowly turn into a sense that he'd been heard. Sometimes that was enough to ease the weight he carried and the anxiety. Other times, it felt like a colossal waste of time, but that was usually when he was fighting against really doing the work to get better.

"We'll do it again in a couple days."

Who knew what would happen between now and then?

"I look forward to hearing your progress." Dr. Porter always tried to leave things on a positive note.

Chase hung up hoping he actually made progress over the next couple days, because he was tired of being tired and sliding back and clawing his way forward.

He checked the time and headed back to Eliza's room, where he'd begun assembling her bed but never finished. He curbed his desire to sit on the couch, watch TV, and not think about anything anymore, because that only led to him not getting anything done and feeling like he'd wasted yet another day.

Plus keeping busy helped keep his mind in the present, where he wanted to be.

He surveyed the wreckage in the room. He needed to pick up all the packaging crap he'd left strewn all over the floor, break down the boxes, and prioritize what he still had left to do. He'd probably start on the dresser next, then the decals for the walls. Or maybe he should hang the valance and shade.

He tried not to get stuck in analyzing one choice over

the other and knelt next to the footboard for the bed.
He found the screwdriver and got to work assembling
the footboard and attaching it to the rest of the frame.
It would have been nice to have some help, but he managed. Bending over and reaching for this or that made
his back ache. He tried to ignore the pain and complete
the task.

His little girl needed a bed and a room all her own.

He'd missed so many things in her life because he'd
been away. He couldn't make up for that, but he could
show her how much he cared and wanted her with him
now. This was a step in proving that to her.

He reminded himself she was only two. She wouldn't
remember him being gone. But maybe she'd remember
this room and the time she shared with him here in this
house he hoped to make their home.

He lost track of time working on the bed, safety bar,
nightstand, and finally the dresser. He had it nearly finished. Just one more drawer to complete the hours of
work he'd put into assembling everything.

When he went to put the drawer in the slider bar, his
aching back seized up. The drawer fell to the floor, and
so did he as agonizing pain shot up and down his spine
and the muscles in his back clenched so tight he couldn't
breathe.

He pulled his knees up, hoping that would help release the tension, but it didn't do a damn thing. He
stretched his legs out straight. That amplified the pain,
making everything infinitely worse. He planted his feet
on the floor and pressed his back into the hardwood,
trying to find any kind of relief. He wrapped his arms
over his watering eyes and just tried to breathe through
the pain.

He'd thought the surgeries to repair the damage the bullets caused would make everything better. Far from it. The muscles in his back took the worst damage and healed with the most scar tissue. Stretching helped, but he'd been remiss in doing that for quite some time now.

Every little movement hurt, but he needed to let Shelby know he couldn't do dinner tonight.

"Fuck." He hated to cancel. He wanted to see her. He wanted to kiss her again. He wanted them here with him.

It hurt like hell, but he managed to pull his phone out of his back pocket. He shot Shelby a text.

CHASE: Need to cancel dinner sorry ☹
SHELBY: Why???

He hated to give her such a lame excuse. He should have paced himself, instead of rushing to have the room ready by the time they arrived tonight.

He should do the exercises the physical therapist showed him so this wouldn't happen.

CHASE: Hurt my back
SHELBY: Do you need help?
CHASE: I'm fine

Far from it.

Chase stared at the phone for a long moment, but Shelby didn't text anything else. Was she angry? Upset?

He didn't know, and that set off a whole new round of anxiety to go with the pain in his back and the disappointment that he'd probably fucked this up. Again.

He tried to keep his breathing shallow so he didn't set off a new round of agonizing spasms. Shadows fell across the room, and before he knew it, he was dragged back into hell, until he awoke and grabbed the wrist of the person attacking him.

"Chase. It's me. Shelby. Wake up."

The disturbing images in his head evaporated, and he stared up into Shelby's eyes, confused and fighting off a panic attack.

"Let me go," she said.

Chase stared harder at Shelby, trying to figure out why she was here and what was wrong, because she looked very concerned.

"Let go," she snapped.

He finally realized he had her wrist in his locked grip and let go like her skin burned, though the only thing on fire was the muscles in his back and the self-recriminations in his head for laying a hand on her. "I'm sorry. Shelby, I . . . I'm so sorry."

She rubbed at her wrist. "I shouldn't have spooked you like that. I saw that you were having a nightmare . . ." She shook her head. "I should have called out to you instead of touching you. You must have thought . . ."

Chase rubbed his hands over his face, setting off a whole new round of spasms in his back, then reached out to Shelby, only to pull his hand back at the last second. "I'm sorry. It's not you. And yeah . . . I thought you were the enemy." He covered his face with both arms crossed over his eyes again. It helped alleviate the pain in his shoulders and made it so he didn't have to look at the fear in her eyes he'd seen when he had her in his grasp. "I'm sorry, honey. The last thing I ever want to do is hurt you."

A little body snuggled up to his side. He kept one arm over his eyes and rubbed his hand over Eliza's back.

"Dada fell down." Eliza patted his chest with her little hand.

Chase uncovered his face and stared up at Shelby. "What are you doing here?"

"You did that thing where you say you're fine, but I know you're not, so I came to help you even though you didn't ask. And you should have."

"I can't get up off the damn floor right now. There's nothing you can do to fix that, and I didn't want you to see me like this."

"So we should only be together when we're acting like we're at our best?" She cocked one eyebrow and stared him down.

He couldn't believe they were arguing while he was flat on his back. "No. It's just . . ." He didn't know what to say.

"You do realize I'm a physical therapist, right?"

"Yeah," he reluctantly admitted, knowing exactly where this was going.

"So you hurt your back and you thought canceling dinner with me was your best option?"

"The last thing I wanted you to see is me lying helpless on the floor."

"Do you think it is a surprise to me that you're still recovering from your physical injuries and that after being shot multiple times, some of those injuries mean you'll be dealing with chronic pain and reinjuries for the rest of your life?"

"No." He sighed, not liking where this was going at all.

"And that given your addiction, you'll need to learn to manage this pain without addictive painkillers, and that I might be the perfect person to help you do that?"

"You are perfect." He hoped that brought a smile to her face. No such luck.

She put her hand on his chest. "Do you believe that I care about you?"

He bit back the pain and put his hand over hers. "Yes."

"Then let me help you."

"You've done so much for me already. I don't want to be another thing you have to take care of."

"Isn't that what a relationship is? You agree to be there for the other person. It's not always fifty-fifty. Sometimes one person needs more than the other. Right now, you need some ibuprofen and a good back rub to work out those knotted muscles."

His back hurt so bad, and she seemed so sincere, he was ready to beg. "Please, Shelby. Can you help me? Because this is agony, and all I want to do is numb the pain, but going down that road leads me to ruin, and I don't want that."

"I don't want that for you either. That's why I'm here. Let me settle Eliza with some dinner and get what I need for you."

He nodded. Big mistake. It set off another round of spasms.

Shelby leaned over and kissed his forehead. "Be still. Relief is on the way."

"It got here a couple minutes ago. Just seeing you . . . it always makes me feel better."

"We'll see if you still think that after I work on those tight muscles, or if you think I am the terrorist you thought I was when I woke you."

He shouldn't smile at that, but he did. "You scare me more than them."

She cocked her head. "Why?"

"Because I need you," he admitted.

She leaned down and kissed him softly. It was the first time she'd done so without him starting things first. She pressed her forehead to his and looked him in the eye. "You scare me, too, because I want to be needed by you."

He didn't care how much it hurt. He reached up, took her beautiful face in his hands, and pulled her back in for a kiss that told her how much he needed and wanted her.

And if he was capable of moving without yelling in agony, he'd show her how deep his need ran for her.

Chase chuckled against Shelby's lips when Eliza nudged her way under his arm and laid her cheek on his chest.

"Dada, fly."

Shelby backed away, giving Eliza room to plant her hands on his chest and stare down at him.

"I'm sorry, baby, but Dada is hurt. I can't fly you in the air right now. But Mama is going to make me feel better, and maybe tomorrow we can play." If only he could move.

She gave him an amused smile and head shake. "I don't think you're going to be in any shape to do the things you want to do for a couple of days."

He slid his hand up her thigh and squeezed her hip. "You have no idea how motivated I am to feel better."

She brushed her fingers over his hand, placed it gently on his belly, stood, and stared down at him, that sweet smile still on her lips. "We'll see how you feel after I get my hands on you."

"Now you're flirting with me."

She giggled. "I'll be right back." She left him with Eliza, who found it fascinating to pull and push the drawer open and closed on her dresser. His head began to pound along with the annoying sound.

He hated being laid out like this and not delivering on dinner. It seemed he fell short too often with Shelby, and she had to come through for him.

Shelby returned a minute later, carrying a bag and a glass of water. "Any chance you can get up and walk to your bed?"

"If I could, I'd take you there with me."

Shelby glanced at Eliza, then stared down at him. "I need you to be straight with me right now. One to ten, what's your pain level?"

He sucked it up and admitted, "Eight." He could really use some good drugs about now, but that wasn't going to happen.

Shelby kneeled beside him again and set the water on the floor. She pulled a bottle of ibuprofen out of her bag, uncapped it, and shook out several pills. "Take all four." She dumped them into his hand.

He popped them all in his mouth and chewed the bitter pills so they'd work faster. Then, with Shelby helping him hold up his head, he took a gulp of water and swallowed.

She gently laid his head back on the floor. "Okay. Let me get Eliza settled. Then I'm going to turn you over and get to work on those muscles."

"I can't wait." His tone told her how much he was *not* looking forward to this, even if she would have her hands on him.

Shelby pulled out a plastic container from her bag. "Eliza, come have dinner." She took the lid off and set the sectioned dish on the floor in front of Eliza, who dug into the cut-up grapes, cheese cubes, shredded chicken, and diced cucumbers. Shelby opened a snack bag filled with broken breadsticks.

Eliza stuffed her hand in the bag, grabbed one, and chomped into it.

"She loves those." To Eliza, she said, "Eat the chicken and other stuff first. Don't fill up on the breadsticks."

Eliza stared at her mom and bit into another one.

Shelby rolled her eyes and tried to hide a grin. She took the breadstick from Eliza's hand and replaced it with a chunk of chicken.

Eliza scrunched her lips in disapproval, then ate the meat.

Shelby glanced at him. "Stay put."

Where would he go? He couldn't move a single muscle without setting off an explosion of pain through his back.

Shelby rushed out of the room, then back in a moment later carrying the pillows from his bed. She laid them right beside him. "Okay, I'm going to help you roll over onto the pillows, so you'll have some cushion under you while I work on your back and you can rest your head on something soft."

He appreciated the thought, but the pillows weren't going to help with the pain he was about to experience. No way around it. He raised his arm over his head and rolled onto the pillows, biting back the cuss words he wanted to spew as the wash of pain hit every cell in his body and every muscle tensed against it, making things worse.

Shelby leaned over him and put her lips to his ear. "Easy, Chase. Breathe." Her hand gently rubbed up and down his back along his spine where the muscles hurt the worst. "Breathe," she whispered.

He tried. First in pants, then slower, until he could take in a long breath as he relaxed into the pillows that stretched from his head down his torso to between his thighs.

Shelby stopped rubbing his back and went to his feet. She tugged at the laces on his work boot and pried one off, then the other. She moved up to his waist, gripped his shirt, and worked it up his back to his shoulders.

He closed his eyes against another wave of pain.

"I'm sorry."

"It's not you," he tried to assure her, but it took a hell of a lot of effort to even speak through the pain. He closed his eyes and focused on breathing and listening to Shelby move beside him.

And then her warm hands pressed into his lower back. She'd used some kind of oil that allowed her hands to glide over his skin. She pressed her thumbs deep into the tight muscles, then smoothed them along the knots.

It hurt like hell, then felt better all at once as her magic fingers worked over his skin, pressing out the tense muscles. She started soft and slow, from his lower back up to his shoulders, then back down again, increasing the pressure.

He fell into a trancelike state of relaxation as the tension eased and the pain dulled.

She didn't seem to mind rubbing her hands over the puckered scars, though it gave him pause when she did. He didn't want her to be repelled by them. Her hands and touch didn't reveal that. Still, he wondered what she thought of the ravages his body had been through and the marks left on him from a war he'd never wanted to fight even as he did his duty.

"How are you doing, Chase?"

"Still alive," he assured her. "Better," he admitted, knowing he should have asked for her help in the first place. She had the experience and know-how to ease his pain and help him get back his strength and mobility.

"Great." She pressed the heels of her hands into his lower back and rubbed them up to his shoulders along his spine. The muscles had finally let loose, and her hands moving over him felt so good now. "When you can move again, I'm going to give you instructions on some stretching and strength training you can do so this won't happen anymore."

"'Kay." That's about all he could manage as she gently moved his arm, then worked on his shoulder where he'd been shot.

"And you're going to do them every day until I say you can stop."

"'Kay," he readily agreed, holding his breath when she found a particularly tender spot. "Ow."

"Breathe out."

He did, allowing her to dig deeper into the sore muscle.

"That's it, Chase. Go with it." She eased off the deep tissue massage and gentled her touch, easing the pain and allowing him to breathe easy again.

"If this is payback . . . I know I deserve it . . ."

Her hands went still. "Do you think I want to hurt you? Because I don't. It kills me to see you like this."

"No," he hurried to assure her. "I didn't mean you."

"Then what?"

"I've done some things . . . things happened over there I want to forget. My mind won't let me. Even my body won't let me. And maybe it's what I deserve for—"

"No. You did what you had to do to survive and come home to your little girl. Every night, you promised her you'd come back. And you did. And whatever it took for you to do that . . . It was worth it, Chase."

"I wanted to make it back for her, but I *needed* to get back to you, because I wanted a whole other life than the one I got stuck in."

"Then try to find a way to let the past go and be here with me."

"I'm not going anywhere." Not to the bottom of a pill bottle again. And definitely not dead, though he'd come close to that twice since he got home. This time, he'd endure the pain for a long and happy life with Shelby and Eliza.

Though he had a long road to recovery ahead of him. He'd keep working at it. He'd ask Shelby for help when he needed it, knowing she wouldn't judge him but help him.

"I'm glad to hear it." She pulled his shirt down his back again and pressed her hand over the middle of his spine. "Do you think you can get up now with my help? I think a hot shower would do you some good, then ice."

"This is not what I had in mind for tonight," he grumbled, planting his hands on the floor, then slowly pushing up so he could sit back on his heels.

His back muscles protested, but he definitely felt better. Looser.

"Go slow."

"I'm good. Thanks to you." He spotted Eliza sitting on her new bed, watching something on a tablet. He turned to Shelby. "Does this mean you're taking her home now?"

She eyed him, then gave him a shy smile. "I thought we'd have a sleepover tonight."

He perked up. "Really?"

"Well, you're in no shape to be left alone. What if your back seizes up again?"

"So, not the kind of sleepover I was hoping for, but . . . I'm glad you're staying."

"Shower. Hot water on those muscles, then we'll ice them while you get some sleep."

"Sleep is not what I want." Besides, he never really slept. But he managed to get to his feet.

Shelby picked up the pillows and followed him down to his room.

"Wanna help me get undressed?"

She carefully arranged the pillows on the bed and avoided looking at him, though he caught the pretty blush washing over her cheeks. "Do you need me to help you get undressed?"

"I can probably manage, but it would be a hell of a lot more fun if you helped."

"And you'd undo all my hard work."

"Worth it," he told her, smiling because she made him happy and he liked teasing her.

She finally met his gaze. "I know it would be, but . . ." She'd asked him to go slow, and he kept pushing to get them where he wanted them to be without all the steps in between that she'd never had but deserved.

"I'm sorry about dinner and being an ass."

She touched his arm. "I know you want us to be together."

"I do. I know you want that, too, and I want it to be perfect. And this isn't even close."

Her hand slid up to his bicep. "I don't need perfect."

"You deserve it."

"Let's take that word out of our thinking and conversations. It's not about that. It's about us being there for each other. Tonight, you need me to help you. Let me do that. Let it be a step toward more."

He loved the sound of that, but he wanted her to understand how he felt. "Do you know why I'm so impatient? I feel like I've been doing for everyone else for so long that I just want it to be my turn to have what I want."

She stared up at him, understanding and joy in her eyes. "I'm here. You're here. We're together."

"Are you at least going to sleep in that bed with me?"

"I will be right beside you."

He took that as a promise for a whole lot more than just being in his bed. "Okay."

"Okay," she echoed him, then stepped around him and headed for the bedroom door. "I'll get Eliza settled for the night and meet you back here after your shower."

Best thing he'd heard in a long time.

Chapter Thirteen

SHELBY WALKED into Chase's bedroom and stopped short. He was sitting on the side of the bed wearing nothing but a towel wrapped around his waist. His dark hair was wet and dripping on his broad shoulders. He kept his hands planted on either side of him as he stared at the floor, quiet and intense.

"Chase, are you okay?"

"You were right. The shower helped. Now I'm just wiped out." Pain and fatigue drew lines across his forehead.

"You need to sleep." The stress, nightmares, and losses he'd suffered had clearly caught up to him. She read it in the sag of his shoulders and the quiet admission that tonight he had nothing left.

She dropped the ice packs she'd brought with her on the end of the bed, walked into the bathroom and grabbed a dry towel, then went back to him. She draped the towel over his head and gently massaged the thick cotton against his scalp to help dry his hair. She pulled the towel off and raked her fingers through his short, dark hair. "There now. That's better."

He gripped her hips, pulled her closer between his

knees, and laid his forehead to her chest. "Just having you here makes everything better."

She wiped the droplets of water off his back and used her other hand to massage the stiff muscles at the back of his neck. "Eliza is asleep in her new bed. I know you're not finished yet, but her room looks great."

"Do you think she'll sleep okay in there?"

"She'll be fine. She fell right to sleep."

He sighed. "Good. I want her to be happy here."

She brushed her fingers across his forehead. "She's always happy when she's with you."

He leaned his head back and stared up at her. "What about you?"

"I'm here. Right where I want to be."

Chase's hands tightened. "It's been a hell of a few days. I really just want to crawl in bed with you and hold you close to me."

She traced her fingers along his brow. "That sounds amazing. But first you need to ice your back." She lifted her chin toward his pillow. "Come on. Lie down."

Chase sighed, stood, and casually dropped the wet towel from his waist to the floor.

She gasped at the sight of all those rippling muscles, the scars on his legs she hadn't seen, and tried not to stare too hard at his impressive, even when not fully erect, penis.

"You're blushing."

She heard the smile in his voice and tore her gaze from his crotch to his wide and equally impressive chest. "You're naked."

He chuckled, drew back the covers, and slid onto the mattress on his stomach, bare ass up for her to admire. "You've seen me naked up close and personal, honey.

I've got nothing to hide, and all of it is for you if you want it." He slid one arm under the pillow, the other over it, and laid his head down. Eyes closed, he settled into the bed without pulling the covers over him.

She suspected he couldn't move enough to do so, but also knew he didn't care if she looked her fill at his buck-ass naked body. Lean. Lined with defined muscles. Crisscrossed with scars and puckered burn marks. All of it drew her to him and made her want to touch him.

"Come to bed, honey. I want to feel you next to me." The soft words rumbled out of him, filled with desire and a deep need for closeness she felt echo through her heart.

"What if I just want to look at you?"

"That's fine, but touching me is better."

So tempting. So right. "I remember." She remembered exactly how he looked and tasted. How his hands molded her body to his. The way he moved in and out of her. Over her. Beneath her.

Most of all she remembered how lying next to his big body felt like it was the only place she wanted to be.

He needed that from her tonight.

She pulled the blankets over his hips and the sheet up his back, then placed the ice packs along his spine.

He grumbled about the cold, but didn't move.

She went to the bedroom door and flipped off the light, then toed off her shoes at the end of the bed, placed her socks, leggings, and the bra she slipped off through the sleeves of her comfy T-shirt on the end of the bed, then slid under the covers. She lay on her side next to him, feeling his body heat, listening to Chase breathe beside her, wanting so badly to feel his hands on her.

"Closer," Chase whispered.

She scooted toward him, her breasts brushing against his ribs as he breathed, her legs touching his.

"You're still too far away," he grumbled. "I want to feel you against me. Then I'll be able to sleep."

She wondered if he added that last part to get her to comply, but it didn't really matter because they both wanted the same thing. She wriggled a bit closer, one arm under her head, the other down her side.

"Better, but not close enough."

"I don't want to hurt your back."

"You won't."

She took that to mean, he didn't care, and draped her bare leg over his, tucking her knee between his two legs. She draped her arm over his waist below the ice packs and spread her fingers wide over his hip. She found his hand with hers at the top of the bed, pressed her palm to the back of his hand, and laced her fingers through his. She settled her cheek on his shoulder and snuggled in against him.

"Except for the fucking cold ice . . . Perfect."

She hugged him. "I've got you. Now go to sleep."

He answered by squeezing her hand and letting out a soft, satisfied sigh.

She was wide awake, taking him in, listening to him breathe as he drifted off. Her mind spun dreams of them together every night like this, only making love before they went to sleep. She thought about Chase being content enough to let everything go and finally sleep through the night without being haunted by his past.

She wanted that for him. She wanted it for them.

And as the quiet night surrounded them, she whispered something she'd wanted to say to him for a long time. "I want you back." She pressed her lips to his skin and kissed his arm, then drifted off to sleep, perfectly content wrapped around him . . . until sometime in the night he jerked in his sleep and startled her. He went quiet again and she settled against him, until his big body bucked again. The thawed ice packs dropped to the floor with four thuds.

All of a sudden, Chase's big body covered hers. "Stay down," he warned, his voice thick and urgent.

She struggled under his weight, but he held her down, his arms covering her head. "Chase," she called out, trying to soothe him, knowing he was probably having a nightmare or flashback of some kind.

Chase abruptly sat up beside her and grabbed her arm. "Wake up," he shouted. His eyes filled with fright, unmistakable even in the dim light. "No, no, no, no, no. You can't die. Wake up," he shouted again, shaking her by the arm.

She reached up and touched his face to soothe him. "Chase, it's me. Shelby. You're okay."

He didn't let go. He just kept shaking his head, and silent tears spilled down his cheeks. "Wake up," he pleaded, and shook her arm harder.

The grip on her arm tightened to the point she couldn't stand it. "Chase, please, let go." She tried to pry his fingers off her.

"You can't die. No one else can die."

"Chase, let go!" Frantic now, she slapped him to wake him up. The crack of her hand against his face echoed in the room, and Chase went eerily still.

"Shelby." Confusion sounded in his voice.

"Let go." She tried to keep her voice calm and soothing despite the tears spilling down her cheeks and clogged in her throat. She tapped her free hand to his wrapped around her arm. "Let go!"

As soon as he realized he had her in his grasp, he released her and shot into the corner of the bed, his back against the wood wall, and stared at her wide-eyed.

She felt a distance as wide as a chasm opening up between them.

She crossed that distance and wrapped him in a hug, her arms locked around his neck. He didn't hold her back, so she held on tighter. "I've got you, Chase. You're okay. I'm here. You're okay," she repeated, feeling his stiff body start to relax against hers. "I'm so sorry she died. You couldn't save her. No one could. It's not your fault."

His arms went around her, and he crushed her to his chest. "She's not the only one I lost."

"I know." She slid her fingers into his hair and held him to her as he wept for the friends he'd lost and a woman he barely knew but meant something to him all the same because she'd been like him. A lost soul, starting over and forging a new path.

Hers ended tragically and way too soon.

Chase probably felt like it could have been him. In some ways, maybe he believed it should have been him because of what he'd seen and done while serving overseas.

But Shelby wanted him to know and believe that wasn't true.

He deserved to live. He deserved to be happy.

And no matter what, she wasn't going anywhere. "I'm here. I've got you."

She felt the energy wane from his big body. She managed to shove a pillow up against the headboard behind her. She leaned back and pulled Chase toward her. He settled his head in her lap and she brushed her fingers through his hair over and over again. "I'm here," she whispered again.

His arms contracted around her waist, and he fell back to sleep. She wondered if he'd even remember this in the morning. She hoped not.

It scared her a little to think he could do something in his sleep and not remember it when he woke up.

Chapter Fourteen

CHASE WOKE up with a jolt. Shelby's grunt punctuated his nightmare as he unknowingly smacked her leg and shoved his shoulder into her ribs. The visions of war, death, and blood dissipated along with the racing of his heart and the rush of adrenaline.

Somehow he'd fallen asleep in her lap, his arms wrapped around her waist. He backed away, not wanting to hurt or disturb her again. He lay on his side and stared at her. She had her head cocked at a weird angle as she tried to sleep sitting up against the wall.

The second he moved away, she reached out for him, finding his shoulders and brushing her fingers gently over his skin. "Shh. I'm here," she assured him, pulling him back into her body without fully waking up.

She couldn't be comfortable. At all. So he hooked his arm around her waist and pulled her down the bed until her head was on the pillow, her body lying down the length of his.

She patted his arm and snuggled into his chest. "You're okay," she mumbled.

Yeah, with her here, he was better than okay. He hugged her close, let the feel of her and the light and joy she brought into his life warm him from the inside out, and realized he actually felt like he'd slept most of the night.

Except . . .

All of a sudden, his skin went cold, and he remembered waking up in the night, caught in the nightmare of losing Juliana, and he'd . . . He tossed the covers back and lifted the sleeve of her shirt, revealing dark red marks circling her bicep.

He laid his forehead to her belly and silently cussed himself out for hurting her.

Again, even in her sleep, she brushed her fingers over his head to soothe him.

Disgusted with himself for hurting her, he slowly rolled out of bed, ignoring the ache in his back, and gently covered her with the blankets. He wanted to rage and weep over what he'd done, but his insides had turned to ice and the contempt and loathing he'd tried so hard to escape before rehab raged inside him.

He quietly backed away from the bed, hoping she'd continue to sleep. She needed it after he'd kept her up last night. He found a pair of sweatpants and dragged them on along with a T-shirt and headed out of the bedroom just as Eliza called out, "Mama."

He stood in her bedroom doorway and took in his little girl rubbing her eyes as she sat up in bed, a blanket tucked around her. He sucked in a breath, found the strength to be calm and smile. "Hey, sweet girl. Sleep good?"

She nodded. "Where's Mama?"

"Still sleeping. You hungry?" He'd missed dinner last night. And though his stomach soured at even the thought of the marks he'd left on Shelby, it grumbled for sustenance that probably wouldn't easily go down.

He'd feed Eliza and get her dressed for the day so Shelby could take her to Abby's on her way to work. And out of his life, because there was no way in hell she'd forgive him for bruising her beautiful body.

He'd never forgive himself.

He'd well and truly ruined everything this time.

A lump formed in his throat, and his gut went tight.

Eliza jumped out of bed and ran to him. He scooped her up and hugged her close, loving her sweet baby scent and soft skin.

She squeezed his neck. "Love you, Daddy."

"I love you, too, baby. Never forget that."

"'Kay." Eliza pressed her cheek to his, then pulled back and scrunched her lips. "Scratchy, Daddy."

He rubbed his scruffy chin against the tip of her nose and made her giggle, then carried her through the living room to the kitchen. He set her little butt on the counter and stared down at her. "Cereal or waffle?"

She tilted her head and eyed him. "Eggs and waffle."

He couldn't help the grin when she was that adorable. "Sounds good." He scooted her back so she wouldn't fall off the counter and went to the fridge. He pulled out the carton of eggs and the milk, then grabbed the box of frozen waffles out of the freezer.

He slid two waffles into the toaster oven and grabbed the pot of coffee that brewed automatically this morning after he made and reset it yesterday. He poured himself a cup, hoping it didn't hurt his sour stomach more. He tried to focus on scrambling the eggs and pouring them into a pan and not his rising anxiety that this was probably the first and last time his little girl stayed the night with him.

"Butter," Eliza said, pointing to the eggs.

He grabbed it out of the fridge, dumped a dollop into the eggs, and added some salt and pepper, too. "Okay." He wanted to be sure he'd cooked them enough for her. He hated when eggs were overdone and rubbery.

"Good job, Daddy."

Another smile came and went on his face. "Thank you." He split the eggs between their two plates, buttered the waffles, put one on each plate, then held up the bottle of syrup.

Eliza shook her head no.

He set both plates on the table, then picked up Eliza and plopped her in the chair where he strapped her booster seat, then buckled her in. "Water or milk?"

"Milk."

"Good girl." He got her a small glass and set it in front of her, then took his seat.

Eliza ate her food, content to be there with him. He found it hard to chew and swallow and not choke on the loathing and remorse writhing inside him.

He abandoned even the pretense of eating and watched Eliza devour her food. He wondered at her carefree spirit and the energy radiating from her as she kind of bounced in her seat and kicked her feet back and forth. He remembered being that energetic as a kid. Now, he needed someone to give him a massage just so he could get up off the floor.

He thought last night could have been the start of something. He'd had Shelby right where he wanted her. Beside him.

It took some coaxing to get her there, but the second she settled in, he'd felt like everything was finally right in his world.

Until . . .

"Mama."

His head snapped up, and he stared at her coming toward him, waiting for the totally warranted attack on his character.

But she walked in like nothing happened, still looking a little sleepy. She kissed Eliza on the head, picked up a piece of waffle, and pretended she was going to eat it.

"Mine!" Eliza glared up at her.

Shelby popped the piece into Eliza's open mouth, making their little girl smile as she chewed. Shelby grinned at him, went to the coffeepot and poured herself a mug, then came back to the table. She stood in front of him and studied his face for just a moment, but it felt like an eternity. "You look like you actually got some sleep." She ran her hand over his hair, then sat in the chair between his and Eliza's and sipped the coffee.

It took him a second to find his voice. "Are you okay?"

She rubbed her hand over the back of her neck. "I tweaked my neck."

"I'm sorry." He didn't know what else to say even if he owed her a hell of a lot more than a simple apology that didn't fix or erase what he did.

"No worries. I'm just glad you finally got some sleep." She put her hand over his fisted one on the table.

He pulled his hand away. He didn't deserve her touch or her company. "You should go now." He couldn't take looking at her much longer, knowing what he'd done, and stretching this out until she walked out with Eliza.

Shelby turned to him, blocking Eliza behind her. She stared at him for another long moment, pressed her lips into a tight line, then pushed her chair back, picked up

Eliza, who had finished her breakfast, and walked out of the kitchen toward Eliza's room.

It felt like someone wrapped a band around his chest and cinched it tight. He could barely take a breath. The pain of losing her just might kill him this time.

Shelby walked back in, still only wearing her T-shirt and leggings, no shoes. She stopped two feet in front of him. "Okay, Eliza is watching cartoons on her tablet. I've only filled up to about a quarter tank of caffeine, so I'm just going to ask and you're going to answer, and we'll figure it out. Okay?"

It took some effort, but he met her steady and confused gaze and nodded.

"What's wrong?"

Like she didn't know.

"I hurt you."

She rubbed her hand over her neck again. "It's just a stiff neck. You can return the favor and give me a good rubdown." She gave him a sexy smile to back up the innuendo.

He didn't let her get away with dismissing his deplorable behavior. He sank deeper into the seat, tried not to choke on his regret and remorse, and shook his head. "Don't. Say what you really want to say." He deserved it and more for what he'd done.

She held up both hands, palms up. "You first. Because I don't understand why you want to tear down what we've barely started building between us." Her hands dropped back to her sides, and her eyes pleaded with him to listen to her. "I thought we made some headway last night. I was so happy to be able to help you feel better. I didn't plan on spending the night, but I found I didn't want to leave you. I wanted to be next to you. I wanted to wake up with you this morning." Her words were thick with emotion and longing.

Hope was a fickle bitch. It rose up so quickly at her words, but he knew how this ended. With her walking out the door and all hope of the future he wanted dead.

"But I woke up alone."

He hated the sorrow in those words.

Her eyes narrowed. "And you're pissed off and trying to shove me out the door. Well, no. I'm not going." She plunked herself right back in the chair, picked up her coffee, took a long sip, and stared straight out the front windows like nothing and no one was moving her.

Chase reached out a shaking hand and brushed his fingertips featherlight up her arm, pushing her shirt-sleeve up and exposing the marks he'd left on her. "I am so incredibly sorry." That band around his chest tightened, and his throat clogged as he waited for her to say something.

She put her hand over his on her shoulder and finally turned her head and looked at him. "You had a nightmare. One of many last night. You thought I was her. It was extremely . . ."

He held his breath, waiting for her to tell him how scary it was for him to attack her like that.

"Eye-opening," she finally said. "I knew you weren't sleeping well. I never thought it took so much out of you, physically and emotionally. I mean, I could see the fatigue and that you were reluctant to talk about the nightmares, but . . ."

"Who cares about any of that? I hurt you. I put my hand around your arm and shook you. You begged me to let you go and I didn't."

She leaned close to him. "Who cares? I care," she

shouted at him. Her gaze softened on him. "I care that you're hurting, Chase."

He knew that, but he didn't want to worry her. He didn't want to burden her with his problems. He wanted to make her feel the way she made him feel.

She gave him a half frown and shook her head. "And I didn't beg. And you did let me go when you woke up and realized you were hurting me. And then you held on to me in the sweetest way, like your life depended on it."

Because it felt like it did, and it might be the last time he ever got the chance to do it. "You can't dismiss this. You can't make an excuse that I was dreaming and didn't know what I was doing. It's unacceptable no matter what the circumstances." He was not that guy. He didn't hurt women. He never wanted to hurt her.

"Fine." She threw up her hands and let them drop into her lap. "Don't do it again. Okay? Okay. Now let it go, because I'm fine, and you will be, too."

He softly brushed his thumb against her arm where he still held it. "I'm not fine. *This* is not fine."

"So that's it. I'm supposed to walk out the door and leave you here beating yourself up for something you didn't even know you were doing. You've said you're sorry. I accept the apology. I know you'd never hurt me on purpose. Isn't that enough? Can't that be okay? Can't you just kiss me good morning and tell me that you liked having me with you last night? Can't you be the one person who wants to hold on to me instead of dismissing me and pushing me away?"

That sad statement hit him right in the heart.

He heard the tears in her voice before the first one spilled down her cheek, and she stood and tried to walk away. He moved his hand to hers and pulled her back to him, wrapped his other arm around her middle, and drew her between his legs and right into his chest. He wrapped her up close and pressed his cheek to her ribs. "I didn't just like having you here with me last night. I fucking loved it." She had to know how much he wanted her. How much he cared. But how could she, really, when no one in her life ever loved her the way she deserved to be loved? He'd only shown her that one night. She needed more from him to believe that he wasn't like the rest of them.

"If I had it my way, you'd be here every day. Every night. Every second I could get with you. Knowing you were in that bed last night, a breath away from me and the darkness that descends in my mind . . . I knew if anything could, you'd pull me out of it. You made me feel safe and . . ." He didn't have the words to tell her he hadn't felt that way in longer than he could remember.

She wrapped her arms around his head and held him close. "You made me feel wanted and needed."

Everyone wanted to feel that way. But no one else ever made her feel that way. Not her mother, who tried to kill her rather than find a way to love her, because of how she was conceived. Not her grandparents, who only saw her as a reminder of tragedy and loss.

She'd practically been alone her whole life.

He knew how that felt.

He also knew how it felt to be Shelby's everything, like he'd been the night they shared so long ago.

He wanted that back. Desperately.

And she needed to know that.

"I want you with every breath I take. I need you with every beat of my heart." He stared up at her. "But I cannot stand that I hurt you."

She swung her leg over his and sat on his thigh, bringing them closer together and her face inches from his. "Yes, it hurt," she admitted. "And I ache for you right now." She slid even closer to him, her thigh nudged up against his dick and balls, her center softly rocking against his leg. "Are you going to apologize for that, too?"

He gripped her hips and helped her rock against him again. "I can make that feel better."

"Just like the brush of your fingers made my arm feel better. Just like your heartfelt apology and how desperately you want to erase what happened makes me feel better. You truly care about me, Chase. That's what matters." She sighed when he rocked her hips against him again. She nudged her thigh up against his thickening cock to let him know she felt that, too.

"I don't want you to go. I don't want to lose you." To prove it, he held her hips a bit tighter.

"Then stop pushing me away. I'm not going anywhere."

He admitted a truth he hated. "I keep giving you reasons to leave."

"You also keep working on being the man I need and the father Eliza deserves. If you take credit for all the bad, then own the fact you've worked really hard to make up for it. You were doing so well at the end of rehab. I heard it in your voice and how optimistic you were about coming home and starting fresh. The thing with Juliana, it set you back, but it doesn't have to derail you. I think you need to talk about her and why her death impacted you so deeply."

"I couldn't save her." He couldn't save any of the ones who died fighting beside him.

"You nearly lost your life trying, Chase." She wrapped her arms around his neck and held him so tightly he wasn't sure she'd ever let him go. "I don't want to lose you." The softly whispered words hit him right in the heart again and made it expand in his chest.

He squeezed her back. "You won't. I'm not going anywhere either." He buried his face in her neck and inhaled her sweet citrus scent. "I'm trying to work everything else out in my muddled head."

"I know. That's why I'm giving you a pass on what happened and the time you need to recover from the trauma you've suffered. I don't expect you to be well overnight. You shouldn't expect that of yourself either. It's a process. Just like healing from your physical wounds, your mind will need time to mend, too."

"I wish everything could just be the way I want it."

"Don't we all? But some things take time. Everything takes effort. And I admire you for not giving up when things get tough."

"I have given up and had to start over many times."

"But you keep trying, Chase. That's what counts."

A little hand settled on his thigh, and though he was happy to feel his little girl hugging him and her mama, he really wanted a few more minutes alone with Shelby.

He missed the closeness the second Shelby leaned back, twisted on his lap, and picked up Eliza. "Daddy needs a big hug."

Eliza settled against his chest between him and Shelby, who wrapped them both up in a hug. "We're a family, Chase. Maybe it doesn't look exactly like you want it to yet, but if we keep trying, we'll get there."

He held both his girls and sighed with perfect contentment.

If Shelby forgave him for what happened last night, he'd let it go, even if he did worry that it could happen again. When he got lost in nightmares that seemed so real, he didn't know what he was doing sometimes. But he didn't want Shelby to pay the price for his messed-up head.

He'd talk to his shrink. Maybe there was something more he could do. He definitely needed more sleep. That alone would help his anxiety, lessen the nightmares, and improve his brain fog and disposition.

Maybe it was time to reevaluate what he was taking and add in the mood stabilizers Dr. Porter had suggested but he'd been reluctant to add to the other meds he took. If they'd help him be more present and focused and get the sleep he desperately needed, he'd take them.

He wasn't looking to escape this time. He was looking for a nice steady balance in his life. A little normal would go a long way to making him feel good.

Shelby stood, taking Eliza off his lap with her. "Time to get ready to go."

"I stay with Daddy." Eliza held her arms out to him.

He wanted to take her immediately, but held Shelby's gaze. "I wouldn't mind if she stayed." He hoped Shelby didn't either.

"So you two get to have fun while I go to work? Totally not fair, but . . ." Shelby paused for dramatic effect. "Okay."

Eliza cheered. "Yay!" She smiled really big when he took her into his arms.

He reached for Shelby's hand and held it. "Call in sick. Stay with us."

She squeezed his hand. "I wish I could, but today is one of my busiest days. Back-to-back appointments through the afternoon." An apology and regret shone in her eyes.

Chase wished she could stay, but a day with his little girl would kick the funk he sank into this morning. "Then it looks like it's you and me, sweet girl. What should we do?"

"Play," Eliza said.

"Sounds good." He needed a fun day. "But first, we need to finish your room."

Shelby frowned. "Your back."

"Is a thousand times better, thanks to you." He didn't want her to worry about him. Yes, his back still hurt. It always hurt. But he could deal with the dull ache.

He'd learned to deal with a lot these last many years.

"Are you sure about this?" She meant keeping Eliza for the day.

"Yes. But if you're worried I can't handle it . . ."

Shelby shook her head. "It's not that. I just thought you might have other things you needed to do today."

He took that to mean she wanted him to check in with Dr. Porter. Because he wanted his life back to normal, he intended to do just that. "I can do what I need to do while she takes a nap." He'd email Dr. Porter and set up the appointment. If Dr. Porter couldn't video conference with him today, they had their meeting tomorrow. That would have to be soon enough.

"Okay," Shelby easily agreed. "Then I'm going to grab my stuff and head out. I'll stop by my place to shower and change, then head in to work. You can reach me on my cell if anything comes up. I'm off at five. Let me know by then if you want to drop her off with me, or I can come pick her up."

"Meet us here for dinner." He wanted her to come back tonight so he could make things up to her. He wanted her to see that he could take care of Eliza today, make dinner, and they could spend the evening together like a normal couple.

"Sounds good. If the day gets away from you and you want me to pick up food on my way here, just let me know." She was always trying to make things easier for him.

"I'll text you."

"Great." She bent in front of Eliza. "I'll bring you some clean clothes. Do you want anything else?"

Eliza shook her head, then scrunched her lips and blurted out, "Bosco and Splat. The story reader. And sparkles."

Chase sighed. "I plan to get her some toys and stuff she can keep here."

Shelby tapped her finger to Eliza's nose. "I'll bring a few things that maybe you've forgotten about at the bottom of your toy chest. Until then, I know you and Daddy can find something fun to do today."

Someone knocked on the front door.

Shelby raised a brow, because who would stop by this early in the morning?

Chase went to the door, wondering if his father was going to make a habit of showing up just after dawn. He opened the door, shocked to find Max standing there in wrinkled clothes with bloodshot eyes. "Hey. What's up?"

"Any chance you can drop by the ranch today? I could use your help with something."

Eliza squeezed between his leg and the door and stared up at Max. "Who you?"

Max dropped into a squat and stared Eliza in the eye. "I'm your uncle, Max."

Eliza beamed at the news and looked between Max and Chase, then back again.

Max read the confusion on her face and pointed up at Chase. "We look alike, huh. He's my big brother."

"We play today."

Max sighed. "I wish I could play, but I've got work, and I need your dad's help."

"I come."

Chase glanced back at Shelby to see what she had to say about it.

"Keep her safe." Shelby turned and headed toward the bedroom.

Chase wondered if she thought he couldn't, or if she just meant that a ranch could be a dangerous place for such a little one. The last thing he needed right now was to return Eliza to Shelby later tonight in less than perfect condition.

Nothing, not even being with his little girl, seemed easy anymore.

He hated the way he second-guessed everything, too.

He turned to Max. "Eliza is staying with me today. Can whatever you need wait?" He needed to make Eliza his priority today. Every day.

"Dad said you're coming back full-time. We're getting ready to send some of the cattle to auction. It's a good time for you to look over the herd. I'd like your read on things and which animals you think should stay or go to auction. Dad likes to do things old school. I think the herd needs more diversity. He doesn't listen to me. Maybe your feedback will get him to change his ways. I'm following your plan after all." Max's frustration rang loud and clear.

And Chase understood it all too well. No matter how hard Max tried to do things right or how much he succeeded, their old man never thought it good enough. Max needed backup. Someone to be on his side.

Chase needed the comradery he'd lost when he left the military and hadn't had with his brothers in a long time.

Chase sighed and glanced down at Eliza. "Want to go see some cows?"

"I need puppy?"

Chase wanted to say yes, because he had the house and land, but that seemed like a decision he should make with Shelby. "You can pet a cow. And a horse." He hoped that appeased her.

Eliza smiled. "Okay."

Chase had so far screwed up taking care of the people in his life. He probably should wait on the dog until he had his shit together. But the thought of getting one and making his little girl happy seemed like a simple way to make up for his absences in her life and get her to like him even more. Yet he'd come back this time to be her dad, not just the guy who showed up with gifts and had fun with her, then left again.

Chase pointed down at Eliza and spoke to Max. "Watch her for a minute. I need to talk to Shelby alone."

Max gave a reluctant nod. "Hurry up. I'm not good with kids."

"Fly me." Eliza held her arms up to Max.

Chase smiled. "You'll do fine." He turned and headed back to the bedroom.

Shelby sat on the edge of the bed and tied her shoe. "Are you sure you want to keep Eliza today? If your brother needs you to—"

He cut her off. "I want to keep her. She wants to stay with me today."

"Okay." Shelby didn't comment on his defensive tone and stood to leave.

He stepped into her path. "Hold on. I want to say something."

She stopped in front of him and waited, nothing but patience in her eyes.

He tried to find the right words. "I'm sorry about what happened."

"You've already apologized."

He planted his hands on his hips and hung his head. "It doesn't feel like enough."

"Chase, I'm fine." She took him by the shoulders and held on. "I'm not harboring any ill will toward you. I'm not thinking bad things about you. I'm sorry that you're hurting. I wish I knew how to make it stop so you could just live your life without all this stuff that happens to you shaking you up all the time."

"I wish I knew how to let it go."

"It's going to take time for the work you're doing to really take effect. I see how hard you're trying and how much you want it. Let that be enough for now." She put her hand on his chest. "It's enough for me."

He loved it when she touched him. He loved her for saying that to him.

It took him a second to get out what he really wanted to know. "Are you afraid of leaving Eliza with me?"

"I know you would never hurt her intentionally or allow her to get hurt. I know you love her. I trust that you will do everything you can to keep her safe." She understood that he couldn't promise nothing would happen, but he'd try damn hard to protect Eliza from harm, even if that meant he had to use Max as backup.

"I will keep her safe. I swear."

She put her hand on his arm. "I also know that sometimes you lose touch with reality. That's not your fault. And you know it can happen. So I expect that you'll be cautious and aware of things that could trigger you."

"Up until last night, I thought I'd gotten that under control. I hadn't had an episode in weeks at rehab before I left."

She frowned, and her gaze filled with sorrow. "And then you suffered another trauma. It's natural that your mind would try to resolve that and make sense out of something beyond your control." She took another small step closer. "I don't expect you to be perfect. I expect you to do the best you can in the moment and ask for help when you need it. So take Eliza to the ranch. Show her where you grew up. Reconnect with Max. Enjoy the day without spending it thinking I'm judging every tiny little thing you do, because I'm not."

"Hurting you last night was not a tiny thing."

She sighed, then gave him a quick, unexpected kiss. "Let it go. Have fun today. I need to get to work." She tried to step around him, but he took her arms and pulled her back, then kissed her the way they'd kissed in the kitchen. He'd like her sitting in his lap again. The bed behind her tempted him to do a hell of a lot more than kiss her. But he kissed her again and again, feeling the tension go out of her until she clung to him.

They both let go of everything and lost themselves in each other and the kiss. Reluctantly he remembered he couldn't keep her here all day, pulled back, and said, "Have a good day at work, honey." He brushed his thumbs across her soft cheeks.

Her eyes looked a little dazed, and he took satisfaction in that. "Use some of the confidence you have in doing that to get through today," she said.

"Good advice." Kissing her made him happy. It erased everything else from his mind but enjoying being with her. Next time those bad thoughts and memories creeped in, he'd think about kissing her. And if she was around, he'd distract himself by doing just that with her.

Her hands slid from around his neck to his chest. "Relax, Chase. You've got this." She nodded to let him know she really believed that. "Dinner. Tonight. We'll see where that goes."

He took her hand. "I'll walk you out." He loved the feel of her hand in his as they moved to the wide-open front door.

They both stopped in their tracks on the porch and stared as Max held Eliza like a sack of potatoes over his shoulder, his arm banded around her little legs as she draped down his back. He turned in a half circle, saying, "Where'd you go? Your dad is going to kill me for losing you."

"I here," Eliza squealed.

Max turned the other way. "Where?"

"Here," Eliza shouted.

Max turned again, making Eliza laugh. "I don't see you."

She smacked her hands on Max's back and pushed herself up. "Here."

Max hoisted her frontward over his shoulder and held her against his chest. "There you are."

Eliza hugged Max's neck and laughed again. "Silly."

Max held her close. "That's what all the girls tell me."

Chase smiled for the first time and squeezed Shelby's hand. "I think our little girl has him wrapped around her finger already."

"Just like she has you."

"Yeah." He pulled her to his side. "I hope you know you've got me that way, too."

She glanced up at him. "If that's true, then promise me you'll drop what happened last night. Focus on her and dinner together tonight."

He kissed her softly, falling into her and not letting the past intrude. "I'm looking forward to you coming back to me tonight."

Her hand fisted in his shirt, and she stared at his chest. "That sounds like so much more than I ever thought we'd be."

He smoothed his hands up her back and gently tugged on her ponytail to make her look up at him. Her shy eyes met his gaze. "I'm hoping we'll be a hell of a lot more soon."

She kissed *him* again. "Tonight. Dinner. More of you and me." Shelby turned at Eliza's cheerful giggle. "And her."

He liked that she was getting more comfortable being affectionate with him. He hoped that over time, she'd not even have to think about reaching for him.

She walked down the steps, her hand still in his, until she reached the bottom and he had to let her go.

Max flew Eliza in for a landing in front of her mom.

Eliza stared up at her. "Bye, Mama."

Shelby fell into a squat and looked Eliza in the eyes. "Be good for Daddy today. Follow instructions. Okay?"

"Okay." Eliza threw her arms around Shelby and hugged her tight, then let her go and ran to Chase.

"Bye, Max." Shelby headed to her car.

"Bye, Shelby." Max joined him by the steps as Eliza chased a bug flying across the yard. "So you two . . ."

"Don't start."

Max shrugged. "I get it. You have a kid together."

Did Max finally believe Eliza was his? Or was he just going along? "And you think that's the only reason we're together?"

"She's not like any of the other women you've dated."

"You keep dating the same kind of women. How is that working out for you?" Chase thought back to the one woman Max had spent quite a bit of time with. "Or maybe you don't want to admit you let the right one get away."

Max's gaze hit the ground before he eyed Chase again and avoided answering his question by shooting back, "You sure she's the right one?" Max held up his hand. "Don't get me wrong, she's pretty and all. It's just . . . she's quiet compared to the others."

"She's got so much more going on than the other women I dated. She's compassionate. She's kind. She listens. And when I'm with her, everything seems like it's going to be all right."

Max cocked his head and watched Shelby drive away. "I see that. The way you look at her . . . It's like you see everything everyone else misses."

"That's because they see her past, not her."

"So, you do know about what happened to her mom? Dad, Hunt, and I thought maybe you'd forgotten the old story."

"I got an up close reminder when Kyle Hodges confronted her outside Cooper's bar after our date."

"What the . . ." Max stared at Eliza picking a tiny wildflower. "I can't believe he's out." Max shook his head. "I feel sorry for Shelby. It can't have been easy for her growing up with that hanging over her head. You're older than us, so you probably didn't know much about her, but I remember how some of the kids were unkind to her in school about how her dad was evil and her mom went crazy, tried to drown Shelby, and killed herself. They teased and taunted her." Max shook his head. "Kids can be cruel."

"That probably only made her feel more alone and unwanted after her grandparents treated her like an unwelcome obligation."

Max nodded. "Dad and Hunt, they thought maybe she used Eliza as an opportunity to take financial advantage of you."

"When we discussed child support, she asked for far less than *I* decided to pay her. Shelby is the best person I know. This is the last time I'm going to say it. Eliza is mine."

"I know. I see that. Hunt does, too. But you know him. He needs facts. Evidence. He's always been that way."

Chase knew that, but it didn't help when he knew Hunt hated him because of how he'd helped their mother find a peaceful, quiet place where she could live out her final days, so that the ones she loved most didn't have to watch her die.

Max hooked his thumbs in his front pockets. "Are we going to the ranch to check out the cattle, or what?"

"Eliza. Come on. It's time to go." With that, Chase picked up Eliza and headed back inside to get himself and Eliza ready for a day at the ranch.

All he really wanted to do was spend time with Eliza, finish up her room, and make Shelby dinner tonight. He wanted to see her walk through the door and not want to walk back out until morning again. Then he'd like to repeat that for, oh . . . the rest of his life.

Chapter Fifteen

SHELBY TAPPED her phone to send the incoming call from an unfamiliar number to voice mail.

"That's it, Cyn. Five more reps." Cyn was so different from Shelby. The exact opposite. Outgoing. Outspoken. Sexy. She didn't care what people thought about her. She didn't care that people gossiped about her carefree attitude and wild hair. Today it was a bright purple that suited Cyn like she'd been born with that vibrant color.

Add in the curves filling out a pair of black leggings and a deep V-neck emerald green T-shirt that had men's eyes bugging out, and someone like Shelby, with softer curves and dull brown hair that didn't have a hint of style, had no chance whatsoever of being noticed next to Cyn.

Shelby looked like a wilted dandelion next to a gorgeous rose.

Even Cyn's name made men take notice. They saw the package, heard the name, and wanted her. And Cyn had the self-esteem and confidence to back it up.

"I can't believe I slipped at the shop and messed up my knee like this. So stupid. Now, if I'd stumbled in a pair of platform heels while drunk and dancing my ass off at the bar . . ." Cyn nodded and pressed her lips together. "Now, that I could understand. That would make sense."

Shelby chuckled. "Your dancing days aren't over."

Cyn smiled. "We should go out. You're never at the bar. I mean, I know you have a kid, but . . . you deserve to have fun, too."

It wasn't that she never went out anywhere. But the first time she went to Cooper's—the place most people in town went for a good time—she ended up with a kid. And the last time she went to the bar, it was to make sure Chase wasn't giving up on his hard-won sobriety.

If Shelby could call anyone in town a real friend, it was Cyn. They weren't besties. Cyn probably had a dozen friends she hung out with all the time. But for whatever reason, Cyn liked her. Whenever they saw each other around town, Cyn always stopped to chat.

"You hide inside too much. In your house. In your head. In those drab, too-big-for-you clothes. Behind the shy facade. You need to stop thinking about what everyone else thinks, or what they'll say to you, and live your life like no one is watching." Cyn finished the last rep and let her knee rest.

"You say pretty much the same thing to me every time we see each other."

Cyn held her gaze, hers intent and direct as always. "Because it's true. And I hate to see someone as nice as you spend her whole life alone."

"I have Eliza."

"Yeah. That's not the same as having someone in your head, heart, and bed, messing things up and making them all right." Cyn had a point. "What's going on with your Wilde man?" Cyn gave her a wicked grin. "I heard he's back in town. Rumor has it his daddy had a change of heart and is bringing him back on at the ranch." Small towns. Everyone knows everything.

"He's there right now with Eliza, helping Max." She hoped everything had gone well today. She tried not to worry, but . . .

"Max is the youngest, right?"

Cyn had only moved to town about ten years ago. Probably why she didn't care about the gossip about Shelby's past.

"Yeah. Chase is the oldest. Hunt's in the middle."

"The cop, right? Feels like he's in the middle of a lot of what goes on in this town. But does he do anything about the scum who are getting away with shit? No."

Well, there had to be a story there.

Shelby wondered what scum had Cyn so fired up.

She picked up Cyn's ankle and raised her leg so she could check her range of motion and any discomfort Cyn might still be experiencing. "How does this feel?"

"Not bad." Cyn winced, and Shelby backed off. "I hate cops," she blurted out, narrowing her eyes.

Shelby imagined Cyn's excitement for life and fun had landed her in trouble a time or two. Cyn thought laws were mere suggestions when it came to things like speeding down back roads. She complained about her many speeding tickets every time she cut Shelby's hair. But Shelby never had the courage to ask about the indecent exposure charge. Apparently Cyn had been caught skinny dipping with an equally drunk cowboy in the Thompsons' pond. Mrs. Thompson took exception when she caught her teenage son watching the couple cavorting in the shallow water and called the cops.

Shelby silently admitted to her jealousy. She wished she could be more outgoing like Cyn and not care what anyone thought. She wished she could take the initiative with Chase, throw caution to the wind, and take what she wanted. Because she really wanted him.

"You're blushing. Please tell me that's because you're thinking about that sexy Wilde man of yours."

Shelby wanted to disagree that Chase was hers, but closed her mouth on the denial. He'd made it clear this time around that he wanted her. Not only that, but he wanted them to be a family. "Chase and I are . . . getting to know each other better." It seemed like they'd known each other for a long time. Shelby let her insecurities get in the way of them having a more intimate relationship.

She had a hard time believing he really wanted her.

Until last night, when that nightmare had him wrapping his arms around her and holding on like she'd anchored him to safety in a storm. And he'd fallen right back to sleep. Deep and peaceful, he'd finally rested. She'd given him that and shown herself that she did have something to offer him. Her heart. Her desire to hold him and make everything all right. She wanted to be the one he turned to when things got tough. And in the night, he had come to her, looking for comfort.

She wanted to give him so much more.

"Sounds like you're both still holding back, letting your fear of getting hurt keep you from having what you really want."

"It's not easy to believe *he* wants *me*."

One of Cyn's perfectly sculpted eyebrows went up. "Why not?"

Shelby didn't know how to explain years of feeling like no one wanted her and how that made her feel like she didn't deserve it. She didn't want to believe that, but it had been ingrained in her from a very young age.

That's why she worked so hard to make sure Eliza always felt loved, and that no matter what, she was enough.

Because Shelby had never been enough for anyone.

Cyn touched her arm. "Maybe you should look at it a different way. You're kind and caring and you have a good heart. In my book, that's more important than anything. Your heart drives you. It tells you what the right thing to do is, and you follow it even when it's hard. So ask yourself, does he have that kind of heart? Does he deserve someone like you? Will giving him your heart mean he'll protect it? Maybe it won't always be easy, but will you be happy with him?"

Yes.

The answer came without her even thinking about it. Her heart warmed just thinking about the life she and Chase could have together.

Cyn took her hand, reading her. "Stop stalling. Stop putting off your happiness. Stop denying yourself what you want. Time is precious. Time is short. Stop wasting it thinking and start really living."

Good advice.

Shelby squeezed Cyn's hand. "I think you've helped me more today than I've helped you."

"I've watched my sister waste her heart on a man who doesn't deserve her. I've seen him take pieces of her. Pieces I'm not sure she'll ever get back. She's so busy holding on to hope that she can change him, that he'll finally love her the way she deserves to be loved, that she can't see the reality right in front of her. She's headed for disaster. And still she keeps barreling toward it."

"I'm sorry to hear that. It must be hard to watch her

stumbling, knowing what's coming, and not be able to stop her fall."

"Our decisions have consequences. We all make good and bad ones. But watching someone I love so totally devoted to someone who is ruining her . . . I wish I could get her to see what's coming and that he'll never change."

"I guess all you can do is let her know you will always be there for her."

Cyn's blue eyes turned stormy. "I hope she realizes that before it's too late."

Shelby saw the fear in Cyn's eyes. "Do you think she's in danger?"

"I feel it all around her. I can't explain it, but I'm worried she has no idea what she's gotten herself into. I don't think she knows how dangerous her boyfriend really is."

"If he scares you that much . . . isn't there anyone who can help?"

Cyn sighed and shrugged. "What would I say? I have a bad feeling about the guy? He comes off nice enough. He's got a job, friends, my sister. I bet people see them and think everything is fine. Abusers make sure that's what others see. I think this guy makes my sister feel like if she just tries harder, does better, says the right thing, they'd be happy. And so she works that much harder to please him. But she'll never achieve the unattainable because he will always make her feel that way. It's how he controls her. It's how he keeps her, by making her think if the man she loves doesn't think she's good enough, why would any other man ever want her?"

Shelby pressed her hand to her aching heart. "That's really sad."

Cyn slid off the bench. "Tell me about it. It's hard to watch. It sucks to see her pushing me and everyone else away because we want to help her and she doesn't see that she needs help." Cyn sighed again.

Shelby didn't like seeing the vibrant and outgoing woman so disillusioned and unhappy. Her carefree spirit had been weighed down by her worry and fear for her dear sister.

Shelby wished she had someone in her life who felt that deeply about her.

Chase popped into her mind. He cared. He wanted to love her.

If only she'd let him.

She didn't want to be like Cyn's sister, thinking she wasn't good enough for Chase when he'd made it clear she was what he wanted. She didn't just measure up in his eyes. She was the one who made him happy. And it was time she started believing she was the one he saw beside him for the rest of his life.

Because that's what she wanted with him, too.

Cyn rallied and gave her a smile. "Sorry to bum you out. I don't really have anyone to talk to about my sister, and you're a good listener. So thanks."

"Anytime." Shelby squeezed her hand again. "I mean that. And your knee appears to be improving. How does it feel after the weights?"

"Good. Better. Last time it swelled quite a bit, but this time it isn't."

"I still suggest you ice it. After a long shift at the salon, put your foot up and rest it. It won't be long before you're a hundred percent again."

"I can't wait. And you should come into the salon. Let me show my appreciation for lending me your ear by giving you a really cute, fun haircut. You'll knock that Wilde man on his ass."

Not a bad idea. "I'll be in soon." It had been a while since she'd had her hair done, and it was growing quite long. Plus, she needed to step out of her comfort zone. Nothing much happened there. She needed to shake things up. Live, like Cyn said.

She needed to stop wishing and start doing.

If she wanted to move forward with Chase, then she needed to act on it and stop stalling, or whatever it was that kept her from giving in to her impulses and holding back.

Her phone vibrated in her pocket again. That made three times since she started working on Cyn's rehab.

Cyn pointed to the phone. "Someone really wants to talk to you."

"I don't recognize the number."

"Live the adventure," Cyn encouraged her, picking up her bag to leave. "If you don't answer, you'll never know if you're missing out on something good." With that, Cyn headed for the door, waving goodbye over her shoulder.

Shelby answered the call. "Hello?"

"Thank God. Finally." Relief and something desperate filled his voice.

"Max?"

"Yeah. You need to get over here. Chase . . . Something's wrong. He lost his shit, and now he's hunkered down in one of the sheds, acting like there's an imminent attack coming or something."

Her heart nearly pounded right out of her chest. "Where is Eliza?" Panic sent a bolt of adrenaline through her.

"She's with me. I was able to get her out. She's fine."

She breathed a huge sigh of relief. "Okay. Good. What's he doing?"

"Shouting orders. Hiding . . . I don't fucking know." Max sounded frantic to help but also helpless.

"Stop swearing around Eliza and put me on speaker so Chase can hear me."

She ran into the office and grabbed her purse, digging out her keys as she walked back out into the main part of the building. Thank God, her last appointment canceled and she could leave early.

"Chase, man, Shelby's on the phone."

"Get down! They're coming! They're all around us." Panic made Chase sound desperate.

"There's no one here. You're safe. We are all safe," Max tried to reassure his brother.

"Chase, baby, it's me. Shelby. Please, honey, you need to calm down and listen to Max. You're safe. You are at the ranch. Eliza is there with you. She needs you, Chase. I need you."

"Where are you?" Hesitation, longing, and an unspoken plea filled that question.

"I'm on my way to you right now. I will be there soon. Do you see where you are now?"

The quiet unnerved her.

"Chase, baby, you need to talk to me. You need to tell me what you need."

"You."

She barely heard the whisper, and his plea broke her heart.

"I'm coming to you right now." She put action to words and rushed out of the building.

"I'm sorry," Chase said, his voice a bit stronger.

"It's okay," Max assured him. "If I hadn't dropped the tool and set you off . . ."

So that's what happened. Something triggered a flashback, and Chase got lost in the past.

"Come out of there, man." Max spoke softly without any judgment. "Let me help you get past this barricade you built."

"Just give me a minute." Chase's breathing was loud and labored.

Max must have gone into the shed to get Chase.

It broke her heart to hear the weariness in Chase's voice.

"Chase, are you okay now?" The long pause made her hold her breath.

"I'm getting there. I thought this was behind me." He'd worked so hard to confront his issues and overcome them.

She didn't know what to say to that because this wasn't the kind of thing you just got over. It wasn't a virus or a cut that needed to heal. It was a volcano. Sometimes dormant. Sometimes, a rumble. Worst case, an all-out eruption.

At least today, it didn't seem like a catastrophe.

No one got hurt.

She hoped Chase could focus on that.

"You've had a lot to deal with, take in, and adjust to since getting out of rehab. Flashbacks are unpredictable. You're more susceptible to triggers when you're under a lot of stress."

"I messed up this morning. I'm sorry." The emotion in that apology made her heart sink.

She didn't want him to think she still blamed him for what happened.

"We already worked that out." She jumped in her car and tried to get him to focus on other things. "How is your back?"

"Sore, but better thanks to you."

"Yeah? Well, I'll give you another back rub tonight."

"Something to look forward to." He sounded hopeful and a lot less tense.

"You have a lot of good things to look forward to."

"You're on your way here." He always made it clear how much he wanted her. Not just in the physical sense, but as a real part of his life. And up until now, she'd been holding back for no other reason than she was afraid it wasn't real, that he only wanted them to be a family because of Eliza.

But that wasn't true.

This didn't have anything to do with their daughter.

"Did you get an appointment with Dr. Porter for to-day? You were going to talk to him about getting a new medication to go with what you're already taking."

"Tomorrow. And I will get the meds. I promise. They'll help."

"Okay." That was a relief. "Until then, we'll work together to help you through this."

"I need you here." The desperate plea made her wish she could be by his side with a snap of her fingers. He was hurting and he needed her.

"I'm on my way."

"I'm sorry to take you away from work."

"I was done for the day," she assured him. "I'm driving as fast as I can and will be there soon."

"Slow down. Be safe." The urgent request touched her.

"I just want to be with you." Her heart ached to get to him. She needed to see that he was okay.

"Do you really mean that?"

They'd been pushing and pulling at each other but never really coming together.

"Yes, Chase. You'll see when I get there." Because she planned to take Cyn's advice and really live her life with Chase.

Chapter Sixteen

CHASE NEEDED to get a grip on his anxiety. He shouldn't rely on Shelby to make everything seem better. But when he thought about her, the noise in his head quieted down.

It wasn't fair to put that on her.

He needed to work out his own problems, but thinking about her, seeing her, being with her, was better than any pill. Though he'd take those religiously to keep this from happening again.

She eased him. She made him believe in a future where he was happy and healthy and whole again.

And he'd do anything to prove to her that he could be those things for her. For the both of them. He had to heal, accept the things he couldn't change, and live with the things he'd done or couldn't do. It was the only way to be the man she deserved.

He'd keep working with Dr. Porter. He'd take his meds. He'd try to be more open and honest about what he needed and not try to do this all on his own and expect to be better all at once.

He'd been advised not to start a relationship in the first year out of rehab, and the flashback was a setback, but he'd waited too damn long and almost didn't make it to this point at all. His feelings for Shelby were so strong, giving her up wasn't an option.

He'd do everything possible to get better, but he'd do it with Shelby by his side.

Chase pushed Eliza on the swing his dad hung from the tree in the yard just for her. His dad and Max walked out of the stables and headed in his direction. He didn't want a lecture about what happened and taking care of himself.

"I don't want to hear it," he snapped at his dad and brother, preemptively shutting them down.

His dad and Max exchanged a look. Then both of them focused on him.

Dad went first. As always. "So you don't want me to tell you that I think your plans for sorting the herd are sound and we'll get started on that tomorrow."

"Uh . . ." He didn't know what to say.

Max added, "It's nice to finally have a second opinion to push for some change around here."

His dad rubbed his hand over his neck. "I know I'm stubborn."

"As an ass," Max agreed.

Dad smacked Max on the chest with the back of his hand for the smart mouth. "But I'm trying. Because the last thing your mother would have wanted is for me to push you all away. Chase has been gone far too long. Max, you're ready to up and quit on me because I'm set in my ways. And Hunt is . . . well, I don't know what's gotten into him lately, but he's barely around anymore."

Chase brought up what they avoided for the past half hour. "Things got a little intense today. I can't control it, but I'm taking meds and working on my issues."

His dad waved it off. "You're okay now. That's all that matters."

Max nodded. "No problem, man. It's all good."

"I hope Shelby thinks so too, because this was the first time I had Eliza on my own, and . . ." Chase hated that he'd lost it in front of his daughter.

Max hooked his thumbs in his front pockets. "She's fine, and thank God, so are you. I tried to get you to hear me, to understand what I was saying to you. You calmed down the second you heard Shelby's voice. Two words out of her mouth and you were right back here in reality."

Chase hung his head, then met their gazes again. "When I was overseas . . . I missed this place, you guys, everything about what it used to be like living here. This was home. I belonged here. Until I didn't anymore. And it cut deep. And then she came along. I thought, one and done. We'd have our night, and I'd go back to my new life and endure like I'd been doing since I left here. I spent months thinking about her and wishing I could find my way out of there and be back here with her.

"Finding out I was going to be a dad stunned me. No joke. I never expected that, but then, I'd been the one to go back for more that night, risking it because I wanted more of her.

"I wasn't sure about being a dad. But then I realized that I'd lost one family and had a chance to build another one. Eliza connected me to Shelby, the woman who followed me everywhere I went. I didn't know if we would ever be more to each other than Eliza's parents until she let me into their life like I was always meant to be there. She showed me that someone could be kind and generous and connect me to something better than where I was. She took me out of that place and gave me a home." Choked up, he took a second to gather himself.

His dad and Max hung on his every word.

"When things were really bad over there, I always had her. Didn't matter the time or my mood or if I talked to her or not. She was always there, my connection to Eliza, but also my connection to her and that night we shared and the feeling that rushed over me every time I saw her or heard her voice."

Chase raked his fingers through his hair, uncomfortable dumping his emotions like this to them, but feeling like it needed to be said so they'd understand. So they'd get it. So they'd know how much she meant to him.

"She's everything I ever wanted."

His dad gave him a firm nod. "I'm sorry for the way I treated her and trying to push her out of your life."

"Me, too." Max's gaze went past him to Eliza. "I really enjoyed watching you with her today. She cracked me up and made me smile more than I can remember doing in a long time."

Eliza had charmed Max just as Shelby had charmed Chase.

"More than anything, they are the life I want."

His dad stepped forward and clamped his hand on Chase's shoulder. "Then you need to take care of yourself so you can take care of them."

"I'm working on it."

"I know you are. Today, well, that was something you can't help. Max was here to get you through it, along with Shelby. Whatever you need, son, we're here for you."

Chase appreciated so much that his father had finally

come around and accepted Shelby. Chase wasn't the same man who'd been booted off this land and out of the family. He was something different. Broken. But worthy of their love. He hoped.

Shelby's car came to a skidding stop in the driveway. She leaped out of the car and ran toward them.

"She's all I need." He took a couple steps to assure Shelby that Eliza was okay because she looked worried, but before he got any words out, she launched herself into his chest, wrapped her arms around his neck, and kissed him. Everything in his mind evaporated. All his worries, gone. Anxiety, vanished. He held her close and fell into the kiss, then took over to show her just how much he wanted her and appreciated that she'd *finally* stopped holding back and came for what she wanted. Him.

He wanted her to know all the way to her soul that she would never be alone again. She had him.

He forgot about their audience and everything else until Eliza's little arm wrapped around his leg. "Mama. Up."

Shelby broke the kiss and pressed her forehead to his. "Are you okay?"

"Right here, right now, I'm fantastic." He meant every word.

She smiled, and it was real and bright and just for him. "Good."

"Up." Eliza tugged on his jeans.

Chase set Shelby back on her feet and reluctantly released her to pick up their little girl. "Tell Mama what you did today."

"Rode horse."

Shelby looked impressed. "You did?"

"With Daddy. And Unc Max."

Shelby poked Eliza's belly. "Sounds like you had a great day."

"Daddy hid from us. Unc Max found him."

Shelby looked to him to explain. "Max kept Eliza at a safe distance while I . . . hid."

"Thank you, Max. For taking care of Eliza and Chase and calling me."

Max shrugged. "He couldn't really hear me. I hoped you could get through to him since you two have been together through a lot of the tough stuff. I figured you'd know what to do or at least get him to listen to you. You were exactly what he needed."

Chase hooked his arm around her shoulders. "You *are* everything I need."

"Good. Because I'm keeping you."

Shocked by her words, he stared down at her and couldn't find anything to say back to her that would adequately describe how she made him feel.

Eliza hugged his neck again. "Mine."

Chase hugged Eliza back, his heart melting at his little girl's sweet heart. Then he caught Shelby's eye, letting her know with a look how much Eliza meant to him. How grateful he was to have them both in his life.

Shelby shocked him again by leaning up and kissing him softly. "Mine."

He stared down into her gorgeous eyes so filled with love for him that it took him a second to really take it in. Overwhelmed with emotion, he touched his forehead to hers. "I've been yours since the moment we met. All I've wanted is for you to be mine."

"You had me the second you smiled at me and didn't laugh at the ridiculous drink I ordered."

He laughed now. "I was completely enthralled by

your peachy choice and the shy way you kept checking me out."

"You're just pure eye candy." Her bold words made him laugh. But the bright smile made him believe she'd finally opened herself up to really being with him.

"You got a good, long look last night. Want another?"

"I'm not sticking around for more of this." Max smacked him on the back as he walked toward his truck. "I'm going to find my own woman at the bar." Max turned back before he hopped in the truck. "Thanks for coming today. It was . . . like old times." Max gave Eliza a lopsided grin. "See you soon, munchkin."

"Bye Unc."

Max shifted his gaze to Shelby, standing in the crook of his arm. "Keep keeping him sane."

"I will." Shelby waved goodbye to his brother, then turned her gaze up to him. "You promised me dinner."

"Let's head home."

"Sounds good to me." Shelby acknowledged his father for the first time. "Nice to see you again, Mr. Wilde."

"It is really good to see you all together." He looked from Shelby to Eliza and finally to him. "That's a nice-looking family, Chase." With that, his dad headed up to the house.

Chase watched him go.

Shelby broke the silence. "He's happy for you."

"It's a nice change," Chase admitted. "And so was the greeting you gave me when you got here."

"I just wanted you to know I'm here. I'm in this with you. And I don't want to wait anymore for any of it. Let's just be . . . us."

That "us" hit him right in the heart. "I like the sound of that."

Chapter Seventeen

SHELBY REACHED over and put her hand over Chase's. They'd just finished dinner, and Eliza sat playing with her favorite stuffed animals, Bosco and Splat. But Shelby sensed that Chase had checked out about ten minutes ago. He sat staring into space. She didn't like the uneasy quiet about him. Or the sadness she saw in his eyes.

Depression had settled over him, thick and heavy. Even her touch didn't penetrate the wall she felt between them.

She needed to break through. "Chase." She'd said his name twice already. "Chase." She squeezed his hand and didn't let up until he blinked and focused on her.

"Huh. What? Did you say something, sweetheart?"

"What's wrong?"

"Nothing. I'm fine. Tired. That's all." His gaze went blank again for a moment before he focused on her again. "Where's Eliza?"

She shifted in her chair so he could see Eliza behind her in the living room.

"Oh." He looked at her empty plate, then his barely touched food. "I guess I wasn't as hungry as I thought."

"You took your medication. If you don't eat, you'll get an upset stomach."

"I'm fine."

"Are you?" She didn't mean to snap at him, but she wanted him to focus and stop avoiding what was so obvious.

He wasn't fine.

"It's been a long day." He rose and grabbed his plate. "I'll give Eliza her bath and read her books. Relax. You had a long day, too." He kissed the top of her head, deposited his dish in the sink, and scooped up Eliza with a wince that told her his back was bothering him again.

Shelby sat at the table, disheartened that the hope she'd seen in his eyes at the ranch when she arrived had dipped back into the sadness he couldn't seem to keep at bay.

He needed something to help him put what happened with Juliana in perspective and find a way to move forward and out of the darkness that came over him.

Maybe not something. But someone.

She eyed the cell phone he'd left on the table. She didn't want to go behind his back, but something had to be done to help him.

She picked up his phone and quietly walked out of the house and onto the porch. She slid her finger across the screen, tapped on his contacts, found the number she needed, and made the call before she thought better of interfering.

Chase might see the call later, but if she called from her phone, more than likely his friend wouldn't pick up, and she didn't have enough time to leave a message and wait for him to call her back.

"Hey, Chase, I'm sorry I haven't gotten back to you, but things have been difficult here."

"Um, I'm really sorry to hear that." Shelby meant it. "But that's why I'm calling. Chase needs your help."

"Who is this?" Drake asked.

"Sorry. My name is Shelby. I'm . . ." She didn't know how to end that sentence and went with how she felt and what she and Chase had said they wanted to be to each other. "I'm Chase's girlfriend." She didn't exactly know how Chase would feel about her saying that, but she hoped it would make him happy to know she'd embraced this next step in their relationship and that it showed him she really wanted to move forward. With him.

"Hey. Yeah. He told me about you. You're Eliza's mom."

"Yes. I'm so sorry to call you out of the blue like this, but Chase . . . He's really having a hard time. He feels responsible for Juliana's death and that he should have done more to save her. I know you're grieving her loss, too, but I was hoping that maybe you could talk to him."

Drake let out a heavy sigh. "Juliana's death hit us all hard. We got the bastard who killed her."

"Chase will be very happy to hear that, but I think it would go a long way if he heard it from you. He's having nightmares about her death. His flashbacks of the war have come back. I don't want to speak for him, but I think he feels like all the hard work he's done means nothing when he lost another life. Does that make sense?"

"Yes." Drake sighed again. "It makes a lot of sense. I should have called him before now. I know Adria wants to thank him for trying to save her sister."

"I understand. It's been hard on everyone. All I want is for Chase to finally have the life he wants, but I'm worried."

"I hear you. I've been where Chase is at, wallowing

in the past and taking all the blame for everything that went to shit."

"He could definitely use a friend who understands. I'm trying, but I know I'm not enough."

"If you're reaching out to him, to others for him, then you're doing everything you can. Hang on a sec."

Shelby heard a muffled conversation between Drake and someone in the background. She glanced through the front window, hoping Chase was still occupied with Eliza.

"Shelby."

"Yeah?"

"Adria and I talked. She and I agree that the best thing for Chase is for us to come and see him. I work with another friend and fellow soldier who I think can provide some additional help, too. We can be there tomorrow afternoon."

She hoped Drake could talk to Chase and ease his mind, but seeing him and Adria in person might help even more. "I think he'd love to see you. Thank you. I appreciate anything you can do for him."

"Is he there? I'd like to check in with him, but we'll keep the visit a surprise. I don't want him getting anxious and overthinking why we're coming to see him."

She hadn't really considered that and appreciated that Drake understood Chase in a way she didn't. It made her feel better about calling Drake without telling Chase first. "He's inside. He doesn't know I called you."

"No worries. Hang up with me. I'll call his cell right back, and you can give him the phone."

"Perfect. And thank you, Drake. I really didn't know what to do. I hoped you and Adria could help, but I wasn't sure . . ."

"Chase and I have been to hell and back. If he's down, I'm here to pull him back up. I want him to know that. I want him to count on it."

"That's exactly how I feel. I just want to help him."

"That's why you called me. Together, we'll support him until he's all good again."

"Thank you, Drake. You have no idea how much I appreciate this."

"Anything for Chase. And . . . I can't wait to meet you. Although he talked about you all the time. I kind of feel like I know you."

"I can't wait to meet you and Adria. I'll see you soon."

"I'll call right back."

Shelby hung up, quickly snuck back into the house, and walked toward the bathroom as Chase's phone rang again. She stepped into the bathroom doorway just as Chase plucked Eliza out of the tub and wrapped a towel around her.

"Hey. It's for you. Caller ID says Drake."

Chase snatched the phone from her hand and swiped the screen. "Drake. Man, are you okay? How is Adria?" Chase listened to Drake.

She touched his arm. "I've got her," she whispered, then picked up Eliza and took her into her bedroom.

"Dada. Books."

"He's on the phone with his friend. Mama will read books tonight, but he'll come kiss you good-night."

"Dada," Eliza demanded, wriggling away as Shelby tried to dry her hair.

Shelby tried to hold on to her patience. "Let's get dressed and brush your hair. Maybe he'll be here by then." Shelby didn't think so, but she'd get Eliza ready for bed one step at a time.

Eliza cooperated and pulled her panties and kitten pajamas out of her bag. Shelby really needed to stock some clothes here for her. Luckily she'd packed the bag this morning after she'd showered at home before going to work. Too bad she didn't bring anything for herself. And she should have, but she'd been in a hurry and running late.

And after her talk with Cyn today, she'd planned to stop at home, put on something more appealing than her scrub pants and work polo, and pack some other things.

Though the evening looked promising when she arrived at the ranch and kissed Chase hello, his mood had changed considerably since they got home, and he'd gone quiet on her.

Maybe tonight wasn't a good night to stay.

She could take Eliza home, and they could try this again another night.

She'd helped Eliza put on her pj's and attempted to run the brush through her hair, but it only got tangled as Eliza fidgeted and tried to go find her dad.

Shelby stopped and held Eliza by the shoulders. "Be still, please. Let me finish."

"Dada."

"He's on the phone," Shelby reminded her, then ran the brush through her hair as quickly as possible without pulling at the knots. "There. Now find the books I put in your bag."

"Dada read."

"I'll start. Dada will be here soon."

Eliza climbed up onto her bed, dug the three books Shelby packed out of her bag, and set them in her lap.

Shelby wished she'd remembered Eliza's night-light.

She'd have to keep the hall bathroom light on again if they stayed. She really wanted to talk to Chase and see where his head was at tonight. Maybe he wanted to be alone. A little peace and quiet after having Eliza with him all day. Maybe he just wasn't feeling like having them here with him right now.

Chase filled the bedroom doorway, the phone still to his ear. "Thanks for calling, Drake. It means a lot. I'm so happy to hear that although Adria is grieving, she's okay, and you two are together."

"Dada," Eliza called.

Chase held up his finger. "Yeah. Sure. We'll talk soon." Chase ended the call and sucked in a huge breath, then let it out and looked at Shelby. "They got the guy who drugged Juliana. Adria and Drake are together. Everything seems like it's okay."

"That's good. Like you said, they're grieving. Like you. In time, things will get easier." She didn't know what else to say.

"Dada," Eliza said, her little voice insistent.

Shelby stepped between him and Eliza.

He stared down at her, a question in his eyes.

"If tonight's not good for you, and you need time to be alone, and—"

Chase took her by the shoulders and pulled her into a kiss, cutting off her words. His mouth was warm and soft and oh so tempting. "No. The last thing I want is to be alone. Stay." She heard the plea in that one word and in his eyes.

She put her hand to his scruffy jaw and nodded.

His tense body relaxed, and relief filled his eyes.

"Eliza insists you read her books. I'll go clean up the kitchen and meet you in the living room when you're done." She went to Eliza and kissed her good-night. "Be a good girl and go right to sleep after books. Okay?"

"Okay."

"Love you."

"Love you, Mama."

Chase brushed his hand down her arm before she left them alone. At the door, she turned back and smiled at Chase sitting on the bed beside Eliza, her hand on his arm, and her adoring eyes staring up at him as he started reading her a story.

Chase glanced her way.

"Sweet," she said, and left Eliza to enjoy having her dad home and in her life, ending a great day with him with a story and the kiss she knew Chase would plant on his little girl's head before he settled her in bed.

Shelby hoped her night would end with a kiss—and a lot more—in his bed tonight.

Chapter Eighteen

CHASE STARED down at his sleeping little girl. For the second night in a row, she was tucked into her bed in his house. She looked so peaceful. He thought back on their day. It started out so well. Everything had been fine until Max knocked over a tool. He'd heard the crack of it hitting the cement floor, and he was right back in the thick of things overseas.

Rationally, he didn't understand how his mind could make him see and believe he was somewhere else. But he wholeheartedly felt and saw the past as if he was right there. As if it could actually touch him.

He wished he still had the innocence and peace of youth that Eliza enjoyed without knowing how precious it was. He'd seen too much. He'd done a lot worse. And it left a mark on his mind and heart.

It made it difficult to see a day when he'd ever sleep so carefree as his little girl.

Would he ever be the person he used to be?

He refocused his thoughts on the happier parts of the day. He'd hold on to the memory of Eliza's bright smile and excited joyful gasp when she stood beside a horse for the first time, and the squeal she let out when she got to pet the mare. He'd remember the way she felt sitting tucked up against his chest as they rode in a circle in the paddock, her whole body vibrating with excitement. She'd wanted more, but for safety's sake, he'd handed her off to her grandpa while he and Max rode out to look over the herd.

She'd had complete faith and trust in him to keep her safe because he was her dad.

He didn't want to let her down ever again.

Which meant that even though he'd had a shit day, he'd keep trying and working toward the new normal that had seemed so elusive and out of reach until Shelby opened her heart and made the future look so much brighter.

He left the door to Eliza's room cracked so the bathroom light seeped in just in case she woke up during the night. He still needed to put the finishing touches on her room and get her a night-light, books, and toys for her to have here.

His goal, though he hadn't said it out loud, was to ask Shelby to move in with him.

In his mind, they were already permanently here. He'd try to be patient and not push too hard to make it their reality before Shelby was ready for that kind of commitment. He might be struggling with his past, but he knew exactly what he wanted for his future. Her.

And he didn't want to mess things up by pushing her to move in before she was ready.

He found her in the dark living room, backlit by the lights in the kitchen, staring out the window. He walked up behind her, slipped his hand around her waist and planted it on her stomach as he leaned in, pushed her hair back with his chin, and kissed her neck. "You look a million miles away."

Her hand settled over his on her belly. "I'm right here with you."

He pressed his cheek to the side of her head and looked at their reflection in the glass. He loved the way they looked together and especially the way she leaned into him, like she needed the contact as much as he did.

"How was your call with Drake?"

It shouldn't have surprised him that she'd ask about his buddy after the way he'd lost his shit today, but he wondered if her quiet intensity meant she was having second thoughts about them. "Drake told me that Adria is having a hard time right now grieving."

"As are you," she pointed out.

"He thanked me again for trying to save Juliana."

She reached up with her free hand, held his arm, and pressed back into him like she could wrap him around her. "You did everything you could to help."

He slipped his other arm around her and held her close. "I wish I could have done more."

She didn't say anything, just nodded, because she understood how he felt, but also that there was nothing else he could do. She was gone. And he was here.

And as lucky as he felt for still being alive to spend the day with his daughter and hold Shelby in his arms, he still felt like he didn't deserve it. But that didn't mean he'd give it up either.

The mixed emotions made it all so muddled.

"I'm sorry about what happened today." He didn't know what else to say. He hoped the episode didn't make her change her mind about letting him spend time with Eliza.

"You don't need to apologize. I know it's not your fault. You're doing what you need to do to get better. That's what counts."

"It feels like it is taking forever to get to the place where the good days outnumber the bad."

"But you will get there. Don't give up on that. And know that when you have a bad day, I'll be there to help support you. I'll do whatever it takes to help you get better."

And that's what sucked the most. Even she saw him as damaged.

He pressed a kiss into her hair, then tried to explain his wild emotions. "I want to be who you thought I was the night we were together. Not this. Not what I've become with a shitload of regrets and nightmares about what I've done. I want to hold on to you and let go of my baggage, but it feels like I can't get close enough to you fast enough, and I can't escape the past at all."

She turned in his arms, wrapped her hands around the back of his neck, and stared up at him. "You are the man I was with that night. Strong. Kind. Thoughtful. Determined. And sexier than any man should be allowed to be."

He couldn't help his grin or noticing the blush rising on her cheeks.

"You will unpack the past and put it away as you settle into your new life and accept that you can't change the past, but you can move on and have the life you want."

"I want you." It always came down to that for him. "But every time something happens with my fucked-up mind, I feel like you could slip right through my fingers, and I'll never get to have that future. I spent all that time in rehab healing, so I could get to the point where I finally believed it would happen. And now that I believe it, and you said you want me, I want us."

"I've wanted you every day since that night," she

confessed, going up on tiptoe, her body sliding against his. She held his gaze as he held his breath. "I'm not going anywhere, Chase, because the only place I want to be is with you."

He crushed his mouth to hers, knowing how hard it was for her to admit that to him because of her past. He rewarded her vulnerability and trust with a deep kiss that he hoped showed her how much he appreciated and cared about her. "Promise me," he demanded against her lips, needing her to make that vow and keep it.

"I promise." She tilted her head to a better angle and took the kiss deeper, sliding her tongue along his as she clung to him, telling him with her whole body that she was right here with him.

He hooked his hands at the backs of her thighs and pulled her up to straddle his waist, bringing her soft center to his hard cock. She immediately tightened her legs around him and rocked against his hard length, moaning at the sheer pleasure of the contact.

He loved that sound and wanted to hear her do it again, so he planted his hands on her ass and rubbed her up and down his length.

She broke the kiss on a sigh, then demanded, "More."

That required fewer clothes and a bed before he went all caveman and laid her out on the floor, stripped her bare, buried his dick in her lush body, and pounded away until they both found the release they needed.

Chase spun around and headed for the hallway with his hands full of Shelby and her lips pressed to his neck, that wicked tongue of hers sliding along his skin.

Suddenly she stopped. "Your back."

He squeezed her ass. "I can't feel anything but you." His body hummed with the sensation of hers pressed to his. Not close enough. Not nearly as good as having her skin sliding against his.

She dropped her legs the second he walked into his room. Her feet hit the floor, and she released him to start stripping off his shirt. He hadn't even gone two steps past the threshold when she pulled the shirt over his head, and he managed to kick the door shut as her fingers tackled the button and fly on his jeans. He reached for her shirt, but stopped with it halfway up her torso when her hand slid over his rigid cock and she grasped him in her palm and squeezed.

"Fuck." It felt so damn good to have her hand on him. It had been way too long since he'd been with Shelby, and his memories of that night they shared didn't compare to the way she made him feel right now. She didn't hold back. She went with instinct and whatever felt good to her.

He loved that so damn much, especially when he was the one benefiting from her desire to touch and taste him like her life depended on it.

He felt like it did, because if he didn't get her naked and under him, he might explode from the passion rampaging through him.

"I love that you let me touch you." She slid her hand down his length and cupped his balls as her lips pressed a trail of kisses from one shoulder, across his chest, to the other.

"Sweetheart, you have an all-access pass. Whatever you want, it's yours."

She leaned back and stared up at him. "I want you inside me."

This woman was going to kill him with honesty.

"Your wish is my command." He gently slid her hand

away and missed her touch immediately, but it gave him the freedom he needed to pull off his work boots and the last of his clothes. She tore her shirt off over her head, unhooked her bra, and let it slide down her arms to fall on the floor. "My mouth is watering with just the thought of licking those pretty pink nipples."

Shelby surprised him and cupped her breasts, caught those tight nipples between her fingers, and squeezed. "You want these?"

"I want all of you. Naked. Now."

It took everything in him to stand there and watch her hands release those two perfect round breasts, slide down her belly, slip inside the waistband of her unflattering scrub pants, and push them down her gorgeous legs. His gaze locked onto her breasts pressed against her thighs as she took off her shoes and socks and stripped the pants off. She stood up wearing nothing but a pair of black cotton boy short panties that hugged her hips.

"You're staring." The soft smile on her lips told him she liked it.

He boldly grabbed his aching cock and gave it a pump up and down, a momentary relief.

Her eyes went wide but filled with even more desire for him.

"Just the sight of you makes me so damn hard."

For a second she was quiet, her eyes locked on his hand wrapped around his hard length. Then she smoothed her hand over her hip and dipped her fingers inside those little shorts. She slipped her fingers deep between her thighs, and he imagined them sliding through her soft folds.

His dick jerked in his hand.

"I'm so wet," she whispered.

He couldn't take it anymore. He closed the short distance between them, pulled her hand free, and brought it to his mouth so he could suck her middle finger and taste her on his tongue once more. "I will never forget the way you taste." He licked her other finger. "Did you lie in bed at night when I was gone and think about me and touch yourself?"

He saw the shyness return to her eyes, and though it was dark, he knew she blushed. He backed her up to the bed until she sat. He took the panties in his hands and tugged. She scooted back as he dragged them down her legs, and he whispered to her in the dark. "Tell me, sweetheart, that I wasn't the only lonely one thinking of our night together and touching myself, wishing it was you making me come."

She fell back on the bed, pulled her knees up and wide, and slid her hand over her mound, her fingers stroking her slick pink center. "I wanted your hands and mouth and body on mine."

She was so damn perfect for him.

"There's a condom in the drawer beside you."

She rolled sideways to get it.

He slid onto the bed, caught her leg, and draped it over his shoulder as he pushed one finger into her wet center. He heard her hand slip from the drawer handle as she sighed and rocked against his hand. "That's it, sweetheart." He licked her clit with the flat of his tongue, and she moaned. "I missed you so damn much. My memory . . . Nothing is as good as this." He slid another finger into her tight core and used his mouth to bring her to the brink.

"You taste like fucking heaven."

Loving her this way aroused him to the point of nearly going over the edge. "Did you find that condom yet?" He thrust his fingers deep inside her and circled her clit with his tongue.

She moaned. "You make it hard to think straight."

"I want to be inside you when you come."

She was close. He kept her right on the edge. He wanted to give her the release she needed, but for their first time back together, he wanted to be a part of her when he did.

"I . . . I have an IUD. I haven't been with anyone else." She pushed her hips hard against his hand. "Chase, please . . . I need you."

Those words unlocked him. He hovered over her body, the head of his dick pressed against her entrance. "I haven't been with anyone since you." He thrust into her, burying himself deep. He stared down into her wide, surprised eyes. "It's only you, sweetheart." And then he proved it to her, taking her mouth in a deep kiss as he pulled out, then thrust back into her, making love to her like he'd wanted to do since the moment he left her the first time.

"I should have never left you," he said against her lips. He'd have been happy to live in that moment forever in that crappy motel room in the lumpy bed they shared that night.

She cupped his face and stared into his eyes. "Don't ever leave me again."

He touched his forehead to hers and thrust deep. "I won't," he promised, meaning it with everything inside him. Then he lost himself in her steady gaze as their bodies moved against each other's until the pleasure of it overtook them.

Watching her . . . it amazed him to see the passion consume her, knowing he was the one who made her feel that good.

He hoped she finally saw that she did the same to him. Because there was no doubt he'd keep that promise to her.

He'd die if he ever lost her.

Chapter Nineteen

CHASE POURED his first cup of coffee, leaned back against the counter, and took a sip, his mind on last night and Shelby. He couldn't stop thinking about her. In his mind, he saw her smile at him, and the lingering unease from the nightmare he woke up to this morning disappeared.

He'd spent the night mostly making love to Shelby. After the first time, he held her close, his body recharging before he started the dance all over again. After nearly three years, he couldn't help himself. He couldn't get enough of her. But for all his need driving him to show her how much he missed her, how good they were together, she was the one to take the lead that time. In bed with him, all her shyness evaporated. He loved how she pushed him to his back, straddled his hips, and sank on top of him in a slow glide of pure pleasure. She took her time, riding him to her own rhythm, drawing every stroke and push and pull of her body over his like she wanted it to last all night. Like she never wanted it to end.

He'd have been happy to live in that moment with her forever.

He couldn't help but take advantage of her position. He ran his hands over her body, fondling those oh so tempting breasts, suckling one and then the other and teasing her tight nipples with his tongue. She'd rode him harder and faster until they were both panting and desperate for each other. He'd taken her hips in his grasp and raised his own, so he was buried deep inside her. He'd rocked her hard against him. She'd gone off like a rocket, and his ass hit the bed on an explosive climax.

Sex had always been good, but never mind-blowing amazing like it was with her.

When he and Shelby were together, it wasn't just sparks flying. It was a connection he'd never felt and didn't want to lose.

She righted his tilted world.

And for a little while, in her arms, he found peace again.

Until he woke up this morning. But today the nightmare faded quickly from his mind and didn't haunt him with the same anxiety that wound him tight most days.

Instead, he had a sense that last night had been a real start to the relationship and life he wanted to build with Shelby.

"Why are you up so early?" Shelby walked into the kitchen, her hair a haphazard mass of tangles and waves, her eyes barely open, wearing his T-shirt and he hoped nothing else.

"I thought you'd sleep longer." He hooked his arm around her shoulders and pulled her in to his bare chest.

She pressed her cheek over his heart and snuggled up close to him, wrapping her arms around his back. "Nightmare?" she asked, because he'd avoided her question.

He'd tried not to disturb her after he'd shot up in bed trying to escape the unescapable. She'd reached for him immediately, but he'd soothed her to sleep by rubbing her back and whispering sweet words to her.

"I'm fine." Not the answer she was looking for, but this morning it was true. Because of her.

She leaned back and stared up at him. "Did you sleep at all?"

"Some. But that's mostly because you were much more tempting than sleep." He brushed his fingers through the side of her hair and held her head. "Morning, sweetheart."

She studied him for a moment, then smiled instead of voicing any more of her concerns. "Morning." She snagged the mug from his hand and took a sip.

He set the mug on the counter beside him, then cupped her face and stared down at her. "You look adorably rumpled and incredibly sexy in my shirt."

She ran her hands up his chest. "You're sweet." She rose up on her tiptoes, sliding her body against his as her hands gripped his pecs and her belly rubbed against his swelling dick. "And hard all over."

His arms and chest flexed as he grabbed her ass and pulled her snug against him.

"You make me that way every time I see you."

"I guess you didn't get enough last night."

"With you, it will never be enough." To prove it, he kissed her, hard and deep, letting her know with his tongue what he wanted to do with his dick.

She responded immediately, her breasts crushed to his chest as she pushed her ass into his hands and made room between them so she could slip her hand over his cock and stroke him from tip to base and back up again.

He groaned against her lips. "Do it again."

She did. She always gave him what he wanted.

Right now, he wanted her. Again.

He slid his hands over her rump and up under the T-shirt, disappointed to find she had put on her panties. He broke the kiss. "I was hoping there would be nothing but you under my shirt," he teased, but she took it to heart, slid the black little shorts down her hips, and kicked them off.

"Better?" She cocked an eyebrow, watching him watch her.

"You are so fucking amazing."

"Because I know how to take off my clothes?" she teased him back.

"Because with me you drop your guard and do what you want."

"I've never really had anyone who . . ."

He waited for her to finish that statement. He wanted to know what she had to say. He wanted to know if she understood she had him. All the way. He'd do anything to make her happy.

But in the end, she simply looked him in the eye and spoke a truth that floored him again. "I'm not comfortable taking emotional risks. But with you, it seems easier. It's worth it to be with you."

He cupped her face and kissed her softly, taking his time, showing her exactly how he felt.

Her words meant everything to him.

Overcome with emotion, he pressed his forehead to hers and looked her in the eye. "You make everything in my life better." He didn't know what else to say.

She did. "I love that I can make you forget the past, the nightmares, everything for a little while. I love that in some miraculous way, I make you want me. I don't know how or why I do, but . . . it makes me feel like I matter."

"More than anything," he assured her, because no one else in her life had ever made her feel that way.

Well, except for their daughter. But with him, it was different.

It was a different kind of personal. Not familial, but based on attraction and a desire to be together and understand each other. A connection that seemed easy but would take work to hold on to and strengthen over time.

He had a lot of work to do on himself so he could be the man Shelby deserved. But in this, the physical part of their relationship, the part that worked for both of them and opened up Shelby and allowed her the freedom to take what she wanted, he didn't have to hold back. He didn't have to think. He just had to give everything Shelby gave to him.

Right now, he wanted to give her the kind of pleasure that would have her thinking about him—them—all day. And hopefully made her want to stay and hold on to this—and him—forever.

"You're everything." He kissed her, long and deep, with his arms wrapped around her. All of her pressed against him, but he needed and wanted more.

He slipped his hand over the sweet curve of her bottom, his fingers parting her soft folds, one finger diving deep and sliding out wet with her desire for him. "You can't get enough either."

He loved the cute blush and the bashful grin contrasted with the desire in her eyes.

All of it, combined with her lush body, had him standing in front of her, pushing his sweats out of the way to free his aching cock. He hooked his hands under her arms, lifted her, turned them around, and planted her ass on the counter. He pressed between her thighs, spreading them wide, and rubbed his hard length against her wet folds. Up, then down, the head grazing her swollen clit and sinking in just an inch as they both watched. Her breath hitched at the barely there invasion.

"Chase." She punctuated his name by using her feet at the backs of his thighs to pull him into her welcoming warmth.

He sank deep and moaned right along with her.

Shelby wrapped her arms around his neck as he pumped in and out of her in long, slow glides. They lost themselves in the steady rhythm until she whispered in his ear, "Harder," and he lost all semblance of slow and gentle and let loose his overwhelming need for her.

He kept a firm grip on her ass. She steadied herself with one hand clamped to the back of his neck, the other planted on the counter. She rocked her hips into his and he pumped harder and faster until her inner muscles locked around his cock and they both climaxed with a quick intake of breath as they were caught in the moment and a slow exhale as the aftershocks subsided.

He ended up holding her close with his arms wrapped around her back, his ass hanging out of his sweats, and her arms draped around his shoulders, her cheek pressed to his.

"That was a damn good 'good morning,' sweetheart."

She giggled at his ear, and he smiled. She always made him smile. "Are you trying to make up for lost time?" she teased.

"Just showing you what we've been missing and what we can have from now on." He felt her smile against his rough jaw. Then he admitted a hard truth. "I know I've given you a lot of reasons to think us being together isn't the best idea right now, but I hope you feel how much I want to make this work."

She leaned back, placed her hand on his face, and brushed her thumb across his cheek. "I know you're working hard on healing, Chase. I see how much you like having me with you. I feel the way you relax when we're together. That my presence . . . eases you in some way means a lot to me and also makes me feel like it's more than just . . . sex."

"Amazing sex," he corrected her. He leaned into her, touching his forehead to hers and looking her in the eye. "But it is so much more than that." He wished he could explain that, yes, having her near eased him. Hearing her voice drove out the negative thoughts in his head, and her touch anchored him in reality and made him feel good when he'd felt nothing but pain for so long.

"You make me believe that one day the past will have faded to nothing but a memory, and everything will be happy and normal in my life again."

"If I inspire you to do the work, it makes me even happier to be by your side with a front row seat to you taking back your life."

"Your support and understanding help so much, but it's your way of pushing me without judging me that's helped the most." He kissed her softly and reluctantly separated their bodies.

Just in time, it seemed, because he heard a sleepy voice from down the hall call out, "Mama."

Shelby squeezed his shoulders, then hopped off the counter. "Last night . . ."

"Yeah?" For some reason, he held his breath, waiting to hear what she had to say.

She put her hand on his chest. "It changed things for me."

"How so?"

"I thought maybe the first time we were together, it was just two people looking for a distraction and sharing a connection they both knew was one night only, so why not go all in?"

"Now you know it's a hell of a lot more. What we have is something special. My feelings for you are real."

"Yes. And I'm sorry I didn't see that when you came home. I'm sorry I held you at arm's length and wasted so much time."

"You had good reason to protect your heart. And Eliza's."

"I trust you, Chase."

Coming from her, that meant everything.

And it felt like a lot of pressure. The last thing he ever wanted to do was hurt or disappoint her again.

"Mama!" Eliza had become impatient. Little footsteps padded along the hardwood, coming their way.

Shelby snagged her underwear off the floor and shimmied them up her hips. "Alone time is up."

"Until tonight?" He hoped she'd come back and stay over again.

Her lips pressed together. "About tonight . . ."

"What?" He didn't want to hear her say they needed to slow things down.

"I only work a half day today. Will you meet me here this afternoon at two?"

He liked the sound of that. "I'll be here. I've got some stuff to finish up around the house."

"Great. I'll bring everything for dinner."

"And some stuff to leave here for you and Eliza." He

picked up his little girl, smiling at her disheveled hair. "Morning, baby girl."

"Hi." She put her head on his shoulder and stared at her mom.

"I'll bring some essentials."

He wanted her to bring everything and move in, but he didn't want to push things.

"Will you feed her breakfast while I shower? I need to get her to daycare so I can head into work a bit early."

"No problem."

Shelby came close, kissed Eliza on the cheek, then went up on tiptoe and kissed him softly. "I like this." She fell back on her flat feet and smiled up at him.

"Then stay," he blurted out. He meant forever.

Her eyes went wide for a second. Then she turned and headed toward the bedroom, calling over her shoulder, "Maybe we will."

He stared at her until she disappeared from his view, hoping she meant it and that he wouldn't spend another night without her.

"Pancakes," Eliza said, breaking the silence.

"Okay. Let's make breakfast." Just like they did yesterday. Just like he hoped to do every morning with her.

He and Eliza were a good team, which meant she followed his instructions well, even if she made a small mess in the process. He cut up strawberries to go with the pancakes and placed his and Eliza's plates on the table.

He settled Eliza in her chair and secured the booster seat strap. "Start eating. I'm going to take Mama a cup of coffee."

Eliza dug into her food.

He poured Shelby's coffee, checked to be sure Eliza

was working on her breakfast, and headed back to his bedroom. Shelby walked out of the bathroom wearing nothing but a towel. His gaze locked on the swell of her breasts.

Shelby smiled at him.

He stilled and stared at the marks on her arm. In the dim light last night, he hadn't been able to see her so clearly. "Shelby. I . . ."

Her eyes narrowed. "What's wrong?"

"Your arm."

She brushed her fingers over the black-and-blue bruises. "It's not as bad as it looks."

"It looks pretty fucking bad." His hand shook, and he nearly spilled the hot coffee.

Shelby took the mug from him, set it on the dresser, then cupped his face and made him look her in the eye. "I'm fine. We already talked about this. You didn't mean to do it."

He couldn't stand that he'd hurt her. "I'm so sorry."

"I know you are. It's okay."

It wasn't okay at all. But he tried not to get sucked into self-loathing and trap himself in negative self-destructive thoughts, not when they'd had such a great night and everything seemed so promising this morning.

He wished he could say this would never happen again. But the reality was that his mind hadn't healed yet. And it scared him to think he could hurt her again. "I have my call with Dr. Porter later this morning. I'll get the meds. They'll even out my mood swings and help me sleep better. I'll do whatever it takes to make sure this never happens again." He took her hand and leaned down. With featherlight brushes of his lips, he kissed the marks he'd left on her arm to show her and himself that he could be gentle. "I wish I could take this back."

She squeezed his hand. "I'm aware now that I need to be careful when you're in the grip of a nightmare or flashback and that you don't know what you're doing when they take you. Just understand that I will always call you back to me."

"I've been trying to get back to you since the day I met you. I will always find my way to you."

Her eyes glassed over. "I know you will."

He sighed. "It's late. Get dressed. Drink your coffee. I'll have Eliza ready to go." He stepped away, but Shelby tugged on his hand to get him to stop and turn back.

"I'm not going anywhere, Chase." She didn't mean today. She meant ever.

He didn't know how much he needed to hear that and how afraid he was that his issues—the PTSD, the anxiety, the anger that sometimes came over him—any or all of it could make him lose her.

Meds. Therapy. Whatever it took, he'd do it so he could be healthy and happy and as close to whole as he could get.

"Trust me, Chase. Trust in us."

"I trust you with my life."

She'd saved it enough times just by being there and standing with him. But there was only so much a person could take. He'd put her through a lot. A pregnancy on her own. Raising their child, mostly on her own up until recently. His drug abuse, bad behavior, and not making her and Eliza his priority.

He was working on all of it. But what if he didn't get his act together before her patience and understanding wore out?

"I keep my promises." She'd sworn last night that she wanted to be with him.

"I'm holding you to it. And I will keep my promise to you to keep working with Dr. Porter, taking my meds, and talking to you about how I'm doing and what I need."

"One day at a time," she reminded him, accepting there wasn't a quick fix and they'd take things as they came.

He leaned down and kissed her softly. "Hurry up. You'll be late, and you said you'd be home early."

He hoped she thought of this place as home.

If not now, then soon.

Chapter Twenty

CHASE WALKED out to the porch, happy to see Shelby and Eliza getting out of the car. That joy turned to excitement when he saw the two big duffel bags Shelby pulled out of the back seat.

She glanced at him and smiled, though it seemed strained. "Can you get the box of toys and books I brought?"

He met Eliza on the path and scooped her up. "Hi. How was your day?"

"Good. Finger paint." Eliza wiggled her fingers in front of his face, showing off the vibrant prime colors painted on her nails. Each finger was a different color.

"Aren't you supposed to paint on paper?"

"I did." She scrunched her little lips tight. "And this." She wiggled her fingers again.

"Okay." He didn't see a problem with her leaving the paint on her fingernails. More than likely it would wash off in the bath tonight.

Chase set Eliza down and went to take the two heavy bags from Shelby. "Let me carry those. I'll come back for the box."

Shelby shook her head. "I've got this. You get that and her in the house. We need to talk, and there isn't much time." With that grenade dropped between them, she walked up the porch steps and into the house.

Eliza stared up at him. "Toys."

Right. She wanted to have something to play with while she was here.

He went to the open car door and pulled out the heavy box. "You must have a lot of toys if you've got this big a load to bring here."

She smiled. "Mine."

"Come on. Let's go inside. I finished your room this morning and set up a spot for you to play in the living room." He'd finished everything in the house after his call with Dr. Porter and running into town to pick up his new prescription. He was officially moved in and ready for Eliza to stay over as often as possible.

If he could convince Shelby to move in with him, everything would be perfect.

Eliza headed up the porch steps. He rushed to get behind her just in case she stumbled. She made it up and ran into the house just as Shelby walked into the living room.

"The place looks great. I love the huge picture of the forest on the green wall." Shelby smiled at the room. "And you bought her the same little table and chair I have at my place."

"I wanted her to see familiar things when she's here."

Shelby smiled at that, too. "Her room turned out so cute."

He'd finished putting the big tree and all the forest animal decals on the walls this morning. When she got older and liked different things, he could peel them off.

"Go ahead and put your stuff away in our room. I'll unpack these toys and put some in the wood crates I have in here and the books and other toys in Eliza's room."

Shelby stared at him with a look of concern he didn't understand. "Um. We don't have time for all that. I need to tell you something. I should have told you last night, but I didn't want you to worry and stress over it all day, waiting for it to happen."

He set the box on the floor by the door and took a step closer to her, not liking one bit the way she spoke too quickly and explained nothing. "What do you want to tell me?"

She glanced out the still open door at the truck pulling into the driveway. "Drake and Adria are here for a visit."

He glanced at the truck heading straight for the house, then back at Shelby, who looked concerned.

His hand started to shake. A wash of anxiety and adrenaline consumed him. His palms went sweaty, and his heart raced. "How did you know they were coming?"

"I . . . um . . . I called Drake last night before he called you. I'm sorry I went behind your back. I just thought you could use someone to talk to who understands what you're going through." She bit her bottom lip. "Are you mad?"

"No. Just . . . surprised."

"You looked so lost after dinner. I didn't know what to do for you, and I know how much you've wanted to talk to them about what happened."

"Did you ask them to come?"

She shook her head. "No. Drake and Adria decided to come see you in person because they thought it would help."

Chase rubbed his hands down his thighs, then one

across the back of his neck. "I don't know what to say to her." Panic set in. He didn't know if he could face them. Adria lost her sister. She chose to save his life over trying, despite the terrible odds, to save Juliana's. He couldn't imagine how she felt about him being alive while she'd had to bury her twin.

Shelby rushed to him and cupped his face. "It's going to be okay. They came because they care."

Chase turned as Drake and Adria walked up the porch steps hand in hand. Adria met his gaze and gave him a soft smile.

All he saw was her twin, Juliana, and his breath caught at the sight of her.

Drake put his hand on Chase's shoulder. "Breathe, man. It's okay."

Choked up, Chase whispered, "Juliana," like that said everything. But it didn't.

Somehow, Adria understood, released Drake's hand, and walked right into him, wrapping her arms around his neck. "Thank you for trying to save her."

The softly spoken words hit him like a wrecking ball in the chest. "But I couldn't save her." He admitted that around the lump in his throat.

"I couldn't save her either," Adria admitted, tears in her voice and wetting his cheek where hers pressed to his. She hugged him tighter.

He finally wrapped his arms around her and held her close. "It shouldn't have ended that way. You should have given her the naloxone."

"I'd seen her OD before. I knew this time it was too late. She was already gone. I wanted her back so bad. But I couldn't bring her back. You were fading fast, and I knew I could save you. I didn't choose you over her,

Chase. The only choice was to save you. And I'm so glad I did, because I couldn't live with losing you both. We don't know each other, but I understand what you mean to Drake. In the war, you saved him. He saved you. And you saved me in a way, because now I have Drake, and I'm not alone. I love and need him so much. So you see, I kind of owed you. I still do, because of what you tried to do for Juliana." She leaned back and held him by the shoulders. "Stop blaming yourself for something you didn't do. Drake and I got the asshole who dosed you and Juliana. Let this be the end of what happened and the start of us being friends. I could certainly use another one."

Chase pulled her back into another hug and whispered in her ear. "I'm sorry she's gone."

"Me, too. But we are still here. We get a chance to have what Juliana wanted. A happy life." She looked him in the eye. "You've got a lot of trauma stored up inside you, like Drake. Let this one go. Juliana wouldn't want you blaming yourself for what someone else did to her. *I* only blame him. Not you."

He nodded and reluctantly said, "Okay."

"Good. Then give her back," Drake grumbled, making Chase smile and hold on to Adria for a few seconds longer.

He glanced down at Adria. "You sure you want this big grump?"

Adria slipped free and walked into the crook of Drake's arm. "I'm sure."

Drake nodded toward Shelby. "Besides, you've been in love with her forever."

Chase caught the surprise in Shelby's eyes. He'd never said he loved her out loud.

Drake held out his hand to her. "It's nice to finally put a face to the name and all of Chase's pining."

Shelby shook Drake's hand. "Thanks for saving his life and sending him back to us." Shelby shifted her focus to Adria. "Thank you for coming during this difficult time. It means so much to me that you'd drive all this way to help Chase heal."

"I know what it's like to love a man who's lost in another world sometimes."

Chase knew Shelby loved him. He felt it in the way she took care of him, the way she made love to him, and the way she understood him.

He'd needed this meeting with Adria to come to terms with losing Juliana. He could already feel the heavy guilt fading away as he accepted what happened, his part, and that Adria and Drake really didn't blame him for being too late.

Adria looked at him. "Anything I can do to help you stay in the here and now and find peace . . . Well, I hope my coming has done that."

"It means a lot," Chase choked out, his throat tight with emotion. He'd felt alone for so long.

But he had his family back in his life now, friends like Drake and Adria, and most important, he had Shelby and Eliza. They brightened his whole world.

He wasn't alone.

He didn't have to do all of this on his own.

"We didn't come empty-handed. Come out to the truck. I've got something that will help you stay grounded in reality." Drake held his hand out toward the still open door.

Chase cocked a brow.

Shelby touched his arm. "I'm going to check on Eliza."

"Oh, can I come? I can't wait to meet her," Adria said.

"Absolutely." Shelby waved for Adria to follow her.

Chase walked behind Drake out to his truck. "What did you bring me?"

"Remember I told you that I'm working with Jamie Kendrick. She runs an equine therapy program at her ranch."

"Yeah. She's one of Dr. Porter's patients. You guys have gotten a bunch of ex-soldiers together and do a group thing for those of us who have PTSD."

Drake opened the truck door and let out the two barking dogs. "Well, she also started training service dogs. She helped me train Sunny." Drake bent and patted the multicolored Australian shepherd, then hooked his arm around the chocolate Lab licking his face. "This is Remmy. He's yours."

"What?" Chase didn't know what else to say.

"Jamie trained him for someone like you. He knows what to do if you get lost in a flashback, or you have an anxiety attack. He'll even wake you up out of a nightmare."

"I'm sure there are other soldiers who could use a dog like him."

Drake stood and stared him down. "Do you think you don't need him or that you don't deserve him?"

Chase took a step back, not knowing how to answer.

Drake didn't relent. "You've been struggling for a long time. I'm sure there are days you don't know which way is up. The nightmares steal your sleep. The anxiety makes it impossible to do anything productive during the day. The guilt keeps you from enjoying anything in your life. And the flashbacks make you act out and feel like you're crazy. We've only been here for a few minutes, yet you've checked the tree line three times to be sure we aren't about to be ambushed."

Busted.

He couldn't help it.

It was part of his training and the hypervigilance he'd lived with overseas but didn't need here at home. Still, he couldn't seem to shut it off.

The Lab walked over and nudged his nose against Chase's clenched fist.

"He's already feeling your anxiety and trying to get you to relax," Drake pointed out. "Look, I didn't want a dog when Jamie foisted a puppy on me. I wanted to be left alone. I felt like I was a menace to everyone and everything around me, and I was better off pushing them all away instead of lashing out at them because I couldn't control my emotions. Believe it or not, the dog helped. Sunny shifted my focus away from the unrelenting thoughts and voice in my head. You need this, Chase. You deserve to live your life free of the past. I'm not saying Remmy will erase everything, but he can help keep you from sinking into that deep dark pit you spent two months in rehab pulling yourself out of. Shelby told me how you get lost in the nightmares, and they overlap with Juliana's death."

"I'm dealing with it."

"Bullshit." Of course, Drake was right.

Chase thought of the marks he'd left on Shelby. How afraid he was that he'd wake up in some other nightmare and hurt her.

Drake squatted next to Sunny again and rubbed his hand over the dog's soft coat. "Living through it, and with it, isn't the same as living. If you work on it, there will come a day when you don't think of the past at all.

That day will turn into another. And one day you'll wake up and realize you haven't thought of it in a week, a month, a year."

Chase couldn't even fathom that ever happening.

"Believe me, I didn't think it was possible either. But it is. And you deserve to have a happy life." Drake stood before him again. "With your meds, therapy, and Remmy all put together, you can live a normal life."

Remmy sat and leaned his whole body against Chase's leg. The steady pressure and his sweet face did make Chase start to relax.

"He likes you. And what do you have to lose? If nothing else, your little girl is going to love him." Drake smiled and stared past him.

"Doggy!" Eliza yelled from the porch.

Shelby caught her hand before she tumbled down the steps in her rush to get to the dog.

Chase was surprised that Remmy didn't run to greet Eliza. He stayed right by Chase's side.

"He's trained to remain next to his person until the anxiety fades. You're still tense and unsure about keeping him. He knows you need him." Drake gave Sunny a hand signal, and Sunny walked over to Eliza. "Your girlfriend invited us to stay for dinner. You and I will spend some time working with the dogs so you know how to keep Remmy working for you. I've got his service animal vest in the truck. Use it. Use him."

"I don't want a big banner following me around that says I'm broken."

"It's not forever, Chase, just until you've got yourself under control. What's worse, letting people see a wounded service vet or losing your shit in front of them and possibly hurting yourself or someone else?"

Good point.

Still.

Chase relented because if Remmy helped him heal and not get lost in the past and his nightmares, he'd do it, because Shelby and Eliza were worth it.

And he needed his sanity back for good.

Chase slipped his arm around Shelby when she and Adria joined them. "Looks like we have a new dog. This is Remmy." Chase patted the sweet boy on the head.

Shelby crouched low. "Hello, Remmy."

The dog licked her cheek.

"That's a good boy," Shelby praised him, then stood next to Chase again. "Eliza is going to love having him around." She glanced at Drake. "Is it okay for her to play with him? Will that distract him from helping Chase?"

Drake shook his head. "Chase will want to spend the most time with him in the beginning. He should be with Chase as much as possible so they bond and Remmy gets used to Chase's moods and behaviors. But yes, Eliza can play with him. Chase just needs to make it clear that Remmy is his dog. Chase needs him."

Shelby slipped her hand in Chase's and squeezed. "Then that's what we'll do." She looked up at him. "He'll love spending the day with you at the ranch while you work."

Chase hadn't really thought about it, but yeah, most of the time he'd be working at the ranch. Having Remmy around wouldn't be a big deal. And when he went into town, well, he'd take the dog with him, because Drake was right. He needed Remmy's help. He needed all the tools he could get to fix himself and have the life he wanted with Shelby and Eliza.

"It'll be nice to have a pal by my side. I haven't had

a dog since I was a teenager. And Eliza looks like she's keeping both dogs."

Eliza sat on the grass, the dogs lying alongside her. She had an arm around each of them.

Shelby smiled. "I think she'll be all too happy to keep Remmy. We'll need to make some rules for her, so that she'll understand Remmy has a job."

He appreciated so much that Shelby went along as if it was perfectly normal to introduce a service dog into their lives because he was messed up.

All she sees is that you're broken.

He hated that voice in his head.

It wasn't true, he reminded himself. Shelby saw what he could be once he healed. She wanted him to get better. That's why she'd contacted Drake and asked for his and Adria's help.

As tough as it was to face Adria when she arrived, he felt better for seeing her and talking to her. She looked sad and haunted by the loss of her sister, but she still smiled at Eliza as she squealed with delight when Sunny shook hands with her.

Remmy sensed his anxiety again and came over to stand by his side. He leaned against Chase's leg, and automatically Chase reached down to pet the dog. It shifted his focus and soothed him.

Drake clamped his hand on Chase's shoulder. "You'll get used to having Remmy at your side. And I hope you'll consider coming to the group rides I do with Jamie. There are seven of us now, vets, who get together, share stories, support each other in whatever stage of recovery someone is in, that kind of thing. It's good to be around people who know exactly what you're going through. We meet once a week, but I hoped you'd come at least once a month, since it's a drive from here up to Montana."

"I'm back to work on Monday, and I've got Shelby and Eliza to think of, so I'll need time to settle into those new routines, but yeah, I'd like to come. I think it will be good for me."

Shelby always listened to him. She tried to understand. But it would be nice to spend time around people who had been there, done that, and didn't require a long, drawn-out explanation. They'd get it. Like Drake got him.

Shelby made everything in his life better.

It just wasn't the same.

And she'd understand that, too.

Shelby touched his arm to get his attention because he'd become lost in his thoughts again. "Adria said you and Drake are going to work with the dogs, so I'll take Eliza inside and start making dinner."

"I'll help." Adria gave Drake a quick kiss, then followed after Shelby and Eliza.

Chase waited until she was far enough away that she couldn't hear him ask Drake, "How is she really?"

"Sad. Lonely without her twin. But also happy to be with me. She talks about our future together like she already sees it, just like me. I know her grief will eventually subside. I just wish I could do or say something to erase it. But just like what you and I have been through, nothing will make it magically disappear. She needs to work through it. *You* need to do the same."

"You coming and bringing her today . . . It helped more than you know."

"Oh, I know. Sometimes words aren't enough. You need to see it. Adria showed you that she's happy you're alive and doesn't resent it or you one bit. Now you believe it."

"One less fucked-up story I tell myself."

Drake grinned. "Dr. Porter has gotten into your head. Good." Drake nodded. "I fought him for a long time before I really listened and put what he told me to use. It took Adria's love and patience and a push in the right way to get me to see I could have a normal life again. I deserved it. And so do you."

"My life is inside that house. Shelby and Eliza mean everything to me. I'll do whatever it takes to hold on to them. I can't lose them." Without them, he had nothing.

Chapter Twenty-One

SHELBY SLID the lasagna into the oven and set the timer. She wanted to make a good impression on Chase's friends. She wanted to be a real part of his life.

Adria chopped a cucumber to go in the salad. She was so quiet and looked a little lost. Shelby understood loss, but she'd never had a twin. That bond . . . It had to hurt to lose someone who looked exactly like you and knew you as well as they knew themselves.

"I'm so sorry about Juliana."

"Thank you. I miss her every second of the day." That truth was written all over Adria's face.

"Chase talked to me about her. He said she'd worked really hard to move on with her life and that she'd been working with you at your shop."

Adria slowly cut another slice off the cucumber. "We resolved the issues and healed most of the pain from our past. We were always close, but I felt like we were closer than ever right before she died. Close enough that we could finally live our separate lives and have what we wanted for our futures. For me, that's Almost Home-made and Drake. She had plans to go to art school. She was always doodling in her journal."

Adria held up her arm and showed off her wrist tattoo. Two hearts nestled up against each other. "One of Juliana's last drawings. Two hearts filled with love. Connected. When you have love, you can get through anything." Her eyes glassed over. "I can get through losing Juliana because she loved me. Drake loves me. Chase will get through what he's dealing with because he loves you and you love him." She said it as a statement, but Shelby caught the question in her eyes.

"I do. It's just . . . things have been complicated between us. We had a baby together before we ever really got to know each other. Then it seemed after all the calls and him talking to Eliza over the baby monitor that I knew more about him than anyone."

"He shared the pieces of himself he hides from others. That's how Drake and I connected. We had secrets we didn't want anyone to know, but it seemed so easy to share them between us."

"Yes. I've told him more about my mom and father than I've ever told anyone."

"It takes a lot of trust to share the broken pieces of yourself with someone. Drake was drowning in his PTSD until he had me to stand beside him while he worked to recover. Chase has you. And I know how hard it is to stand by and watch the man you love struggle."

"I try to give him what he needs."

"You're probably the only one he listens to, the only one who can push him to keep fighting. And he will, because he wants to be better for you. And that sweet little girl of yours."

Eliza was in her room, taking the nap she missed because Shelby picked her up from daycare early today.

Adria touched her arm. "It can be hard to know that

his recovery is in part linked to your love and support. Just know that when things get tough, and they do sometimes, that it's not your fault. Drake and Chase have to choose every day to live in the here and now and not get lost in the past."

"Is Drake better now?"

Adria smiled. "Every day he's a little bit better. I've seen him at his worst. I've been there when he couldn't see me, but a living nightmare. It scared me."

"Chase has lost touch with reality."

"It's got to be scary as hell to wake up and know you've lost time and you have no idea what's happened. I remind Drake that he's safe. I'm here. The war is over. It didn't always work. Now it does."

"Chase isn't quite there yet."

"He'll get there."

Shelby appreciated so much the absolute certainty Adria put into those words.

"Remmy will help," Adria went on. "The less Chase gets pulled back into the past, the better and more grounded he'll feel. I've seen it with Drake. Working with Dr. Porter will be the biggest help."

"I made that one of the conditions of his having access to Eliza. I hated to put stipulations on it, but—"

"He left you no choice." Adria gave her an understanding nod. "Sometimes you have to kick some ass to get them to do what's good for them."

"So that's it. You take care of Drake and because of it, he's worked to get better."

Adria nodded, but added, "He takes care of me, too." She studied Shelby for a moment. "You should let Chase take care of you. It will help him to know that you rely on him, too. The more purpose he has, the more he'll feel like the man he wants to be."

"Chase is wonderful with Eliza. He's so good with her."

"That's not what I said. You deserve to have someone on your side and by your side who will hold you up when your world gets too heavy to carry on your own. Believe me, I know what it feels like when you only have yourself to rely on. Then Drake came into my life, and I opened myself up and really let him in. It made a difference for me and for him."

"Chase and I . . . we've got this insane connection. I swear I can feel him. Read him. He does the same with me. He senses when something is off. He knows just how to push when I hesitate or hold back. I've never been bold. I've never put myself out there for anyone but him. It's only ever been him," she ended on a whisper.

Adria's hand settled on her arm. "If you two are anything like me and Drake, destined to be together, then I can tell you, when you've been through the worst, it only gets better."

Shelby thought the worst had been watching Chase destroy himself with the pills and the regrets and guilt about his past. She'd spent every day since he came home watching him grieve for Juliana and blame himself for her death.

She hoped with Drake and Adria's visit, his grief subsided and he remembered Juliana as the woman who fought her demons and tried to build a new life for herself just like Chase was trying to do now.

They were at the very start of finally building a solid relationship and being a family. For them to succeed, Chase needed to be healthy in mind, body, and soul.

She wanted that for him.

And he was working on it, because he wanted them all to be happy together.

CHASE DRAPED HIS arm over the back of Shelby's chair and played with her hair with his fingertips. "Dinner was really good, sweetheart." He loved having Drake and Adria there.

Remmy lay under his chair. The dog hadn't left his side since he arrived.

He hoped having Remmy with him would help.

He'd see over time.

Shelby put her hand on his thigh under the table. "I'm glad you liked it. You ate really well tonight."

The comment reminded him that Shelby was always trying to take care of him and watching for signs that he wasn't okay.

Chase lifted his chin toward Eliza. "I think she's got more on her bib than she put in her tummy."

Eliza smiled at him, and his heart lightened just looking at her.

Shelby sighed. "I better get her cleaned up in the bath and ready for bed."

They'd been sitting around the table after dinner. He and Drake talked about old times. The good things they remembered about their military service. Shelby and Adria seemed to get along great. They talked about Adria's store and exchanged some recipes. Shelby talked Drake through a couple of exercises to help strengthen his bad leg and scolded Chase for not doing the ones she taught him this morning.

Drake stood and helped Adria slide her chair back.

"We better get going. It's late, and we're leaving early in the morning for Montana." Drake and Adria planned to stay in a hotel in town.

Chase gave Remmy a pat on the head to let him know he needed to move and waited for the dog to slide out from under his chair. Chase stood to see his friends out, and Remmy was right by his side again. "Thanks for coming all this way. It means a lot, especially now, during this difficult time."

Adria hugged him. "I really wanted to see you and thank you for what you did. I know what happened set you back, and I'm sorry for that."

Chase shook his head. "I'll be okay." He'd said that a lot since he returned home. This time he meant it. "I needed to hear you say that you didn't blame me."

Adria squeezed his arms. "You rushed in to help when that asshole had to be pushed into calling an ambulance."

Chase released her.

Drake stepped in and rubbed his hands up and down Adria's arms. "He's locked up now."

That seemed to soothe Adria. A little bit. "He deserves worse." She sighed. "Sorry. Sometimes it just hits me, and the anger inside me boils over."

"We get it," Shelby assured her. "I hope we'll see you again soon."

Adria found a smile. "Me, too. *When* Chase comes to Drake's group ride, come with him. We'll hang out. You can meet Drake's sister, Trinity, who is also my best friend and business partner."

Chase didn't miss the look in Drake's eyes that he better show up for the group meeting.

He'd started opening up to Shelby and his family, but

he didn't want to burden them with all the gruesome details.

His talks with Dr. Porter helped, but this could be a way to connect with fellow soldiers and talk about how they transitioned back into civilian life and how they overcame the hurdles of feeling sometimes like home was a battlefield, not four walls and a roof.

And while Dr. Porter got him because he'd served, talking with others who shared the same kinds of experiences and maybe had different feelings about it might help too.

After spending time with Adria and Drake, he felt like he could grieve for Juliana and shed the guilt and regret.

One step forward.

And if he made enough of them, he'd eventually get to where he wanted to be.

Drake and Adria each gave Shelby a hug and said goodbye to her and Eliza.

Chase gave Eliza a quick kiss on the head, then glanced at Shelby. "I'll walk them out, then come back and help you with Eliza's bath."

"Take your time." Shelby smiled at Drake and Adria once more and walked with Eliza down the hall.

Drake put his hand on Chase's shoulder. "You look happy here."

"I am."

"Maybe next time we see you, you'll have good news to share with us. Something that will include wedding bells," Adria hinted.

"We'll see." He hoped so. It felt like things were heading in that direction, but they had a little ways to go. Especially him. Before he and Shelby had a real shot at forever, he needed to be sure he had his shit together and he'd never hurt Shelby the way he had the other night.

She forgave him. She understood.

But if it happened again . . . He couldn't expect her to keep going through that and letting it slide.

He was wholly responsible for his actions whether he was conscious of them or not. And if he thought he was a threat to Shelby or Eliza . . . He didn't want to think about what he'd have to do to keep them safe, because all he really wanted was to be with them.

But maybe that wasn't possible.

He didn't want to go there.

Remmy nudged his nose into Chase's palm. Chase immediately got out of his head and patted the dog's head.

Drake lifted his chin toward the dog. "He's doing his job. Work with him. Let him help you. Pretty soon, you'll notice that you're calmer, because he'll stop you from going down the rabbit hole in your head."

Chase stared at Drake, then down at Sunny sitting right next to him. He nodded. "I can't thank you enough for . . . everything."

"I've got your back. You've got mine. That didn't end when we came home. Remember that." Drake held the truck door open for Adria and Sunny to climb in, then shook Chase's hand and walked to the driver's side door. "I'll see you soon."

Chase heard the order in the goodbye. "See you soon."

Before Drake closed his door, he added, "It gets better, Chase."

He hoped so. It was up to him to do the work to make sure things didn't get worse.

Chase waved one last time as Drake drove away, then squatted and stared into Remmy's brown eyes. "I need your help. If I start having bad dreams tonight, you need to wake me up and keep me from hurting Shelby. Okay?"

Remmy let out a soft woof.

Chase stood and headed back up to the house, Remmy beside him and, he hoped, a better future in front of him.

Chapter Twenty-Two

CHASE CAME up behind Shelby in the kitchen and kissed her neck. "Morning, sweetheart."

She reached up and slid her fingers through his hair. "Sleep well?" She didn't really need to ask. The last five nights had been a transition from Chase waking from a nightmare several times a night to him barely twitching in his sleep last night.

The new medication combined with the relief he clearly felt after talking to Adria and Drake, plus having Remmy, had helped.

She turned and stared at Chase and wanted to cry with relief that he'd slept the entire night and looked like it.

The dark circles under his eyes were gone. He smiled, bright and open with real happiness shining through. "I did. My back isn't even aching this morning."

The exercises she'd taught him had been working as well.

"Did you stretch this morning?" She'd risen early to get Eliza dressed and ready to leave for Pancake Tuesday breakfast at the diner in town. Eliza was currently kicked back on the sofa, watching cartoons.

"Yes. Right after Remmy let me out of bed."

She smiled and looked down at the dog. "Good boy."

Remmy let out a soft woof and wagged his tail.

"He did his job. It's working," Chase admitted with hope and a little trepidation.

They were both in awe that Remmy slept right beside Chase's side of the bed every night now. As soon as Chase showed any sign of distress, Remmy jumped up, lay next to him, and licked his face or pawed at his chest to wake him up. Once Chase settled, Remmy would take his spot on the floor again. Over the last few nights, Remmy learned to read the cues from Chase and snuggled up close to him when there was a change in his breathing or he twitched. Any sign of distress and Remmy was right there to soothe Chase, allowing Shelby to get the sleep she needed, too.

Of course, Chase still reached for her in the night, and Shelby was used to Remmy sliding in between them if need be.

But Chase slept more in the last five days than he'd probably slept this whole month, and she was so grateful everything was coming together.

She needed to send Drake and Adria a thank-you for all they'd done, coming here to reassure Chase in person and bringing Remmy to help him.

She turned to him and put her hand on his cheek. "You look better."

"I feel better. The first night we had him, I was still worried about falling asleep."

"Why?" The nightmares, of course, but it seemed like something more.

"I was so afraid of hurting you again. I didn't think you were safe with me, but I wanted you with me so damn bad." He touched his forehead to hers and held her gaze. "But then Remmy woke me in the middle of a nightmare. You were still sleeping peacefully next to me. I breathed a little easier and pulled you close. I didn't settle right away, so Remmy lay at my back. You were tucked up against me. I held you and tried to think only about good things. Eventually, I fell back asleep. Remmy woke me several times that night, but you were always right there, safe. I hadn't grabbed you or hurt you."

"Chase, honey, I'm not afraid of you."

"I'm glad, but I was afraid of me." He leaned back and brushed his hand up her arm and over the fading bruises on her bicep. "I can't stand that I did that to you. And now I have Remmy to help me make sure I never do something like that again."

"How was it having him at the ranch yesterday?" She wanted to steer the conversation away from the past and focus on the future.

"Good. He reads me really well. Better than I recognize the signs that something is going on with me. When he feels my anxiety amping up or my training kicks in and I'm on high alert for a threat that isn't there, he's right at my side, distracting me, making me take notice of my behavior. It helps. A lot."

"That's really great, Chase."

"Having you and Eliza here . . ." He choked up on her.

She put her hand over his heart. "It's been really nice, us, living like a family here the past several days." She and Chase couldn't seem to stand being apart anymore. She'd never had someone who wanted her around all the time and missed her the way he did when she was gone. Except for Eliza, of course, but it was different having Chase miss her like that and be so happy to see her at the end of each day.

"I'd like to make this a permanent thing." Chase made that clear in every way.

She loved being here with him. She didn't really feel like going back to her place and missing a night with him. It felt like the last two years had been a huge missed opportunity. She wanted to be with Chase. She wanted Eliza to really know her daddy and make as many memories with him as they could.

They'd already fallen into a routine that worked for all of them. She and Eliza arrived for dinner each night. She cooked most nights. Chase barbecued once. Chase did bath time, and they read Eliza books together. Once Eliza was in bed, Shelby and Chase relaxed in the living room, talking about their day, watching something on TV, but mostly just cuddling together until it was time for bed. There, they came together with the same kind of need and desire they'd always shared. The connection between them seemed to grow stronger. And in the morning, they woke up smiling at each other.

They were happy.

And Shelby hoped it lasted forever.

But Chase was still working on his mental health. She was so happy to see that finally going well for him. But she didn't delude herself that a few good days of sleep and no new flashbacks meant Chase was well.

A chill went through her.

"What's wrong?" Chase studied her face. "You said you like being here with me."

She immediately reassured him. "I do. I love being with you." That's as close as she had come to telling him she loved him. She thought she fell in love with him a little that first night they spent together, but dismissed it, because what did she really know about love? No one had ever really loved her. She'd always felt a distance with her grandparents. With everyone. Until Chase.

The feeling he left her with that night grew stronger with the birth of Eliza and seeing how invested and in love he was with their daughter. And now, it really felt like this was their chance to let their feelings grow into something good for all of them. She finally had someone in her life who really cared about her. He showed her in so many ways that he was good for her and Eliza, especially in the way he kept working on himself.

But in the back of her mind lingered the one thing in her life that could ruin it all for her. Kyle Hodges. The bastard wouldn't leave her alone. Right now, he'd only asked to speak to her. He'd only watched Eliza playing at the park. But how long until he got tired of her dodging him? How long until watching Eliza from afar wasn't enough? How long until his desires became more important than common sense and urgent enough for him to do something drastic and dangerous, just like he'd done to her mother?

"Shelby. Shelby. Where did you go?" Chase raised his voice and stared her down. "What's wrong?"

"Sorry." She brushed her fingers through her hair. She'd left it down this morning because Chase seemed to like it that way. She'd also packed her work clothes in a tote and wore jeans and a cute top. She'd worn them not to impress Chase, but because she wanted to look good. And the second she put them on this morning and saw herself in the mirror, she felt good as well. It made her wonder why she didn't wear the nice things just for herself more often.

She focused on Chase, who now looked really concerned. "Do you like my outfit?"

"You look great. You always do."

She scrunched her mouth into a derisive pout. "Seriously. You think I look great in my work stuff?"

"I see a lot more than your oversized clothes." He stared into her eyes and brushed his thumb across her cheek. "I see you, Shelby."

That had to be the nicest, most romantic thing anyone had ever said to her. "Thank you. I appreciate that a lot." She glanced down at her outfit. "I feel like this is more me." She looked at him. "The me I am with you." She really did feel like she could be open and relaxed and just herself with him, which made her want to be that way all the time.

What good was it having nice clothes and never wearing them?

She'd bought so many things she hoped to wear for a date or special occasion that never happened. Stupid. She should have been wearing them all along. She should have at the very least replaced her baggy scrubs after she lost the baby weight, but it never really mattered enough to spend the money.

She'd ask her work for new shirts today and order new pants, so that she felt just as good at work as she did in her casual clothes.

She was going to wear what made her feel pretty from now on.

Chase smiled at her. "I like the you who is with me, and I like the outfit. You're beautiful in purple. It makes your green eyes stand out all the more."

"They're the same shade as my mother's."

"And Eliza's, though hers have a hint of blue in them, too."

"That's from you."

"That's from my mom. Hers were darker than Dad's," Chase pointed out, a dash of nostalgia in his eyes. He missed his mom.

She wished she knew her own. The real her. The girl she was before Kyle Hodges broke her. But he'd taken her mother's life and made Shelby's life miserable.

"Pancakes," Eliza yelled as she stepped into the kitchen.

"Time to go," Chase declared, scooping Eliza up into his arms. "Ready?"

"Yes." Eliza nodded, smiling at her dad and warming Shelby's heart.

She liked that Chase was finally a part of their routine and traditions.

Shelby grabbed her tote and purse and Eliza's backpack. They'd have breakfast, and then she'd go to work. Chase would drop Eliza at daycare and head to the ranch.

Shelby followed the two out of the house and locked up. Chase buckled Eliza into her seat in his truck, and she climbed behind the wheel of her SUV.

The drive into town gave her time to really think about a future with Chase and what that would look like. They'd still do Pancake Tuesday because Eliza loved it and traditions were important. It wouldn't just be her and Eliza on holidays. Chase would be with them. They'd get to make more traditions. And since his family was trying to mend their relationship with Chase, maybe there'd be a few more people at the table.

She thought of Cyn and how she'd asked Shelby to go out for drinks. Why not make a point to connect with her? They had the beginning of a good friendship.

She'd make an appointment with Cyn to get her hair done and ask Cyn out to lunch. That would be fun.

It wasn't easy for her to put herself out there. Years of feeling unwanted, being teased in school, and being talked about behind her back made her cautious and shy. She really hadn't learned how to make friends.

That's why she'd start with Cyn, who was outgoing enough to approach Shelby and not get discouraged when Shelby remained standoffish.

If she could be open and honest with Chase, she could do it with others who were good and kind like him.

She pulled into the diner parking lot behind Chase, but had to park around the back. Before she exited the car, she took a minute to scan the area for any sign of Kyle. It pissed her off. It drove her a little crazy. And it made her think of her poor mother and how he'd made her life hell.

She wouldn't let him do that to her.

She wouldn't let him anywhere near her daughter.

The parking lot looked clear to her, so she got out and walked to the front to meet Chase, Eliza, and Remmy, who with his service vest was allowed inside the restaurant.

"What's wrong?" Chase saw the worry she couldn't hide.

"Nothing. I'm just being paranoid."

He hooked his arm over her shoulders. "I know it's not nearly enough, but keep doing what you're doing. Stay vigilant. Don't give him a second of your time. And if you ever feel unsafe, call me. I don't care why or when. I'll come."

She leaned into him. "I know you will."

They walked into the diner, and both she and Chase pulled up short when they spotted his father and Max waiting for them and seated at a table for six.

She glanced up at Chase. "Did you know they'd be here?"

Chase shook his head. "No. I told them I'd be a little later than usual showing up because it's Pancake Tuesday with Eliza."

Mr. Wilde stood and waved them over. "We heard this is a family thing."

Chase sucked in a surprised breath.

Shelby didn't know how to respond, but her heart warmed that they'd invited themselves to Pancake Tuesday because it was a family thing. Traditions were meant to be happy memories.

And when Eliza ran to Max and held her arms up saying, "Unc, up," and he scooped her into his lap, Shelby softened toward him and Mr. Wilde.

They were really trying.

So would she. She smiled at the men, then asked Max, "Would you mind moving to the other side of the table? Chase will want to sit with his back to the wall, and a view of the exits."

Chase touched her shoulder. "It's okay."

Max stood with Eliza and rounded the table. "It's no big deal."

A couple of gentlemen at a nearby table stood and approached Chase. He immediately put his back to the wall, and his whole body went tense, proving her point that he needed to situate himself in a position that made him feel safe.

Remmy leaned against his side.

"Chase. Good to have you home again. Thank you

for your service," the first man said, holding out his hand.

Chase shook it. "Thanks for the support."

She'd seen this exchange many times since Chase came home before he went to rehab, but this time Chase seemed more at ease and willing to accept the thank-you without his eyes clouding with guilt, remorse, and a lot of other emotions that made him go quiet.

"How long are you back this time?" the second man asked.

"For good," Chase said, giving Remmy's head a pat. "I'm back working at Split Tree Ranch. My girlfriend and I have a new place, and we're raising our little girl." That was a lot of words for Chase. Under other circumstances, he'd kept quiet. It showed that rehab and working with Dr. Porter had changed him. He was much more open with her and everyone else, it seemed.

Someone nearby leaned into the person they were dining with and said none too softly, "He really is dating *her*." She made it sound like something completely unbelievable.

Chase's gaze shifted to the blonde. Her flirty smile vanished when she saw the disgruntled look in Chase's eyes.

Another person in another booth whispered for all to hear, "Her father's a rapist, the worst kind of scum."

Shelby agreed wholeheartedly.

"There's some bad blood in that family," the old guy added.

Shelby didn't believe that, but for a long time she did believe there was something wrong with her, because she'd been made to feel that way.

But Chase made her feel special and loved and worthy.

Eliza made her feel important and needed.

Kyle Hodges was nothing to her.

And she was nothing like him.

Chase looked fit to kill. But instead of going off half-cocked, he sighed and shook his head.

The guy who'd shaken his hand said, "Don't pay them any mind."

She'd ignored people talking about Kyle around her for her whole life.

"Shelby is the best person I know." Chase's deep, rich voice carried across the entire diner. "She's an outstanding mom and a great woman. She's smart, kind, and generous. There isn't a bad thing in any cell in her body." Chase stared down at her. "There's no one better than you, sweetheart." And right there in the middle of the diner, Chase kissed her in front of everyone.

A few gasps went up.

Someone let out a catcall whistle.

Eliza clapped her little hands together.

Shelby simply got lost in the sweet, tender kiss Chase laid on her and the love in his eyes when he pulled back and smiled.

She'd seen that look before but never admitted to herself that what she saw was real. But here and now, she couldn't ignore it.

He loved her.

Her heart felt too big for her chest.

The guy still standing beside Chase smacked him on the back. "That'll only get them talking more." He chuckled and moved away with his friend to go back to their booth.

Chase held a chair out for her, and she sat down, feeling the heat in her cheeks.

Max smiled at her. "That's one way to shut them up."

Chase took his seat and sighed when Hunt walked in, took the seat across from him, and set an envelope on the table between them.

Before either of them said anything, the waitress came by to take their order. "You want your usual, Hunt?" Mia, the waitress, asked him.

"I think I've lost my appetite," Chase chimed in, petting Remmy's head.

Hunt glared across the table, but answered Mia. "Yes, please."

Mia moved on to take Mr. Wilde and Max's order before coming back for the rest of theirs.

Hunt leaned in and spoke to Chase across the table. "This is not what you think, so give me a chance to explain."

"Shelby did not lie to me."

"I know. It was never really about Eliza. I've known she's yours since you took responsibility for her the second you found out she was coming."

"What?" Shelby didn't understand why Hunt would continue to pursue getting the DNA test if he knew Eliza belonged to Chase. "Then what has all this been about?"

Hunt finally shifted his gaze to her. "You."

"Me?"

"Be careful what you say next," Chase warned, not caring one bit that his brother sat across from him in his sheriff's uniform and armed with a gun. "If you upset or hurt her again, I'll deck you."

Hunt held her gaze. "At first, yes, I wanted the test to prove the baby was Chase's, but I also had another reason for asking for it. I wanted it for you."

She cocked one eyebrow. "I knew *for sure* Chase was the father."

Hunt shook his head. "Like I said, this is about you, not Eliza."

At her shrug, Hunt tried to explain. "When I found out about you and Chase, I pulled the case file because I kind of knew the story, but I wanted the facts, especially after I found out Kyle was due to be released. I mean, you were going to be part of the family. I wanted to know what kind of threat he posed to you, Eliza, and potentially Chase."

She fell back in her seat, taken aback that even though she and Chase weren't married, he considered her family. "I thought you hated me."

"When Chase came home and you'd call for my help with him, the stress, anger, and helplessness I felt watching Chase fall apart kind of spilled over onto you. I wanted you to fix him. I know that's not how it works or fair to you, but . . ." Hunt frowned. "I'm sorry."

She understood all too well how that helplessness made him feel back then.

"Anyway. Chase is better now. You guys are together. I have a niece." He pressed his index finger on the envelope. "My hope was to thank you for pushing Chase into rehab by giving you something that would maybe change your perspective on who you come from and ease your mind."

"What do you mean?"

"Did you know there was another person questioned in your mom's kidnapping?"

Her heart thrashed in her chest. "What? No. I never heard anything about that. Who?"

"According to the case file, the guy had been seeing

your mom for several weeks, making him the likely suspect in your mother's kidnapping."

"Okay."

Hunt continued, "So not only was he a potential suspect in her case, but also—"

"Potentially my father?" She couldn't believe it.

Hunt nodded. "I hoped she was already pregnant with you before Kyle took her, because that would change everything for you."

She didn't want to hope, but it rose up inside her like the biggest wish she'd ever imagined.

Chase took her hand and linked his fingers with hers. "And what did you find out?"

Hunt met Chase's gaze, then turned to Shelby. "I'm sorry I got your hopes up, but I had Eliza's DNA compared to Kyle Hodges's from when he was arrested. I wish I had better news, but it was a familial match. Kyle Hodges is your father."

Shelby took a calming breath, hating that the disappointment felt so huge and crushing. "It doesn't matter. He has no place in my life." Nothing had really changed, except now she knew Hunt wasn't calling her a liar about Chase being Eliza's dad.

"Still, I wanted to give you good news. I hoped this would give you and me a solid reason to make Kyle back off." Hunt glanced over at Eliza happily sitting in her Uncle Max's lap. "She's got all the family she needs right here at this table." Hunt looked at her. "And so do you."

She really appreciated that he'd basically just welcomed her to the family.

Hunt turned his gaze to Chase. "We're both angry. We're both having trouble trusting each other. I hope you see now that this was never about trying to hurt you."

Chase put his forearms on the table and leaned forward. "I get that you're upset about Mom. I wish things had been different, but I wouldn't change what I did for her. I appreciate what you tried to do for Shelby, but I'm not exactly thrilled at the way you went about it."

"In addition to finding out who Shelby's real father was, I did want to protect your parental rights. I knew for sure she was yours the second I held Eliza in my arms." Hunt grinned.

Shelby sat forward. "When did you hold her?"

Hunt shrugged. "The day she was born. In the nursery."

She gaped at him, shocked. "They let you in?"

"I wear a badge, and I told them I was her uncle and her dad couldn't be there to welcome her to the world. They let me in and handed her over to me, and I told her that her dad couldn't wait to meet her."

Chase sat back. "I'm surprised you waited all this time to throw it in my face that you got to hold her first."

Hunt chuckled. "I kind of liked having a secret with Eliza that neither of you knew."

Shelby shook her head. "If you'd told me why you wanted the DNA test, I would have gone along with it."

"And you would have obsessed over it for weeks until the results came in. This way, you had no idea and simply thought I wanted to verify Chase's paternity, which you already knew would come back in your favor. I didn't want to take the DNA sample without your permission, but then I simply couldn't let go of the idea that your life would completely change if Kyle wasn't your father. I thought you deserved to know that. And I really wish it had turned out that way. I thought about keeping the results to myself. You'd never know there was another possibility and just go on hating Kyle. But I felt I needed to come clean. One, because I didn't want you to think I'm a complete asshole, even if I've acted that way sometimes. Two, because I didn't want there to be a lie between us. And last, because despite the fact that Kyle Hodges did turn out to be your biological father, I thought you might like to know that your mom had someone in her life before him who made her happy."

Mr. Wilde touched her shoulder. "I pushed Hunt to pursue the DNA test because I wanted to protect Chase. I didn't know anything about Hunt's suspicions about your father. I just wanted to be sure Chase got shared custody, since you two didn't really know each other." Mr. Wilde raised his hands and let them drop to the table. "I see now that he didn't need a lawyer or judge. He just needed you."

Eliza held her hands out to Mr. Wilde. "Pop-pop up."

Shelby smiled at her daughter. "Look who learned a new word."

Mr. Wilde plucked Eliza from Max's lap and held her to his chest, his eyes a bit misty. "I wish your grandma was here."

Shelby saw the exact same sentiment on all the Wilde boys' faces.

The waitress came with a huge tray and started serving everyone.

Shelby leaned over to Chase. "Would you mind grabbing a booster seat from the hostess station?"

Chase slid out of his chair and grabbed one, strapped it to the seat next to her, then picked up Eliza from Hunt's lap, where she'd crawled to steal a bite of his pancakes. Chase settled her in the seat, buckled her in, kissed her on the head, then went around the table to sit in the chair beside Shelby. Remmy watched, then laid down on the floor beside him.

She cut up Eliza's pancakes and handed her a fork to get started, then turned to her plate, but got lost in the fact that Chase was deep in a conversation with his brothers and dad about last night's hockey game. They talked about goals and members of the team who played well. Or didn't. But what struck her was that after all the tension and anger they'd had between them, they came together today for Pancake Tuesday with Eliza and fell right back into being family.

Chase slid his arm across the back of her chair, leaned in and kissed her on the head, then turned back to Hunt. "I'm telling you, they're going all the way this year. They'll win the cup."

"Not if Granger is out for more than one game because of the knee sprain he suffered during that rush on the goal."

"He'll be back next game. You watch. Nothing will keep him from playing. He's their best player."

"Which means they can't afford to lose him for more than one game or they'll be out of the running," Max pointed out.

Shelby met Mr. Wilde's gaze across the table. "Are they always like this?"

"It's like old times." She didn't think Mr. Wilde's grin could get any bigger. And then it did when he glanced at Eliza. The love in his eyes when he looked at her couldn't be denied. "Only this is better," he added. He leaned over toward Eliza. "Wait until we take you to your first game. You'll love it."

Shelby ate her breakfast, transfixed by the men around her and how light and carefree Chase seemed in the middle of a crowded restaurant with his family. They joked and teased and even brought up a few other memories about their mom. She got a glimpse of what growing up a Wilde must have been like for Chase, and how much he'd missed them these last many years he'd been gone.

He had a lot of support here at the table. A lot of love.

She hoped this was the start of a tradition they'd have for years to come.

She hoped Eliza sat here one day, all grown up, surrounded by these men, and knew without a doubt they had her back. They loved her. This was her family.

It's what she'd been missing in her life.

And if Kyle Hodges thought for one second he could ruin this for her and Eliza, he had another think coming, because Shelby would protect her daughter from that vile man at any cost.

Chapter Twenty-Three

CHASE WOKE up with Remmy snoring on the floor below him and Shelby's warm body pressed all along the back of him, her arm draped over his waist. He put his hand over hers on his stomach. She snuggled in closer behind him, her breasts pressed to his back.

He loved every morning he woke with her beside him, which meant the last two weeks had been heaven. Shelby and Eliza came home to him every night. They ate dinner together. Eliza chatted about her day and whatever nonsense her two-year-old mind conjured. She had a vivid imagination, and she often made him laugh. Once Eliza went to bed at night, he and Shelby cozied up together on the couch. She got him hooked on an old TV show they'd both missed when it originally aired. He loved that they could binge the eight seasons on Netflix. Mostly, he just enjoyed having Shelby snuggled up next to him.

She made the end of a hard day feel like the best part of his day, even though waking up next to her felt just as good.

They didn't talk about where this was going. They didn't talk about her staying with him every night. It just seemed to come together like it was always meant to be.

Which made him think of the night this all started. Three years ago today.

The anniversary of the day they met had hung in the back of his mind since he returned from rehab. He wanted to make today special.

And since he'd risen early and they had time before Eliza woke up, he'd start right now.

He rolled over and faced Shelby, who immediately tried to get close to him again by burrowing into his chest. He reached one hand behind his neck, grabbed his shirt, and tugged it up and off, tossing it to the end of the bed.

Shelby's hand slid over his skin, her cheek pressed to his chest, and she sighed with pleasure even though she hadn't really woken up. Yet.

He dipped his head and kissed her neck, sliding one hand up her side to cup her breast. Her back arched, and her breast pressed into his palm. She combed her fingers through his hair.

"Good morning, sweetheart."

She rocked her hips into his swelling dick. "You're up early." He heard the smile in that innuendo, but he didn't see it. He was too busy pushing *his* T-shirt that she wore up so he could lick her tight little pink nipple and make her moan.

"Mmm." Just like that. One of his favorite sounds, especially when it was followed by "I like that."

He palmed one ass cheek, pulled her snug against his hips, and slid his hard cock along her soft folds. "I'm supposed to ride with Max this morning, but I think I'd much rather go for a ride with you." He sucked her nipple into his mouth, slipped his hand between their bodies, down her panties, and slid one finger into her wet core as she rocked into his hand.

He loved that she was always so giving and in the moment with him. Whatever shyness she'd had in the beginning had evaporated as the trust between them built and she figured out anything she wanted, he was willing to give.

And that went both ways, because she never failed to make him feel every ounce of pleasure she poured over him. Like right now. Her hands slid up his back, rubbing taut muscles, and her fingers splayed wide and raked down again, sending a wave of pleasure through his system. She squeezed his ass and rocked her hips into his hand again as he plunged two fingers deep, then brushed them softly up her soft folds to her swollen clit. He kept his fingers there as she rolled her hips, her clit rubbing softly against his fingers until she was panting and moaning.

He hated to leave her wanting, but he needed her naked with his cock buried deep inside her. He hooked his fingers in her panties, shifted his weight, and dragged them down her legs. She tore the T-shirt off over her head and sent it sailing across the room. Her hands came back to his chest and slid up to his shoulders as he kicked his boxers off and settled between her thighs again. He took one breast into his mouth, her tight nipple hard against his tongue as he sucked and laved the pink tip. He gave her other breast the same attention as her hips shifted, seeking what she wanted deep inside her.

He gave it to her, lifting himself above her, the head of his dick nudging her slick entrance. She pulled him down for a kiss and raised her hips just as he thrust home. The wave of pleasure that came over him being seated deep inside her nearly had him coming right then and there, but he clenched his jaw and held back because he wanted her right there with him when ecstasy took the reins.

Her hands mapped the scars on his body, the same way they did every time they made love. Her fingers slid along the scar that made a half circle from his ribs, around his side, nearly to his spine. Then her fingers trailed up and over one bullet wound near the center of his back, and the other high on his shoulder. Her hands trailed down his spine to his ass, and she pulled him close as he thrust deep. Her leg hooked over his and another bullet wound scar there. He didn't think she even knew she did it, but in his mind he heard her unspoken, *You survived this, and this, and that, all of it, and you're still here.*

The wounds had all healed, though most not even close to what he'd been before the bullets ripped through flesh and muscle and whatever else on their path of destruction. He'd deal with the aches and lack of mobility and nerve damage the rest of his life. And yet her touch, her caring made it all seem better.

He took her mouth in a deep kiss, sliding his tongue along hers, tasting her on his lips and tongue and needing her to feel all that she made him feel.

Her hands came up to cup his face, and she whispered his name like a prayer as their bodies moved together, their lips touched, and their hearts beat as one.

That connection they shared cocooned them. It lived and breathed around them. It was up to them to keep it alive just like this, both of them open and honest and giving everything to each other.

He pressed his forehead to hers, stared into her eyes, and saw everything in his heart reflected back to him. Love. So overwhelming and impossible and wonderful and frightening and perfect.

Her eyes went bright, and he knew she saw it and felt it, too.

And in the wonder of it, her body tightened around his, and he moved in and out in deep, long thrusts. They never took their eyes off each other as the pleasure overtook them.

He brushed his thumb along the slope of her cheek, held her green gaze, and said the thing he'd never said to anyone outside his family. "I love you."

Her eyes went wide with surprise, then softened as she placed her hand on his scruffy jaw, her thumb pressed to his bottom lip. "I can't believe it."

"It's true," he assured her.

"I know." She surprised him, because she'd always had such difficulty accepting how much he wanted her. "I love you, too. I think I have from that first night three years ago, exactly from today."

"Happy anniversary, sweetheart."

"And a very happy birthday to me, too."

This time he was shocked. "What? It's your birthday? Today?" He should know this. He meant to ask her when her birthday was when he celebrated his six months ago, but it had gone to hell because he'd taken a few pills and downed a couple shots, and the next thing he knew she was slamming the door in his face instead of letting him see his little girl.

Fuck.

"How do I not know after all this time that our first night together was your birthday?"

"Well, I never said anything then or since, so you're off the hook."

He absently brushed the hair away from her face. "Explain."

"You know the story of how I was conceived, and nine months later, it's a girl!"

"Smartass. No. Explain why you were in a bar on your birthday drinking alone."

"I have no friends, except for coworkers and Cyn, but she's really an acquaintance I'm planning to make my best friend here really soon. I have no family. My grandparents never liked to celebrate, because you know, yeah, a monster raped our daughter, and it's a girl." The words dripped with sarcasm, but she couldn't bury all that hurt underneath the sad truth.

"I'm sorry, sweetheart. I wish I'd known."

"Doesn't matter. You gave me the best birthday present ever."

"Eliza."

She cupped his face again. "Yes. And no. You gave me *you*."

He took the blast of love in the heart and wondered how he got so lucky to have someone so amazing in his life.

"That night, you made me feel beautiful and special and wanted and needed. For the first time in my entire life, I felt like I was enough. You didn't know anything about me, except what you saw and what we shared. I thought it would be quick and you'd be gone after the first time. But you stayed, and you wanted more, and I didn't want you to go, because you saw only me. That was the best gift. And from that I got another. Eliza. This morning, you gave me one more when you told me you love me. No one has ever loved me the way you do."

"I feel the same way, Shelby. I thought I was lost. I thought I was worthless. And every time I felt like my life was over, there you were, waiting for me. And if we're talking about gifts . . ." He shook his head. "I don't need anything the rest of my life because I have you and Eliza." He kissed her softly, then pulled back. "Unless you want to give me another little one to love."

She tilted her head, surprise in her eyes. "You really want another child?"

"Why does that surprise you? I love Eliza. And I missed all of your pregnancy. I wasn't in the delivery room when she arrived. I had to watch it like a bizarre sporting event."

She smacked his shoulder for that comment.

"I missed all the baby stuff because I was overseas for nearly all of it." He stared down at her, trying to read her thoughts. "Do you want to have another one?"

Please say yes.

He really would like to have another child and be there for him or her from the beginning and share it all with Shelby and Eliza this time.

"When you first came home, I'll admit, I kind of thought about it. But then . . ."

He'd gone off the deep end and didn't present her with a steady partner, who'd be there for her and the kids.

She'd done it alone once. He understood that doing it alone again, this time with two little ones to look after by herself, wasn't her idea of a good plan.

"We didn't plan Eliza. We can do that this time. It doesn't have to be right away, but sooner rather than later, I hope."

She gave him one of those shy smiles. "I'd like to give Eliza a brother or sister. Maybe two," she added, giving him hope. "But I'd like things to be more . . . permanent."

He cocked his head. "What do you mean? I'm not going anywhere. I've got a job. I'm working with Dr. Porter, I'm taking my meds, which are helping way more now, and Remmy has been a huge help in making sure I don't get lost in the past or nightmares. Sleep," he said with enthusiasm, "is a good thing." It made a world of difference in his life. The brain fog had lifted.

Granted, he was a long way from where he wanted to be, but he finally had hope he'd get there.

She touched her fingers to his lips and shook her head. "All of that is great. But I'm talking about between you and me."

Permanent.

Marriage.

They hadn't talked about it, but it made sense that they'd eventually get married.

She stared at his chest. "I don't need or want a big to-do. I just want . . ."

"Forever," he finished for her, because that's all he wanted, too.

She met his gaze. "Yes. A promise that we make to each other that we will choose love and each other every day."

He smiled down at her, excited about planning their future. "Anything else?"

"Chocolate cake with vanilla frosting wouldn't hurt."

He laughed. "Absolutely. Forever and cake."

She brushed her fingers along his jaw. "And one more thing."

"What's that, sweetheart?" He'd give her anything.

"For you to say it again."

He had no problem saying it a hundred times a day. "I love you." He sealed that promise with a soft kiss. "Forever," he whispered and kissed her again.

"Mama! Daddy!" Eliza called out to them.

"I really want to show you how much I love you."

She pressed her hand to his heart. "You already did. And you will again. Later."

"Daddy!"

Shelby smiled, all her love in her eyes, and his heart melted. "Your girl wants you."

"About having another child?"

"I guess how soon is up to you." Meaning if he gave her a ring, a promise, and forever, they'd start making a baby again.

"Got it."

She nudged him off her, so he landed on his back beside her. "Smart man. Now hurry up before she runs in here and catches us. I need to get ready for my day."

Chase rolled out of bed, grabbed a pair of sweats and his T-shirt off the end of the bed, and pulled them on. "About your birthday . . . How about I ask Max to babysit and I take you out to dinner at The Rustler's Steakhouse?"

"Really?"

"Yeah. Of course. Let's celebrate it right." He'd never forget her birthday again, and he'd make sure they marked the day with something special every year from now on.

"Okay. How about you have Max drive you into town and drop you off at my place? I'll call Abby and tell her that Max is picking up Eliza today. I'll go to my place after work, shower and put on a dress, and we'll leave from there in my car and drive back here tonight together after dinner."

"Sounds like a plan," he said, heading for the bedroom door, but he turned back and stared at her sitting up in bed with the sheet tucked around her breasts, all that long hair a mass of waves and tangles around her pretty face. "But I have one problem."

"What's that?"

"That you keep calling that house *your place* when this is *our* home now."

"If it bothers you, then you should give me a permanent reason to stay and sell my place."

"You should keep it and rent it out for extra income. We'll need it to send our children to college."

She smiled when he said *children*. "How many little rascals are we sending to college?"

"At least two, but if you want to go three or four, I'm happy to keep you in that bed to make it happen." He caught Eliza under the arms seconds after he opened the door and she ran right at him.

"Four what? Puppies?"

"Not puppies," Shelby said to Eliza. "But you can help Daddy feed Remmy his breakfast before you have yours."

As he left, he held Shelby's gaze. "Tonight. You and me. I can't wait."

She smiled. "Me, too."

He tickled Eliza's belly. "Tell Mommy happy birthday."

"Happy birthday," Eliza cheerfully called out. "Presents?"

"Later." Chase added a shopping trip to his to-do list. "We need to hurry up or we'll make Mommy late."

"Someone woke me up very early," she reminded him.

"My pleasure," he shot back, giving her a wicked grin as his eyes roamed over the rumpled sheet.

He needed to get going because once Shelby left with

Eliza he needed to drive over to the ranch, do whatever
needed to be done immediately, then head into town so
he could pick up a very special surprise for Shelby.

He couldn't wait for their night out and a chance to
show her what their future could look like from now on.

Chapter Twenty-Four

Iᴛ's ʜᴇʀ birthday."

"She's not going to want to celebrate it with you." His mom knew just how to spoil Kyle's good mood.

"Stay home. Leave the poor girl alone." His father gave him that look that said not to defy him.

"I'm an adult. I don't have to take orders from you anymore. Besides, today of all days she'll want to see me. Birthdays are celebrated with family. I'm her dad. I have a gift for her, something only I can give her."

"Don't," his mother warned. "You'll only make things worse."

"You'll see. She'll love it. And we'll finally be together." He closed the door on them.

"Don't do it," his father called.

"You can't stop me!" No one would keep him from his daughter on her birthday. No one.

Chapter Twenty-Five

⟊⟋

SHELBY RUSHED into the salon and smiled at Cyn, ready for a change.

"I have been waiting to do this forever." Cyn waved her over toward the chair.

Shelby made the appointment first thing this morning when she got in to work, hoping Cyn could squeeze her in at the end of the day for a cut and style for her date tonight. A birthday treat. Something fun and frivolous. Something to make her outside reflect the changes she felt on the inside.

Shelby dropped into the chair and waited while Cyn wrapped the drape around her neck. Then she leaned back so Cyn could wash her hair in the sink behind her.

"I'm trusting you to make me look . . ." She wasn't quite sure what she wanted to look like.

"*Hot* is the word you're searching for." Cyn turned on the water, made sure it was the right temp, and wet her hair. "You didn't give me enough time to do a full color, but I can definitely give you a cut that will flatter your face and knock your Wilde man's socks off."

Shelby settled in and enjoyed the scalp massage while Cyn shampooed her hair. "You've got magic fingers." Shelby relaxed like she hadn't been able to do all day, because she'd been thinking about what she and Chase talked about this morning.

"You're not the first to compliment me on my hand job," Cyn teased. She really had it down to a science.

Shelby chuckled. "I bet you've left a man or two smiling in your wake."

"A few," Cyn confirmed. "But less than some people in this town think. And let's face it, you were totally tense when you walked in. Now you're nice and relaxed and probably thinking about your hot date tonight."

"It's my birthday," she blurted out. "Chase promised me a great night, just like the one we had together three years ago."

"Anniversary and a birthday. Big night. You two are getting serious." Cyn rinsed her hair and laid a towel over her head.

"He told me he loves me. We talked about getting married someday soon."

Cyn stopped rubbing her hair dry and stared down at her, eyes wide but filled with happiness for her. "Wow. I guess it's been a long time coming."

Shelby had never thought so, but had harbored hope that maybe she and Chase would be together again. And then it happened and felt a little unreal until she took Cyn's advice and started living her life, which freed her up to see Chase cared for her. He wanted to be with her. And now . . . it looked like they were really going to make a life together.

"I didn't think so at first, but now I can't see my life without him. I mean, I knew we'd always be connected by Eliza, but this . . . Despite how hard it's been to get to this point with Chase having to deal with his physical and mental health—"

"And you having to get over your fear of being rejected before you even gave him a chance," Cyn pointed out.

"Yes. And that. Still, we're good together. There's the connection, of course, but there's also this honesty between us. We don't hold anything back. We see each other for who we are."

"It's important that the person you're with can see the things we think we hide so well and others don't look close enough to see in the first place. Someone who takes the time, pays attention, that's someone who cares." Cyn's gaze turned sad.

Shelby took a chance and reached out and touched Cyn's wrist. "How is your sister?"

"Not good." Cyn shut down for a second, then plastered on a bright smile that didn't reach her eyes. "Let's get you over to my station so I can fancy you up for your date."

Cyn helped her up. They walked over to another chair, where Shelby settled in, and Cyn pulled the drape out from behind her.

"Okay. Length?"

Shelby met Cyn's eyes in the mirror. "Whatever you think works best. I'm open to whatever you think flatters me. The only thing I ask is that you make it something I can easily do myself."

Cyn ran her fingers through the long strands and played with her hair for a minute, watching in the mirror to see how a part this way or that looked before she settled on whatever she saw in her mind's eye. "Your hair has some wave to it, but the length is weighing it down. I think if we go for a shorter cut, say shoulder-length, that wave will really make your hair fuller and frame your face better." Cyn rolled the ends of Shelby's hair under so she could get a look at the length Cyn suggested.

Shelby's stomach fluttered with anticipation and anxiety, but she went for it anyway. "Sounds good."

"Okay. Once I cut it off, I can't put it back."

Lopping off a good foot of hair that included an inch of split ends looked like a lot, but Shelby was ready for a change. She was tired of the same old ponytail and flat hair when she wore it down.

Cyn got to work, sectioning off her hair and pinning it on top of Shelby's head so she had less to work with at a time. Shelby watched in the mirror as Cyn made the first drastic cut and a long chunk of hair fell to the ground.

"So, where are you two going tonight?"

Shelby appreciated the distraction. "Um, out to dinner at The Rustler's Steakhouse."

"Fancy. Perfect for a celebration."

"I'm just happy we'll get to be alone for a little while. Max is watching Eliza for us. I love her, but . . ."

Cyn kept cutting. "Mama needs some I'm-also-a-woman time."

"Don't get me wrong, Chase and I find time alone together after she goes to sleep, but it's not the same as going out, sharing a meal, talking, and . . . I don't know, not having to think about anything but the two of us."

"Then take some advice and don't talk about Eliza tonight. Focus on the two of you. Enjoy each other's company. Maybe stop by Cooper's afterward. The bar will have a live band. You two can dance."

"I've never actually danced with anyone."

"It's fun and easy. Just hold on to your partner and

move with him." Cyn gave her a sexy grin and eyebrow raise in the mirror. "You know what I mean."

She did, because Chase had taught her how to dance in bed. She bet they could do something similar and a lot less carnal on the dance floor.

"We've spent every night together for weeks, yet I'm nervous about going out on a date with him." She pressed her hand to her quivering stomach. "I don't know why."

"Out at your place, it's just the two of you. Tonight, it's out in public, where everyone will see you two together." Cyn let loose a section of hair and combed it out. "I heard he claimed you right there in the diner and nearly set the place on fire with the kiss he laid on you. I'm sorry I missed it." The grin came with a twinkle in Cyn's eyes.

"I couldn't believe he did that."

"Why not? He loves you. He wants everyone to know it. You're a great person, Shelby. That's why I picked you to be my friend."

Shelby met Cyn's gaze in the mirror. "I'm lucky to have a friend like you, too. We should get together for lunch once a week. We both work in town. I'm not too far from here. We could pick a place and meet up."

Cyn smiled. "I'd like that. And a girl's night once in a while. I could use a wing-woman to help me weed out the bad apples, so I can find me a man like yours."

"Chase has two brothers," she reminded Cyn.

She rolled her eyes. "One is too young and wilder than me. The other is . . . a stubborn ass."

"Hunt does come off that way sometimes, but I think under all that law and order, he's got a good heart."

Cyn's eyes went wide with surprise. "What made you change your tune about him?"

"Well, I get that legally his hands are tied when it comes to Kyle Hodges. And the DNA thing—"

"What DNA thing?"

"He asked me for a DNA test. He and his family wanted proof Chase was the father so he could get legal visitation rights, even though Chase never wanted any of that because he knew I had no intention of keeping him from his daughter. But that wasn't the only reason Hunt wanted the test. He found out there was another suspect in my mother's case. He hoped that her boyfriend at the time was really my father."

"Wow. I had no idea."

"Me either."

Cyn stopped cutting and caught her eye in the mirror again. "So was he able to find out who the daddy really is?"

"Unfortunately, Kyle is my father. Hunt didn't tell me the real reason he wanted the test because he didn't want to get my hopes up and make me wait weeks for the results. He came clean for a few reasons, but mainly so I'd know that my mom had someone in her life who really cared about her before Kyle ruined everything."

"Did it help to know that?"

"Actually, yes. My grandparents never talked about her. All I really know is the tragic parts of her life. It makes me feel closer to her knowing she was a normal teenager before that, going to school and out with her boyfriend." Shelby imagined a whole world where her mother was happy and living her life thanks to Hunt giving her that little bit of information.

Cyn set her scissors on the counter, stood in front of her, raked her fingers through Shelby's hair and shook it, then scrunched it in her hands. She stepped back and out of the way of the mirror and asked, "What do you think?"

Shelby had been so distracted talking to Cyn, she hadn't realized she'd finished cutting all the length off. She stared at herself in the mirror with her hair cascading to her shoulders in soft waves. It made her whole face, and especially her green eyes, stand out. "Oh my God, Cyn."

"I'm not done. I'll add some product to hold the waves and blow it out, but yeah. You look beautiful."

She turned to Cyn. "Thank you for seeing what I couldn't."

"It's all you, Shelby. You always had that pretty face and those gorgeous eyes. You were just hiding it under all that hair."

"Thank you." Shelby's eyes watered. "I love it." She really did. It made her feel different. She hadn't known a simple haircut could do that, but it made her feel more like herself.

"I suggest you use some bronze eyeliner to highlight those green eyes, a little neutral shadow, black mascara to bring out those long lashes you were blessed with, and a soft pink lip. Let all that natural beauty shine through."

"I kind of like your electric-blue eyeliner. It pops just like your purple hair."

"I'm bold. You're more—"

"Boring," Shelby interjected.

"Classic," Cyn corrected her. "And believe me, that's not boring. Your Wilde man's eyes are going to pop out of his head when he sees you." Cyn gave her a firm nod to go with the smile that said she knew what she was talking about. "Now, let's finish this look so you can get home and put on something sinful and pretty."

Shelby thought about the sexy underwear she planned to wear under her simple but curve-hugging dress. No, not simple. *Classic.*

She liked that word. It did suit her. At least it fit who she was now.

And when Cyn finished her hair and she looked at herself in the mirror, her first thought kind of stunned her. *This is how I was meant to look.*

"You even hold yourself different now. You see it. This is the real you." Cyn beamed with pride. And she should. She'd helped uncover the real Shelby.

"I should have let you lop off my hair a long time ago."

"Everything in its time. You weren't ready then. Now you are."

She hadn't been ready for a lot of things until now. What a difference a few weeks of seeing herself through someone else's eyes made, especially when it was someone who loved her.

Chase loves me.

Every time she thought about it, it made her heart soar and sent a rush of happiness washing over her.

Cyn undid the drape and pulled it off her.

Shelby couldn't take her eyes off her image in the mirror. "Cyn, I really can't thank you enough."

"You're happy, so I'm happy. Come on, you don't want to be late for your big date."

Shelby paid for the haircut at the register and left Cyn a huge tip.

"That's too much," she protested.

"Take it. You earned it. And I'm now your loyal cus-

tomer for life. Lunch next week is on me, too. I really
want us to be the best of friends."

Cyn's eyes softened, and she looked really touched.
"I'd like that. And happy birthday, Shelby."

"Thank you. See you soon."

SHELBY SLIPPED THE dress on over the black lace bra and
panty set she thought made her look amazing. She was
still riding the high of her new haircut and how it made
her feel. She tried to be careful and not flatten her hair,
but it seemed no matter what she did, it stayed put.

Thank you, Cyn.

She found the black strappy high-heeled shoes she'd
only worn once and slipped them on, making sure the
tiny buckles were secure.

The doorbell rang, and she gave herself one last
check in the mirror. Cyn was right about the makeup.
It highlighted her green eyes, and the soft pink lipstick
she'd chosen complemented the hunter green dress. The
dress color also made the golds in her light brown hair
stand out.

A glance at the clock told her Chase was early. He
must be as excited as she was about their date.

She rushed out of her room to the front door and
threw it open wide, eager to see Chase's reaction to her
new look. But the bright smile on her face fell into a scowl
the second she spotted the man standing on her porch.
All her happiness vanished under a wave of anger.

"Shelby, you're . . . stunning. You remind me of your
mother."

The compliment and the comparison from Kyle left
her cold. "Leave."

Kyle's eyes narrowed. "I just want to talk to you. Please."

"You are not welcome here." She grabbed the door to slam it in his face, but he slapped his hand against it, held it open, and took two steps inside her house. Heart jackhammering in her chest, she shouted, "Get out!"

His shoulders slumped. "Happy birthday, sweetheart. It's the first one we can celebrate together."

"That is never going to happen."

"Why not?"

"Because I hate you."

"Don't say that. We'll get to know each other. You'll see. I'm a good guy. Let's finally talk."

She held her ground and didn't back down. "I have nothing to say to you."

One side of his mouth dipped into a half frown. "You could tell me about my granddaughter."

A knot of pure rage formed in her belly. "She is none of your concern. Neither am I."

"Don't be like that. I'm your father."

That soured her stomach. "You're a monster. You kidnapped, raped, and killed my mother."

He shook his head. "We had something special. I would never have killed her."

"You sent her over the edge."

His hand went to his chest. "I loved her. I love you." He reached out to her, but she took a step back, not wanting him near her, let alone in her house. "Please, Shelby. I never meant to hurt her. I would never hurt you."

"You do every time you show up and remind me that I grew up without her. I don't even know her. All I know is the only story people tell about her, that you kidnapped her because you were obsessed with her. I didn't even know until recently that she'd been seeing someone."

His sharp gaze narrowed with anger. "He didn't love her the way I loved her."

She rolled her eyes as the fury built inside her. "You forced yourself on her. You terrorized her. That is not love."

"I loved her! I will always love her! Just as I love you."

"You don't even know me. And you will never know me, because I don't want anything to do with you. Now get out of my house!"

"I'm your father. I have a right to see you and my granddaughter."

"You have *a right*!" Her hands fisted at her sides. "You think DNA gives you a right, but it doesn't. I choose who gets to be in my life, and I will never choose you."

"We're family."

She scoffed. "You destroyed my family. You made it impossible for them to see me as anything other than the unwanted outcome of your brutality. You made me a living reminder of your mistakes, misdeeds, and cruelty, and you think you have a right, you selfish asshole."

"What about Chase's mistakes and misdeeds? You forgave him. You let him into your life. Why does he get to be a dad, but I don't?"

Her fury exploded. "Don't compare yourself to Chase. He's a good man. He has *two* Purple Hearts and served this country even when he was asked to stand up and defend freedom with his life. He loves his little girl. He'd do anything for her, even if that means staying away from her so that he can heal, so that he's better for her. What the hell have you ever done in your life that required that kind of sacrifice? Nothing," she answered for him. "You took what you wanted, damn the consequences. You didn't care if my mother suffered. You wanted her to because she didn't want you. You took her from me. It was because of *you* that she took her life and tried to take mine. You took her from her parents and made it impossible for them to ever really accept me or love me, because who can love the person who reminds them of the worst things that ever happened in their lives?"

"I love you," Chase said, carrying a huge bouquet of flowers and a wrapped gift as he walked in the door with Remmy at his side. He came around Kyle, moving closer to her, his body tense, gaze sharp and filled with anger that Kyle was in her house. But his words were soft and heartfelt when he said, "I would do anything to make you happy."

She pinned Kyle in her gaze. "Would *you* do the same? Because the only way you can make me happy is to disappear from my life and never come near me or my daughter again."

Chase, keeping Kyle in his sight, set the flowers and gift on the side table next to the sofa. "Leave. Now."

Kyle stared at her. "You forgive him everything, you believe he's healed and changed, but you can't even imagine that I have too. All I'm asking for is a chance to prove it to you."

"You've already proven you haven't changed. You've been lurking around us, watching, and approaching me when I've made it clear I want nothing to do with you."

"I gave you time to get used to having me around and the fact that I will be part of your life."

"That sounds like a threat."

"It's not. I just want you to listen," he implored with an edge to his voice that set off a warning inside her.

"I don't want to hear anything you have to say. There is no excuse for what you did. There is no apologizing for what you did. You cannot heal it or erase it. It will never go away. My feelings will never change. I hate you."

Those words hit home. Kyle actually took a step back, but he narrowed his eyes like he wanted her to see he wasn't giving up.

Well, she would make him see that he would never get anywhere with her. "You are not my father."

Kyle stepped close again. "I am. Whether you like it or not."

"Not," she spat back. "I am not your family. Chase and Eliza are my family. Because of you, I have no one else. You made me the gossip of this town, the one people stare at and whisper about. You made me believe there was something wrong with me, that I didn't deserve to be loved or treated like any normal person. Everything bad that's happened in my life is because of you. Why the hell would I want you in my life? So people can talk and point and stare even more? I will not put Eliza through what I went through growing up. I'm done being associated with you. I'm building a life with Chase and Eliza, and it doesn't include you. At all."

"If you'd just give me a chance."

"Do you really think I would let a rapist near my daughter? Are you crazy? I've given you my answer over and over again. No. No, I do not want you in my life. No. Never. Don't make me say it again."

Kyle looked to Chase.

"Don't look at him," she snapped, standing up for herself. "I'm talking. I'm telling you no. I will not change my mind. And if you think Chase would let you near his daughter . . ." She shook her head like he really was crazy if he thought that.

"You heard her. Leave," Chase ordered, stepping close, his body right next to hers. Remmy let out a warning growl.

She appreciated that Chase had let her handle Kyle, that he knew she needed to stand up to him the way her mother never got a chance to.

She had years of pent-up anger and things she'd wanted to say to the monster who ruined her life by simply creating her. She'd lived too long in his shadow and with his existence making hers so difficult. Not anymore.

She wasn't going to be Kyle Hodges's daughter anymore.

She was going to be Shelby, Eliza's mom, and hopefully soon, Chase's wife, a woman who stood up for herself, loved her family, and lived the life she wanted, not the one people projected onto her.

She had people who loved her now.

Kyle sighed like she'd done something wrong and he'd make her see that. "I served my time, Shelby. I am a free citizen again. And I have rights. Those rights include seeing my granddaughter. And if you won't give your permission, then I'll fight for her in court." He made the threat, and she wanted to rage at him for daring to try to force her hand, but she kept her head.

"And how will you do that? Do you have a job? How will you pay for an attorney?"

"There are a lot of hours in the day when you have nothing to do in prison but read. I made sure I knew the law when it came to facing the charges against me and my appeals."

No one could accuse Kyle of being stupid. He'd been exceptionally smart, a straight-A student in school without really trying. And cunning when it came to his plan to take her mother and hold her hostage.

In the end, he'd been found because a man hunting out of season spotted smoke at the abandoned cabin, investigated, saw her naked mother tied up in bed, and called the cops.

Without that man's help, who knows how long Kyle would have kept her mother tied up in the woods?

"So this is how you want to be a father and grandfather, by going to court and trying to force me to do what you want."

"You're the one forcing me to do this."

"Is that how you justify it? I say no, so you make me. Is that what you said to my mother, too? Did you tell her you wouldn't have had to force her to be with you if she'd just done what you wanted?"

She saw the guilt in his eyes. "Right," she said. "Now tell me again how you've changed."

Kyle shook his head. "We could have done this the easy way. You could have been reasonable."

"You could have accepted that my mother wanted nothing to do with you and left her alone. You created this. You ruined us."

"Give me a chance to fix it." It wasn't a plea but a demand.

"You can't. What you've done is unforgiveable. And I will fight to my last breath to make sure you never go anywhere near my daughter."

For some crazy reason, that made her think of her

mother and how she'd tried to end both their lives. So Kyle never got his hands on either of them again?

She wondered if that had been what her mother was thinking when she committed that desperate act.

Chase stepped in front of her now, Remmy at his side, and took another step to make Kyle move back toward the door. "You've had your say. You made your request. It's been denied. Now get out and don't come back. You won't like what happens if you do."

"That sounds like a threat. Something I could use in court against you."

"Try it. I have more in my favor than you do. Shelby and Eliza are *my* family. I will protect them at all costs." Chase took another step into Kyle's personal space.

He didn't back up this time. "I've dealt with men like you in prison."

"I don't think so. You see, they have nothing to lose. I have people worth fighting for, who I love more than my own life, so you can bet if you come after them, I'm coming for you. Now get out, or I'll call the cops and make my brother toss your ass in a cell for trespassing."

Kyle glanced around Chase at Shelby. "This isn't over." He pulled an envelope out of his back pocket and dropped it on the table by the door where she kept her purse and keys. "I thought you might like some pictures of your mom and me. Happy birthday, Shelby."

"Just another day you've ruined."

Kyle finally walked out the door.

Chase slammed it at his back and turned to her. "Sweetheart, I'm so sorry I wasn't here sooner. Are you okay?"

She pressed her hand to her tied-in-knots stomach. "No. Yes. I'm furious."

"Did he hurt you?"

"No. He surprised me. I thought it was you at the door, and before I knew it, he was standing in my house!" Her anger got away from her and she shouted the last, making Chase's eyes go wide. "Sorry. I just can't believe he keeps coming at me like that. I say no and he keeps coming back. It's infuriating."

Remmy actually pressed against her side to comfort her this time.

Chase took her shaking hand. "Breathe. Eliza is safe. You held your own against him. He knows exactly how you feel and that we are never going to let him near our daughter. It's time to get that restraining order."

"And what if he tries to take us to court?"

"Let him try. No judge is going to give him visitation. He's a stranger to you and Eliza. He raped your mother. He served additional time in prison for violence he committed while in there. He can't have a reasonable expectation that he'll get what he wants."

"That's what I'm afraid of, that he knows he can't get it, so he'll take it. He'll take her." That was her worst fear.

"That is not going to happen."

A chill raced up and down her spine. She wished she could believe it, but something told her Kyle was not going to back off.

One would think rapists lost their parental rights if a child was conceived as a result of the rape. Sadly, not so. Not in every state. But she was too old for Kyle to seek custody of her. He wanted visitation with his grandchild. She had no idea if there were any laws that pertained to that on the books in Wyoming, let alone anywhere in the country.

She'd need a lawyer.

Chase cupped her face. "You're letting your thoughts spin out of control. I know the feeling. I'm angry, too. If something happened to you . . ."

She hooked her hands on his wrists. "I'm fine."

He gave her a pointed look.

"Yes, he scares me. But I was so angry, I didn't have time to be scared. The thought of him being around Eliza . . . No. It is never going to happen."

"Exactly. We won't let it. And we won't let him ruin tonight either."

"Chase, I don't know . . . I . . ."

"You are going to remember you told him off and kicked him out, and you won't let him ruin your birthday and our anniversary. We're celebrating tonight. Tomorrow we'll take on Kyle and his ridiculous demands."

There really was nothing she could do about him tonight. She didn't want to cancel their plans. She deserved to celebrate and be happy.

"Kyle can suck it," she said. "We're going out."

"That's my girl. And damn, honey, you look amazing."

She'd totally forgotten he hadn't seen her hair and her in a dress. She found a shy smile. "Do you like it?"

"I love all of it, especially you." Leave it to Chase to make everything seem better.

She closed the distance between them and wrapped her arms around his neck.

He hugged her back immediately and kissed the side of her head. "It's going to be all right."

She needed to hear that right now. And in his arms, she felt that way, too. "I know. I just wish he'd leave me alone. I want to have the life we talked about without him in any part of it."

"And we will, because we choose to leave him out of it. If we have to do it legally, we will."

"Or I'll take one of the jobs out of state and leave with her. He'll never find us."

Chase held her at arm's length. "What are you talking about?"

"Before you came back from rehab and he started spying on me and Eliza, I thought the only way to get rid of him was to leave, so I sent out résumés to several places out of state. I got job offers from all of them."

"Is that really what you want to do? What about us?" Fear and hurt filled his eyes.

She wasn't thinking straight and quickly reassured him. "I'm not taking any of the offers because of us." She pressed the back of her hand to her forehead and the headache starting just behind her eyes. "I'm sorry. I'm upset and . . ." She threw her hands up and let them drop. "I just want him to go away. We can't let him get visitation rights. That's not happening. Ever."

"Agreed. But if he won't go away, are we making plans together, or do I have to chase you wherever you run?" He had a right to be angry that she'd done things without clueing him in.

She went up on tiptoe and kissed him softly. "I love you. I want our life together." She dropped to her flat feet.

He pulled her back up and into a scorching kiss. "From now on, it's you and me. We do things together. Agreed?"

She readily nodded. "That sounds so good to me."

"Then I'll talk to Hunt tomorrow. We'll get a lawyer and find out our rights and what his shouldn't be."

She liked the way he put that, because Kyle had forfeited any right to be a father or grandfather when he raped her mother.

"Now, how about we start our night together." Chase leaned over, grabbed the flowers from the table, and held them out to her. "For my beautiful girlfriend."

She loved that he called her that. "Thank you. They're lovely." She buried her nose in the blooms and inhaled the sweet scents of the lilies, roses, alstroemeria, and peonies. The pink, white, and red blooms were filled out with greenery in a huge bundle that barely fit in her hand. "They're the same flowers you sent when Eliza was born. I love them."

"You seemed really happy with them the last time, so I thought, why not remind you of happy things." He picked up the small wrapped box and held it out to her. "For you."

"Chase, you really didn't need to buy me a gift."

"Yes, I did. It's your birthday. That requires something special. Open it."

She couldn't wait to see what it was and passed the flowers back to him so she could use both hands to pull off the ribbon and tear the paper free. She opened the box and found a velvet jewelry box inside. She pulled that out, flipped the lid open, and stared at the gorgeous diamond earrings. "Chase, this is too much."

"Do you like them?"

"They're amazing. Nicer than anything else I own." All the other pairs of *nice* earrings she had were dainty little things. These were the size of chocolate chips. Not big and ostentatious, just right. "They're really beautiful."

"Classic. Like you."

Cyn had said the same thing about her. She liked it.

Chase's steady presence, the wonderful gifts, his support all helped to dissipate the fury her father stirred in her. She wanted to share this night with Chase without bringing along her baggage.

"Give me just a sec to find a vase for the flowers and put on my earrings, then we can go. I don't want to miss our reservation."

Chase waited in the living room while she rushed into the kitchen to find a vase big enough to hold the huge bouquet. It really was sweet of Chase to buy things for her. They'd never done the whole dating and getting to know you thing the conventional way, and she appreciated that tonight he was giving her a little of the experience.

She unwrapped the bouquet, dropped it into a vase with water, and separated the flowers a bit to give them room to fully bloom. She carried them back into the living room and set them on the coffee table. "We'll have to come back here tonight so I can take them to your place, and I can enjoy them there."

"It's *our* place," he reminded her as he stuffed something into his back pocket.

"What's that?" She lifted her chin to indicate whatever he'd hid from her.

"What?"

She raised a brow. "Seriously?"

He held his hand out toward the door. "Let's go to dinner."

"Chase." She stood her ground even as he opened the door.

"Please," he implored. "It can wait." He stepped close and slipped his hand up under her hair at her nape. His touch centered her and eased the building anxiety making her tense. "I want to put what just happened out of our minds for a little while. I want to take you out on this special day and spend time with you where we talk and think about only us. We'll celebrate with good food and a decadent dessert, then go home and kiss our girl good-night. Then I want to slip that sexy dress off you and get my hands on you because damn, sweetheart, you just make me feel lucky."

She couldn't help but smile and fall a little bit more in love with him.

She leaned into his touch. "Okay. Let's go."

Chapter Twenty-Six

KYLE BURST through the front door of the house and didn't even consider going up to see his parents. He wouldn't give them the satisfaction of rubbing it in his face that Shelby had denied him what he wanted most.

She actually yelled at him and called him a monster.

And that boyfriend of hers stood between him and his daughter and kicked him out.

He didn't get to spend Shelby's birthday with her. He hadn't even gotten a glimpse of Eliza.

He walked into the living room, furious beyond belief, and shoved the sofa over in a fit of rage, sliding it along the hardwood and toppling it. He went into the kitchen and knocked everything off the table with one swipe of his arm. Cereal scattered across the floor, along with some cookies that exploded from a bag that hit the wall. Most everything else survived.

He kicked a can of stew across the floor and right into a cupboard door. It cracked down the middle.

His mother would have a fit about his outburst, but he didn't give a damn.

He pulled out his phone and scrolled through the dozens of photos he'd taken.

Gentler than how he actually felt, he brushed his

thumb over Eliza's pretty face in one of his many photos of her playing at the park. She looked so sweet and
innocent and kind.

She'd love him.

She'd be happy to see him.

He switched the picture to one of Shelby. She'd defied
him today. She refused to let him be a part of her birthday. He'd missed so many, and now she wouldn't even
let him make it up to her.

She wanted him to stay away.

She'd forced him to use the law to get what he wanted.

He deserved to see his granddaughter.

She wouldn't keep him away.

Not now. Not ever.

He stared down at her face. If she wouldn't grant
his request, she'd have to obey a judge. And if it didn't
work, if the judge wouldn't help, well, he'd have to take
matters into his own hands like he did with Rebecca. "I
will put my family back together."

Chapter Twenty-Seven

SHELBY WOKE up happy, warm, and naked in Chase's arms and thinking about their wonderful dinner date last night. The food was amazing. The company even better. Chase had no trouble distracting her from Kyle's unexpected intrusion into her life again and the threat he posed. And as distractions went, Chase was the best one she could have in her life.

He opened up last night about the good things he remembered about serving overseas, giving her a glimpse of his life and his experiences of other countries. He was sweet with his many compliments and the way he flirted with her all through dinner. She'd never seen him that relaxed and unguarded. It was in the way he spoke and how he treated her. Everyone in the restaurant surely saw what she did. He never took his eyes off her. He touched her constantly, holding her hand, brushing his fingers along her arm, his hand at her waist when they walked in and out of the restaurant. He gave her a sedate but sexy kiss when they brought out dessert and sang happy birthday to her.

She owed him a sock in the shoulder for embarrassing her like that. But she loved it. All of it.

It had been one of the best nights of her life.

All because Chase cared enough to make it a great night.

And he hadn't stopped at dinner. As promised, he'd brought her home to an astonished Max, who gasped with surprise when he saw her in her new dress with her cute haircut. Chase actually ordered him to stop staring.

She was seriously considering never putting her drab work clothes on again.

Max left after telling them how much fun he'd had with Eliza and that they'd played hide-and-seek and topple-the-block-castles, which Max built and Eliza relished knocking down.

She and Chase checked on Eliza to be sure she was sound asleep. Then Chase took her by the hips and nudged her to follow Remmy to their room, where he closed the door and proceeded to get her naked and worship her for God knows how long before they both collapsed in exhaustion and fell asleep entwined together.

But the contentment from last night faded as her birthday-slash-anniversary high wore off and reality set in.

Kyle wanted to spend time with Eliza. He wanted to get to know Shelby.

She didn't want anything to do with him.

She didn't want a man like him around her daughter.

And he planned to make her fight to keep him away.

She hated him for what he'd done to her mother. That hate only grew as he forced his way into her life.

She let out a frustrated sigh that had Remmy standing up and putting his front paws on the bed. He stared at her over Chase's chest where she was snuggled up against him, her head on his shoulder as he slept.

She didn't want her tension to cause Remmy to wake Chase, so she slowly slipped out of bed.

She spotted their clothes strewn across the floor and smiled. They went at each other last night, tearing off clothes as if their lives depended on it. But like always, there'd been a moment when everything paused and they just stared at each other as if they couldn't believe the person in front of them wanted them so badly.

But they did. It still made her weak in the knees to see Chase look at her the way he always did. His body did the same to her. All those strong muscles covered in tan skin, his strength so evident but controlled when he touched her. The scars still took her aback sometimes and made her throat tight. She hated how much and how often he'd been hurt.

He survived.

And she was so grateful he came back to her.

Smiling at the memories of them tossing clothes last night, she reached down to pick them up, but stilled when she held Chase's black jeans and found the white envelope Kyle left for her last night.

She pulled the envelope free, dropped the clothes, found one of Chase's thermals he'd tossed on the dresser, pulled it on along with her leggings, and walked out of the room. She walked to the kitchen, poured herself a mug of coffee, then sat at the table and stared at the innocuous envelope, mustering the courage to look inside and see a past she didn't know enough, and too much, about.

Kyle said he left her pictures of her mom.

She'd only ever seen a few. Her grandparents had tucked them all away because they were too painful to look at.

They couldn't tuck Shelby away, though she was too

much for them to look at some days, so they ignored and avoided her sometimes. Often enough that Shelby still felt the pain of not understanding what she'd done.

Chase and Eliza chased those feelings away with their love.

Shelby left her coffee cooling and stared at the envelope, lost in her hurt and loneliness.

Chase's hands settled on her shoulders, and he leaned down and whispered, "I love you," knowing somehow that she desperately needed to hear it this morning even after the night they'd shared.

She glanced up at him only to see so much worry and regret in his eyes.

"Don't open that," he implored. "There's nothing but pain in there." He reached down to take the envelope, but she put her hand over his and held it there.

"I need to see."

"You know their story. You don't need to see it." He was trying to tell her something about what the pictures showed.

Her heart raced in her chest because of his warning, but it didn't stop her. She had to know. She needed to see. She couldn't keep running from a past that all too often was thrust front and center in her life.

She slipped the envelope free and pulled out the dozen or so Polaroids.

The one on top was a picture of her mother in a sundress standing in what looked like a park or maybe a field, smiling and looking at something in the distance. It didn't appear she even knew someone was taking her picture.

"You look so much like her." Chase stood close, his hand on her shoulder now. "You have her smile."

Shelby hadn't smiled often enough in her life before Eliza showed up and made her smile every day. She wished her mother had been able to smile like that when she'd had Shelby.

She started to switch the picture but stalled when Chase said, "Don't. Just hold on to that one. That's all you need. That's her, happy and smiling and carefree."

She looked up at him. "I want to, but I can't." Because she'd never been allowed to forget what happened.

And right now, she wished her grandparents had been able to tell her all the stories about the happy, smiling, carefree mom she never knew, instead of just the horrible end of her life.

He brushed his hand over her hair. "What he sees in the next pictures is not the reality of what they show. I don't know why he gave these to you, but it's clear that he's hoping you see them together and believe that he really loved her, that she loved him back. That's not what you'll see at all." He pointed to the picture of her smiling mom covering the rest of the Polaroids. "He captured her vibrant spirit in this one shot. This is who he saw while he held her hostage and looked at her all the days he held her. Her beauty. Her joy. And that's what he took from her. *You* do not need to see how he destroyed her."

A tear slipped down her cheek. She understood exactly what Chase was telling her. Knowing what happened and seeing it . . . two very different things. She knew it wouldn't be easy, but she also couldn't look away.

"I don't know how to explain this, but I feel like she needs me to see him for who he really is so that I'll know the monster in the story truly is as evil as I've been told. So I'll know exactly what I'm up against when he tries to come for our daughter, and I'm prepared to see past nice words and softly spoken pleas to the conniving and brutal man he really is."

"I won't let him anywhere near either of you ever again."

She appreciated the sentiment, but they both knew Chase couldn't protect them 24/7.

She spread the photos on the table in a haphazard collage of sadness and madness.

Her focus shifted from one image to the next. Kyle smiling like the happiest man alive in all of them. Her mother's face close to his in the selfies, the emotion in her eyes ranging from fear, to terror, to wide-eyed horror. The ones he took of just her, she looked scared in most, helpless in one, resigned in another, and always desperate. But one showed her looking off into the distance just like the first shot Shelby had seen, only she wasn't happy and bright. No. She sat up against a metal bed, shoulders slumped, hands tied behind her back, wearing a dirty white men's T-shirt, knees tucked into her belly, feet by her hands, bruises on her arms and legs, a split lip, a bruised cheek, and her face devoid of any emotion, her eyes as flat and dead as a corpse's.

She held that photo up with the first one and stared at what Kyle Hodges had done to her mother.

Chase squeezed her shoulder. "What kind of man, a father, gives something like this to his child?"

"A monster," she answered.

Chase crouched beside her, took her face in his hands, brushed his thumbs over her wet cheeks—it took her a second to realize she was crying—and turned her face to look at him. "We will use this and what he did to her to make sure he never sees Eliza or you ever again.

We'll start with the restraining order and getting a lawyer to fight any attempts he makes for visitation with Eliza."

"Why can't he just stay away? All I want to do is forget. But he won't let me. This town won't let me. Maybe it is time to leave and start over somewhere else."

Chase shook his head. "Running away isn't going to solve this. If you and Eliza are his new obsession, like he had with your mom, he's not going to stop. It doesn't matter where we go."

That scared her all the way to her soul because they were talking about her precious Eliza.

She also loved that he said, *where* we *go*. Meaning he was in this with her, and if they had to run to protect Eliza, he'd be right there by her side.

"Sometimes, sweetheart, you have to stand and fight."

"Sometimes retreating is the only way to save lives."

"We have to at least try. We'll meet with a lawyer and find out what our rights and his are. He probably doesn't have a case. We are Eliza's parents. We make decisions in her best interests. If a judge says no and backs us up, then we can legally keep him away. I know that doesn't solve the problem, but it's a start. Then we go from there. No matter what, Eliza will be watched and protected. The next time he shows up at your place or here, we call the cops and have him arrested for trespassing and going against the restraining order. I know it's not much, but it's something."

"He's going to try something drastic. He knows we aren't going to voluntarily let him see her."

"Maybe this isn't about her at all, but getting you to talk to him and form a relationship."

"That is the last thing I want to do."

"I know, but let's do this one step at a time before we give up our lives here. Because that kind of feels like we're letting him win. And when does it end? If he finds us wherever we go, do we run again? Start over again?"

She sighed. "You're right. I know that. I just don't want anything to happen to Eliza."

"Neither do I, which is why I'm going to call Hunt, tell him what's going on, and ask him to help us. I'll also tell Max and my dad what's happening, so they know to keep a close eye on Eliza and you, too."

"I'm not worried about me. I can take care of myself."

Chase raised a brow and shook his head. "I'm sure your mother thought the same thing."

"You're not making me feel better or safer."

"Good. I want you on alert. I want you watching your surroundings. I don't want you to be surprised. If he grabs you, fight like hell. Don't let him take you to a second location." He touched his forehead to hers. "Come back to me no matter what."

"Nothing is going to happen to me. And I don't want anything to happen to Eliza. We'll be careful. *All* of us."

Chase stood. "We're going to need to implement some security measures you may not like."

She turned in her chair to face him. "Like what?"

"We've settled in here together. We've talked about making it permanent. We've done everything else in our relationship out of order, so moving in together before a proposal and wedding seems right. And I don't think it's a good idea for you and Eliza to go back to your place unless I'm with you."

"Agreed. I'm not going to fight you on protecting Eliza. We want the same thing."

"Then I need you to acknowledge that you could be

his target, too. You're his daughter. He wants a relation-ship with *you* and Eliza. If he can't get your coopera-tion, he might just force you."

She placed both hands over all the pictures on the table. "I'm well aware of what he's capable of and that he's not rational when it comes to what he wants."

"Then we'll get a security system here. I'll call Drake. He can probably set me up with whatever we need, and I'll install it."

She nodded her agreement, because she'd sleep better knowing they had the protection.

Chase gave her a look that said she might not like what he told her next. "Maybe it's not safe for Eliza to go to the babysitter for a while. I know she loves being with Abby and the other kids, but . . ."

"Kyle has already been lurking around outside her place and the park. It's not fair to put such a burden on Abby. I have some vacation time—"

"No. You'll need those days if we have to go to court. I don't like that you'll be out of my sight, and I'll worry like hell whenever you're at work, but I don't want you to jeopardize your job either. I know you love it, and it's important to you to maintain your independence. Be-tween me, Max, and my dad, we can all watch Eliza. And I think it would be a good idea if we set up a tracker on your phone. That way, if something happens, I can find you."

"Maybe we should put one on Eliza." She was only half kidding.

"I'm sure Drake can help me find something that could work."

"This is all getting a little crazy. Are we overreact-ing?" She wanted him to tell her they were.

"I'd rather someone called me paranoid than not know where my daughter or you are because that asshole came after you." Chase rubbed his hand over his neck. "I can't lose either of you." He shook his head. "It's not going to happen."

She felt Chase's rising irritation and panic, stood, and placed her hands on his chest just as Remmy nuzzled his nose in Chase's hand. "Relax. We're both here and safe. We'll take precautions. We'll hire a lawyer. We will not let that man in our life."

"This feels a lot like the enemy plotting an attack against us, and I just need to be prepared."

She took his hand and looked him dead in the eye. "We will be. We'll start today."

He squeezed her hand. "Promise me you'll be careful."

"Always."

The only way she knew she and Eliza would be safe was to fight Kyle for her daughter's security and well-being and for the peaceful, happy life she wanted with Chase.

Chapter Twenty-Eight

Eliza in his arms, Remmy by his side, Chase walked out onto the porch and closed the door behind him just as Shelby pulled into the driveway. He helped Eliza down the stairs and released her on the path so she could run to her mom.

Shelby climbed out of her SUV, her wavy hair softly blowing in the breeze, a bright smile on her face for Eliza. She put one hand on Eliza's back and pressed her close to her legs as Eliza wrapped her arms around Shelby's thighs. "Hey, baby. How was your day with Dad?"

Chase had kept Eliza with him for the past week.

Abby had called three times to let them know she'd seen Kyle either lurking at the park or parked on her street, watching the house.

They'd had good reason to keep Eliza home.

"I pet horse. Pop-pop made cookies."

"Sounds like you had a good day."

He and Shelby had one yesterday when they went to court with their attorney and the judge denied Kyle visitation with Eliza. The judge didn't even give Kyle any chance to argue his side of the case and Kyle stormed out of the courtroom. In Wyoming, rapists forfeited their parental rights if a child was conceived during the rape, so the judge simply said he had no rights to his grandchild either and denied his request.

The whole thing had been an act of futility for Kyle, and he had to know it.

Eliza walked back toward Chase with Shelby, but then ran after Remmy to play tug-of-war with Remmy's favorite rope.

Shelby stopped in front of Chase, studying him. "You don't look happy."

"I'm fine. Just worried." He pulled her into a deep kiss to say hello and show her he was happy to see her.

She brushed her fingers along his jaw. "That's more like it." Her head tilted, and her lips dipped into a frown. "Kyle?" She read him so well. "He didn't get what he wants. God knows what he plans to do next."

Chase knew all too well what evil could do. He'd been to war. He'd seen what people would do for a cause and something they believed in.

Kyle didn't want a family.

He wanted to possess those he thought belonged to him, the ones he "loved."

Chase knew it was a twisted kind of love. That only made Kyle all the more dangerous. And dedicated to getting what he wanted.

Chase pulled Shelby close. "If he comes for her, we're ready."

He'd installed the top-of-the-line security system Drake overnighted him. He also put a tracker on his and Shelby's phones. And because he'd learned a good dose of paranoia and gut instinct saved his ass on more than one occasion, with Shelby's permission he had Shelby wear a digital watch with a tracker in it, and Eliza wore a silver bracelet with a charm that was actually a tracker, too.

It kind of gave Chase the creeps to put tracking devices on his two girls, but he'd been left with no choice. If something happened to either one of them . . . he couldn't go there or he'd drive himself crazy. Well, crazier.

The last few days had been hell on his anxiety and paranoia, but he'd talked it all through with Dr. Porter, who advised him not to get caught up in the what-ifs and focus on being in the moment.

He reminded himself a hundred times a day that Eliza and Shelby were safe. They were with him. He wouldn't let anything happen to them.

Still, it weighed on his mind and heart.

He thought coming back meant they'd only have to deal with his issues. He'd have to work on being better for them.

He never expected there to be another threat to their happiness and future.

He hated it.

He wanted Kyle out of their lives. For good.

Chase pulled Shelby in for another searing kiss. He hadn't seen her since she left this morning for work, and his need for her grew through the day. He'd slake that need tonight. She looked great in a pair of black leggings and a black-and-white-plaid flannel shirt. He loved her new haircut and her new sense of self. It showed in her eyes and her easy smile.

Shelby kept her arms around his waist and leaned back to look up at him. "We have the restraining order now."

The judge had been all too happy to sign off on it for them right in front of Kyle.

Chase didn't think a piece of paper would do anything to keep Kyle away. "Hunt and his buddies on the force are aware of it and ready to help if we need them."

She rolled her eyes. "We both know Kyle is never going to stop."

"We stay alert. Hunt will be doing some drive-bys of your work when you're there."

"How are things between you two?"

He shrugged, unsure how to answer. "Better. I think. He's hard to read. But he's willing to help us out with this."

She smiled up at him. "He showed up for Pancake Tuesday this past week."

That was encouraging. Chase hoped he showed up every week, so they could continue working on getting back to the way things used to be when they were all best friends.

Eliza ran past them, chasing Remmy. "I want pancakes," she called out.

Shelby smiled. "Breakfast for dinner it is."

Chase cupped her cheek. "I know you say you're fine even though you're worried. We'll get through this thing with Kyle."

She smiled, but it didn't reach her eyes. "I know. I just wish he'd go away and never come back."

If only he could make that wish come true.

If Kyle came for his family, Chase would take him down.

Chapter Twenty-Nine

KYLE HATED the smug looks on his parents' faces.

"We told you this wouldn't work. Nothing will. You're nothing to Shelby and Eliza." His father's condescending voice echoed in his head and fueled his desire to prove him wrong, yet again.

"I will have the family I want. Just like I had the woman I wanted."

"That girl didn't want you. She didn't love you. Who could love someone like you?" His mother sneered at him. She'd never helped him. She'd always stood with his father against Kyle.

"What you've done," his father began.

"What I've done! What about what you've done? You made me this way!" He shook with rage and fisted his hands so tight they ached.

"You were an obstinate child. You always misbehaved. You never did what you were told." His mother's disapproving gaze and disappointment only made him angrier.

"You blamed the child when it was your fault! You locked me in this room. You forced me to bend to your will. Get used to being in here, because you're never leaving!"

He spun on his heel and left the room, slamming the door and locking it behind him.

"Don't do what you're thinking of doing," his mother called out. "You'll only make things worse." Her favorite refrain to him.

There had been many times he'd made things worse for himself, but not this time. This time, he'd get what he wanted. He'd have what he deserved. If he couldn't have Rebecca back, he'd have his daughter and grandchild.

No one would stop him.

Anyone who tried . . . well, he'd eliminate them.

Chase . . . he had to go.

"Don't do it," his mother called out.

"You can't stop me!"

No one could now.

Chapter Thirty

THE SECOND they arrived in the grocery store parking lot, Shelby realized something wasn't right. She swore someone was watching her, but when she scanned the lot, all she saw were other shoppers.

Still, the ominous feeling didn't dissipate.

Chase got out of the truck, holding Eliza in his arms, with Remmy by his side. "What's wrong?" He read her so well.

"I don't know." She scanned the lot again. Nothing. And yet something kept her on edge.

She kind of felt a little like how Chase described his PTSD. That sense of always being on alert and expecting a threat to come out of nowhere.

Kyle was driving them all crazy.

"If you're uncomfortable, we can go back to the house and—"

"No."

Remmy pressed his body against Chase's leg.

She shook her head, feeling like her bad vibes were infecting Chase, and that's the last thing she wanted to do. "It's just . . . Every time I'm out in the open now, I'm looking for him."

"As you should be. But I get that it's wearing on you."

"Let's pick up what we need to stock the fridge before this little one starves to death." Shelby tickled Eliza's belly, making her giggle and Chase smile. It also helped ease her mind. She'd focus on them, not her paranoid thoughts of Kyle coming after them. Justified though they might be, they were taking away from her happiness.

Chase hooked his free arm around her shoulders, and they walked toward the store. He grabbed a cart and went to lift Eliza into the seat up top.

"No, Daddy. I shop." She loved to pick the items off the shelves. It took more time to allow her to do it, but it made her happy.

Chase set Eliza on the ground because carrying her for too long hurt his back. He took her hand, and Shelby pushed the cart next to them.

"Let's start with the produce," she suggested, turning the cart toward the left of the store. They'd work their way across the store to the bakery section, where she planned to pick up something sweet and chocolatey.

Eliza tugged free of Chase's hand and ran for the strawberries and grapes.

Chase smiled at her. "She knows what she likes."

"I'll grab some lettuce and broccoli. You keep an eye on her." Shelby moved to the wall of vegetables, pulled down two plastic bags, opened one, and chose a large head of green leafy lettuce. She set it in the cart and moved a few feet down to the broccoli crowns, picking out four and putting them in the other bag. She dropped it in the cart just as Chase came up beside her and set Eliza's finds in the cart, too.

Eliza plastered herself to Shelby's leg like she always did.

"I think we still have tomatoes at home, but we probably need another cucumber." She set her purse in the cart seat and rummaged through it to find their list.

Remmy barked and let out a low growl.

She immediately turned to him, because he never growled and only ever barked at the squirrels in the yard.

Chase grunted and fell to his knees beside her.

At the same time, Eliza was suddenly pulled away from Shelby's leg.

Of the three other people she could see in the produce aisle, one froze, one ducked behind the apple display, and the other ran.

Shelby looked over Chase's head and stared into Kyle's cold, flat eyes, then saw the knife in his hand dripping blood onto Eliza's arm where he held her up against his chest, his other arm tight around her waist.

"Don't do anything stupid. I'll kill her."

Despite the panic in every cell of her being, Shelby didn't want to believe he'd kill his own granddaughter.

Chase launched himself toward Kyle. He tried to grab Kyle by the legs and take him down but missed when Kyle shuffled away, bringing the knife down and plunging it into the back of Chase's shoulder before he ripped it right back out again.

Eliza screamed and squirmed to get free. Kyle held her tighter.

Blood spread across Chase's army-green T-shirt until it reached the splotch of blood on the other side of his back, down by his waist. Remmy whined and lay over Chase's back to protect and soothe him.

Shelby rushed to Chase's side and pressed her hand on the wound.

Chase moaned in agony even as he tried to crawl forward and grab Kyle again. "Give me back my daughter!"

Kyle pointed the knife in Shelby's face. "Leave the purse and your phone and come with me and Eliza now, or stay with him and watch him die." Kyle pointed the knife at a guy inching his way closer and stopped him in his tracks as Kyle backed through the swinging doors that led into the employee-only stockroom.

The doors closed. She only had a moment to exchange an apologetic glance with Chase and then sprint after their daughter.

CHASE CAUGHT THE look of anguish and fear in Shelby's eyes that he really would die and the sorrow that she couldn't stay to help him before she rushed after Kyle. It took him too long to get the fifty-something-pound dog off his back. He made it to his feet and wobbled with dizziness.

Remmy and a couple of people from the store followed, someone shouting, "Stop! You're bleeding!"

No shit.

But his family was in danger, and Kyle needed to die.

He didn't stop until he burst through the side door of the building and caught a glimpse of Shelby getting into Kyle's car seconds before he tore out of the parking lot with Eliza sitting in his lap.

"Sir, are you okay? We've called 911. The cops and an ambulance are on the way," the store employee assured him.

He didn't need a trip to the hospital. He needed Shelby and Eliza back.

He pulled out his phone, blood dripping down his arm from the stab wound to his shoulder. He hit the speed dial and swore when Hunt didn't pick up on the first ring.

"Sir, you're bleeding really bad. Maybe you should sit down until the paramedics get here."

Chase ignored the guy, the pain, the dizziness setting in, and spoke the second Hunt answered. "Kyle just took Eliza and Shelby. I'm at the grocery store. Pick me up now. We need to go after them."

"Sir, you're bleeding," the grocery store guy said again.

"Are you hurt?" Concern filled Hunt's voice.

"The only way I'm not going after them is if I'm dead. Hurry up." He wanted to run to his truck and leave this second, but if he did that and the bleeding was worse than he thought, he'd lose them and probably end up dying never knowing if they were safe.

He needed to be smart. He needed Hunt's help.

Kyle wasn't going to kill Shelby. Not right away. He wanted to get them alone so he could convince Shelby they could be a family.

He'd held Rebecca for days, trying to convince her she loved him and they could have a life together.

Chase told himself he had time. He'd find them before anything else bad happened to them.

And when he did, he'd put Kyle down, so that he never hurt the ones Chase loved ever again.

Chapter Thirty-One

SHELBY PULLED Eliza away from Kyle and used her shirt to wipe Chase's blood off her baby's arm.

Eliza sat in Shelby's lap, her face buried in her chest, crying softly. "Daddy owie."

Shelby glared over at Kyle. "You didn't have to hurt him."

"He was keeping you from me. You're my child. No one can keep me from you."

She snarled at him. "Yet you just took his child from him. You would have taken her from me."

"I gave you a choice. But I knew you'd come with us. You want us to be a family, the one you never had. The one I missed out on with Rebecca."

"She didn't belong to you. You took her from her family. You held her against her will."

"No!" He slammed the knife against the steering wheel, then pointed it at her, Chase's blood still smeared on it and his hand. "*She* wanted to be with me. *She* loved me. I showed her how good we were together. I promised her a life where we would be happy away from everyone who wanted to keep us apart."

"Did she even know you before you took her? Or did

you just not hear her when she told you she didn't want anything to do with you?"

Everything about him, his shoulders, his eyes, the grin on his face, went soft. "Rebecca smiled at me from across the room. She wanted to go away with me. Every time I looked at her, she'd feel me watching, and she'd turn to me and smile." Delusional asshole. He saw what he wanted to see in Rebecca. He'd created a story in his mind that Rebecca's smiles meant something more than a polite gesture. He actually believed she secretly desired him. All from a look and a smile.

"And you believe that after losing my mother because of you that I would want anything to do with you?"

"They poisoned her against me. It made her crazy to be away from me. She felt like the only way out of the pain of losing me was to take her own life."

"She tried to kill me as well."

"That's how distraught she was to lose me." He really couldn't see reality.

Kyle took a turn too fast and sent Shelby into the passenger door.

"Slow down before you kill us," she snapped.

"We're almost there."

"Where?"

"Where we can be a family."

She would never be able to get Kyle to understand or believe that she wanted nothing to do with him. So she saved her breath, held her baby in her arms, glanced at the watch on her wrist with the tracking device, and prayed someone got to them in time.

CHASE LET THE paramedics look at his shoulder and side. He bit back a yelp the second they pressed thick gauze pads to his wounds. He'd been here, done this before, but you were never quite ready for the searing pain.

Hunt showed up five minutes after the paramedics, took one look at him, and swore. "He's armed."

"Hunting knife. Stings a little."

Hunt swore again and lifted his chin to indicate the phone in Chase's hands. "You tracking them?"

"We were wrong about him planning to take her to the cabin in the woods where he hid Rebecca."

Hunt squatted next to him and looked at the map on Chase's phone. "Where are they going?"

"Looks like he's headed to his parents' old house where he grew up. The one they lived in here before they moved their business down south."

"That makes no sense. You'd think he'd want to hide them."

"Why? He thinks they're going to be a family. So why not go home."

Hunt shook his head. "I called in the highway patrol and state police to help track down his ass." Hunt winced. "You're bleeding really badly."

Chase glanced over his shoulder as the paramedic taped a new thick pad to his shoulder. The movement made the wound on his side scream with pain. "I'm fine."

Hunt glared at him.

Chase stood and wobbled on his feet before he caught his balance, thanks to Hunt grabbing his arm.

The paramedic looked up at him. "Hey, you need to go to the hospital. You probably need surgery, especially on the wound to your side. You might have some organ damage and internal bleeding."

"It's going to have to wait," he said to the paramedic,

then looked at Hunt. "They're eleven minutes ahead of us. Let's go." Chase headed for Hunt's squad car.

Hunt got on his radio for an update on the search for Kyle.

Chase settled in the passenger seat, trying his best to ignore the pain and focus on saving his family. "You have what I need?"

"In the trunk." Hunt started the car, hit the lights and siren, and took off after Kyle. "You sure about this?"

"He's not going to give them up without a fight. He lost Rebecca that way. He won't lose them, so I'm going to have to take him out to get them back." They'd known this was coming. He'd planned for it with Hunt and Shelby.

He wasn't the same monster who took Rebecca.

He was worse, because he somehow thought he'd get away with it this time.

He'd had all these years in prison to think about what he wanted and how he'd take it.

He just never counted on Chase and what he'd do to get them back.

Kyle's plan was flawed in many ways because his mind was warped and he couldn't see past having Shelby and Eliza with him. Then what?

That's the part Kyle never planned for with Rebecca or Shelby and Eliza.

But Chase had a plan. He just hoped Shelby was able to help him carry it out.

Chapter Thirty-Two

SHELBY STARED at the old mansion with the boarded-up windows, weathered paint, sagging porch, dead plants and weeds, and thought this was what had happened to Kyle's mind while he was in prison: time had decayed it.

Kyle smiled at the house. "Do you like it?"

She knew he didn't see what she saw. "It's beautiful." Once, the two-story white house with black trim, beveled leaded glass windows, and expansive yard had probably been gorgeous. Now it felt desolate.

His family ran a huge lumber company. They were well off, and it showed in this home. But that didn't mean they'd been happy. Because something had gone terribly wrong inside those walls that had turned Kyle into a monster.

"There's not much left inside, but we'll make it home."

She doubted the place even had water or electricity.

"Pee-pee," Eliza whispered.

"She needs to use the bathroom."

Kyle opened his door, climbed out, then peered back inside at her. "Run away and Eliza and I will just have to live here alone."

She would not leave her child. Help was on the way,

even if Kyle believed she'd come willingly and there'd be no consequences.

He held his hands out. "Come here, sweetheart."

Shelby cringed at the endearment and about letting Eliza go to him, but she didn't have a choice. She needed to bide her time and look for her opportunity.

"I'll bring her inside."

Kyle shook his outstretched hands. "Give her to me!" The biting tone made Eliza shake and her bottom lip wobble.

"It's okay, baby. Go to him. You'll be okay." She hated Kyle for making her do this to her child. She lifted Eliza toward him, and he took her. Hands empty, her heart breaking, and the fury inside her stirred to a white-hot inferno, she exited the car and ran after Kyle as he walked into the house, leaving the door wide-open for her.

He thought to control her by keeping her daughter by his side.

She'd just have to outsmart him and get her daughter back.

It took Chase a little extra effort to climb out of the cruiser and meet his brother at the trunk. Five other police cars had gathered at the perimeter of Kyle's property at the end of the long driveway, out of sight of the house.

Hunt tossed him a gray T-shirt from a duffel bag, then pulled out the long black gun case.

The paramedics had cut off his other shirt, so he pulled the new one on, though Hunt had to help him tug it down after he got stuck trying to move his left arm.

"And you think you can shoot." Hunt shook his head.

"Gun stock goes in my right shoulder. I'll be fine."

Hunt didn't look convinced. "I told you we have someone who can shoot."

"They're not as good as me." He'd been trained in the military and used that skill with deadly precision more times than he'd like to remember. He'd promised Shelby it wouldn't be him. She didn't want one more death on his conscience. But he would not spare a thought for Kyle once he put him down. And there was no way he was putting Shelby's and Eliza's lives in someone else's hands.

"Chase, you don't have to do this. My guys are good. We can get them out of there."

"That's my life in there. I will not trust it to anyone else. It has to be me. I promised her I'd protect them. She knows I will with my life."

"You're bleeding out as we stand here. Pretty soon, you won't be able to even hold a rifle, let alone fire it."

"I've got this."

Hunt swore and rubbed his hand over the back of his neck, just like he and their dad did all the time. Family trait. He bet it would be cute as hell to see Eliza do that someday.

"Let's figure out where they are in the house so you can set up. If you get any paler and pass out on me, I'm having the ambulance take you to the hospital."

If this took too long, Chase would have no choice but to trust Hunt to finish it for him, because he was no good to Shelby and Eliza dead.

He followed Hunt over to where his guys had set up at the back of a cruiser, discussing a plan to surround the house.

Hunt stepped in and took the lead. "My two-year-old niece is in that house, so we're not going in guns blazing." The seven men nodded their agreement. "If we can get a shot at Kyle through one of the windows, we'll take it. Until then, let's set a perimeter and get eyes on our target and the hostages. I want to know where they are and the best vantage point to shoot that asshole." Hunt looked around at all the gear. "Who's got the thermal imaging camera?"

One of the guys raised his hand. "Get as close as you can behind cover and see if you can confirm how many people are inside and where." Hunt looked at Chase. "If he's got one of them locked up in a room, maybe we can get them out first."

Chase feared exactly what Hunt hadn't said in so many words. If Kyle locked Shelby up alone in a room and kept Eliza with him, it would be that much harder and more dangerous to get Eliza away from him so they could take down Kyle.

"One step at a time," he said to Hunt, reminding himself as well that he couldn't let his mind spin out of control with what-ifs and likely scenarios. He needed to focus on facts.

They'd start with this and plan their next steps to eliminate the threat.

Chapter Thirty-Three

KYLE STOOD in the doorway, the knife still in his hand, watching while Eliza went potty. Shelby helped her with her pants and took her hand. She turned and waited for Kyle to move away from the doorway so they could exit.

"Follow me. I want to introduce you to my parents." He waved the knife in the air, indicating for her to come along. "They never got to see you when you were born. Your mother's parents told them to stay away. They gave up. They blamed me for making it impossible to see you. They said it was painful to know you were out there, their only grandchild, and they couldn't see you. Like I wasn't suffering without Rebecca, locked in a cell, surrounded by savages." Kyle led them back down the hall, through the empty foyer, and up the stairs.

"Did you know that after I was found guilty and sentenced, my parents never came to see me? They wanted to forget me."

She understood that very well.

"I wrote them letters, begging them to send me information and pictures of you. When they would answer my calls, all they'd say was to stop calling them." Kyle paused on the landing of the second floor and turned to her, pointing the knife in her face again. "What kind of parents turn their back on their child and refuse to give him what he wants?"

"What kind?" She asked because she'd really like to know what he thought. He didn't seem to understand the pain he'd caused. In his mind, he'd done nothing wrong.

"The kind who liked to punish me for every little thing."

Eliza stood beside her with her face buried in Shelby's thigh and Shelby's hand pressed to her back. She hoped Eliza couldn't feel her hand shake.

"I'm sorry they mistreated you." She hoped a little sympathy calmed him down.

He pinned her in his angry gaze. "They're sorry now."

She caught a whiff of something that drifted on the stale air in the house that had been closed up for nearly three decades. It wrinkled her nose. "This place looks abandoned. Are your parents even here?"

"Of course they are. I told them to wait for us. They didn't think you'd come. They told me not to even try. But I needed to show them that I would get my family back." He waved her forward with the knife again. "Come. They've wanted a reunion for a long time. They told me they hoped to one day meet you and Eliza."

His agitation turned to a kind of euphoria she didn't understand as she followed him down a long hallway. The odd smell became more pungent as they passed two closed doors and stopped just outside the second to last door. Light filtered in through the dirty window at the end of the hallway. Too far away for the police to see them. If they'd even found them yet.

The knots in her stomach tightened with every passing moment.

Kyle put his hand to the door and stared at it, smiling.

She nudged Eliza behind her legs and backed them both up as far away from the door as possible in the wide hallway.

"I was a mischievous boy." He tapped the tip of the blade against the dead bolt, completely out of place on an interior upstairs room, with the lock on the outside of the door.

"They didn't like the games I played. I could only do what they said and go along with what they wanted for so long. And when they didn't approve or got tired of me, they locked me in here to teach me a lesson." He kept his hand on the door and turned his head to look at her over his shoulder, his eyes menacing. "What did they think I'd learn in the dark?"

Looking into his cold, dead eyes, she saw the answer. He'd learned to not feel.

And it had warped his mind and turned him cruel.

"Stay here with me. Be the family I know we can be, and I will never put you in the dark." He unlocked the dead bolt and opened the door wide.

Light from the window spilled into the small space, a walk-in closet about five-by-five, with Kyle's parents sitting in two chairs staring out at her, their faces gray, eyes closed, their bodies sagging and desiccated.

How long had they been dead? Weeks? Months? A long time by the looks of them.

Eliza whimpered from behind her, startling Shelby out of her shock. She used both hands to hold Eliza at her back, hoping she didn't see anything.

Kyle put his hands on his hips. "See. I told you they'd come."

Shelby looked from Kyle to his dead parents and back.

"I told you I'd get what I wanted." He paused. "No. I won't let them go. They want to be here." He shook his head. "Yes, they do."

Shelby trembled.

Kyle actually believed he was having a conversation with his dead parents.

Oh God, this is bad. Really, really bad.

So much worse than she, Chase, or Hunt thought.

"Shelby understands. She wants us to be a family." Kyle looked at her, then turned back to his parents. "Stop. Just stop." He put both hands to his head, the knife still firm in his grasp. "I don't want to hear it anymore."

She wondered if that's what he'd said to them before he killed them.

Her gaze drifted to the door as something caught her eye. Dark smears and jagged lines carved into the wood. Dried blood and claw marks, most likely from a young Kyle trying to get out.

She imagined him as a little boy crying in the dark, pounding on the wood, desperate to be free. To be in the light again.

Sympathy welled in her heart for that young boy.

Though she wondered if his parents were ill-equipped to handle a troubled hellion, or if they were cruel and put him in that dark box and turned him into an unhinged monster.

She'd probably never know the whole truth.

Did abuse make him who he was?

Or was he born that way?

Could that disturbed child have been taught to be kind with patience and discipline?

Or was this inhumane punishment the only recourse for parents who felt they had no other way to stop someone they couldn't reason with, who didn't care how he hurt others?

Had they sought help for their son, or given up on him?

Kyle grabbed the door, slammed it shut, locked it, then turned to her. "I'm sorry you had to hear that. I thought they'd be happy to see you. Instead, they lecture me. They disapprove of everything I do." He spun back to the door. "Stop being so critical! I'm leaving. Maybe if you behave, I'll bring them back for another visit." Kyle met her gaze and shook his head. "They always said stuff like that to me, but they never did anything they promised."

Perhaps Kyle never behaved. Therefore, he never got whatever it was he wanted.

Or maybe his parents taunted him with something and never gave it to him no matter how hard he tried. Until he simply stopped trying and took whatever he wanted anyway.

All of those disturbing thoughts left her head spinning and her no closer to understanding Kyle.

There was only one thing she knew for sure. She needed to get out of here before he put her and Eliza in a closet and kept them to fulfill his delusional family fantasy.

Chapter Thirty-Four

CHASE WAS going crazy with worry and fear every second that passed. Not even Remmy's constant comfort kept his darkest thoughts at bay about what might happen to the two most important people in his life.

He played mind games with himself while waiting for Hunt and his police buddies to feed him information. He denied the situation was as bad as it seemed, or that Kyle was as deadly as they predicted. He bargained with God, the universe, whatever higher power was out there listening that he'd be a good man, give his life, whatever they wanted to just bring Shelby and his daughter out of this alive and well.

Nothing worked.

The front door never opened to them walking out and right back into his arms.

He was ready to do whatever had to be done to make that happen.

His injuries were serious. He could feel the drag on his mind and body from the blood loss. The pain wouldn't cease.

But he'd been through a hell of a lot worse and made it out alive.

He'd hold on as long as it took to get Shelby and Eliza out safe.

And to put Kyle down.

The cops wanted a peaceful end to this.

Chase knew in his bones that was never going to happen. Kyle had played his hand. He took them. And just like when he took Rebecca, he had no intention of giving them up. Ever.

When Kyle realized they were outside and he was surrounded with no way out, he'd know the only options he had left were to surrender, which Chase believed he'd never do, or hold on to Shelby and Eliza the only way he could and take them out with him.

Murder-suicide seemed the most likely outcome for a man as unhinged as Kyle. Chase didn't believe for a moment they'd even scratched the surface of what Kyle was capable of.

Shelby was smart, intuitive, and empathetic. She understood hurt people because she'd been hurt. She knew the deep pain others felt about being misunderstood. She knew loneliness and regret. She'd use those abilities to try to connect with Kyle.

She knew Chase was coming to help her. He'd never leave anyone behind. He'd do anything to get her back.

Hunt finally arrived with an update. "They were upstairs in a hallway just inside that window."

Chase had set up in the barn loft, thinking it the best vantage point for the largest portion of the house. He could practically feel her in there.

"They stood in the hallway for the last few minutes. Then they turned back and went downstairs." Hunt pointed to the boarded-up windows along the back. "That's the kitchen. They're standing in there." He pointed to the French doors leading out to a patio. "That's the main living room area. We haven't seen any sign that he's checking out the windows or that he's even concerned about the cops showing up."

Odd.

Did he really think he could take Shelby and Eliza and no one would come for them?

It didn't make sense.

Nothing Kyle did made much sense.

Chase tried to think. "I have no clue why they went upstairs and came back down. I'd think he'd lock them in a room together." That would give Chase a chance to rescue them, possibly without Kyle even knowing about it.

Hunt shrugged. "Maybe Eliza got hungry and they're getting her something to eat?"

Maybe. Still. "Look at this place. It's been abandoned a long time. The elements have worn it down, and nature has taken over." The whole landscape was overgrown, giving him cover, thankfully. "Why bring them here? He has to know that we'd check out all his family's properties."

Hunt nodded. "I've already contacted the police where his folks live down south and asked them to go out and interview the parents, see if they know what their son is up to."

Chase wondered what they knew and if they even cared. As far as he knew, they'd never contacted Shelby. Maybe because they felt like they didn't have a right after what Kyle had done. Maybe because they too didn't want to be reminded about what he'd done every time they saw her.

Either way, they'd missed out on knowing a really great woman.

One he hoped to spend the rest of his life with. And after all this, he didn't plan to wait for the right time, whenever that might be, to ask her to be his wife. He loved her now. He'd love her forever. So why wait? Why put it off? Why miss another day without being able to call her his wife and know that they'd committed themselves to each other?

Why not start working on building their family and their lives together right now?

Kyle threatened to take it all away.

Chase was not going to let that happen.

"We need to get them out of there. Now."

Hunt's phone rang. "Looks like we don't have to wait to find out about his parents." Hunt stepped away to take the call.

Chase checked the rifle he'd checked a dozen times since Hunt handed it to him. It was ready to go and so was Chase. He never thought he'd have to look down the barrel of a gun again and shoot someone. He'd wanted to leave that part of his life behind him. But for Shelby and Eliza, he'd take down however many bad guys he had to, to keep them safe.

Hunt came back much too quickly. "This isn't good."

"What?" Chase really didn't want to know.

"No one has seen the parents since Kyle was released from prison a couple months ago. The mail has piled up at their home, so local law enforcement went inside, concerned for their well-being."

"And?"

"They weren't there, but there were obvious signs of

a struggle and even some blood. Not much. Not enough to suggest a major injury or death, but . . ."

"Yeah. But." That left a lot of room to speculate about what Kyle had done to his parents.

"They've opened an investigation into their disappearance."

Chase stared at the boarded-up windows. "The answer is inside that house."

Hunt followed his gaze. "You think he planned all this in prison, got out, killed his parents, then came after Shelby and Eliza?"

"I think he blamed his parents for . . . Who knows what they did to him. They didn't love him enough? They abused him? They didn't help him get out of the mess he made for himself when he took Rebecca? God knows. But I think he really thought Shelby would give him a chance and welcome him into her life. He doesn't believe what he did to Rebecca was wrong. He loved her. He wanted her. He thinks their time together in that cabin was them living out his fantasy."

Hunt rubbed at his neck. "That is really fucked-up."

"He's not in his right mind, yet he was competent enough to stand trial. Who knows what all those years behind bars did to him. All I know is that Shelby and Eliza are not safe with him, and he's not thinking rationally enough to see that Shelby will never forgive him for what he's done."

"Then we give him an ultimatum. He comes out peacefully, or he doesn't come out alive." Hunt meant that, but of course he'd have to use protocol.

Chase wasn't bound by any restrictions. He had no qualms about killing Kyle. The man was a threat to his family, and he'd take him out without a second thought.

Chapter Thirty-Five

SHELBY FEARED the horrifying sight of Kyle's dead parents would haunt her forever. She'd probably have nightmares about that gruesome scene the rest of her life. But right now, she needed to focus and plan her next moves.

She held Eliza in her arms, her little head on Shelby's shoulder. Shelby looked around the kitchen, noting the flat of bottled water, the nonperishable groceries on the counter, and wondered what Kyle planned. "What are we doing here?"

"Dad."

She cocked her head, not understanding.

He prompted her, "What are we doing here, *Dad*?"

Hell no. Even the thought of calling him that made her stomach knot and sour.

"I've never had a dad. That's something other kids had and I missed out on. I don't know what it feels like to have a dad like Chase has been to Eliza, like his father was to him."

Kyle had been the monster in her family's story. He was someone who had to be locked up because he was not fit to be around good and decent people.

She wished they'd never let him out.

Kyle leaned against the counter, careful to stay away

from the boarded-up windows, even though no one could see in through these.

The kitchen was dark, though he'd turned on a battery-powered lantern that cast a soft glow in the room.

"We have all the time in the world to make up for the things I missed. I can be your dad and Eliza's grandpa. You'll see. It will be everything you ever wanted."

"I wished you weren't my father my whole life."

His eyes narrowed and filled with anger. "You don't mean that."

"I do. Look at what you've done to my life. Because of you, my mother took her own life and tried to kill me. We're the town's most talked-about gossip. This will only make that worse. For me. For Eliza." She hated to think of her daughter growing up with people talking about her behind her back, or worse, kids teasing her because of her madman grandfather. "You stabbed Eliza's father, the man I love." Choked up, she tried to hold it together. "I don't even know if he's alive." She prayed he was okay and being taken care of at the hospital right now.

Kyle waved that away with the knife. "He's probably fine. I made sure I stabbed him where it would do the least damage." Kyle rolled his eyes. "I knew you'd be upset if he got really hurt, but I needed him out of the way so we could talk and you could see that we can finally be together as a family."

"You stabbed my boyfriend so we could talk, and you think that's okay and I won't be upset about it?" She really hoped he'd see the crazy in that statement.

"Don't be so dramatic. He'll be fine. If you'd simply let me speak to you all those other times . . ."

"Are you saying that it's *my* fault you stabbed my boyfriend?" It dawned on her that she was talking about

Chase being stabbed and whether he was dead or alive in front of Eliza, who seemed to have grasped the danger of the situation and gone quiet on her. It gave her an opportunity to do what she needed to do.

"Would it have killed you to have a simple conversation with me?" Kyle eyed her, like this truly was all her fault.

And maybe it was, because she hadn't given him the time of day.

He scared her. For good reason. Look where she was right now.

But could it have been different if she'd just talked to him?

"I planned to bring you here sooner, but Mom and Dad kept telling me that I needed to give you time."

She didn't think that had been a real conversation. "How long have your parents been back here?"

"For a while."

Judging by the state of decay of the bodies, she was guessing a couple months. Kyle hadn't wasted any time when he got home eliminating two of the people he thought wronged him. But he hadn't escaped them. They were still in his head.

She didn't want to become his next victim, dead in a room upstairs and alive in his warped mind.

She thought about the living room they'd walked through and how she could get him in there by the windows.

"Eliza is tired. Do you mind if I put her down for her nap in the other room?"

Kyle waved the knife out toward the living area. "Make yourself at home."

She walked through the living room, noting that

while most of the contents of the house were gone, there were still some pieces of furniture left behind. The console table in the entryway. Two leather club chairs and a table near the fireplace. A love seat near the entrance to the kitchen. She found it odd that he seemed to be using it to sleep on in the darkest part of the room.

She wouldn't think he liked the dark anymore.

She set Eliza down by the fireplace, pushed one of the heavy club chairs toward the windows, then moved Eliza to the chair to curl up and rest. She kissed Eliza on the head, then whispered in her ear, "Daddy is fine. We will see him soon. I need you to stay right here and be quiet. Do not move." She met Eliza's worried gaze and got a nod that she understood.

Kyle stood just inside the room. "You're a good mother. You protect her."

Shelby walked toward the windows. "I will do anything to keep her safe." She grabbed one of the heavy drapes and shook it.

"Stop. What do you think you're doing?"

She turned to Kyle, hoping he understood. "Eliza is afraid of the dark. I'll open the drapes and let in a little light so she's not scared."

He was about to say something, but stopped short when Hunt's voice rang out over a loudspeaker. "Kyle Hodges. This is the police. We have you surrounded. Come out with your hands up."

His gaze narrowed, and a stillness came over him. "How did they find us here?"

Her heart pounded. She glanced at Eliza curled up in the chair, her eyes wide and watchful. Even she sensed the change in the mood in the room. "This is your family's home."

"Everyone knows my parents moved away." He tilted his head. "They got here awful fast. Especially if they didn't look for me anywhere else." He took a couple steps toward her. "They knew we were here because you told them."

"How would I do that? I don't even have my phone. I've been with you, in your sight, the whole time. It's logical they'd check *both* your parents' homes to find you. This is the closest one, so they probably came here first and found the car parked out front."

"Kyle, we know you're in there. Come out with your hands up."

"You should surrender now." She didn't think he'd do any such thing, but she wanted him to have the opportunity before things got worse.

"And let them take me back to jail? I won't be put in a box! Not again!"

"Kyle, please," Hunt implored. "Send Shelby and Eliza out. Let them go, and we'll take you into custody safely." Hunt's pleading tone said he meant it.

Kyle only grew angrier. "You did this! You brought them here."

She shook her head and held her hands out wide. "How would I bring them here?" She hoped Hunt and his officers carried out the plan they'd made with Chase. She needed to get to him at the hospital. He was probably worried sick about them.

He has to be alive.

"You stabbed Chase." Her voice cracked. "Of course his brother came after you. Hunt won't stop. He won't go away. Your only choice is to surrender." *Please do it.*

He pointed the knife at her. "All I wanted was for us to be a family. But you kept refusing to speak to me.

You wouldn't listen. And now look what you've done. It wasn't supposed to be like this." He charged her with the knife held up in his hand, ready for him to plunge it into her chest.

She spun around and flung the curtain open a split second before the glass shattered. She spun back around and saw the bloody hole in Kyle's head, his arm still raised in the air, sunlight gleaming off the bloodstained knife, his eyes wide with shock. He simply fell to his knees, his arm dropping as he collapsed face-first into the dusty rug, the knife clattering on the hardwood.

THE SECOND THE curtain opened, Chase took the shot he'd been waiting for. Kyle's face appeared in his crosshairs, and he pulled the trigger and took him down. But then the curtain fell closed again, and he didn't know if Shelby and Eliza were safe and unharmed or not.

He released the rifle and jumped up from where he'd lain in wait on his belly up in the barn loft. He'd taken position the second he'd seen the curtain rustle a moment ago. Shelby's signal to him that she'd made it to one of the boarded-up windows. She'd found the one that had a board halfway pulled off and revealed enough of the interior that he saw Kyle coming at her.

He left the rifle and ran for the ladder leading down to the stalls below. When his feet hit the ground, he sprinted for the house, adrenaline giving him the strength to hold on a little longer. Hunt and the other cops had already rushed in to protect Shelby and Eliza and make sure Kyle was dead.

Chase already knew he was, but he'd gotten a flash of the knife Kyle used on him, and he didn't know if he'd also used it on Shelby or his little girl.

He slowed from the blood loss on the porch steps and burst through the front door. It only took a second to find where his family was since there was a cop standing sentry outside the living room. He ran past the officer, Kyle's body lying on the ground where Chase had dropped him, and right to Shelby, who was holding Eliza against her chest.

"Chase! Why aren't you in the hospital?"

Chase pulled his girls into his chest, hugged them tight, and finally breathed. He ignored the fiery pain in his side and shoulder and just held them close. "Are you okay?"

"We're fine." The death grip she had on his waist said otherwise.

Eliza squirmed between them.

Chase leaned back and looked down at the two of them to be sure they were indeed okay. He caught Shelby's eye. "You did so good."

Her sorrowful gaze dropped to Kyle's body. "He didn't give me a choice." She'd wanted him to surrender like he did when he got caught with her mother.

"You know he wasn't going to let you go."

Tears gathered in her eyes. "His parents are locked in a closet upstairs where they used to keep him to punish him."

That shocked him. "Are they okay?"

"No," Hunt said, walking into the room. "They've been dead quite a while by the looks of it."

Shelby held Chase tighter and buried her face in his neck. "He talked to them like they were still alive."

He brushed his hand over her hair. "He wasn't in his right mind." Now that the worst was over, Chase took a deep breath, but it didn't help the spots in his eyes or the spinning of the room.

Shelby looked up at him. "Chase, baby, are you all right? Chase!"

He wobbled. She tried to hold on to him. The darkness crept into his vision until it tunneled into a tiny dot of light that quickly winked out.

Chapter Thirty-Six

SHELBY TRIED to hold Chase up, but while holding Eliza on her hip, she only had one free hand. Chase's weight started to take her down. Hunt rushed up and grabbed Chase under the arms, pulled him back, and gently laid him on his side on the ground. Blood covered his shirt from his side down to his jeans.

"Shit. I thought we stopped the bleeding." Hunt called out to one of his men, "Get the paramedics in here." He looked at her. "I've had them on standby at the end of the driveway."

She sighed out her relief. "Why did you let him come here?"

"Because no one was going to take that shot but him. No one could have done it better. *He* needed to protect you. After everything he's been through, he needed to know he could keep his head and do what was necessary to keep you safe."

"There's nothing for him to keep me safe from now."

Hunt shook his head at Kyle. "I wish it didn't have to go down this way." He ran his hand over Eliza's head. "Take her out of here. She doesn't need to see this."

Shelby wasn't thinking clearly. Eliza had to be traumatized after all this. Especially seeing her dad collapse.

"Daddy is going to be okay." She stood and did the hardest thing she'd ever had to do, leaving Chase with the paramedics. She walked down the steps and spotted Remmy in Hunt's patrol car. "We are all going to be okay." She hugged Eliza, then opened the car door and let Remmy out to jump up and lick Eliza's hand.

"He kissed me." Eliza gave a soft smile, some emotion finally coming back into her greenish-blue eyes.

"He loves you, sweetheart. Just like me and Daddy."

"Bad owie."

"Yes, baby, Daddy has two bad owies, but he's going to the hospital, and the doctors are going to make him all better."

"Promise."

"Yes. I promise." Because there was no way after all they'd been through that Chase was going to leave her now.

CHASE FELT REMMY'S fur against his right arm and wondered what he was doing sleeping between him and Shelby. His heart raced as a wash of adrenaline went through him when he thought about her. He tried to roll to reach for her, but stopped at the shot of pain in his shoulder and side. Someone was holding his left hand, keeping him from moving. He opened his eyes.

Shelby stood over him. "Don't move. You'll tear your stitches."

He stared at her, trying to figure out what was off about her. "What's wrong?"

Her eyes filled with tears. "You could have died?"

"What? I'm fine." At least he thought he was, until he saw her. On second thought, his shoulder and side ached, the pain intensifying the more he moved.

It took a second for the memories to come back. The old mansion. The window. The feeling of immediacy to pull the trigger. The way time seemed to slow as the drapes drew back and Shelby shifted away just enough for him to see Kyle coming at her with a knife. The slam of the rifle stock hitting his shoulder as he fired.

He squeezed her hand. "Are you okay? He didn't stab you. I got him in time."

"Yes." She nodded, wiping away a tear. "But you shouldn't have been there. You lost too much blood. They had to rush you into surgery."

He had a vague memory of her holding his hand just like this but in an ambulance, a paramedic's face over his asking him questions as he jabbed a needle into his arm and started giving him fluids.

"I'm sorry I scared you, sweetheart." He wished he could hold her and make the fear and sorrow disappear.

"I'm the one who's sorry. I brought this on myself. If I'd just talked to him, maybe—"

"No." He shook his head, but stopped the second his shoulder protested the movement. "He was coming for you no matter what. He lost his damn mind a long time ago. You didn't do anything wrong. No one expected you to accept your mother's rapist in your life."

A light dawned in her eyes. She hadn't thought about it in that way. She'd simply been worried about him and upset he got hurt and took the blame on herself.

He squeezed her hand again. "Seriously, how are you? You must have been so scared."

"There was blood all over your back, and they took you directly into surgery because you were bleeding internally. They gave you a blood transfusion, and the surgery took a couple of hours, but you should have full range of motion in your shoulder after some physical therapy. Your side is going to be tender for a while. I don't know how he didn't hit anything major, but you are mostly muscle." She shrugged and held his hand tighter.

A smile tugged at his lips. "I meant, you must have been scared when he took you and Eliza." But of course, she'd been more worried about him than what happened to her.

"Oh." She raked a shaking hand through her already disheveled hair. "I really haven't had time to think about it. I've been here with you all night."

"Where's Eliza? Is she okay?"

Shelby nodded, her eyes filling with tears again. "She shouldn't have seen those things." Her earnest gaze met his. "Do you think she'll remember any of it?"

"No," he assured her. "She's too young to remember. It will fade away soon," he promised. He believed it, but also feared that she'd somehow been affected by what happened and it would stay with her in some way.

He'd talk to Dr. Porter and ask him how he could help Shelby and Eliza survive this trauma and put it behind them.

He knew from experience the thing that helped him most was spending time with them as a family. They needed each other.

"Sweetheart, it kills me when you cry."

She gave him a weak smile. "I really am happy you're awake."

"Me, too. But I'd be even happier if you kissed me."

She leaned down and brushed her lips against his in a soft, sweet kiss. He loved it, but wanted more. He needed to feel their connection surround him again.

He brushed his right hand over Remmy's head, then reached for Shelby, sliding his fingers under her hair and behind her neck as he drew her down and kissed her like he hadn't seen her in forever, because it felt that way.

She broke the kiss, pressed her forehead to his, and stared into his eyes. "I can't lose you."

"Never." They'd been through so much, mostly because of him. "We're forever."

"Is that a proposal I hear?" Hunt walked in with his usual cockiness.

Chase kissed Shelby quick before turning to his brother. "Are we good?" He didn't think there'd be any repercussions after killing Kyle, but . . .

"All good. He had a knife and was about to kill Shelby. It was a righteous shot." Hunt sighed, and whatever weighed on him sagged his shoulders. "I also want to say, I'm sorry I didn't put you in an ambulance the second I saw your wounds at the grocery store and go after Shelby and Eliza without you. When I saw you fall, I thought . . ." Choked up, Hunt's gaze dropped to the floor. "I thought you died." His gaze came up and held Chase's before it moved to Shelby. "I'm sorry. You and Eliza could have lost him because I didn't do my job, and I wasn't the brother Chase needed me to be."

Shelby let Hunt off the hook. "Let this be a new start for the two of you."

Chase had to admit, he was choked up, too, and it really hit home how close he'd come to dying. Again.

"Thanks for showing up, Hunt. I know things haven't been easy between us for way too long, but I hope that changes."

Hunt held out his hand. Chase shook it, though it hurt his back to hold his arm up. Remmy sat up and pawed at Hunt to pet him. Hunt obliged. "Good boy. You kept him calm all night."

Chase was actually surprised they let Remmy stay in his room.

Shelby squeezed his thigh. "You were restless in the ambulance and when they were taking you away to surgery. I thought maybe going full-on military mode might have messed with your head and brought back all the bad memories. Not that they're ever too far from your mind. Anyway, I kept Remmy here with you. The doctor and nurses were completely sympathetic, especially when Remmy jumped up and sat with you and your blood pressure went down."

Chase rubbed Remmy's chest. "Good boy." He really appreciated all Remmy did for him. Drake had been right. He didn't have as many panic attacks. His anxiety went down just petting the dog and shifting his focus to him.

He'd made progress. He had a long way to go still. But with Remmy and Shelby and Eliza by his side, he saw a brighter future, one where he didn't lose himself in the past but enjoyed the moment and looked forward, not back.

His dad and Max walked in.

Max had Eliza in his arms, her little head on his shoulder as she slept. "She conked out about twenty minutes ago."

Chase smiled at his sweet girl, then met Max's gaze. "Looks like I'm not going to be much help at the ranch for the next couple weeks."

"No worries. I've got it covered." Which meant Max would try to do all the work, expecting to have his effort overlooked again.

Chase thought Max deserved more and turned to his dad. "I think it's time you made it clear to everyone who works on the ranch that Max is the boss."

Max's eyes went wide. "You're not coming back?"

"I'll be back as soon as the doc and Shelby say I'm fit, but that doesn't change the fact that you run that place. Yes, with my help, but you've been carrying the load and getting none of the respect you've earned and deserve."

Max rubbed his hand over Eliza's back. "I like how things have been these past few weeks. I like working together."

Chase appreciated the sentiment and the words. "And we'll continue to do so, but you and the men need to know I'm not running things on my own. We do it together. And that needs to come from the top." He pinned his dad in his gaze. "It's time you stepped back and put Max in charge and let everyone know it."

His dad turned to Max. "I should have done it a long time ago. Well before Chase came home. I'll make it official, and you'll get the raise you deserve. You and Chase will be equals."

Max nodded, looking a little overwhelmed. "Thank you. I appreciate it. Now I need to take this one home."

Shelby released his hand and walked around the bed to the cupboard by the window. She opened the door and pulled out her purse, then handed her keys over to Max. "Before you take her, I want to wake her so she can see that her dad is awake and everything is okay." Shelby reached for Eliza and pulled her close to her chest. "Hey sweet girl, wake up. Daddy wants to see you."

Eliza's sleepy eyes opened. She spotted him and held her hands out for him to take her. He couldn't move very well, so Shelby pointed for Remmy to move to the other side of the bed, and she set Eliza on his right side. Eliza immediately lay her head on his chest. He held her close.

"Hey, sweetheart, I love you so much."

Eliza lifted her head. "Ouchy go away?"

"The doctor fixed me up, but it still hurts. I'll be better in a few days."

Shelby laid her hand on Eliza's back. "Kiss Daddy bye-bye. Uncle Max is going to take you home to play and eat lunch."

Eliza leaned up and kissed his cheek.

His heart warmed and he got a little choked up thinking about how close he'd come to losing her and her mom. If something happened to them . . . He couldn't go there.

"Unc." Eliza held her hands out for Max.

Hunt held his hands up. "What about me? I'm Unc, too."

Eliza hugged Max's neck.

Max chuckled. "What can I say? The girl loves me."

Hunt frowned. "You and me, little one, are going to spend some time together."

Chase appreciated so much that his brothers had stepped up to be the uncles Eliza deserved and needed.

He settled into the bed, his body and mind tired even though he'd just woken up. He wanted to spend time with Eliza, but it hurt to breathe.

Shelby put her hand on his shoulder. "The nurse should be here soon with your pain meds."

He stared up at her, and she read his mind.

"Not narcotics, just something to ease the pain and take down the swelling."

He let out a sigh of relief. He didn't want to fall down

that rabbit hole again. "You said something about physical therapy."

"Once you've healed enough that we can start moving those damaged muscles and building them back up again."

"So you'll be giving me back rubs and putting your hands on me soon?"

"Gross." Max rolled his eyes. "I'm taking the little one home." With that, Max headed out with Eliza waving back at them from over his shoulder.

His dad came to the side of the bed and put his hand on Chase's head. "You scared me again, son. Time to take things easy."

He felt the same way and gave his dad a nod just before his dad kissed him on the head, then walked out. Chase thought he might have seen a sheen of tears in his dad's eyes.

Not so in Hunt's. "I know you've been through a lot, but remember Shelby was in that house staring at her dead grandparents while her father acted like they were still alive. Talk about skeletons in the closet." Hunt held Shelby's gaze, his eyes filled with sympathy and worry. "That's got to mess with your head."

"I'm okay," she said.

Hunt looked at Chase. "How many times have you said that and actually meant it?" Hunt gave his leg a pat. "Take care of her, the way she takes care of you."

Chase didn't need to be told, but he appreciated that his brother was looking out for Shelby. Chase would be there for Shelby just like she had always been there for him.

Hunt gave Chase's leg another pat, then walked out, leaving Chase alone with Shelby.

He studied her blank expression and the quietness about her, unsure what she was thinking. "I'm sorry I didn't stop him from taking you."

"You stopped him from killing me."

"Still. If I could have spared you that kind of trauma . . . Eliza, too."

She brushed her hand over his head. "You saved us even though you'd been stabbed two times. We knew he was coming. We were prepared. And even though I thought you'd gone to the hospital, inside, I still knew you were with me."

"I don't want to be anywhere without you."

She leaned in. "Same." Then she kissed him, and he lost himself in her. "I love you."

"I love you, too, sweetheart." And he couldn't wait to get out of here and go home with her. He had plans. Things he wanted to say and do to show her they could both leave the past behind and move on together.

Chapter Thirty-Seven

⁓

So you're all settled in with your Wilde man?" Cyn sat across from Shelby in the diner with a knowing smile.

Shelby had invited Cyn to their first of what she hoped to be many lunches to come while Chase was with Eliza at home.

Home. They'd made it their place after Chase got out of the hospital. His first night home, he'd asked to talk. It made her nervous that maybe he'd had enough and needed some time alone. She'd worried for nothing, because of course he wanted them to be together forever, so he'd asked her to pack up what she wanted from her grandparents' old place and officially move in with him. At Dr. Porter's advice, that focusing on the future and not the past was best to help them both put some space between Kyle stabbing Chase and abducting her, they took a couple days to pack up her place. In that time, she also began the process of settling Kyle's family's estate, because as it turned out, she was heir to everything his parents had built. They'd left it all to her. The granddaughter they didn't know, but thought deserved everything they left behind.

She didn't have an emotional attachment to any of it. In fact, she'd like to forget they ever existed.

But another part of her grieved for the grandparents she never had and blamed, whether deserved or not, for Kyle's cruelty and crimes.

"Chase and I are officially living together. I'm thinking about renting out my place here in town."

"Really? I love your place. It's close to my work and is in a quiet spot, not too close to downtown, but totally walkable. The place I rent now has the oldest, ugliest furnishings, the hot water is only ever lukewarm, and you'd think I'm the noisiest neighbor in the building, but the couple next door are always either fucking or fighting, and they do both at high volume."

Shelby laughed. "If you're interested, I'm happy to show you the place. I haven't had a lot of time to get it ready for showing, but if you don't mind that it's not completely clean and organized after we boxed up my personal stuff, then . . ."

"I'm in. When can I see it?"

Shelby loved Cyn's enthusiasm, and renting to someone she knew was a lot better than a stranger. Which was probably why she'd been dragging her feet about getting it ready. "I can show it to you after we finish lunch if you'd like."

Cyn was still working her way through a French dip sandwich and fries. "You're sure? I don't want to put you on the spot or anything."

"You're my friend. I'd rather rent to you than anyone else." Shelby really meant that. She took a bite of her chicken club burger with ranch and enjoyed Cyn's obvious delight.

"Did your Wilde man like your haircut?"

"Chase loved it. More importantly, I love it. I didn't

realize a haircut could really change the way you feel, but every time I look in the mirror, I see a happy and confident me."

"The haircut is only partially responsible for that. You've changed since you and Chase took a chance on love and each other. You opened yourself up for him. All of us on the outside of that can see it, too."

"After everything that's happened, I feel like we are finally in a really good place."

"What are your Wilde man and little one up to today?"

"I'm not really sure. When I told Chase I had plans this weekend with you, he looked happy to hear that I'd be out of the house for a little while today. I think those two are either doing something they know I won't approve of, or they've got some sort of surprise."

"He looks at you like you're his whole world. I bet it's something good."

"Is anyone looking at you that way?" Shelby hoped she didn't overstep. She wasn't that great at girl talk yet.

Cyn's gaze turned pensive. "You know me. I always have a lot of fun. But lately . . ." Cyn looked a little sad.

"You're hoping for more."

"Watching my sister's dumpster fire relationship and you find love . . . I've had bad and I've had fun-going-nowhere, but I've never found love."

"It'll come calling when you least expect it."

Cyn's phone rang. She glanced from it to Shelby. "You think it's *him*."

Shelby chuckled along with Cyn, but thought about her and Chase. "It'll probably be the guy you least expect it to be."

Cyn held up her phone. "*He* must still be out there. This is my sister." Cyn swiped the screen to accept the call. "Hey, sis."

Shelby finished off her sandwich and glanced around the restaurant, trying to give Cyn some space to take her call.

"Angela," Cyn called out. "Can you hear me?" Cyn's concern piqued Shelby's curiosity.

"Is everything all right?"

Cyn held the phone in front of her, then put it back to her ear. "Angela!" She stood, grabbed her purse, and met Shelby's interested gaze. "I'm sorry. Sounds like she and her boyfriend are going at it again. I need to get over there."

"Of course. Lunch is on me. Take care of your sister."

"Thanks for understanding. Let's do this again soon. And I'll call you about renting your place." Cyn started backing away, looking even more worried and angry as she listened to whatever she overheard on the phone.

"Go. We'll talk later."

Cyn rushed out of the diner.

Shelby pulled out her phone and texted Chase.

SHELBY: On my way home
CHASE: Great! I have a surprise for you
SHELBY: I can't wait
CHASE: ♥♥♥

Shelby smiled, and her heart melted and lightened in her chest. She couldn't believe this was her life. Lunch with a friend. A beautiful little girl who made her life so much more fulfilling and happy. The man she loved waiting for her at home with a surprise.

Maybe her life wasn't extraordinary, but it finally felt normal.

And with Chase in it, she'd be happy with normal forever.

Chapter Thirty-Eight

CHASE'S HEART raced with every passing minute he waited for Shelby to arrive home. They'd gotten through the worst of things. Now he wanted them to have the best of everything for their future.

He patted Remmy's head and checked out the window again, hoping to spot her car.

"She's on her way. Take a breath and calm down," Max advised. "It's not like you don't know how this is going to go."

"I know, it's just . . . I want to do it right."

"You will." Hunt lifted his chin toward the front of the house. "She's here."

"Mama!" Eliza jumped up from her little table where she'd been coloring and ran to the window. "Now, Daddy?"

"Yes, baby, now." His heart sped up, but he also had a sense of relief that Shelby was here.

His dad slapped him on the back. "Go get her."

Chase turned to Max. "Take her and Remmy around the back like we planned. Don't forget to record it and take pictures."

"I've got this," Max assured him.

His brothers and dad took Eliza and Remmy as he

stepped out onto the porch and stood waiting with his heart in his throat for the woman he loved.

He'd tried to think of a special way to do this, and in the end, the only thing that came to mind was to do it here, the place that Shelby got for him to make a home, and start a new life where their relationship really started.

Shelby stepped out of her SUV and walked to the path that led to the front door. She smiled down at the red rose petals he'd spread along the path, leading up to the porch where he'd made a huge heart out of the petals and Eliza sprinkled a bunch of colorful plastic gems. He waited inside the heart for her to join him.

It dawned on him that he should have done this at night with twinkling lights along the porch railing and eaves. But then she stood at the bottom of the steps, her sweet smile growing bigger, her gaze shifting to the half-dozen vases filled with flowers around the rose petal heart on the floor, and he knew she loved it.

"Chase, this is beautiful."

He breathed a huge sigh of relief and held his hand out to her. "I'm so glad you like it."

She took his hand and joined him on the porch. "I love it. Such a sweet surprise."

"There's more." He waited for his family and Eliza to take their places at the bottom of the steps.

Shelby glanced over at them. "Everyone is here." She gave him a curious look and tilted her head. "What's going on?" She looked nervous, and that's the last thing he wanted, though his stomach was tied in knots.

"I love you."

She squeezed his hand. "I love you, too."

"You—" He looked at Eliza, then back at Shelby.

"You and Eliza are the most important people in my life. You saved me in so many ways, but especially when I came home from rehab and discovered that not only were you waiting for me with an open heart, but you'd given me this place to make a home. But it's only home because this is where *you* are. With me. By my side, always on my side."

"Of course I am," she assured him. "I love you."

"I know. And it's been the greatest gift in my life aside from the one you gave me two years ago." He glanced at Eliza again, then dropped to one knee in front of Shelby.

She gasped and put her fingertips to her lips, and her eyes turned misty. "Chase."

"I thought there was nothing left in my battered heart or worth living for when you sat next to me in that bar. You showed me a glimpse of the happy life we could have together if I fought for it."

She dropped her hand from her mouth and held his in both of hers. "And you have. You're better now."

"Because of the amazing love I have for you. I want us to make a life together. I want us to be a family forever. You and me and Eliza and whoever comes along next." She smiled and blushed. He glanced at his family watching them. "You may not have any family left, but if you say yes, you'll have mine, though I'm not sure that won't make you run for the hills."

"Hey," his family all said in unison.

Shelby giggled, and it lightened his heart and made the next part so easy.

"Even with them as part of the bargain, will you be my wife?" He held up the ring he'd bought her the same day he bought her the diamond earrings for her birthday that she wore every day now. "Will you marry me?"

"Yes!" Eliza shouted.

They all laughed, but he didn't take his eyes off Shelby, who stared down at him, a single happy tear trailing down her cheek to the bright smile on her lips. "What she said. Yes!"

Chase forgot all about the ring, stood, and pulled Shelby in for a searing kiss as he held her close.

His family and Eliza clapped for them.

He finally remembered he needed to put the ring on her finger, but first he touched his forehead to hers and looked into her eyes. "You're going to be my wife." Just saying it made him so damn happy.

"You'll be my husband."

"Best thing to ever happen to me." He stepped back, took her hand, and slid the ring on her finger. "Do you like it?"

She gasped when she saw the three-stone ring, the center round stone larger than the trillion-cut ones on the side. "Chase, it's beautiful."

He brushed his thumb over the diamonds. "We're starting with the three of us."

"Congratulations," his dad called out. "I hope you'll be really happy together."

Chase looked down at everyone. "Thank you for being here."

"Welcome to the family," Hunt said to Shelby, then poked Eliza in the belly, making her giggle.

Max bounced Eliza on his hip. "It's you and me tonight, little one. Ready to go?"

Eliza beamed Max a smile. "Yes!"

Chase turned to Shelby. "Max is taking Eliza for the night. You and me, we're celebrating."

She gave him a sexy look. "Oh yeah? What did you have in mind?"

He had planned a very special dinner—for much later—and pulled her toward the front door and their bedroom. "You and me and forever."

Want more of the Wyoming Wildes?

Don't miss

SURRENDERING TO HUNT

Coming Summer 2022!

A Scot is Not Enough by Gina Conkle

Alexander Sloane is finally a finger's breadth from the government post he's worked toward for years. He has one last step—dig up incriminating evidence on the most captivating woman in London. The coy and clever Cecelia MacDonald has never had any trouble using men to do her bidding. But when a mutual enemy proves deadly, she must rely on Alexander for more than flirtation.

The Cowboy Says Yes by Addison Fox

Hadley Wayne is known all over America as The Cowgirl Gourmet, a beloved star on The Cooking Network. Everyone knows all about her perfect life with Zack Wayne, her perfect rancher husband—but it's not real. They're living separate lives in separate bedrooms. But when their work has them leaving the safety of the ranch, they begin to rediscover why they fell in love all those years ago.

All the Duke I Need by Caroline Linden

Philippa Kirkpatrick has been raised at Carlyle Castle by her doting guardian, the Duchess of Carlyle. Preoccupied with the duke's health, the duchess has left the estate in Philippa's hands. When the handsome, scandalously bold William Montclair arrives as the new estate steward, the horrified duchess wants to sack him on sight. Philippa is just as shocked . . . but also, somehow charmed.

REL 0322